Peter

The Shadowmasters Part One
Corruption

BloodBinds Press
www.bloodbinds.com

Published by BloodBinds Ltd

Copyright © 2004 Peter Lancett
peter@bloodbinds.com

The right of Peter Lancett to be identified as the Author of the Work has been asserted by him in accordance with the Copyright Designs and Patents Act 1988

ISBN 0 9547563 0 4

All characters in this publication are fictitious and any resemblance to real persons living or dead is purely coincidental.

Fist Published in Great Britain in 2004 by BloodBinds Press

Acknowledgements

Song lyrics reproduced by kind permission:

'Revelations'
Written and composed by Bruce Dickinson
Published by Iron Maiden Holdings Ltd
Administered by Zomba Music Publishers Ltd

'Moonchild'
Written and composed by Bruce Dickinson/Adrian Smith
Published by Iron Maiden Holdings Ltd
Administered by Zomba Music Publishers Ltd

'Can I Play With Madness'
Written and composed by Bruce Dickinson/Adrian Smith/Steve Harris
Published by Iron Maiden Holdings Ltd
Administered by Zomba Music Publishers Ltd

Prologue

'Spiritus!'
'Sanctus!'
'Spiritus!'
'Sanctus!'

EACH WORD A strident chorus of low voices, formless in a dark void. And each chorus containing more voices than ought to be accommodated, even by the high vaulted emptiness of the room. Then suddenly all was quiet. The darkness was absolute. Even after a period of adjustment, the human eye would have been able to discern neither shape nor form.

Two men, naked within a circle of salt, sat on a tiled floor facing each other, the smaller man's legs wrapped tight around the larger man's waist. They sat close together; close enough for each to smell the spearmint mouthwash on the other's breath. Close enough for their genitals, hard and hot with excitement, to brush tantalisingly together.

The sudden quiet, corrupted only by the heaviness of their breathing, was a signal. The smaller man squeezed his right hand between the two slippery bodies and gripped the larger man's penis. The larger man gasped slightly, a sharp intake of breath as he felt his partner's fingers surround him. They sat, locked like this for several minutes, neither of them speaking, neither of them moving.

And out of the silence came whispers. Formless noises at first, then words taking shape only as their volume grew. Carefully, slowly, the smaller man began to move his hand up and down the shaft of the penis that he had moments before grasped, gripping tight with his thumb and the palm of his hand, his fingers

1

playing in gentle contrast along the underside.

The larger man's breathing became more laboured. His chest heaved and rubbed against his partner's. The whispering continued to echo around the room, unseen voices gaining in volume and in number with each passing second. Separate words were now clearly discernible. But the language remained unidentifiable, a meaningless jumble of syllables and sounds. From somewhere came a crazed giggling. Still the men continued with their act, seemingly oblivious to the noise, but reacting to the increasing volume and intensity with their actions.

'Herrrr. . .' A deep, guttural growl, heavy with breath, the sound clear and sharp for all that, cut across the bedlam of whispering and giggling. The two men stiffened, ceasing momentarily from their labours.

'Herrrrmmm. . .' There. Again.

The two men looked at each other. Through the totality of the darkness they could see nothing. The look was pure instinct. If lights had been switched on at that moment they would have been staring each other directly in the eye. The larger man leaned back, resting on hands stretched out behind him. The smaller man reached back with his left hand and, placing it on the larger mans' thigh, lifted himself up and forward. His right hand still gripped the larger man's penis and he manoeuvred himself carefully so that the tip of the penis rested at the entrance to his anus. Just a few seconds now... Then they would reap the fruits of their labours. Five days of preparation and meditation... The ritual purifications... The pain... Oh yes, more than anything, the exquisite pain. Come now O God!

The Whisperers could sense it! Their babble became subdued, all the voices crushed and relegated to a far corner of the room. Here was power greater than theirs... Here was Knowledge... Here was Death... Here was Eternity... Here was... THE GUARDIAN OF THE WEST!

'HERRRMMM...' the smaller man tried to relax his muscles in order to lessen the pain and found that he couldn't – but there was no backing out now. He took a deep breath and rammed himself down savagely onto the hard flesh beneath him '...EEEESSS!!!'

'AAAAAAAAAARRRRGGGGHHH!!!' He felt his flesh tear

2

as the penis ruptured its way deep into him. The larger man threw himself forward, clamping his arms over his slender partner's shoulders, forcing himself even deeper inside as that same wretched partner squirmed and writhed in an effort to flee the violence of the pain that ripped through every nerve of his body. But the larger man had great strength. There was no escape. The slender man slumped forward, cradling his head on the larger man's shoulder. He was almost unconscious with the pain now and this caused him to relax. Made the pain more bearable. It was coming in huge throbbing waves, dull and obtuse rather than jagged and predatory. He could feel a trickle of fluid running out of him, wetting the cheeks of his behind. He knew that it was blood. Still neither of them uttered a word.

The room was quiet again now. But both men could feel that they were not alone. The air was full and heavy, pregnant with power. They were not finished yet. They were expected to take this ritual to its conclusion. It would be disrespectful not to. And Power would always be honour-bound to punish disrespect.

In the silence, the larger man began to move his pelvis. Each thrust caused a groan of misery to come from his pain-wracked partner. Each groan caused a ripple of giggling to issue from the Whisperers in the corner. Unseen, the Guardian of the West continued to cast a formless shadow over all.

The act was coming to its conclusion. The two men could feel their minds melting, fusing together, becoming one. Instead of darkness there was now light, no less real for existing only in their collective soul. Clouds rushed past, silver and grey, and in the distance a spot, growing larger by the second as they approached. Faster and faster they went, drawn to the spot, which glowed with gold and yellow fire. Closer they came, the clouds all gone now, pure black void surrounding the golden orb.

And physically they were there. The orgasm was shared as the larger man emptied himself deep inside his partner, whose own semen pumped thickly between them coating their bellies with its white stickiness. And at the zenith of their pleasure came the voice, as clear and vivid in both their native tongues of French and English – one voice equally intelligible to each.

'THIS PLACE IS TERRIBLE!!!' it boomed.

And their collective mind understood. Time had no meaning

there. They became aware of Secrets. Became aware of Arcane Wisdom that had long been lost to man. They absorbed and then leaked out again an infinity of knowledge. And came within a whisper of seeing that infinity. But it was not to be. They were not yet ready to cross the Abyss.

It had been successful enough though. They had surely been rewarded for their efforts. They had encountered the Face of God.

It seemed as though they had been in the realms of the pan-dimensional for aeons, but in time as counted by their terrestrial bodies, the span of their leap into expanded consciousness could have been measured in nanoseconds.

Slowly, their minds began to separate, and each became his own being again. Exhausted, they slumped in unison to the cold, tiled floor. They spent a few moments catching their breath. But for themselves, the room was truly empty now. Even in the all-pervasive dark they could tell that. With touching tenderness, given what had so recently occurred, the larger man reached down and gently extracted himself from his friend. The intensity of this act caused the now limp and exhausted smaller man to whimper and then finally, mercifully, pass out.

The larger man got to his feet. He could not see, but he knew the layout of this room perfectly and without hesitation walked the few short paces to where he knew the light switch was situated. His shuffling feet scuffed the salt-ring, breaching its perfection, but that didn't matter now. It had done its job. And done it well. For were they not still alive and sane?

Approaching the far wall by the door, he reached up, feeling for the light switch. He found it and flicked it on. He squinted as his eyes grew accustomed to the light and looked about him. He was mildly disappointed that the room had not changed somehow. For he could feel a change in himself. Even through his weariness, he could feel that he was... different. But nothing more concrete than that. Still, the nature of the change would make itself apparent sometime. There was no hurry.

In the middle of the wooden floor, he looked at the large square of black and white marble tiles, laid out like a chessboard. And in the middle of that lay his slender friend. He could see the blood still oozing from his friend's anus, mixed no doubt

4

with his own semen. He looked down to his own now flaccid penis to notice with no surprise, that it, and indeed his whole genital area, was covered with the sticky red liquid.

Beyond the salt circle, in the far-left corner of the tiled chessboard was a rough stone block. In the right corner a smooth, even, polished block. And ranged behind the chessboard were three truncated marble pillars, carved in the Roman style. The large man smiled to himself as he remembered the effort and the expense that had gone into getting this place just right. And into keeping those efforts secret.

A movement from the centre of the floor caught his eye. His friend was beginning to stir.

'Be still Michael, be still,' the large man whispered gently in his native French. 'I will fetch Dr. Lebrun. He will help us. And he will be discreet. He is one of us. As you now are. *Courage mon brave.*'

He reached for the door handle, opened the door and stepped out through it. Seconds later he returned with a heavy woollen blanket which he carefully draped over the still unconscious Michael. He checked Michael's pulse and satisfied that there was no immediate danger, stood and went out of the room again.

Outside, in an elegant hallway, he walked over to an antique hallstand on which was situated an ornate, gilded telephone. He picked up the receiver and dialled a number.

'Dr. Lebrun please.' There was a brief pause. 'Hello, Pierre? It's me Henri. Henri St. Clair. I would be grateful if you could come round right away. We need your assistance...'

Chapter 1

5.30am. THE SUN HAD already begun its climb up over the horizon. Even at this early hour the temperature, which had never dipped below sixty-five during the still night, had risen to seventy. It was going to be another sweltering day.

Several hundred million dollars worth of sleek yachts lay still at their moorings in the harbour. For the most part, their occupants would have only recently returned from the casino, nightclub or whatever. The idle rich, like owls, being a nocturnal breed.

Midway down the left harbour wall along the *Quai des Etats Unis*, a beautiful seventy foot steel-hulled ketch, painted a gleaming white, stood out among the ranks of almost exclusively motor yachts which dwarfed it to either side. From the jack staff rising from the transom at the rear of the aft saloon deck, the Red Ensign hung limply in the still morning air barely denoting its British registration. On the transom itself, printed in large gold letters was the boat's name, *The Hasler*.

At this early hour, the streets around the harbour were deserted. There was no one to see as the saloon doors, set just below *The Hasler's* high, enclosed centre cockpit, burst open. A man, naked save for a pair of plain yellow shorts stumbled out and through, onto the saloon deck itself, where he lay gasping for breath. Perspiration beaded him from head to toe.

The man just lay for a while as his breathing became more relaxed and his pulse dropped back to its regular fifty-two beats per minute. Slowly, he picked himself up off the deck and climbed the four steps up into the cockpit. A pack of Marlboro Lights lay atop the Icom ICM80 VHF radiotelephone, along with a battered steel Zippo lighter. The man took a cigarette from the

6

near empty pack and placed it between his dry lips. He peeled his tongue away from the roof of his mouth, which was as dry as a desert. He really needed a drink; fruit juice or water or something. But that would mean going back down into the galley, and right now, a few minutes in the fresh air would help clear his head.

He made his way forward, the cigarette dangling unlit between his lips, until he stood, thighs braced against the bow guard-rail, looking out beyond the harbour wall to the emptiness of the open sea. So the nightmare was returning, he thought to himself as he stared at the still blueness beyond. It was always the same one...

...It began with darkness, a sense of pitch black. He was kneeling in mud. All around was deadly quiet. He felt uneasy - something wasn't quite right, but he could not figure out just what. It seemed as though unseen heavy weights were pressing in on him from all sides, and he couldn't move. Except for his head. He could twist his head around to the left where suddenly there was a brightly lit shopping precinct visible beyond the black expanse. People were milling around, going about their business. Crowds of them. And there were coloured lights, strung between the shops... and there - a man dressed in red robes with a long white beard. Yes! It was Christmas! Then, more sinister, a figure all in black - black boots, black pants, black sweater, black balaclava - steps out of the darkness and into the brightness of the precinct. This figure, man or what you will, is holding something hidden from the sight of the crowd, behind its back. The black figure takes a few steps further into the precinct. No one seems to notice it. Slowly, from behind its back it pulls... Oh my God! It's a machine pistol! Look out, *for pity's sake watch out!!!* But the words of warning just will not come. The black figure lets rip into the crowd. People scatter, trip over each other in their haste to escape and it cuts them down where they lie, giving no quarter, showing no mercy. It walks among them firing to left and right, the magazine seeming never to empty. And finally the black figure is stopped in its tracks as it is hit by a fusillade of bullets from a patrol of British army soldiers. It sinks to the ground and the whole scene begins to fade into blackness as his head is twisted, by some unseen force to face front. Again, all is blackness as from somewhere comes a quiet, low-pitched giggling. He feels his arms begin to lift, once more against his will. Stretched out in front of him they rise to shoulder height as the giggling gets louder, becoming a raucous laugh. A mocking laugh. And then at last he can see. In his left hand is a knife, its blade dripping sickly with dark, red blood. But his right hand; oh God. Right before his face he is clutching the hair of a severed head. And it's the head that is laughing. The tongue is animated in the open mouth inches before his face, as bright red - almost luminous - blood gushes in a steady torrent from the crudely torn neck. He forces his head down, anything rather than face it. And then he sees that what he has been kneeling in is not mud after all. It is the butchered remains of human flesh; hearts, lungs, kidneys, muscle tissue, ligaments, intestines, stomachs; all of God's creation in a steaming pile. But that isn't all. This pile of offal is anything but dead. It moves and writhes, rich with life. Hearts continue to pulsate, lungs inflate and deflate, grasping for air; stomachs squeeze and twist, spewing their foul smelling contents into the festering mess. And when the snake of lower intestine slides up over his chest to probe at his open mouth, he begins to scream and scream and scream...

...Christ! It had been five years since his breakdown. He remembered little of the night itself. Just opening his eyes as the Sea King hovered overhead, the wind from the massive rotor chilling his soaking wet frame to the marrow. They had found him just in time as hypothermia in its final stages was beginning to ebb his life away. Huddled beside him, the rescue having come too late to save his life, was the trooper who had dragged him away from Wireless Ridge, a battle that had raged just prior to the recapture of Port Stanley. Only an hour before, that trooper, a superb soldier named John Robertson, had fallen into a sleep of death from which he had never awoken.

The helicopter crew had pulled both men from the sea and flown them to HMS Hermes, the floating command centre for the South Atlantic Task Force. For twenty-four hours, he had been kept warm and quiet while being force-fed hot sweet tea to bring up his body temperature. Then came the debriefing. He had been able to remember waiting on Wireless Ridge for the assault to begin, but after that, all was a blank until his rescue. And that was all that he could tell the SAS Major who had conducted the debriefing session. The Major had simply looked at him pensively and it had been impossible to fathom what had been going through the man's mind. Finally, the Major had just got up and left, without saying a word. That night, the nightmare had come to visit for the first time. But certainly not for the last. He had eventually been evacuated back to England, to the Hereford Headquarters of the SAS.

Here the nightmares had continued almost nightly. A year had been spent undergoing psychoanalysis – the Regiment always strove to take care of its own – and gradually, trouble free nights came more and more and the nightmare came less and less. But no one would ever tell him what had happened back on Wireless Ridge. The two surviving troopers who had been with him that night had been quickly re-assigned to new Sabre teams and he had never seen them again. However, the shrinks had made it plain that his propensity for violence now bordered on the psychopathic. He had been living so high on adrenaline during his time with the Regiment that the anticipation of impending action would send the stuff pumping through his system in such quantities as to render his actions unpredictable. Dangerous. He would perhaps get well though, in time. If he behaved.

Obviously the Regiment could not keep him under those circumstances. And there was no way that he would consider being returned to his old unit, where even back with the Parachute Regiment, the best they could offer him was a desk job. Anyway, the shrinks had said that peace and quiet would be his salvation. His body would re-adjust, eventually. His system would begin to lessen its adrenaline output and he would be able to lead a perfectly normal life. And so eighteen months after the enigma that had been Wireless Ridge, he walked away from the army forever.

He had continued to follow a course of mild tranquillisers that the army doctors had prescribed for him, and the nightmare had gradually come to haunt him not at all. Six months into

9

Civvy Street it had come for the last time, and in recent months, he had been able to put the memory of it behind him completely. Until now.

A light breeze, which chilled his still sweat-dampened body, brought him back into the present. On the open sea, a large grey freighter lay at anchor about three miles out. Alongside sat a huge black bloated tube, lying low in the water. So the Americans were back in town. The man allowed himself a brief smile. He enjoyed drinking with the American sailors who came ashore during the days and nights that the sixth fleet chose to make its submarine replenishments off Monte Carlo. One of the perks of an otherwise mundane life at sea for them, putting in at glamour ports like this.

A movement to the stern of the freighter caught his eye. Just coming into view was a large motor yacht. It must have been hidden by the freighter's bulk before, and undoubtedly it was heading for the harbour. He looked down at himself. Standing around in one's underwear was hardly *de rigeur* in the millionaires' playground. He tossed the cigarette, still unlit, over the guardrail, hoping that none of his neighbours had been watching. Nimbly, he made his way back down to the boat's cockpit and disappeared through the saloon doors leading below decks, to shower and dress. After all, he had a busy day of nothing to look forward to…

It was a good fifteen minutes before the man came back up on deck. He had not bothered to towel himself properly dry from the cold shower, and his tee shirt and white tennis shorts stuck to him in dark mottled patches. The motor yacht - another multi-million-dollar job he noted - was making its way carefully through the gap in the harbour wall. He watched as the yacht reversed engines and came to a standstill before being manoeuvred skilfully by its Captain stern first into an empty bay, four berths down the line.

The man stepped off the saloon deck of *The Hasler* and onto the quayside. He wanted to get a better look at this vessel because even though a purist sailing man, preferring wind and canvas to diesel or gas turbine, he was able to appreciate the sleek beauty of the modern custom designed cruising palace. And this one looked a real gem.

He was about to wander over to get a closer look when the panoramic glass-doors at the rear of the boat's saloon deck, slid open. Two crewmen, dressed smartly all in whites, emerged and jumped swiftly onto the quayside and began securing the vessel to its mooring points. The man smiled, admiring their efficiency, then he noticed two more crewmen who were somewhat roughly frog-marching a young woman off the boat. One of them pushed her so that she fell to the concrete.

Quickly, the two crewmen then re-boarded the vessel and stood, arms folded like guardsmen, on the transom. Their demeanour forbade anyone to cross that threshold, but they stared in particular at the girl with intimidation as their obvious intent.

The girl herself lay sobbing on the ground as a boy, barely in his twenties, waddled out onto the saloon deck. His fat bulk was accentuated by the too-tight bathing trunks that he wore and there was no mistaking his Middle-Eastern origin. *Wealthy* Middle-Eastern origin at that, the man noted as he continued his casual observation. In his hands this boy clutched two faded rucksacks, one red, one blue. These he threw after the girl not caring to take any real aim. The blue one hit her on the shoulder; the red one dropped into the scum-surfaced water below.

He began to scream at the girl in Arabic, and the man, more and more intrigued, listened. And he understood every word.

'Whore! Whore's spawn! Mother of whores! Begone. Take your filth and your pox with you. You are cheap, to be stoned in the market place. I would not spare my piss for you.' His spleen vented, the boy turned on his heel and waddled back through the smoked-glass doors followed by his crewmen. The doors slid shut with a hiss behind them.

Pleasant bastard, the man thought as his eyes scanned the aft deck of the yacht. In the back of his mind there was a flicker of recognition. Still, it hadn't been worth his getting involved. He didn't know the full story, and anyway, it was none of his business. No one had been hurt. He looked at the girl who had picked herself up and now sat cross-legged on the quayside, clutching the blue rucksack to her chest. Not physically hurt at any rate, he mused.

11

He stood watching the girl for a while. He told himself more than once in those few seconds that he should leave well alone. That he should step back aboard *The Hasler* and cook himself some breakfast. A proper English breakfast with bacon and fried eggs and tomatoes.

Nevertheless, he didn't step back on board. He continued to stand and stare at the girl, though for her part, she remained oblivious to his presence. She sat facing the yacht from which she had been dumped, in a posture of defiance. Then her face sank as she rested her chin on the rucksack that she still clutched tight, and although her hair hung forward obscuring her features, the man could see that she was crying.

Now would be an ideal time for him to turn and walk away. He knew it. *No point in getting involved in someone else's problem: you got plenty enough of your own, boy.* But he didn't turn. To his surprise, he found himself walking towards her. Christ! Just what was he thinking of? Well *he* didn't know, but his feet sure seemed to. And then he noticed that he was standing over her. She still showed no sign of having seen that he was there. He stooped down, balancing easily on the balls of his feet. He didn't know what he was going to say but found himself speaking anyway.

'Need any help?' he asked. 'Speak any English?'

The girl turned to face him, startled. Her eyes were puffy and red. Damp tear tracks washed over her cheeks but there was no self-pity in those eyes. They were set hard and mean. Her tears were tears of rage and frustration. She looked the man over but said nothing.

The man felt a little silly and all he could do was grin at her, which made him feel sillier still. He could literally feel her giving him the once over. Perhaps it would have been better if he had thought before he had spoken. His words, he realised, had not been the right ones.

For her part, the girl had been surprised by the man's approach. She had been concentrating her mind on the fat bastard sitting back in the comfort of his yacht. If the opportunity were to present itself there and then, she would surely take a knife to his genitals and castrate the cowardly shit. Still, that was not this man's fault. He was only trying to help. She regarded him

12

momentarily. He had a handsome face, dark with brown eyes that couldn't disguise a deep-seated loneliness. The nose was slightly crooked, but that just added character. If she had been thinking about it consciously, she would have laughed at the cliché. The mouth was spread in a natural smile revealing white teeth, their brightness accentuated by the deep bronze tan. The kind of tan, she observed, that would lead to wrinkled weathering unless it received daily doses of moisturising lanolin cream. But it was the eyes that she kept coming back to. Mixed in with the loneliness, she could feel honesty. Trustworthiness, even. And she sorely wanted to be able to trust someone right now.

'Y-you American?' she asked, her voice wavering only slightly as her sobs began to die down.

The man continued his friendly smile.

''Fraid not. I'm a Brit. Good try though.'

He stood now, pulling his hands from the pockets of his shorts where they had been buried. Looking at him, the girl noticed that he wasn't quite as tall as she had first imagined, about five feet ten. But he was lean. Almost whipcord thin. She could see his muscles like knotted rope beneath the clinging wetness of his tee shirt. He stepped over to the edge of the quay and looked down into the aquatic murk.

'*You're* American though, right?' he asked as he continued to stare down into the water. 'Southern California at a guess.'

'Right first time.' Her voice had brightened a little, her anger beginning to subside. 'San Diego, and you don't get much more SoCal than that.'

He said nothing, his back still facing her as he continued to gaze at the filth of the harbour water.

He turned to her and asked 'That yours?' extending a hand in the direction of the red rucksack floating on the surface.

'Yes. I...' But it was too late. The man jumped into the filthy water unmindful of its surface skim of diesel oil and assorted refuse. Seconds later, he was clambering up a rusty quayside ladder, rucksack in hand. He pulled himself up and over the side and stood, water dripping from him to form little puddles at his feet.

'Fancy a cup of coffee?' he asked. 'I got a boat over there with

13

all mod cons.' He waved the hand still clutching the dripping rucksack in the direction of *The Hasler*. He used his free hand to wipe the wet hair back from his forehead then extended it to the girl.

'Thanks. That'd be great,' she said, and she smiled as she took his outstretched hand and let him pull her to her feet. Then it was only a few steps over to *The Hasler*; and to the girl - though the man could in no way be aware of this - it felt like nothing less than Sanctuary...

Chapter 2

A SECOND COLD shower and not yet 6.00am, the man noted to himself. He smiled at the thought that occurred to him, that a psychiatrist might consider such behaviour to be obsessive. Smiled because he knew himself to be anything *but*.

He wrapped a towel around himself self-consciously. Normally, he did not have to bother, but with a guest on board, he thought that modesty might be in order. But why was she on board? What the hell was he getting himself into? Right now he didn't know the answer. He was just going to let things run their course and see what happened. There wasn't a charter party due for a couple of weeks and having company might help break the routine. He'd always known that the life of a *Lotus Eater* would never suit him, and that's what he felt like here between charters; a *Lotus Eater*.

See what happened? He was dreaming again. Daydreaming this time. Planning. And hadn't he promised himself never to make plans? Who was to say that this girl would want to stick around for more than a few minutes anyway? A polite few minutes making small talk and drinking coffee then *so long and thanks,* he thought, telling himself that this would indeed be the reality.

His cabin was the master cabin for'ard, and the shower cubicle was en-suite. There was a pair of jeans, Levi 501s, lying on the double bunk where he had pulled them out of the closet and left them draped, and he pulled them on. He stepped out of the cabin and down the narrow corridor flanked on either side by the doors of the three other double guest cabins. The corridor led to the main saloon and there he found the girl, seated at the polished mahogany dining table. In her hands she cupped a large mug of steaming coffee. On a wicker place mat on the other side of the table sat another mug.

'Found everything in the galley OK then?' the man asked.

He sat down at the table facing her. She didn't answer. She was in a world of her own someplace, deep in thought. It occurred to him that she might not even realise that he was there. He waved a hand in front of her eyes, and she came back to consciousness with a start.

'Sorry, I was just thinking,' she answered, saying that and no more. Evidently that was considered explanation enough.

The man picked up the mug in front of him and took a sip. He stifled a grimace. She had put sugar in his coffee. A lot of sugar. The sweetness was cloying and sickly. He put the mug down again. For a few seconds there was an empty silence. The girl was obviously in no hurry to make small talk, polite or otherwise. If there was to be any conversation at all, the man realised he was going to have to make all the running.

He sat looking at her for a few moments then said 'Nice weather we've been having along the coast lately.' He knew it was corny stuff but hey, it was a start.

No reply. So he answered himself 'Yeah sure, really lovely.'

This time the girl did at least look up.

'Look, I'm sorry,' she said. 'It's just that I've got one or two things on my mind.'

The man kept quiet, waiting. Eventually the silence forced her to expand.

'It's my wallet. It's still on that boat with shit-heel back there. I don't care about the money. Just a couple of hundred francs. I can live without that. But my passport's in there. And I want that back.'

Her eyes were flashing signals of violent anger as she spoke. The man could see that it wasn't just getting the passport back that was bothering her. He realised that what was pissing her off mightily was the fact that the fatboy had got her over a barrel. This girl, he realised, was just not used to being tied face down, butt in the air, waiting for the strokes. Somehow her frustrated outrage was a delight to him. No whimpering self pity there. It showed fighting spirit - and he knew all about fighting spirit - and it made him smile.

'And just what the fuck is so funny, huh?'

Her anger directed itself at him now. He was a target, as good

16

as any and at this moment he was in range and she just had to fight something and...

He raised his hands, palms forward in a gesture of surrender, saying

'Hey, hold on. Nothing's funny. Nothing at all.'

Still the narrowed eyes glared at him. They looked to him how he imagined a big cat's must look as it was about to pounce.

'And just to show you how unfunny it all is, I think I'll just wander on down the jetty and get your things back for you, OK?'

But he continued to smile just the same as he rose from the table.

'No, you can't, you mustn't!' Her voice was urgent now, concerned rather than angry. Her hand shot out across the table gripping his forearm as if she realised that her words would not be powerful enough, that physical action would be necessary.

Their eyes met, just for a second, and hers softened. But the hand remained tight on his forearm. Just the touch of her made his body hairs stand on end. It had been months since... But no. It wouldn't be right. Not while she was so vulnerable.

Vulnerable? This girl? Really?

They hadn't spoken about just what *had* gone on aboard the fatboy's yacht, but the man knew. Deep inside he knew. He had seen it all too often on the *Cote D'Azure*. Holiday girl meets rich boy. Rich boy shows girl a good time. Back on rich boy's yacht, all of a sudden it's playtime. And in this part of the world, what spoiled little rich boy wants, spoiled little rich boy always expects to get. Especially when it concerns a return on his investment.

She spoke again and this time her voice was calmer. The man swore that he could sense concern there.

'Look, you've been really nice to me, and thanks for that. But there's no need to go to any trouble, really there isn't. I'll survive, I guess.'

She smiled. A weak smile and, they both knew, a weak lie. Besides, now he *wanted* to go to the trouble. The day was starting to get interesting. It would be no hassle, he knew. But it was a break in his routine. And wasn't that what he had been craving this last few months?

17

'It'll be no trouble,' he said vocalising his very thought 'I'll just go over there, get your things and come back. No problem.'

The girl could feel his confidence. He really thought he could get her wallet back. Just like that. And even more, *she* somehow felt that he could do it. There was something about him. Here was a do-er, not just a sayer. It would be satisfying to let him loose on the *douche-bags* over yonder. Even so, she had her misgivings. She had seen things on that boat and she felt she ought to warn him.

'Well there might be a *little* trouble,' she said. 'There are six of them and…' she paused as if trying to find an easy way of saying the next words.

'And what?'

'And they've got guns.' There! She'd said it. Maybe he'd change his mind now. She wouldn't blame him. After all, it wasn't his problem. Wouldn't anyone think twice about the possibility of getting shot over a few lousy bucks and an easily replaceable passport? And for a stranger, to boot?

But she desperately wanted him to go over there and kick ass. If ever she had felt like Lois Lane calling out to Superman

And she never had, oh no sir. Whatever needs to be done I can do for myself and just don't you forget that bud it was now. Inside though, she prepared herself for disappointment. Might as well go through the motions though. Tell him the rest.

'They keep them in a cupboard beneath the cocktail cabinet in the aft saloon.' She continued weakly. She had turned her eyes to look down at the floor. She didn't want to see the look of horror on his face as he stumbled to find the words that would get him out of this sticky situation that his big bragging mouth had landed him in. She felt no bitterness towards him though. After all he had been so kind up to now and she-

'So what?'

She looked up suddenly. The smile was still cut across the man's face. He didn't seem in the least perturbed by what she had told him. She still gripped his arm and could feel the relaxed strength of his muscles. Perhaps he hadn't heard her right. Give him a few seconds more, then he'll come to his senses. But no.

'Hey, whatever kind of desperados they are, they're hardly

likely to blow me away right here in the harbour,' he said. 'Not just for asking for the legitimate return of your property are they now?' He winked at her conspiratorially and she surprised herself by blushing like a schoolgirl. 'Besides,' he whispered 'I've got a trick up my sleeve. I'll get by, don't you worry'

And by God he would! She knew it. She knew it the way *he* seemed to, as if *his* confidence was being transmitted through to her, seeping out through his skin where she still held him. She lifted her eyes to meet his, feeling cocky now. Selfishly, she felt ready to push him out of the boat in her eagerness to turn him loose on her erstwhile tormentors. Sort this one out, bastards. There was something special about *Smiling Joe* here, something that she couldn't quite place. But it had to do with the application of raw violence. She could sense it within him. She had always been sensitive to these things. But anyone would be able to see it in this guy. *They* certainly would. And they would back off. Because they were cowards. And best of all, because *they* would be afraid.

She knew that this would more than get even with fatboy and his gang. There would be no trouble, oh no. But just having to give up her wallet to this man would make the fatboy squirm with rage. She knew that. And that knowledge warmed her blood. Made her feel *oh* so good.

She relaxed her grip on his arm, and smiled a wry smile at him.

'Must be quite a small trick that you can keep up the sleeve of a tee shirt,' she said. 'Let's hope that it's a good one.'

He winked again, then turned and was through the galley and up onto the deck in a few short strides, leaving her to her embarrassing blushes. Again.

Oh but it was a good one all right, that trick up his sleeve. Fact was, he had recognised the fatboy. He felt relaxed in the knowledge, like a man holding all the aces in a poker game between old friends. Not that the fatboy could be classed as an old friend. Not really.

He stood on the quayside, looking at the motor yacht four berths down. The sun had begun to make its mark now. The heat was beginning to rise. He had to screw up his eyes against the brilliant glare of the sunlight reflecting off the white concrete of the ground and the windows of the yachts that lolled at anchor beside him. He had never taken to wearing sunglasses. He found them somehow restricting and a little claustrophobic. And strangely enough, he also felt that they affected his hearing. Crazy, he knew, but there it was. Just one of those quirks of nature, he supposed.

His mind looped back to the fatboy again. The 'Little Prince'. He hadn't recognised the fatboy by sight at first, and that surprised him now. The fatboy hadn't changed that much in appearance in the seven years since their first encounter. A little taller, perhaps, and certainly fatter. But this was still essentially the arrogant spoiled brat that he had come to loathe. Even so, it had been the voice that had given him away. The voice and the words that its poison brought to life. Unmistakable.

The man looked down at the upturned palm of his right hand. Was it his imagination or was the scar that ran from the base of his index finger down to his wrist, glowing a bright, vivid, pink? Almost as though being in such close proximity to its creator was making it signal a warning. The man smiled at such a ludicrous thought. He needed no warning signal to identify the potential of the Little Prince. Cruel and sadistic the boy was, yes. He knew all that. But he was also cowardly. There could be no danger from that quarter for a man like himself. He had been caught out, taken advantage of, once. It would never happen again.

He looked up and found, to his surprise, that he had walked the short distance to the fatboy's yacht. He stood facing it. The decks were clear, no sign of life. But that was not unusual. The same could be said for all the yachts ranged along the quay. It was still too early in the day for there to be any signs of life from this quarter.

Behind him, a low growl, growing rapidly louder, breached the morning silence as a Ferrari Testarossa flew screaming out of the tunnel that ran beneath the Loews Hotel and down the *Avenue J F Kennedy*. The man did not have to turn and look to recognise the vehicle make and marque. He had come to know the sounds of the cars that were most common to the region until recognition had become second nature. Once it had been tanks and armoured personnel carriers and… but then he didn't like to think of that anymore. That was the past. And sometimes the memories could be blisteringly painful. There were a couple of times when he had cried. Alone. In the dark. That was dangerous. Becoming maudlin was surely the first step onto the downward slope.

Before him, the yacht sat fat and still in the water. Was it mocking him? Did it think there was uncertainty in the way he just stood at its perimeter? Perhaps it thought that he was afraid to proceed, as though the prospect of coming face to face with a portion of his past was somehow intimidating. But this was just bullshit and he knew it. So he cleared his mind and stepped aboard…

Chapter 3

BANG BANG BANG. Standing on the aft saloon deck of the Prince's yacht, he hammered his fists against the thick toughened glass of the sliding doors. Bulletproof glass, he noted. Tinted and polarised. Fatboy certainly continued to take himself seriously.

Heavy velvet drapes hung behind the doors. A dark purple, he suspected, although it was difficult to tell through the smoked-glass effect.

No reply. He'd waited a few seconds. Time to bang again. Wake 'em up if he had to. He was looking forward to this encounter. Truth of it was, he could feel his juices begin to rise in anticipation. And funny that. Although he'd stayed out of real trouble since his release from the army, there had been odd-times when he'd been annoyed, frustrated, angry for whatever reason, just like there were for most people. And at those times he had felt the old, ever-so-slight tightening of his chest, had noticed the shallowness of his breathing. Surely this was when his adrenaline should run? Run out of control according to the army medicos. But it hadn't. Not even so much as a hint of it happening. He'd always been able to control it; walk away from the annoying Saturday night drunk, merely curse under his breath when routine mechanical maintenance turned into a gremlin-ridden five-hour slog. Perhaps the medicos had got it wrong. Perhaps that night back on Wireless Ridge had been a one-off. But then why insist on a Return to Unit for him if that had indeed been the case? Because they could never be sure, that was why, and deep down he knew it. He'd always known it. If it happened once, it could happen again. No way the Regiment could take that kind of risk. They had had to finish him and that was that. He was a potential risk, a liability. Hell, he was the worst kind of monster in a world of symbiotic teamwork. He was... *unpredictable.*

Then maybe it was the pills that were keeping him calm. But in his mind he knew that to be a lie. At first it might have been true, but now? Well, he knew that he had gotten to be a little forgetful of taking them this past year. More than that, there were whole weeks going by without his touching them. And nothing untoward ever happened.

Then a slight touch of logic intruded. Perhaps the medicos *had* been right. After all, they had always maintained that eventually a full return to stability might be possible. No guarantees of course, there never were with them. Could it be that his life of peace and quiet and all that time when he had taken the pills religiously had paid off? He was due back in the UK next month for his annual series of tests and mind games. Could it be that they would give him the all clear then? Whatever, he had made his mind up on one thing. He was never going to touch another one of the *tranx* that had been repeatedly prescribed for him. Never. No matter what.

He stuffed the hand that had been clenched ready to bang on the glass doors deep into the pocket of his jeans and pulled out the small plastic drum that he always carried with him. He had peeled the sticky label off ages ago. It had become a ritual with him, as though he had no desire to be reminded of his own shortcomings. He took one last look at the pillbox then casually tossed it over the side. His hand clenched into a fist once more as he prepared to hammer on the toughened glass. But the necessity was removed. One of the glass panels slid almost silently open a mere nine inches. A slight audible hum from an electric motor betrayed the secret that it was operated by the power of mechanics, and not magic. The man peered into the gap, but there was little to see. A large crewman filled the space, dressed all in white, and only the low-lit dimness of the interior beyond could be discerned by looking over his shoulder.

'I'd like a word with...

fatboy

...the Prince' the man said, stifling an urge to giggle at the unbidden thought.

His request was met with silence, so he added, 'If you don't mind,' laying on the charm just a shade more than was necessary.

Wordlessly, the crewman stepped back a pace and the door

slid shut once more.

The man sighed inwardly. This charade of security and self-importance could get to be very irritating. Still, he'd known what fatboy had been like once before. This was all very much in character.

Looking around him, he spotted the remote security camera, almost hidden but with a field of vision that could cover virtually all of the saloon deck, right up to the doors. He smiled into it, wondering if the fatboy would recognise his features from the distorted image that the bulging wide-angled lens would provide. He resisted the temptation to give a little wave.

Seconds later, the door hummed open once more, this time a more inviting three feet. The same crewman that he had seen before stood to one side and wordlessly gestured him to enter with a sweep of his hand.

The man stepped inside. Hands thrust deep inside his pockets, he seemed casually offhand, as if he were making a regular visit to an acquaintance of some long standing. But his eyes were everywhere. It took him a few seconds to adjust to the dimness of the interior, especially after the brilliant glare of the sunlight outside, but he could see enough. He was in the main saloon, a large room some thirty feet long, which spanned the whole beam of the boat. The décor was plush and elaborate in the Rococo style. The furnishings complemented the décor, each piece a valuable antique of the period. It all stank of great wealth.

To the left, standing midway down the room, the man noticed the two crewmen who had thrown the girl off the yacht. Fatboy's bodyguards, he thought. They both stood foursquare and impassive, grim expressions on their humourless faces, their arms folded across their chests.

Inwardly, the man was about ready to crease with laughter. Bodyguards! And oh fuck, if this don't beat it all, just about the most inept pair of wankers he had ever seen.

He could take out the whole fucking boat, kill the fatboy and be off into the distance inside half a minute. It would be so easy; snap kick left, shattering the first guard's kneecap, sending him screaming and crippled to the ground. By now number two would just about be unfolding his arms. Grab the right wrist and twist outwards. He staggers, off balance, so lunge with straight fingers

24

to the throat and release. No further trouble from that quarter - death will come within seconds as the Adam's apple swells to cut off all breathing. Now turn to face the doorkeeper. He is advancing, perhaps with a knife or baton. Spit heavily into his face, use the split-second of disgusted surprise that this will provide to grab the weapon-bearing arm. Pull this arm towards and behind you, grip the tunic at the throat and pull the man off-balance towards you, catching him full in the face with a head butt. Now, thrust him away again, sharply so that the head is thrown back. There! The throat again. Open and inviting, so hit it. The first bodyguard is still wailing on the floor clutching his ruined knee - yours to deal with at leisure. Because at the far end of the room is -

'Good morning your -

fatboy, don't forget... fatboy!

- Highness.' The man found himself speaking the words of greeting as though on some kind of autopilot, having become carried away with the pleasure of his thoughts.

The massive bulk of the Prince stood shirtless and perspiring behind a heavily gilded cocktail bar which dominated the far end of the saloon. He appeared greasy and unclean as he silently scrutinised the man standing before him.

'Perhaps you don't recognise me,' the man continued. 'I'll never forget you.' He raised his right hand, the palm spread, facing the *fatboy*, and smiled.

The fatboy's eyes narrowed nervously with recognition. His smile was anything but casual and friendly. Indeed, nowhere near as easy as its wearer would have an observer believe. Still, he told himself, he was a Prince. And the odds were stacked three to one in his favour. Surely there was nothing to fear? But in truth he knew that there might be. He *did* know this man; knew him of old. This man was dangerous. But he would not show fear. The man would not have come here simply to open an old, and to be honest, rather trivial wound. He relaxed, feigning sudden recognition and put on his most charming smile.

'That incident -' he gestured towards the man's still-raised hand '- happened many years ago. I was young and spoiled, too used to getting my own way. Surely you can forgive the impetuosity of youth?'

The man glanced towards the two bodyguards. They had not budged but were now glaring at him, as if they sensed that there was a hidden animosity between him and their master that neither time nor sugary words would ever heal.

'I can assure your -

fatboy!

- Highness that there are no hard feelings,' the man lied. 'The wound has healed and the blame for the incident was entirely mine...'

That's true. You were slow back then, weren't you, Dumbo

'...I should have suspected the concealed knife. And after a month of giving lessons in self-defence to you and your brother I should have developed a keener awareness of your nature. As you say, it is many years since I served on secondment to your country.'

'And my country will be ever grateful Captain, make no mistake. But is this a purely social call, or is there perhaps some way that we may be of service to you?'

and wouldn't you just like that service to include a knife in my back somewhere along the way, you fat oily bastard...?

The man continued his mock friendliness. 'Well there is something. There's a girl. A friend of mine. I believe you were kind enough to furnish her with a ride from Antibes last night.' the man watched with interest as he saw the fatboy's eyes narrow again. The little bastard was going on the defensive. Here was the proof that he had been up to some form of no good. He was readying himself for whatever was to come next.

'She left her wallet here and it contains her passport,' the man continued. 'She'd very much like it back.'

The fatboy relaxed visibly. The man wasn't going to accuse him of attempted rape, and that was the main thing. If any hint of a scandal should journey back to his father's ears... He repressed a slight shudder and regained his composure.

'The girl, yes,' he said pensively. 'What a coincidence that she should turn out to be a friend of yours. A sign of just how small a world we live in, yes? However, I regret to say that she took all of her belongings with her when she left us this morning. If she has mislaid her wallet, I can only suggest that she try searching for it back in Antibes.'

26

'She's pretty certain that she left it here, Your Highness.'

'Are you calling me a liar, Captain?' The fatboy, sticking well to his story, now stiffened with outrage. 'Bear in mind that you are a guest in what for the time being is my home. If you do not know better than to mind your manners, perhaps it would be best if you were to leave. My father would have you flogged for such discourtesy.'

How well you lead me into this next bit, the man thought. Time to pull the ace from the sleeve and lay it on the table.

'Your father, yes. Perhaps your father could persuade you to look for the wallet. As a special favour to me. He does still consider himself to be in my debt, I think.'

If it had been possible to see a man's soul retreat from his body, the man could have sworn that that was what he had seen happen to the fatboy.

The fatboy's father was a King of men in every sense of the word. As strong and courageous as a lion, and with a passion for justice and honour, as befitted the responsibility of his station. He was a man beloved of those who served him. And a man to be feared by those who would disabuse his trust. He also owed the last seven years of his life to the quick reactions of a certain British SAS Captain.

The fatboy, of course, would remember this. He had been there when the Captain had spotted the two rebel fanatics who had been secreted into his father's bodyguard, pull the revolvers from inside their tunics. He had seen the Captain throw himself between them and his father. He had seen the captain disarm the pair of them before any shots could be fired, the snapping of limbs clearly audible above the screams of their combined pain. The King would certainly not have forgotten the Captain.

The man looked hard at the fatboy and knew that he had him. And he knew that the fatboy knew it too

'As you said earlier, it's a small world. I dare say that I can be speaking to your father within the hour. I expect that he'll be thrilled to hear of your new lifestyle.' The man paused for a moment to let that thought sink in. Then came the *coup de grace.* 'Particularly when I tell him that the girl is ready to make an official complaint through her embassy. Think of the scandal. I suspect that a few years of penance in the frugality of Islam is

27

the least that you can expect. It's been a pleasure seeing you again Your Highness.'

The man turned to leave but was halted by the fatboy's desperate cry.

'No, wait. That's blackmail. You cannot do it.'

'Call it what you like. I can do it and I will.'

The fatboy was perspiring freely now. The man could see in his features the curling frustration of conflicting fear, rage, and hatred. He waited, smiling again. The ball was firmly in the fatboy's court. It would take him a few seconds to capitulate. After all, he was a spoilt little brat and hadn't had to learn what it was like not to get his way at every turn. This would be a valuable lesson for him, the man thought, though deep down he knew that for the fatboy it was long past too late for that sort of learning. This incident would only serve to increase his bitterness.

Finally, the fatboy's shoulders sagged, although the eyes still blazed with anger. He looked to his bodyguards, but they were not prepared to move with out a direct order to that effect from their master. After all, they had heard everything. If this man was to suffer harm at their hands, they might have to face the wrath of their King. And for all the fatboy's bluster, it was the real and practical displeasure of their leader that they feared most.

'All right,' the fatboy said, 'just let me look. It may have been left down here.'

He reached down behind the cocktail bar and the man tensed. This was where the girl had said the boat's arms cache was stowed. The fatboy straightened again and the man relaxed. In the fatboy's hand was a scuffed, tan-leather wallet. The fatboy tossed it towards the man contemptuously, unable to shake the arrogance from his system even when it might cost him dear.

The man stooped and caught it just before it hit the ground, his eyes never leaving the two bodyguards. He stood and inspected the contents, his own gesture of contempt. The passport was still there.

'Thank you Your -

fatboy! There, back again!

- Highness.' The man said. 'I have to be on my way now. Sorry I don't have time to stay and chat.'

28

The man turned and made his way out into the brilliant sunshine without looking back. The glass door closed behind him as he stepped onto the quayside.

Walking back to *The Hasler*, he removed the passport from the wallet and opened it. He grimaced as he looked at the photograph. It did the girl no justice at all. Why was it that all passport mug shots looked so goddamned awful? He closed the passport and slid it back in the wallet.

Back on board *The Hasler*, he announced his return by whistling 'Hail The Conquering Hero Comes' as he clambered down the steps to where the girl was waiting in the main saloon below. She had made herself another mug of coffee and was sitting at the table reading a book that she had pulled from the shelf, which ran the length of the saloon above the portholes on the starboard side.

The man pulled his right hand from behind his back and tossed the wallet onto the table in front of her.

'Here you go, Astrid Johnson. I told you that there'd be no problem,'

She grabbed the wallet and opened it eagerly, checking that nothing was missing. Nothing was. She stood, about to throw her arms around his neck and hug him but he thrust out his right hand. She shook it.

'I have you at a disadvantage,' he said, with mock formality. 'Allow me to introduce myself. Astrid Johnson, meet David Strachan.'

Momentarily speechless, she curtsied before him.

Chapter 4

IT WAS RAINING in London. A light evening drizzle following the heavier showers of the afternoon. Despite the approach of the Summer Solstice, the grey skies had tainted the atmosphere so that even open spaces seemed dark and shadowy at a time when usually there would be warming light.

Even the people seemed coloured by the pervasive greyness as they walked the streets, going about their business. Heads were bowed as the masses shuffled their way along dim streets, not yet illuminated by street lamps, which had been set to blink into life at a much later hour. They wore their light raincoats and carried their umbrellas with a grudging reluctance. All about was an unnatural quiet, as though the low misty clouds were deadening all sound.

In the north London garden-suburb of Hampstead, a large Victorian house stood back away from the quiet tree lined street in which it was situated. A steep flight of marble steps led up to the deep, red-bricked arch of the porch, at the rear of which, dimmed in shadow, was a heavy oak door.

At the top of the steps, a man stood, catching his breath. He rested his weight on a stout hickory cane, favouring his left side. From the street, he would appear to be getting on in years, the cane and the stoop of his back indicating a long and perhaps not always amicable association with life. Only the young chauffeur, dressed in an immaculate charcoal-grey uniform and cap, could see different. He stood to one side of the man, holding a large black umbrella to shield the man from the steadily strengthening rain.

The chauffeur could see the man's face, boyish and unlined. The face was vigorous and alive, despite the rasping wheeze of the man's breathing. Indeed, such was the incongruity of the man's appearance at close quarters that where the body acted to exaggerate the man's true age, the face had exactly the opposite effect. In fact, the man's real age was forty-three, a nice middling average. It was the only thing about him that was.

After a brief pause, the man's breathing began to steady. He shuffled forward, gripping tight to the cane as it supported him with each step. Inside the porch, the man came to a halt before the imposing wooden door. The chauffeur carefully furled the umbrella and then tugged the brass bell-pull that hung to the right of the doorframe.

A few seconds later the door opened and a butler, resplendent in a black tailcoat greeted the man warmly, but with quiet dignity. He took the man's free arm and carefully helped him over the doorstep and into the hallway. The chauffeur, confident that his charge was in safe hands, turned and walked - he did not run, despite the now pouring rain - down the steps to wait in the car, a Rolls Royce Silver Spur, which was parked at the kerbside. And the grand door shut quietly behind his back.

Inside the house, the butler helped the man off with his overcoat. The hall was large and square, the floor tiled with red and white marble diamond ceramics. At one end and to the left, a wide staircase swept up to access to the floors above. To either side, panelled doors, their natural wood colour stained a deep reddish brown, remained closed, as if guarding secrets. It gave an appearance that the house was nothing but hall, with rooms beyond the panelled door-fronts given life only by the imagination.

The butler stayed with the man, patiently ushering him to the far end of the hall. They made slow progress, the man stopping on two occasions to use a medical inhaler, which he carried with him to stave off the worst effects of his chronic asthma. Finally, they came to their destination.

To the right was one of the closed, panelled doors. Directly in front of them was a pair of tall, wider doors, firmly shut, but giving the impression that they could sweep open to show some magnificent ballroom of resplendent grandeur.

The butler, his hand supporting the right arm of his charge, stopped again, in perfect anticipation of the man's own action. This was a common ritual.

The man looked up, beyond the frame of the double door. Ornate compasses and a square stood out in bold plaster relief, heavily gilded. Below this design was a legend, which the man read out loud:

'For Noah the navigator, and for the Great Architect, work we the temple of our being.'

The man grunted, smiling, as if enjoying some private joke. And if it was so, it was a joke that he had failed to share with the butler on occasions too numerous to count. The butler, like all of the very finest of his craft, made no comment. Indeed, he had the knack of seeming to be some distance away, so as to go unnoticed. Until, that was, his presence was required. Then there would be no need to summon him; he would already be there. It was a trait that the stooped man greatly admired. And appreciated, though he would never so much as dream of saying so. Nor would the butler expect such a display. Indeed, it would embarrass the butler greatly. In their different ways, they were both men of a different order, of older times.

The butler had already reached to open the door to their right. He guided the man through the open portal into a room of dim yet rich comfort. High leather chairs were arranged in loose groups around exquisite hexagonal tables of an age in-keeping with the house itself. The subdued light was provided by ornate shaded wall lamps, once fuelled by gas, but now powered by electricity. To the left of the door was a long wide bar, backed by long polished mirrors, in front of which were shelves filled with glasses, and at the far end, with bottles of exotic liqueurs. A barman wearing a white jacket and black tie stood polishing a cut-crystal whisky tumbler. He did not speak, as if to break the silence of the otherwise empty room would be to commit an unforgivable transgression of the natural order.

In reverent silence, the butler and the man made their way slowly to an alcove, dim with shadow, on the far side of the room. In this alcove was a huge leather armchair. The butler sat the man in it and left, returning moments later with a tumbler of iced mineral water. The man grunted his thanks automatically, his eyes and mind focused elsewhere. The butler set the glass down on a plain cardboard mat on the occasional-table, which stood to the right of the armchair, and giving a short bow, took his leave.

For five minutes the man sat back in his chair, the drink untouched as he spent time alone with his thoughts. He sat corpse-still in this manner until he became conscious of the butler's approach.

'If you will pardon me, sir, a telephone call for you. A Mr St. Clair.'

The man reached out a hand to accept the portable telephone, the deep burgundy colour of its plastic casing trying hard to blend with its lost–age surroundings - but without success. The man held the instrument out to one side, nodding his thanks to the butler, who bowed again and then retired about his business. Only when he was certain that his conversation would not be overheard did the man hold the telephone to his ear and speak.

'Hello Henri. It is good to hear from you. And punctual as ever.'

'My dear Michael, arrangements are made to be kept, are they not? But my time is short, so to business.'

The man, so obviously a master in this, his own domain, would not usually be hurried in such an abrupt fashion. But this caller spoke with a greater authority, and his was to listen and obey, not to question. It had been this way for eighteen years. Eighteen years that had seen his body crippled beyond repair, but which had brought rewards beyond even the imaginings of most men. Rewards that more than compensated for the withering of his corruptible and mortal frame.

'Go on Henri,' the man said, 'I'm listening.'

'It will happen eight days from now. The site has been prepared. Is being prepared still further. Do what you have to do. Make sure that you are there. Without you it will be nothing, as we both know. And if all comes to nothing my displeasure will be aroused. We are approaching a critical time.'

There was a hint of a threat in the caller's voice, but the man pretended he hadn't noticed, though it was not in his nature to miss detail such as that. The excitement was obvious to his ears.

Soon would come the time that he had suffered the last eighteen years for. A time for rewards richer than any that had been enjoyed up until now.

He said: 'I will do what must be done, Henri.' His voice became grave and determined. 'You know that I will.'

And the caller did know. They had come through much together, Michael and himself. Michael would always do that which was necessary.

'Good Michael. Now, we'll meet again in seven days. Let me know when you will arrive in Nice. I will make the usual arrangements for the airport. *Au revoir, mon ami.*'

The line went dead. The man placed the telephone on the table by his side. The butler would be there to collect it within seconds, he knew. But such certainties did not concern him now. Henri's excitement was beginning to filter through to him. He felt strong, physically strong, as if he were performing the ritual, then...

The excitement had become too much. He had broken down in a fit of asthmatic coughing which he had to control by the use of his inhaler. He must watch that. Stay calm. Let events run their course.

The door of the room burst open and a band of well-dressed men poured noisily through, gathering at the bar. Some of the faces were new. The man did not recognise them. But then that was to be expected. These would be new members of the Lodge. Even as he had been sitting there, waiting for the most important telephone call of his life, they had been undergoing a ceremony of initiation behind the grand doors that dominated the far end of the hallway, keeping the secrets of the Temple.

He watched them at the bar, ordering drinks, calling each other 'brother' while not knowing the true meaning of the word. How he despised them their naivety. They thought that they had joined a gentlemen's club for like-minded businessmen. And for them, that was as much as the ceremony had meant. Some of them would even continue to attend church on Sundays, as though the oaths that they had just sworn were in no way at odds with the Christianity they professed to follow. Although if any of them ever had the wit to sit and think about the tenets of pure faith required to make a true commitment to *that* belief, they would see it for the manufactured sham that it was.

The man squirmed back into his chair as best his twisted body would allow, smug in his superiority. After only seconds, the raucous conversation of the crowd was gone, drifted away with his thoughts, as his mind became a void.

Chapter 5

STRACHAN WOKE WITH a start. His body and the single sheet that covered him were bathed in sweat. It was the nightmare again. He was trembling, but this time he hadn't screamed. He was sure of that.

He glanced to his right for confirmation. The girl, Astrid, lay fast asleep. She had not so much as stirred. The cabin was in half-light. Dawn was beginning to break. He sat up carefully, leaning back on his elbows, and looked at the girl again. She was so beautiful just lying there, like a real-life Sleeping Beauty. So still, she was, with her long reddish-gold hair framing her face on the pillow. He loved her, and he knew it. This last week with her had been the best of his life.

Funny though, he had had little enough to do with women up till now. It was not that he didn't like women, far from it; it was just that he had loved adventure more.

His thoughts drifted back to scan the past, as they often did. He had left school at eighteen with his twin brother Jonathan and they had both joined the army. They had worked their way through Sandhurst together but then had come the blow. They were posted to different units, he to the Third Battalion of the Parachute Regiment, and Jonathan to the First Battalion. Same Regiment but even so, it was the first time they had been separated in their lives.

They had always been close, even as small children, living with their parents in the comfort of stockbroker-belt Surrey. And after their parents had been killed when the Piper Cub that their father had been flying home from Northern France had crashed...

Beside him Strachan felt the girl stir.

36

'Whatcha thinking…?' she asked in a croak, not nearly awake yet.

He looked at her for a moment, wondering whether she really expected a reply. 'I was thinking about my brother,' he said finally.

'What's his name?' came the half-awake voice from beneath the sheet.

'Jonathan.'

'And where is he?'

'I don't know,' Strachan replied, somberly.

Jonathan had left the army unexpectedly about a year earlier. He had come to stay for a month, shortly after his return to civvy-street. Strachan had tried to gently push the right buttons but had been unable to discover why Jonathan had wanted to leave the army so suddenly. Jonathan had been evasive and unwilling to talk, so he had not really pressed the matter. Men experienced things on service with The Regiment that they found difficult to discuss even with their closest friends, and more rarely still with their families. It had been best just to let it rest. Jonathan must have had his reasons, and he of all people, had been able to respect that.

He had asked Jonathan what his plans were, and Jonathan had merely shrugged, saying that he had made no plans. They were both secure financially, having been equal and sole beneficiaries of their father's estate, which had been made more considerable by their uncle Robert's sound investment management. Yet they had both opted to continue with their military careers.

David reflected that he was happy with his quiet lifestyle aboard his yacht. He took the occasional charter party to give some variety to his routine, and he had even invited Jonathan to join him. Perhaps they could plan to sail around the world together; Christ, that would be great. But despite David's, and at first Jonathan's, enthusiasm for the project, after a week or two, they had stopped speaking about it, and a couple of weeks after that, Jonathan had become restless and had finally returned to England.

They had stayed in touch by letter, and sometimes by phone, but lately David had found that many of his letters were going unanswered. In the letters that he did receive he had begun to detect a note of melancholy. And Jonathan had become just about untraceable by phone. David suspected that his brother was only now starting to experience the post-Regimental blues that moving from a world of high adrenaline and adventure to the mundane routines of civilian life could bring. He knew that Jonathan's last tour of duty had been bandit hunting in Northern Ireland. A bastard of a job at the best of times. He knew. He had been through it more than once himself. He just hoped that Jonathan would be able to come through it all okay. He felt redundant here on the yacht, but what could he do? He would have to trust that Jonathan would contact him if he needed him. Surely he would.

He looked back at the girl. She was sleeping again. He thought about waking her. Beneath the damp sheet he was hard. Merely being in such close proximity to her was making him feel horny. In the end he decided to let her sleep on. Yesterday had been quite a full one and they had gone to bed late. They had drifted off to sleep even later still, and looking at his watch, Strachan realized that they must have only had about three hours sleep. And if they were to go ahead with the adventure that they had planned for the coming night she would really need all the rest that she could get...

10.30am

Beneath the sheet, sleeping Astrid stirred again. Strachan continued to watch her. It was mid-morning now and he'd been sitting there watching her for several hours. Just sitting there, just watching her. And all he could think of was what he'd promised they would do that night.

Hell, that was getting to seem a silly idea now. Perhaps she would feel as he did when she finally woke, and they could call the whole daft exercise off.

The day before, they had hired a car, quite early in the morning, and armed with a wicker hamper full of food and drink, had set off to explore the surrounding countryside. There had been no set plan so they just drove as the fancy took them, high into the mountain forests that climbed up steeply just a few miles inland from the Riviera coast.

They had made frequent stops, often taking long walks in among the trees away from the infrequent dirt-paths. The cool shade had been a welcome relief from the blistering heat of the summer sun. It had been during one of these gentle walks in the mid afternoon that Strachan had first taken hold of Astrid's hand. They had been walking side by side, this time along one of the rough paths, and he had just let his hand slide into hers. He hadn't dared look across at her in case he saw rejection in her eyes. But her fingers, long and cool, had closed around his, and they had continued their stroll back to the car in comfortable silence.

For the rest of the day, whenever they left the car to walk, or just to sit by the roadside enjoying the sometimes spectacular scenery, they had held hands, had been able to touch each other with the easy familiarity of lovers who also shared a deep and understanding friendship. But were they lovers, he had wondered? They had been together for a week and there had been nothing physical between them. Strachan had been attracted to her from the start. Oh boy, had he ever. But that had been surface lust. And that part of life he did know about. So far, his experiences with the opposite sex had been confined exclusively to sordid one-night stands and nights spent in the company of his army buddies in a variety of the world's more bawdy brothels. These were affairs that could be experienced and then just as quickly discarded, allowing him to get back to the real love of his life; soldiering. No complications. And that had suited him just fine.

Yet with Astrid he felt something that went beyond the obvious surface lust. Something that caught him, not between the legs, but in the pit of his stomach. Something that made him feel queasy and just a little breathless in her company.

He had never known love, and was afraid to apportion these feelings to that complex emotion. But whatever it was, he knew that he did not want Astrid to leave, and was loathe to make any overtures that might push her towards such a course of action. He knew that she *liked* him. Why else would she stay? After all, she had spent the whole summer drifting around Europe on her own, and there was nothing to tie her to *him*, other than the job he had offered her crewing the yacht. He had a charter party arriving in a week's time and on a boat of *The Hasler's* size, that help would really come in handy. But the pay he had offered was cursory, and *she* was well aware that he had managed well enough on his own in the past. Her help would be welcome, but life would go on if she turned him down. So there must be something more. He could make her laugh, at least, and hadn't he read somewhere that that was a good sign? If only he had been able to read her mind.

So far, her willingness to hold hands with him had been the only signal that he had been able to interpret. And if he had interpreted well, it had been a good sign.

He had not wanted the day to end, so they had driven ever deeper into the mountain forest, enjoying each other's company, swapping anecdotes and generally getting to know each other in a way that suggested, though nothing was mentioned, that they both wished to stay together, at least for the foreseeable future.

At nine thirty, the shadows had grown long but being close to midsummer, it was still light. They had pulled in to the side of the road at the top of a steep hill. They decided to take one last walk through the trees that they had come to enjoy before heading back to the bright-lights of Monaco.

They walked, away from the tracks, until they came out of the forest at the crest of a high ridge. Below them the land dropped away to form a breathtaking forested valley. And where the land rose again on the far side they had spotted a magnificent chateau half way up, bursting majestically from amongst the dense pine. Astrid had been truly taken in by the incongruous beauty of it all.

'Christ, look at that' she had gasped.

It had been so unexpected to see it there like that. If they had kept to the pathways, they would surely have missed it.

'C'mon, let's get back to the car -' she tugged at his hand '- I want to get closer. I want to get some pictures.' Suddenly she was fully alive again, tiredness all gone. She had dropped Strachan's hand and put her camera to her face and had taken several snaps before he had been able to react. She took his hand again and pulled.

'Well, are you coming? C'mon, let's go. There must be a road leading up to that place.'

Strachan had not attempted to discourage her. *He* was not in the least bit tired anyway. He had enjoyed the day more than any he could remember and was loathe to see it end, though he knew that they would be unlikely to be able to get right up to the chateau walls. Still, he would humour her as best he could.

They had driven for an hour, losing their way on seemingly unmapped lanes on more than one occasion. Eventually, they had come across an overgrown lane that was flanked on one side by a tall brick wall, which ran in parallel. They suspected that it must be a boundary wall enclosing the chateau grounds. Then, up ahead, they spotted where two square pillars seemed to grow up out of the wall, each topped with a large stone sphere. As the road began to curve they got a better view. It was the entrance gate.

Strachan had pulled the car onto the verge, and they had walked the fifty yards or so to the gates. The gates were made of wrought iron and twisted into intricate patterns. As they got close, they had seen a small wooden booth just behind the left gate-pillar. The booth was open on the side facing them and inside they noticed a uniformed guard.

Strachan had wanted to call it a day at this point. People who valued their privacy enough to employ full-time security personnel were unlikely to take kindly to prying tourists. Not that it was ever likely to get anything like that far. After all, it wasn't as though the guard was likely to even call his master up at the house with such an absurd request. No, they would be quickly shown about their business, politely or otherwise. Strachan, in a rare moment of pessimism figured that it would indeed be otherwise. He guessed that that was how *he* would react at any rate, and said so.

But Astrid had been in no mood to take no for an answer. She had insisted that they at least give it a try. So he had thought *what the hell*, and they had walked up to the entrance and called out to the guard through the scrolled iron metalwork of the gate.

He had been wrong, as it had happened, about the security man sending them away with a flea in their ear. Of course, the man had not opened the gate for them and taken them for a guided tour, but he had been friendly enough. He had left his booth and they had chatted amiably for a few minutes through the bars of the gate. The guard had told them that the chateau, which was not visible from the main gate because of the dense pine forest that flanked the twisty narrow driveway to either side, was owned by an influential French banker, Emile Stopyra. They learned that he was unmarried and lived alone. They had made small talk like this for several minutes. Strachan had supposed that the guard was happy for the break in what must be a dull routine. They had been about to leave, when a car had approached from around the bend, just beyond where their own car had been left. It was a large stretched Mercedes limousine, and the guard had identified it as being that of the chateau's owner.

Strachan and Astrid had stepped to one side to allow the car to turn into the driveway, where it stopped just short of the gates. The guard had gone back to his booth to operate the electronic switch and the gates had opened smoothly, the hum of their electric motors clearly audible.

To Strachan's surprise though, the car had not moved off immediately. Instead, the rear window nearest them had been lowered and they had found themselves looking at a handsome, somewhat distinguished face. Touches of gray in the hair around the temples and deep lines wrinkling the corners of the eyes had Strachan estimating the man to be in early middle age, although the rest of the skin was smooth and clear. Those touches of maturity only served to add character to the face, and Strachan guessed that this was a man who would be devastating in female company if he had charm to go with his looks.

'Good evening,' the man had said. 'It's late to be calling at the chateau. We're quite remote here. Are you in need of assistance, perhaps?'

Astrid had told him how they had spotted the chateau whilst out walking and how they had come to see if they could get a closer look, and even, if possible, some photographs. She had apologized for invading the man's privacy. Strachan had thought that that was going a little over the top. They had done nothing but stand outside the gates on a public road. They hadn't even been able to see the chateau from there. But to his surprise, the man's lips had drawn into a smile and he had opened his car door.

'You have gone to so much trouble to get here and I find myself flattered at the kind attention you pay to my home. Come, it is a fine evening. You shall have your pictures.'

Astrid had clambered in eagerly, and Strachan had followed, wondering cynically whether two male tourists together would have received the same treatment. He made a mental note to be wary of feminine wiles. The more time he spent with Astrid, the more he was coming to discover the lie of the old *it's a man's world* nonsense.

During the long ride up the driveway, the man introduced himself. He was Emile Stopyra, which they knew, and a banker, which they also knew. His family had owned the chateau for over three centuries, and his lineage could be traced back to the times of the Emperor Charlemagne. So he claimed. Strachan and Astrid had told him that they were living on his boat in Monaco. They had made small talk about the beauty of the region, about the weather, the usual things, until finally, they had broken through the tree line.

The chateau stood before them, now in the open, and it really was a spectacular sight. Constructed of brown stone, it was asymmetrical. Wings spread out from the main hall, seemingly at random. Towers rose inspiringly from unexpected junctures. It was a work of inspired madness architecturally, perhaps stopping just short of the wildest excesses of mad King Ludwig, the Bavarian castle builder.

The building was set into a clearing cut out of the surrounding forest, the driveway curving through a hundred yards of immaculate lawn before sweeping up to the main entrance. The lawn was brightly illuminated in the fading light by powerful spotlights mounted on the chateau walls. The car pulled up before the huge entrance and the uniformed chauffeur hurried round to open the door for them.

For the next hour or so, the banker had been gracious enough to give them a personal tour of the property, and Astrid had been able to get many - hopefully - wonderful pictures. Even Strachan himself, not normally interested in architecture, had been impressed with the chateau, whose interior had been as

43

magnificent as its exterior.

But the tour had come to a rather hurried and somewhat mysterious conclusion. As they had strolled outside the rear of the chateau, Astrid had spotted what appeared to be the roof of a large gray stone gazebo, mostly hidden by trees, about two hundred yards into the forest. Two burly men were carrying a stone slab across the lawn in the direction of this outbuilding. The banker had stopped short when he had seen them and had tried to divert the attention of his guests to an interesting carving cut into the stone of the wall above their heads. But Astrid had wanted to know more about the gazebo, and despite the banker's bluster, would not be put off. Eventually, he had told her that he often used the gazebo when entertaining.

'It is old though, and its condition has become dangerous. This renovation work is essential and I have perhaps delayed it for too long,' he had said. Then smiling: 'I wouldn't wish for you to see it at anything other than its best.'

This had sounded somewhat lame even to Strachan, who frankly couldn't have cared less whether he saw the damned building or not.

The banker had sensed that Astrid was not going to be put off easily and had had to cut the tour abruptly short, pleading that he had work to do that had to be finished before morning. He had hinted that one day, when the renovation work had been completed, they would be welcome to join him and his guests for dinner, when he would be happy to show them the gazebo. They had both known this to be a polite way of putting them off, however; a promise made in the same way people promise to keep in touch with strangers befriended on holiday. Strachan had not been concerned. Astrid had been able to see the chateau at closer quarters than she had ever bargained for, and really, that was enough to be satisfied with.

Driving back to Monaco however, she had been animated and excited. She told him that the carvings that she had seen on the stone slab being carried to the gazebo had meant something to her. She had come across them before. She was sure that they were alchemical symbols.

'I'm telling you,' she said, 'Emile Stopyra, respected and respectable French banker and ancient aristocrat, is involved in magic in some way.'

Strachan remembered thinking how ludicrous the whole story sounded, and even if it were true, so what? But she had cajoled and badgered him the whole journey home -

'C'mon C'mon C'mon'

and

'Pleeeeease...aw, pretty-please...?'

and

'Not chicken are ya...?' said with a grin

- until finally, Strachan had given in and agreed to take her back to the chateau after dark the next night. She would see the gazebo and find out for herself. He hoped that she would then be satisfied.

Despite his agreement, Strachan had considered it to be a ridiculous course of action - 'It's fucking ridiculous,' - was what he had said, but deep down he *had* felt excited at the prospect. It would have none of the danger of an illegal East-German border crossing of course, but in his mind, he could already taste the thrill of adventure again, no matter that this was a trivial objective. He could feel himself coming alive. The feel of the earth, the smell of the forest; these were the things that were familiar to him. Out in the open, his wits against the world; that was where he really belonged.

'Okay,' he had said finally 'Okay. We'll do it. Just give me a break, wontcha...?' but she was grinning, and so was he as his mind began to race. They would need equipment (well they wouldn't *need* it, but he was going to treat this adventure as a live operation anyway) and they could buy that tomorrow. In and out with speed and stealth, and no one would so much as suspect their visit until - but whoa, slow down sunshine. This wasn't going to involve explosives! Those days were over. All the same, he could not help thinking about it as a raid. He made do with mental pictures of the gazebo collapsing as explosive charges blew away its foundations. Something to make Monsieur Stopyra sit up and think.

Back aboard *The Hasler*, Astrid had come to his cabin. She was naked and neither of them had spoken as she pulled back the thin cotton sheet that covered him and slipped into the narrow bunk to snuggle up beside him. Her lips pressed hard against his and her tongue forced its wet way into his mouth where it danced tantalizingly with his.

It had been a time for passion and not finesse. He had slipped his hands between her legs and found her wet there, warm and excited. He played with her only briefly, sliding his fingers in and out of her, rubbing the hard bud of her clitoris with his thumb, before rolling on top of her and entering her. She had groaned and come almost immediately and he had quickly followed, pumping his semen deep inside her. That had been sex of the kind that he had known well enough. Later, she had taught him some of the secrets of the art of lovemaking and he had not been embarrassed at being the more than willing pupil, suborning himself to her expertise...

But that was hours ago and these memories were only accentuating the horniness that he now felt, and were leading his mind away from the sensible thought that they should call off the whole business of this return to the chateau. He looked over at the girl again and almost changed his mind about waking her, but at the last moment he rolled himself out of the bunk and stepped into the adjoining shower cubicle. He turned on just the one tap. The cold one.

Chapter 6

THEY LAY STILL in the shadows. The earth smelled sweet, and lying pressed flat as they were, they could almost taste its aroma. All around, the tall pines rose to form a black canopy through which neither stars nor moon could be discerned.

Strachan looked to his right. There was Astrid. She lay, five yards away, her left shoulder pressed tight into the base of a large tree. A classic attacking posture. Her body was angled slightly, using the tree as protective cover. If this had been a military raid, an enemy patrol would have had to virtually stumble over her before discovering that she was there. And if it *had* been a military raid, that would have been too late...

Beneath his full-face black balaclava, Strachan smiled. He himself lay in the open. This was not, after all, a matter of life or death. They had covered the quarter of a mile from the boundary wall much faster and with much less care than they would had it been for real. But all the same, he had to admit that Astrid was taking to the venture like a natural. This rest-and-look position for example. He had not told her to lie like that; she had just gone ahead and done it. And whereas he would have liked to have walked through the forest, keeping a wary eye open for gamekeepers of course, at least until they were within a hundred yards or so of the target, she had taken to playing commando straight away.

Maybe he had gone too far with the clothing. They had taken the train to Marseilles early in the morning. There Strachan had been able to buy camouflage pants and smocks, and German paratrooper boots from a military surplus store. It had been her idea to buy the balaclavas. She had seemed attracted to their sinister look. He had seen that she was intent on this role playing,

47

so he had bought everything - webbing belts, water bottles and webbing pouches, black covered compasses and the latest in-vogue survival knives.

He tapped the knife where it lay in its sheath against his thigh. He'd had a good look at it when they had got back to *The Hasler*. What a cheap piece of crap it was. The low-grade stainless steel blade with its serrated-top edge had not even been forged in one piece with the handle. A poor weld seam ran in a bubbly line where the blade met the hilt. Just one day in a real survival situation and the strenuous tasks that it would be asked to perform would prove too much. It would snap like a twig. And the would be survivalist with it, no doubt. Still, it had been what she had wanted and he had been more than happy to oblige.

Carefully Strachan reached a dark mittened hand out in front of him. He scrabbled around with his fingers in the loose earth and pine needles until he found what he was looking for. A small stone. He lobbed it gently over towards Astrid and it landed almost soundlessly on her back.

Her head turned towards him with a start. She was living on a tight edge, he noticed. Actually taking on the commando persona that he had teased her about all day. He knew how she must be feeling. Not so much tense as high. To a lesser degree he was beginning to feel it himself. The old thrill of adventure for adventure's sake was coming back to him.

He held his right hand slightly away from him, indicating her forward. He had taught her a few basic hand instructions during the day, and she had been a quick learner. He watched as she eased herself forward, staying flat to the ground using her elbows and knees to propel herself along.

They were only about fifty yards from the clearing in which the gazebo stood. At this point even Strachan felt the need to use professional technique. He followed Astrid through the soft bed of pine needles and silently came along side her. The gazebo was now plainly in sight. They lay together sharing the cover of a single large pine a dozen yards from the edge of the tree line. A couple of trees blocked their line of vision, but they could see the gazebo sure enough. And what they saw was not what they had expected.

It consisted of a vast but shallow concrete dome, about sixty feet in diameter as far as Strachan could reckon. The dome was supported a full thirty feet above a luminous white marble base by thirteen - Strachan counted them - marble pillars.

Away to the left, a narrow dirt track disappeared among the trees in the direction of the chateau. From the tree line to the base of the structure there was only ten yards of open clearing.

Strachan thought about the large piece of folded paper that he carried inside his camouflage smock. Written on it in large crayoned letters were the words: 'BOOM BOOM STOPYRA! REMEMBER AGINCOURT.' Beneath was a picture built up of matchstick figures showing a row of archers despatching a mass of mounted knights, a crude depiction of Henry V of England's finest hour. It was childish nonsense, Strachan knew that. But he had intended to leave it as a memento of his and Astrid's visit, a sort of personalised *Kilroy Woz Here*.

But that would not be possible now, he could see. Because the inside of the gazebo glowed with flickering yellow light given off by old–style brushwood and pitch torches which were mounted on the insides of the stone pillars. And by that light he could see six people of indeterminate sex, draped loosely in white robes with pointed white hoods covering their heads as they sat facing each other in a tight circle in the middle of the gazebo floor. Each was sitting in cross-legged silence, deep in meditation...

WITHIN THE CHATEAU... 9.55pm

'So, you have brought it then?'

Six men sat in the comfort of plush deep armchairs in the chateau's elegant library. All eyes turned to face the speaker who had just entered the room. Like them, the newcomer was draped about with a long white robe. Black eyes in deep sockets, fixed upon one man in particular.

'Of course,' replied Michael Brachman, the object of this harsh gaze. 'We have our Magdalene.'

'Where is it?'

'It is in the next room, being prepared.'

'You have done well, Michael, very well.'

Brachman dipped his head slightly, acknowledging the thanks. He began to cough, wheezing slightly. He had been preparing for this moment for years, but so close to the event, nerves were beginning to get the better of him. He managed to control the cough without resorting to the inhaler, which rested on a table to his left. That was good. He would not have the inhaler during the ritual. Its impurity would give offence.

'Let us see it,' said the newcomer, and although he was obviously the great authority at this gathering, he strode swiftly to help Brachman out of his chair. Their host Emile Stopyra joined him, and together the trio shuffled carefully to a connecting door at the rear of the library. None of the others moved to join them. No one spoke.

The newcomer, a nearby wall light reflecting brightly off his shaven head, threw the door open. They found themselves in a small antechamber, ten feet square. The walls were bare, whitewashed plaster. In the far corner was an iron-framed bed. A young girl, with long wavy blond hair lay motionless there. She looked to be about five years old. Sitting in attendance on a hard wooden chair was a middle-aged woman wearing a nurse's uniform. Resting by her feet was a black leather medical bag.

Stopyra gasped when he saw the girl. Brachman and the shaven headed man both looked at him sharply.

'So young...' breathed Stopyra. He turned to the newcomer. 'Oh Henri it is so young.'

His voice though, conveyed no trace of horror. There was, rather, a hint of admiration.

'A virgin, Emile. Her youth guarantees it.'

'But a child. Will she not be missed?'

It was Brachman who answered.

'A missing child. In London she will be one among many. But there will be no hue and cry. The mother from whom I purchased this fine creature was a heroin addict. A prostitute living in a one-roomed slum. She has since been attended to.'

At this, Henri St. Clair, his shaven head thrown back, began to laugh.

On the bed, the child stirred. Her feet rustled beneath the shimmering electric-blue gown that she was wearing. A low moan came from her lips.

'See to it.'

St. Clair's instruction was directed at the nurse. Unspeaking she reached down and opened the bag at her feet. She pulled out a hypodermic and a small bottle. Carefully, she drew some of the liquid up into the syringe and administered the dose into the arm of the child. Immediately the moaning stopped. St. Clair turned to Stopyra.

'Heroin. Of great purity. So you could say, 'like mother like daughter.''

He threw back the glistening dome of his head and laughed out loud again.

And beyond the laughter, Michael Brachman eased himself back into his chair and mused that there were billions of people on the earth. Billions now, he knew, and the count growing relentlessly. And everywhere, it seemed there were seething knots of hatred and violent factionalism and spiritual anarchy. Not necessarily how the Universe had intended things, and on the spinning planet there were those who claimed to know the very intention of God.

They were far from mundane these people – his people - they had achieved great wealth and power and positions of influence in spheres that were beyond the description of most, in not a few cases. Yet their neighbours and colleagues and families would never ever have suspected their inner thoughts and ambitions... much less understood them.

And as the earth continued to spin in the cold emptiness of space, on her surface these men were now stirred from their beds, ready to take the practice of their craft to a new height. And never out of their waking thoughts was a shared ambition as dangerous as it was frightening as it was Glorious... Glorious at least was the way they saw it.

Still yet, the earth continued to spin. And above and around her and through her and within her, God and the Devil frowned as one.

Chapter 7

THE CHATEAU GROUNDS... 10.03pm

IN THE FOREST, Strachan and Astrid had edged forward until together they lay hidden behind the protective cover of a tree on the very edge of the clearing. This was as close as they were going to get. Astrid had been right. Stopyra was involved in some sort of magic circle. But what was going to happen? They had maintained their silent vigil for just over half an hour now, and the tableau before them had not altered. Strachan leaned over, about to whisper something, then thought better of it. There had been movement.

The group of six stood as one, rising up slowly from their cross-legged posture, smoothly and without using their hands. Sill facing each other, they each took three paces back, then stood still, forming a perfect circle, the edges of which touched the outer squares of a black and white marble chess-board effect which dominated the centre of the gazebo's floor. To the right of this chessboard, Strachan could see two stone cubes, one polished and gleaming, the other rough, as though freshly hewn from a quarry. Across the top of these stones lay a marble slab. It was the one that he and Astrid had seen carried by the workmen the previous night. On this slab lay a thin silver baton, topped with a golden five-pointed star, and a shiny silver dagger with a wavy ten-inch blade. Behind this altar there were three stone pillars, supporting nothing, their tops cut roughly short at a height of some twenty feet. A wooden ladder rested against the middle column.

Strachan had been getting a little bored, but now there was some sign of activity, his curiosity was awakened. He watched as the magician nearest the altar retreated until he could reach behind him to pick up the dagger and the wand. He moved back, into the centre of the circle now, and the others moved, so that their spacing would be equidistant again.

The magician with the wand began to sing, a crystal clear tenor voice mouthing words that were beyond Strachan's comprehension. Pressed beside him, he felt Astrid stiffen. Maybe she knew what was going on. He thought about asking her, then changed his mind. He didn't really care. He was trying to work out which of the be-robed figures were women. These back masses always finished with an orgy didn't they? That was what he was waiting to see.

'Metatron Gabriel Oriens Paymon...' sang the voice. Though sickly sweet it was strangely calming. A little hypnotic.

'Azmodee Magog Amaimon Astorot...' it continued. All the while, the central magician, who was, as far as Strachan could tell, doing the singing, danced intricate patterns within the circle of five, pointing here, then there, first with dagger, then with wand.

Had Strachan been paying attention, he would have noticed that the magician was marking out the sacred five-pointed pentacle and six-pointed star of wisdom, latterly known as the Star of David, within the circle.

Abruptly, the singing stopped. The central magician took his place in the circle once more, the others moving to accommodate him. Without a word of command, the six magi turned through ninety degrees so that each faced the back of the man in front. Stooping, they began to move, describing the circle with an odd shuffling gait, each spilling a white crystalline powder as they moved. The circle was completed three times, leaving a perfect ring of salt on the ground. Silently, the magi walked backwards until each rested his back on one of the columns supporting the gazebo's dome. There were two or three minutes of inactivity during which time Strachan was able to make out the features laid out on the gazebo floor.

Before each pillar, so far as he could see, was a symbol drawn in gold. From the angle at which he lay, he could not quite make out the nature of the designs. To three sides of the chessboard, excluding the side facing the altar, were three large painted triangles. The far one was coloured red, the near one was blue, and to his left as he looked at the scene, was a yellow one. He looked sideways at Astrid. She had been strangely quiet, and he could feel that she was still tense. She was staring intently at the scene before them. He wished to God that something exciting would happen. So far, this black magic stuff was to say the least, less than the stuff of dreams. Or nightmares.

IN THE LEE OF THE CHATEAU WALLS... 10.15pm

Outside the chateau walls, seven men stood in white robes. They stood in a line, waiting to begin their strange procession. At the head of the column, a large man, his shaven head glistening in the flickering light of the torches carried by the last pair, held the delicate hand of a little girl who stood by his side. Her eyes were glazed, the pupils wildly dilated. She might as well have been on another planet. The metallic blue of her garment also caught the light from the dancing flames. It seemed more alive than she did. Behind them was an even stranger sight. The next two men each held a silken rope. These ropes were attached to a ring in the nose of a huge bull. The bull had had all of its body hair removed and its bare hide was painted all over, a gleaming gold. After the bull came a frail looking man, his twisted body hunched forward as he sat in a chrome-plated wheelchair, ready to be pushed by one of his brothers. The rear was brought up with rather more sanity; two more robed men holding the flaming torches.

'Let us go,' said the shaven headed man.

The procession moved forward at a reverent pace, away from the chateau through the gap in the trees where a narrow path led deep into the heart of the surrounding forest.

THE FOREST... 10.18pm

Danger. Strachan could feel it. A dry, metallic taste in his mouth, a slight tightening of his stomach. Danger of the worst possible kind, its source indeterminate. Just what the fucking hell was going on here? Up until now it had all been somewhat amusing, if a little dull at times. But events had taken a sinister turn. It had started with the arrival of the horror-carnival procession. He should have laughed; it had all looked so ridiculous. But he hadn't. Something was making the hairs on the back of his neck stand on end. There was something not quite right.

They were all up there on the gazebo now. The original six had removed their hoods and had turned out to be exclusively male. The seven that had joined them had all been men. That made thirteen. Strachan had not been so ignorant as to miss the significance of that number.

And then there was the girl. That frightened him most of all. There was something so inherently wrong about the girl that the natural revulsion of seeing such innocence among so obvious a collection of corruption had been bypassed within his system. Her hand had been held by a shaven headed madman as they had entered the gazebo. And there *was* madness about that man, Strachan was sure. And power. But for all that power, it had seemed for all the world that it was the child that led the man.

The man-child - for this obscene couple seemed inseparable - had entered the gazebo first. The eyes of the man-part were wide and staring, the rich lips drawn back in a sardonic smile. But the child. Oh such terror. Terror of a kind that Strachan had never experienced. It appeared as though the irises of her eyes were turned back, lost to sight somewhere in their sockets. The whites shone unblinking in the torchlight, a Daemon contrast to the otherwise Angel of her appearance.

The madman led her across the chessboard to the altar, helped her up onto the marble slab. She stood facing her congregation, a god-queen welcoming her subjects with unblinking white eyes. Magdalene; Whore of Babylon. And her congregation had come to pay homage to their Magdalene. The first two, bowing as they approached with the bull, stopped in the middle of the chessboard. They turned the bull, placid with drugs, through a hundred and eighty degrees, so that its behind faced the demon-queen. Four of the original six stepped forward while heavy chrome-plated chains were lowered from inside the dome. Loops of chain were bolted around each of the carnival-gold animal's quarters. The chains were then pulled taut, leaving the beast standing rigid and immobile.

Now the cripple was pushed in his shining carriage up into the temple. The unnaturally curved body sat uneasily in the wheelchair, but the face was alive, and the head inclined its homage as he was brought to rest inside the yellow triangle. The cripple sat, eyeball to eyeball with the beast. Finally, up came the last two. Their torches were secured in brackets outside the temple. They walked forward, bowed deep in supplication and took their places within the salt ring. Only the cripple and the Magdalene remained outside its protective custody.

An unnatural quiet fell about the gazebo. Strachan's senses told him to retreat, to get the fuck out. This was all getting out of hand and he wanted no part of it. He could not dampen the alarm signals that every nerve sang out to his conscious mind. The kind of signals that he'd always listened to in the past. The kind of signals that had kept him alive. He was the professional again now. The adrenaline was running, and the doctors could go fuck themselves. He could feel that he was going to need that energy before long. Unconsciously he had snuggled lower to the ground. Pressed tight he would literally *feel* the approach of any hostiles. His hearing had become acute, and his eyes, though watching the events unfold before him, were darting constantly about, on the alert. He could hear his own pulse. The rate was now up to eighty or ninety. Overdrive to him.

Astrid turned her head towards him, about to whisper. He cuffed her sharply in the mouth with the back of his mittened hand. She stiffened in shock, more frightened by the narrow slits of his eyes blazing behind the balaclava than by the force of the blow. His hand remained raised, ready to strike again to stem any vocal protest, but it was unnecessary. She turned to stare, in utter dread, back at the temple.

'Ateh, Malkuth, Ve Geburah, Ve Gedulah; Le Olem, Amen...'

The ritual had begun. The madman faced east, to the altar. To the Magdalene. As he had spoken the opening intonation, with his right hand, he had lightly touched his forehead, solar plexus, right shoulder, and then left shoulder, bringing his hands together for the final phrase.

A wicked silence had descended on the forest. Strachan recognised it as such. And he knew forests. Knew them as home.

The madman's right arm shot out and in one movement drew a cross in the air before him, surrounding it with a circle.

'In the name of Adonai, I open the gateway of the east...' he chanted.

He repeated the process for the south, west, and north, then came back to face the Magdalene once more. She stood, still unblinking, for her eyelids had been stitched with silken thread to keep them open, facing her worshippers. The heroin was blinding her to the pain, a hypnotic trance giving her the strength to remain upright.

'In the name of the light of the world, under the protection of the god name El, I declare this temple open.'

The madman threw his hands dramatically high and shouted:

'In the name of the blessed, I do desire ye strong and mighty angels Choronzon, Magog, Meklbok, that if it be the Divine Will of Him that is called Tetragrammaton, that ye take upon ye some shape as best becometh thy celestial nature and appear to us visibly in this place and answer our demands...'

There was more, but Strachan did not hear it. Beneath the balaclava he could feel rivers of sweat running down his face. Astrid had crushed close by him. But really, he knew that if she was afraid and was drawing close to him for comfort and support, she would be disappointed. He was terrified.

He wanted to cut and run. Not literally; not rise up and stride shrieking through the forest, but to get away. He could do it. He would be fast and silent. Within minutes it would be as though he had never been there. But there was Astrid. How could he leave her? She was tense, hard as stone beside him. Even through his own fear, he felt such love for her as could cut across so ephemeral an emotion. He tried to calm himself; told himself that they were at a safe distance. That they would not be discovered if they could only keep quiet and still. But he knew that it wasn't discovery that frightened him at all. There was something more primal at work here. Something old. Perhaps ancient was a better word...

And here it was. In terrifying silence, the very earth began to vibrate around the temple. The edges of time itself began to unravel as through his fear, Strachan looked up through the canopy of trees to see the stars rushing earthwards. Or was the earth rushing up to meet *them?* The sensation was one of travel, rapid beyond the understanding of man. And it yes it was the earth that moved, ever faster and faster through space, the stars curving in their paths to rush around the edges, this very act screaming defiance to relative dimensional physics as these vast cosmic structures appeared not to increase in size as they were first approached, then passed...

Then it stopped. Suddenly and with a flash of blackness, the exact opposite of a photographic light flash. It was as though light had changed its characteristics. Strachan could see the yellow of the flickering torches where they hung on the temple pillars. But the flames cast no shadows. Indeed, there was no indication that the torches were radiating their light at all. The flames were dancing and visible, but that was all. There were no patches of light and shadow within the temple as there had been before. But strangely, the objects inside the temple and the magicians were all clearly visible, as if they each were their own source of illumination, a light that did not radiate, but rather was linked directly to the eye if the beholder. And in the absence of any beholder would not exist at all.

Strachan felt Astrid's hand find his. She gripped him tight, painfully so. But he did not flinch. This touch had returned him to sanity. He knew what she must be feeling right now. He had been there with her. But now, he knew, he would have to be strong. He was all that she had got. This was his environment, his *home*. The forest. There were things going on here that he could not explain, but the magicians showed no fear. Obscene though the ritual was, they were not afraid of its effects. And he would draw his strength from them.

He was beginning to experience a degree of control again. His pulse had steadied. His breathing was slower, he was more relaxed. Until he noticed...

In the triangle on the opposite side of the chessboard was slime. A beast from humanity's vilest imaginings made flesh. It sat in the triangle neither malevolent nor benign. It simply *was*. The head was solid. It had eight mouths that Strachan could count, no lips; just ragged metal teeth that snapped constantly open and shut. A bilious green liquid ran from the corners of each mouth to drip to the floor of the triangle where it hissed and spattered. A long neck ran from the base of the head. It was slimy and uneven, a leathery blue skin, bubbled and swollen, covered about with open red sores which spat rather than wept, thick green puss. But the body was strangest of all. It seemed to be an amorphous blob, a mottled bluey-green in colour, wet and shiny with liquid. And it was constantly on the move. Hands and arms would grow and reach out from incongruous places, probing and seeking, before retreating back into the body, only to emerge from somewhere else, probing again.

Strachan realised that it was probing up to the edges of the triangle in which it sat, as though the three boundary lines confined it. Even from where he lay, safely hidden in the forest, Strachan could smell it. It stank of piss and shit and decay. And an undercurrent of sickly-sweet gangrenous puss. Strachan wondered if Astrid could smell it. Surely she could. But she was stifling any urge she felt to retch. That was good.

He looked towards her. Her face was buried in the earth. He prayed that she would not look up and see the thing. For both their sakes. But she stayed pressed to the ground. He kept telling himself that this must just be an illusion, some form of induced hallucination. He had to. He wanted to retain his sanity.

And then he noticed the other one. It was in the triangle on the nearside of the chessboard. And he hadn't seen it before because it was invisible to the eye. But not to the mind. His own mind must have inadvertently caught an inkling of it, and having done so, it was now forced to bring its full attention to bear. And oh, this was the worst of all nightmares. It wasn't physical. Its purity was too great for such vulgarity. But it contained power and knowledge so vast that his entire mind was needed to contemplate it. His eyes were open but he could see nothing. His mind's eye was doing the focussing in an abstract way that he had never previously thought possible. And it reflected on a monster. A monster so terrible that it was beginning to tear apart the logic with which he had been able to exist as an earth-bound entity. A monster whose purity and dimensions began to expand inside his head, filling the unused two thirds of the brain and expanding still... and he knew what it was, and this terrified him further. It was... *MATHEMATICS!*

Oh fucking hell, he couldn't move. He couldn't think. His

entire mind was infused with profound exactness, of knowledge that superseded Einstein, the way Einstein himself had superseded Newton. And there were no numbers. Numbers were a human device, useful arithmetical tools and nothing more. This was methodology; it was abstract concepts that showed the reality of the relationship between energy and matter. For a fleeting moment he could see. He could see how the speed of light could be surpassed as matter achieved a state of negative existence. He could see all this and more. A million states of truth that man had not even thought to enquire about, things that were not yet even abstract notions in the minds of the world's brightest and best. And he knew them all. Understood them all. And it was a nightmare.

He was not ready for any of this. Neither the abstraction nor the pain. And there *was* great pain. The Math-Monster was filling him, expanding with geometric progression. Having filled the unused portions of his brain, it now began to encroach on the sentient third, pushing first the memory store, and then the motor controls in its greed for storage space.

And still it came. It pushed out the centre controlling the senses of touch, smell, hearing, sight, and taste. Now it was taking out the motor control centres. His breathing stopped as the part of his brain controlling that reflex was taken over by geometric proofs. The heart control centre would fail next. Then would come release. The body would cease to function, would wither and die...

Chapter 8

'ZAZAS, ZAZAS, NASATANADA, Zazas!'

The words were hissed by a crouching figure, which stood with bended knees on the altar next to the Magdalene. They were ancient words that heralded eternal damnation. They were the words used by Adam to open the gates of hell. They were the words that saved Strachan's life.

Immediately the Math-Monster removed itself from Strachan's mind. Memory, sentient thought, automatic motor control, all returned in a rush, filling what for a split second had been the void left in his mind as it was vacated by the Math-Monster, which for some reason Strachan now knew to be called Meklbok. This searing inrush caused a spasm of excruciating pain making Strachan silently wince. Then all was calm again.

Strachan saw the new arrival standing next to the child on the altar. Visibly it was more acceptable to his eye than its brothers. But something about it frightened him more.

It was fairly humanoid in form, although its features were exagerrated, like cartoon representations. It had pointed ears and a long narrow chin. Its eyes were black and sparkling. It looked about it, and its thin lips curled back in a smile. Its gaze came to fall increasingly on the child alongside it. After a few seconds of scrutiny of this new wonder, it stood upright out of its crouch and began to speak:

'I am Choronzon. I am the master of light and form. In me shall you see the Gateway to Beyond. Where the ancient of days lies blackened and scourged. Where the Secret Chiefs of the Great White Lodge hold counsel for the everlasting. What would you enquire of me?'

The madman, safe within the circle of salt, responded.

'O mighty angel, whose power lies with fiery sword that holds sway in the garden beyond the abyss, we are seekers after truth.'

Choronzon studied the madman momentarily, then the Master of Light and Form erupted, becoming pure orange fire. He blazed silently in a tall orange pillar on the altar. The madman lifted up his hand to shield his face from the heat. The Magdalene, standing only inches away, remained unmoved, as if the great heat was but nothing.

There came a mighty crack as Choronzon drew blue bolts of lightening from the roof of the dome above. The fire-pillar crackled and buzzed as the bolts of electricity danced impishly around it. Then abruptly, the fire pillar split into myriad fragments, each of which flew, erratically at first, then taking the recognisable forms of stellar constellations, around the protected circle of salt. The motion stopped dead. One of the electrified fireballs hovered slowly over to where the cripple sat, hunched forward in his wheelchair, outside the protection of the circle. It hung suspended over his head for a few seconds, then dipped down sharply, spreading itself over his face.

Strachan winced, waiting for the screams and the smell of burning flesh, but they never came. The fire disappeared up the cripple's nose and into his open mouth, from where it glowed in slow pulses of orange light. The cripple did not seem unduly discomfited by this invasion. He merely sat impassively in his wheel chair.

Breaking the silence, the manacled bull managed to roar through his sedation.

The fireballs were on the move again, all of them this time. They bombarded the Magdalene, standing on the altar, until every square inch of her was covered in searing flame. Smoke curled in tight spirals from the fire. This time they *were* burning. This time there *would* be the stench of singed flesh.

Strachan wanted to run into the temple and grab the child. To smother the flames and then blast off into the forest, taking her with him to safety. But he couldn't move. There was Astrid, paralysed beside him, and there was his own fear. Truth or illusion, he did not want to risk another encounter with Meklbok.

Yet there came no stench of burning. The child remained apparently unharmed. The dazzling electric blue robe that she had been wearing had been burned away though. And now the fiery Choronzon was claiming his gift. His fire was drawn into thin lines that disappeared into the girl's mouth, her ears, nostrils, eye sockets, anus, urethra and vagina. Her skin glowed an orange-pink as she stood naked on the altar. Her mouth now curled into a sinister smile, a smile that Strachan felt contained the wisdom of countless millennia. He was glad that he was not near.

She moved. She stepped down from the altar and stood on the threshold of the salt ring, the smile still cutting her face. Her breath carried with it almost invisible blue flames which danced around her mouth and nostrils as she exhaled. Her lips moved and she spoke one word to the Madman:

'Prepare…'

The madman recoiled from the vicious heat of her breath, but it was evident that he knew exactly what to do next. From beneath his robe he produced a long silver dagger. He reached out a hand and placed it on the rump of the golden bull standing beside him. Never taking his eyes from the Magdalene, he walked slowly backwards, his hand brushing the hide of the beast as he moved, until he stood alongside the powerful neck.

The bull must have been well aware of its impending doom. It bellowed and struggled - to no avail - against the heavy chains that bound it tight. It was stuck fast, immobile, able only to swing its huge head from side to side. The madman turned to face it. He plunged the dagger into the underside of its throat, hot blood pumping all over his white robe and face. His tongue flicked out, licking the blood, which lay thick on his lips and cheeks. With quick practised movements, he slit the beast from neck to genitals, spilling its guts, stinking and steaming to the chessboard floor. The beast had at least died quickly. Its carcass remained eerily upright, a golden idol held fast by silver chains.

The magicians in the circle, following the madman's lead, shed their robes. They stood naked inside the perimeter of the circle, waiting. The madman stood facing the Magdalene again. Her sightless orange eyes travelled down his naked body to take in his sex. He was aroused and hard. A long red tongue emerged from between the Magdalene's lips, flicking from side to side in appreciation before disappearing once more into the smiling mouth. The orange fire began to drip more readily from between her legs, a reaction to what she saw.

The madman's pleasure showed on his face.

'We bid you enter,' he said.

The Magdalene stepped into the salt ring, lifting her tiny feet carefully so as not to disturb so much as a grain of its perfection. She stood close to the madman for a second, her chest rubbing against his sex. At her touch, he looked to the temple ceiling, almost lost in ecstasy, but quickly controlled himself. He stood to one side and took the Magdalene by the hand. In that instant, the fire that burned within her was extinguished. She became a five year old girl again and the heroin was beginning to loose its hold on her senses.

Strachan could discern movement on her face. She was trying to blink her eyes, but silken threads held the lids open. Even so - though Strachan had no way of knowing it - she was experiencing no pain; the heroin still controlled *that* centre of her brain. But she was frightened. Even from where Strachan lay silently watching, that much was clear. She was obviously aware that things were not as they should be.

The madman led the child to the centre of the ring. Two of the magicians knelt in the bull's guts to either side. They took the girl from the Madman and lay her face down beneath the beast, her head facing its hindquarters, then lifted her prone form into its empty carcass. Two of their brothers hurried forward with heavy thread and silver needles and sewed her inside the animal, so that only her head remained outside, protruding obscenely from between the animal's hind legs. Then slowly, they returned to their positions within the perimeter of the circle.

The madman approached the girl, his hard sex standing upright before him.

He stood facing her, resting his hands on the animal's rump and introduced his penis to her young mouth. Her lips resisted at first, but then yielded, allowing him to enter. He moved his hips forward, slowly at first, then faster and faster until he was fucking her mouth, savagely in and out. With each thrust, he would chant the name of a seraph:

'Arrabin... Katolin... Baruel'

He was fucking faster now. He was close to coming. Chroronzon had returned to the girl. She was the Magdalene

64

once more. Fire blazed in her eyes.

And then he was there. He came with a great cry, flooding his semen into the girl's mouth, copious amounts so that it dripped and dribbled down her chin. The madman pulled himself away. His breathing was laboured, his chest heaving up and down. He stood to one side. One of the magi from the far side of the bull moved froward to take his place.

Strachan felt as though he had been hit by a baseball bat. This newcomer to the action was known to him. It was... The Prince!

Strachan's mind reeled with this information as one by one the magicians took their pleasure at the Magdalene's mouth. He would be in touch with the Prince's father for sure. This could not be allowed to continue. He knew that he himself would be ridiculed if he tried to make what he'd seen public knowledge. But Prince's father was a King. He would be listened to. And he was a friend. When Strachan gave his word regarding the truth of this abomination, he would be believed.

It was half an hour before the twelve magicians had finished with their Magdalene. Strachan had had his orgy. But it had not been what he'd anticipated. He felt unclean for simply having been a witness. He sorrowed for the girl. Her corruption was now beyond salvation. The mental scars that she would carry would surely prove too heavy and unyielding for her ever to live a normal life.

He cursed the fear that had rooted him to this place. Fear that had prevented him from putting a stop to such obscenity. Poking at his consciousness was a dim awareness of the true horror of the Math Monster, Meklbok and he knew that he still feared confrontation with such as *that*. And he felt ashamed. Looking into the temple once more, he saw the magicians freeing the little girl from the beast's carcass. Gently they lowered her into the slime and offal that lay beneath it.

Strachan hoped that it would all now be over. That soon he and Astrid would be able to leave. Right now he longed for the soothing sanctuary of *The Hasler* as she lolled at anchor on the *Quai Des Etats Unis*. He longed for the lights and sounds of Monaco. When he got back, he would even pay a visit to the casino and lose a few *thou* at roulette. What the fuck? It was only money. But there would be people there. Lots of them. Clean people. Happy people. Even in the hubbub, he would be able to relax. Lose a littler of the horror.

Then as he looked into the temple, he realised that it was far from over. There was the cripple. Until now he had sat beyond the circle, a silent fiery observer, infused with the flames of Choronzon. His chair moved forward, under its own unearthly power, bursting through the sanctity of the salt ring. The wheels cut uncaring through the salt, spraying white crystals to either side. All pretence that the ring afforded the magi some protection from powerful forces that they had called to aid them was now abandoned. That protection had died when Choronzon, in the form of the Magdalene, had been invited to join them inside. The madman had acted of his own free will. At last Choronzon the Cripple sat face to face with Choronzon the Magdalene and with timeless wisdom, the seraph contemplated its own being.

The robe that still shrouded the cripple began to smoulder. Then it ignited fiercely with bright yellow flames. The flames turned blue as their heat–intensity rose, roaring out their power as the robe was turned quickly from silk to ash to dust, carried high by the flames into the roof of the temple. The flesh beneath remained untouched by this furnace-action, remaining visible throughout, a ghastly white. The flames died suddenly. The cripple sat still in his chair, the Magdalene standing a few feet in front of him. For a few seconds their eyes were locked in understanding. Their exhalations of blue white flame, mingled, searing the air between them. Then the fire died in the eyes of the Magdalene. She became a little girl yet again. Now though, the effects of the heroin were receding rapidly. She was aware of her pain and aware of her fear. Her eyes, which had been stitched open, had dried and shrivelled. The pain was crucifying. She could not see, the irises had been turned up inside the sockets and were now stuck fast. She screamed in her terror and suffering. The face, once sweet and angelic now showed the signs of its defilement. Dried semen was pasted on her cheeks and in her hair. Fresher samples still dribbled from between her lips, mingled with blood where her milk teeth had chaffed against some invading penis or other. Some of the magi had scraped away skin in an intensity of face-fucking with the child.

She raised her hands to her face and wailed again, about to sink to her knees. But the Cripple would not let her. Choronzon would not let her. It was not yet finished with its prize. Shafts of fire blazed from the cripple's eyes, bursting the child's hands away from her face. The fire beams caught her own ruined eyes, searing the tissue, which browned and boiled, finally bursting aqueous humour out from her face. Flames entered the girl's head through the eye sockets and she was lifted up on her feet again, held steady by the fire gaze of the Seraph-Cripple.

And very suddenly the fire beams were gone and the screams were gone. Once again, it was the Magdalene who stood facing the cripple. She moved forward to touch him, to stroke a child's soft fingers along the inside of his thigh. Her hand reached down between his legs to cup his balls, squeezing gently, stroking the penis into life. The orange fire dripped from between her legs once more. There was no pain in the face now, only smiles, old and horrible, an antithesis to the youth of the flesh that bore them.

She climbed onto the chair, her small hands gripping the flesh of the cripple's chest, pinching hard. Her thighs were open, his hard penis between them, appearing massive in proximity to her tiny body as the fire of her arousal dripped out to lubricate the excited member with the heat of her passion. She leaned her head forward, her wet tongue reaching out to lick slowly at his lips.

In the middle of the chessboard, the dead bull lifted its massive head. The mouth opened and a deep bass voice boomed:

'Adonai!'

The Magdalene impaled her slender frame onto the cripple as red and yellow lightening bolts fizzled and crackled in an uneven lattice surrounding the temple. And with that moment she was the Magdalene no longer. The little girl became the Whore. The Whore of Babylon.

Strachan, crushed to the pine needle floor between the trees continued to watch in mounting disbelief, disgust and self-loathing. He was gripping tight to Astrid's heavy smock and fear rippled out and over and through them both. He looked up and regarded the madman and the magi standing with their backs to the pillars of the gazebo, and he could see clearly, with his fear-

67

sharpened senses that all of them were every bit as shocked and frightened by the events unfolding before them as he was, at a distance and unseen.

His focus was continually drawn to the little girl. The fire had gone from her eyes and mouth. Her skin had darkened, an opaque olive-green. Black slime dripped from her eye sockets and hideous red sores began to erupt on the newly corrupted flesh of her face and body. The sores burst and ran with yellow puss, which wriggled, alive with maggots, down her skin. The skin itself began to split, exposing the grey green of decaying flesh beneath.

Yet still the cripple fucked harder and harder into this vileness as Choronzon took its pleasure with itself. He came, an eruption of fire that burst in pulses through the flesh of the Whore, ripping her into chunks of rotten meat, which flew to the floor in cascades of blood and body fluids. The fires of creation that had issued out from the cripple burst brightly on the underside of the temple dome where they clung, glowing brilliant in the darkness.

Strachan did not see Astrid lift her head from the pine floor of the forest where it had been buried for most of the ritual. He did not realise that she had watched the ultimate obscenity of this final act. He only heard her scream 'Noooooooooo!!!' A scream that burst through the silence of the forest night, telling the magi and their gods that they were not alone.

Run. That was all that he could think of. Just get the fuck out. Right now!

And this time Strachan's instincts took over. Good instincts. The best. Instincts that had no room in their reasoning for Math Monsters and Slime Monsters. Pure *let's get out of range*, *boys* survival. He grabbed hold of Astrid's wrist and was off, dragging her upright, and for a few seconds, pulling her through the trees behind him.

Then suddenly she was with him, running by herself now, her reasoning returned. She knew as well as he did that they needed to move quickly. If she was shocked by what she had just witnessed, then she could not afford the luxury of reacting to it right now. That would have to come later. When she was comfortable. And safe. And safety was not over the wall where the car was parked. It was not even down the mountain forest among the lights of Nice and Monaco. Safety was home. An ocean away. A continent away. Away from Europe with its ancientness and history. Away from lands where secrets were known, still handed down from times predating Jesus the Christ whom her mummy and daddy did so revere. Home where the skies were big and blue, were daddy could save her from the hurtful and the hateful...

'Come on and hurry the fuck up,' hissed a voice from in front.

She looked up and saw Strachan, a sinister and deadly figure crouched against a tree. He was almost invisible in the dark, his camouflage smock and trousers blending perfectly with the mottled forest shadows. The balaclava made him look frightening.

Even so, she did hurry the fuck up towards him. He was down by the base of the tree and even through the balaclava, she could see that he was scanning the forest behind her, watching the area that they had just left. For the first time she realised just what it meant to be a professional in the shadowy world of military special forces. She could see that he was on top of the situation. She sensed in him that confidence and urgency that she had first seen onboard *The Hasler* that day when he had gone to get her wallet from the Prince. She picked up her pace and was with him in a few strides, sliding on her knees to the dirt floor beside him.

With one hand he grabbed her roughly by the shoulder, half pulling her back to her feet, then shoved her roughly in the back.

'Move!' he said. 'Don't wait don't stop, just keep moving, get over the wall. I'll be with you all the way.'

She stumbled from the force of the shove but regained her balance quickly and was running, unmindful of the low branches, which scraped against her balaclavaed face. Strachan waited a second, still scanning the area behind them, then seeing nothing, took off after her.

They ran full pelt, swerving around tree trunks, leaping over fallen branches. Twice Astrid stumbled and fell, unused to moving rapidly in a darkened forest environment. Twice Strachan stopped, wrenching her to her feet and hurling her on her way with ever more encouraging torrents of whispered abuse.

The boundary wall could not be far away now. Three, maybe four hundred yards. There had been no sign that anyone (anything?) had followed them, but Strachan knew better than to get complacent. Their goal was the wall; then the car; then Monaco. And maybe that wouldn't be far enough. They would have to achieve each objective in turn. So right now, it was the wall they needed to think about. Then, twenty yards ahead, from out of the shadows, from behind a tree, stepped Death.

Reaction. Strachan dived to the left, rolling for cover behind a tree. Instinctively his hand reached down to draw the knife from the sheath strapped to his calf. He had to look again to reassure himself that his eyes had been deceiving him. That an animated skeleton had not stepped out to confront him. The reassurance came, but the reality was somehow nowhere near comforting.

It was a man. Painfully thin, wearing tan cowboy boots, brown corduroys and a plaid shirt with a Trilby hat completing the ensemble. But the face beneath the hat was ghastly. It *did* appear to be skeletal. The flesh had been burned; hideously, irreparably. The skin, such as it was, cleaved tight to the skull, sucked in at the cheeks, white and shining like wax. The mouth, a lipless slit, was cut wide, twisting up at the edges, following the line of the jawbone. And the browless eyes gleamed black from deep in the sockets. The very picture of Death. Not quite the dread Apocalyptic Horseman, perhaps, but not far off. And the scythe that he carried in his left hand; well, Strachan could now see that it wasn't a scythe at all. It was a crossbow. And the skeleton man lifted it. Strachan could only watch as it was pointed at Astrid, standing paralysed and staring in terrified disbelief.

Strachan lifted himself into a crouch, unconcerned that he was giving his position away, preparing to dive at Astrid, to knock her out of the way of the lethal weapon. But it was too late. The grinning-skulled skeleton man pulled the trigger. Strachan felt as if he was watching in slow-mo as the deadly bolt caught his newfound love in the throat. The bulbous nose of the tip crumpled slightly on impact, sending ripples through its fragile casing, before penetrating the flesh of her neck to about an inch and a half. Then the pressure became too much for it, and it ruptured violently, sending beads of mercury cascading through muscle cartilage and blood vessels, propelled onwards and outwards by the momentum of their flight.

Astrid's head was all but torn off in this moment. It was thrown back by the force of the blow, spraying blood and liquid metal high into the air, before hanging loosely down her back, held to her body by nothing more substantial than a few strips of skin. She stood like that for a few seconds, a headless statue, black in the shadows, before crumpling to the forest floor.

The skeleton man had reloaded the crossbow and was turning to Strachan. For a split second, Strachan was frozen with the shock of what he had just seen. He allowed the useless knife to drop to the ground then dived for cover once more. He had to get away. To survive. What had happened back at the temple might conceivably have been a grand guignol of a hallucination, but Astrid's murder had been real. And there would be no revenge for that atrocity if he did not live to tell the tale. For the moment, he felt no loss. No sense of outrage. No hurt. If those feelings were to come, they must come later. For now, survival and escape were uppermost. The professional in him was taking charge once more. He would let that instinct guide him, would follow where it led. He had lost close friends in combat before. *Wireless Ridge???* The time for grief, he knew, came after the battle.

He moved swiftly out of his cover, leaping low, from tree to tree, using their dark bulk as cover, moving erratically, showing no obvious direction to his flight.

Behind him he heard laughter. Loud and hearty. The skeleton man, he realised, was not bothering to follow. But he could not afford to relax. Such complacency, he was sure, meant that the skeleton man would not be alone. There would be others in the forest bent on his destruction.

He rested near some fallen branches to think. The wall was away to his right, maybe a quarter of a mile away. He had slipped far enough away from the skeleton man. Time to make his escape. And then his head seemed to drain of blood. He felt a slight dizziness. And in flashes his nightmare, *the* nightmare, was returning to him, for the first time invading his conscious mind!

In quick bursts it flashed before him; the shopping precinct, the black figure, the mass murder, the killer killed, the hideous bearded head, the living offal. A voice inside his head called out:

71

Daviiiiid!

A wailing, pleading scream of a voice; the voice of a man that he vaguely knew. And then his head cleared and he knew immediately what he had to do. No time to philosophise, just to fuck off out.

So he moved, fast and fluid. Just like the old days. He was an animal of the forest. The pine needle floor barely rustled beneath his feet. He melted into the shadows, running never stopping. His senses were alert, hearing, vision, even smell, seemingly magnified way beyond the accepted human ranges. It was the one-ness with the forest that he had enjoyed so much in his now longed for past. His instincts were remembering; they had never really forgotten. And now it was all flooding back to him.

He could see the wall. There, through the trees, only fifty yards away. He was going to make it. He picked up the pace, more alert than ever. Nothing was going to stop him with the goal now clearly in sight.

But stop he did. Short and sudden, not even bothering to dive for cover. Up ahead, hands in pockets, leaning against a tree just before the wall was a dark figure. It wasn't the skeleton man; the build was too heavy for that. In the night shadow, the features of the face could not be distinguished, but he recognised that figure just the same. Even in the dark at this range he could make out his brother. It was Jonathan.

He blinked, and in a split second, the figure had disappeared. Another illusion? No time to think. A noise, out of the trees behind him. Close and getting closer, fast. He recognised the sound. Another memory, another piece of the jigsaw of his past being slipped into place. It was a dog. A large, powerful animal by the sound of it. And a dangerous one. There was no growling, no snarling to accompany the approach of this animal, just the fast and heavy pounding of its running feet as they carried it through the trees towards him. An attack dog. A silent killer, trained to make no noise, to give no warning of its approach. But Strachan was not afraid. He was the master of this situation. There was, he could hear, just the one animal. He turned around to face it, crouching down, his feet spread to give him balance, leaning forwards to meet it. He was glad of this opportunity, happy to tell himself that in a small way at least, his revenge would start here.

The dog came into view, hurtling at full pelt towards him. It was large all right, a Doberman-Rottweiler cross. A powerful animal. Strachan held his left arm in front of him, protecting his face and throat, giving the dog an obvious target to strike at.

In eerie silence, it pounced, its large jaws opened wide, and Strachan got the timing just right, ramming his raised forearm into the back of the animal's mouth, not allowing it the leverage necessary to inflict any real damage with its bite.

He allowed the dog's momentum to push him over backwards, crushing its body to him with his right arm, and in one movement, rolling over so that the animal was pinned beneath him. He spread his legs wide, pushing hard against the ground, not allowing the struggling animal to roll out of his grasp. His left arm remained jammed hard into the back of the dog's mouth, holding the vicious jaws open. Then he quickly grasped the lower jaw with his right hand and wrenched downwards and sideways, not even wincing at the sound of tearing sinews and dislocated splintering bone. He raised himself to his knees, the disabled animal squealing and writhing on the ground beneath him, its useless jaw flapping hopelessly from side to side in its agony. Grabbing the two front legs, Strachan wrenched them harshly apart, smiling grimly at the sound made by the sternum as it splintered. The animal fell lifeless in his hands, its heart ruptured.

Strachan threw the animal to one side. In his mind, he knew that the animal had only been doing a job that it had been trained by humans to do. In a small way, he felt sorry at having had to destroy such a magnificent animal. But he left it at that. The dog would have killed him, and if its death struck even a small blow at those who had killed Astrid, then all well and fucking good.

He ran to the wall, glancing about, not sure now whether he had seen his brother or not, nor whether it had all been some perverse hallucination. He saw nothing now, and there was no time to stop and look. Certain that he was clear, he scrambled over the wall, never looking back, and ran for the car that was parked half a mile down the lane.

73

Chapter 9

'MAY I ASSUME that everything is in hand, Emile?'

Emile Stopyra was taking the call in the small secluded study that he had had furnished for himself high within the chateau that was his home. Its small scale was much removed from the vastness of his offices in the smart buildings that he owned in Nice and Paris. But the womb-like nature of this place was designed to work wonders when concentration was called for. And a call like this one, from Henri St Clair would always demand clarity of thought and his full concentration. St Clair never made small talk.

Stopyra knew immediately what St Clair was referring to. The events of two nights earlier would not be easily forgotten. It had been an important night for them all. It had confirmed their power to those present. Servitors all, to be sure. But men who counted all the same. From all quarters they had come, and to all quarters they would be returning. Soon the world would be ready to accept a new *renaissance*. A new Age of Light. The Great Work would make all things possible.

However, for Stopyra there was still St Clair's question to consider. It was in his province. It was his responsibility. The girl, and the man. Unfortunate, that. The girl was taken care of. It had been as though she had never existed. And the police inspector that the man had brought to the chateau had seemingly been put off. For the time being, at least. *What girl? What murder? The man must be delirious. What an absurd notion. Please, inspector, see for yourself...*

And the inspector and his men had done just that. They had searched the house, searched the grounds. Always that man was with them, showing them, telling them. And what tales he had

74

told. With each new revelation, the inspector's brow had furrowed further with respectful disbelief. Of course they had found nothing. By the time of this thorough - forensic even - search, there had been nothing to find.

But the man was a worry just the same. He had remained calm throughout. There had been no hysterics. It had been as though he had expected the police to find nothing, as if he were simply pursuing the official channels before embarking on some adventure of his own. It had been in his eyes. Outwardly he had seemed calm and rational, but inside? Those eyes burned with a cold fire. He had not been able to meet them more than once.

And more, that man must have been persuasive, because the inspector had been back, only that morning. His questions had been circumspect but worrying. This Police Inspector would have to be attended to as a matter of priority. The man could wait a day or two. There would be no problem. So with regard to St Clair's question, he had his answer ready.

'Of course Henri,' he said into the telephone 'as the mind thinks it, so it is done.'

ONBOARD THE HASLER... MONACO... JUNE 14th... 7.20pm

The police inspector was dead. Strachan had found that out just two hours earlier.

That had been unexpected. He *had* expected Stopyra's money and influence to bring the investigation to a halt. The group of perverts that had been gathered at the chateau that night; well, he expected that they must all have been wealthy and influential in their own ways. The Prince had been there. *He* certainly was not short of the odd Franc or two. And he *was* a Prince. A bastard, but a Prince all the same. His connections were of the very highest order.

Besides, there hadn't been much to investigate. It had been his word against Stopyra's. There had been no body, the temple had been totally sterilized, not even a hint of the horrors that it had played host to only hours earlier. No, it was amazing that the inspector's keen nose had smelled a rat at all. He had said that he was going to see Stopyra again that morning, just to ask a few questions, see if he could get an inkling of anything suspicious.

Even then, Strachan had been prepared to plan his own revenge. He owed it to Astrid. This was not to be a quest for justice. It would be punishment, pure and simple. After all, what was justice anyway? A word to salve the conscience of the civilized, and Plato could be fucked for thinking otherwise. If the object of justice wasn't punishment, and punishment wasn't synonymous with revenge, he'd eat his own head. If that were not the case, then the punishment element of justice would be wholly redundant. It would be enough to take offenders to one side and explain the error of their ways to them.

But enough of philosophy. He needed no rationale. He was going to rip the fuckers; open their flesh, tear down their walls for what they'd done. He'd loved her. She had been the first one, the only one. And they'd taken her away. For nothing; for no reason, like she'd been just some piece of shit that they'd had to kick out of their way.

For the first time he'd seen light. Seen what it might be like to share the future. And he had liked it; had been looking forward to it. And the cunts had taken it all away.

Well he'd *banjo* the bastards for that. Even though he might die for the effort, he'd take out Stopyra, guaranteed. Nothing would prevent that. Then the fucking chateau, the grounds, the people that surrounded and served Stopyra. As much as he could destroy, and as many as he could kill. He would not stop until none were breathing, and no stone remained standing. And if he stayed alive to see all that through, well, he could be out of the harbour and out east, where in a few days he would be able to lose himself in the Greek islands. And then on to Africa, maybe, or better still, Pakistan. Yes, Pakistan. He would have a welcome there. He had skills that they could use, those Mujahadeen Afghans. They were his spiritual brothers, and he would join them against the Russians. Not because he particularly hated the Russians. But because he loved to fight, loved to soldier. He had lost his new love, so would return to the old. Never, never again would he allow his life to rot in limbo. To live or to die; either way. But to vegetate? Never no more.

It had been decided, sitting there deep inside *The Hasler* amid tears and whisky. God how he missed her already. He had written a letter to her parents, explaining everything, including what he intended to do. If he returned, he would send it to them, along with her things. If not, well, it would be found with those things aboard *The Hasler* and forwarded anyway.

The policeman had intended to return to the chateau. For some reason, Strachan had felt confident about the man. He had sensed the honesty there. He had owed it to this man to allow him the opportunity to bring Stopyra to civilised justice. And now the policeman was dead, shot in the head by a pillion passenger riding on a motorcycle, as he walked along the *Rue D'Angleterre* in Nice.

Strachan had found this out when he had telephoned, as arranged, to see if the policeman had been able to discover anything from his visit to the chateau. A part of him had hoped that the inspector would turn up trumps, but after this – well he was happy to be going about his own business. He would visit Marseilles again in the morning. There were things that he would be needing.

Chapter 10

DARK AGAIN, JUST like it had been on *that* night. But a different mind was at work here now. Then he had been the Lover, the Adventurer, the Play Actor. Now he was the Killer.

He was in the grounds. That was never going to be a problem, and it hadn't been. Acres and acres of forest surrounded the chateau, enclosed by literally miles of wall. Stopyra's interests in security obviously ended a few hundred metres from the chateau itself, to where the powerful spotlights beamed out front.

Strachan couldn't see the spotlights from where he was, just inside the wall, about a mile from the chateau. But he remembered them from his first visit. This op was going to have to be played largely by ear. He would have to rely as much as he could on the memories of what he had seen on that first guided tour. It would be enough.

He was wearing camouflage gear again. And the balaclava, and the webbing belt. But there were extra pouches on the belt this time. An anti gas respirator, an AGR, was tucked into one; nine-millimetre ball ammunition filled another. A small rucksack on his back contained some highly unstable explosive charges that he had concocted using common household detergents. Each of the five charges was packed in a tin biscuit-barrel and was attached to its own battery-powered timing device. Not as powerful as *plastique*, but it would do the job. Another pouch contained infrared binoculars. All these things had been easily purchased over the counter from the military store in Marseilles, along with a *real* knife this time, a Gerber BMF. It had cost two thousand francs, but was worth every centime. The balance was perfect, the steel tempered and refined. It would serve him well.

78

And there was the Browning. An old world-war-two model purchased in a seedy waterfront café. Not for nothing had he gone to Marseilles. A major port and France's second city, it was also the garrison town of the French Foreign Legion, and had its seedier quarter. He had felt at home among the current and ex Legionnaires. They spoke the same language. Had shared many the same experiences.

He had been discreet and the weapon had not been hard to come by. Nor the ammunition. Two hundred rounds of *nine-milly* ball. And five magazines. And all for five thousand francs. A bargain. There had been no questions asked nor explanations offered. It had been a straight business transaction, completed in minutes.

On his back he carried a small rucksack; not as large and voluminous as the more familiar Bergen, used by the SAS, but large enough to carry the 'extras' that he had brought with him.

He moved quickly through the forest. This time it was for real. He knew how to move in silence, keeping to cover, never allowing his presence among the trees disturb the natural order of things. It was as though he belonged to the forest, had become part of it.

His eyes and ears were constantly alert, seeing, hearing, everything. There would be no human patrols, not this deep into the forest. But dogs. There might be more dogs. He had to be careful. The knife felt good in his left hand, the handle pleasantly filling his grip. There was going to be no pissing about with any animals tonight. Just rip the fuckers and be gone. He had more important matters to attend to.

And then, at last, came the tree line. His sense of direction had been reliable. There had been no mistakes, no back tracking on himself in the dense forest. He squatted, four trees in from the clear edge, where the forest ended and several acres of manicured lawn, blazing yellow rather than green with the intensity of the halogen spotlights, stood between any would-be intruder and the chateau.

East Germany. He couldn't stop his mind going back to that. How many times had he crossed that devil's hell? Too many times, it seemed. And at one time it had seemed like a siren, calling to him. He had come to know the border, all of its strong points, all of its weak points. He was the world's unacknowledged number one back then. But what was past was past. The job in hand occupied his every thought. And rightly. This wasn't the border, after all, for all the floodlighting. There would be no electrified fence to negotiate. No minefield, no watchtowers manned by unforgiving take-no-prisoners guards, whose lives, whose families' lives depended on pure vigilance. No trip wire operated machine guns. Fucking hell, this was a piece of piss by comparison. Just a floodlit stretch of open ground, and maybe some attack dogs. Nothing. Easy. For a man like him.

He watched for a few minutes, and saw nothing. Then, from round the corner of the chateau they came. Two men, walking two Alsatian dogs, controlling them on short leashes. They were walking in an anti-clockwise direction around the chateau, about twenty yards from the walls. Ex-police rather than ex-military. Their bearing was too casual, unprofessional. They were chatting amiably, rather than watching the tree line. Dangerous. Without doubt, men who had never had their lives depend upon sentry patrols. Men who had never been in a position where a highly trained and motivated enemy might sneak amongst them unawares and take the lives of them and their comrades. And patrolling together. Strachan shook his head in disgust. They should have at least been patrolling separately, one clockwise, one anticlockwise, in constant radio contact.

He waited and watched again. It took them twenty minutes to circumnavigate the chateau at their casual pace. He would like more time. There would have to be a diversion. And he knew just the one. He was going to have used it anyway. Let them know that he had opened the batting. Let them know that Davy-boy was here.

Inside the chateau, Emile Stopyra sat back in a Louis XV armchair in the small study, which adjoined his chamber on the first floor of the east wing. He sipped peppered Russian vodka from a tiny thimble glass that he constantly had to refill from a bottle wedged firmly into an ice bucket by his side.

He was worried. He would be worried until that dangerous

Englishman was dead. Tonight, and it would be over. It had been fortunate that the Prince had known the man. He had had his doubts about the Prince. Too much the playboy. And they were involved in serious business. Was this really a man who could play any part in the evolution of mankind on earth? It was a question that he had asked himself many times. And the answer had not usually been positive. But higher minds than his thought otherwise. And that greater wisdom needed to prevail for the plan to achieve Glory. He knew that. And now the boy Prince had shown his worth. They had dined together aboard the Prince's yacht the previous night. The problem had been discussed. The Prince had known of the Englishman. The Prince had offered to deal with the problem. Had been eager to do it. He had agreed of course. God knew, there were enough incriminating pathways leading to his door as it was. Yes, let the boy Prince prove his worth. It would make the bonds that joined them tighter still. Would make them more than brothers.

The music that had been playing unobtrusively in the background, Debussy's "The Submerged Cathedral," came to its conclusion. In the silence, Stopyra rose from his chair and walked over to the compact disc player. He removed the disc, replacing it in its plastic case, and inserted another. He sat back heavily in his chair as the first few misty occult notes of Erik Satie's *Trois Gnossiennes* oozed darkly from the speakers.

The explosion, when it came, shocked him into throwing the thimble glass of vodka down onto the deep pile carpet beneath his feet, where the liquid stained dark against the bright golden colour of the pile. It was *him*. Come to extract revenge. He knew it. It had been in those eyes when he had come with the policeman. Those eyes had been windows to a soul that knew no mercy. A soul black and with scorched wings, a soul that brandished a golden sword of vengeance. He had seen it there, that morning. And he had seen the dog the night before. Just one man. A fanatic, but just one man. Surely he was safe, here, locked in his study, his guards standing between him and this Nemesis? Out of the small leaded windows to the east, a pillar of smoke and yellow flame billowed skyward from beyond the darkened tree line. This was no time to take chances. He reached to this right and picked up the telephone...

Strachan crouched low beneath a ground floor window on the western flank of the chateau. He had pulled on the AGR, having first smeared the insides of the glass eye-pieces with washing-up liquid to prevent them from misting up. There would be no gas, he knew, and in the event of fire, the AGR would provide no protection against smoke. The black rubber mask was worn for a distinct purpose. To inspire terror. He remembered his times in the Killing House back in Hereford during siege busting exercises. When the attack team stormed the building, when tensions and adrenaline were running high, God, how terrible they had seemed, clad all in black, with faces black and angular, and for that crucial split second, seeming non human, insectoidal even. And the natural urge had been to turn and flee. Well, they would know that feeling inside the chateau before long. *Fuckin' A* they would.

The distraction had worked well. The charges were more powerful than he had expected. It had been difficult to be precise. He had strapped fifty firework bangers to each of the two charges to increase the noise level. And a bloody good bang they had made. He had not stuck around to see after planting the charges, but he hoped that they had been powerful enough to bring down the two pillars of the gazebo to which they had been attached, hoped that the whole obscene edifice had come crashing to the ground. Maybe he would get to find out later. Now it was time to move.

He scurried along the base of the wall, leaving the two thin cables that had run down from below the window sill where they disappeared underground, split in two, curling slightly at the ends where the knife had parted them neatly. There would be no telephone calls that night. He had circumnavigated the chateau, scouring every wall with his binoculars, looking for those telephone cables. He had crossed the illuminated lawn after the charges had detonated. He knew that the guards, such as they were, would all head off in the direction of the blast and he had been right. Now the communication links were broken, the next task would be to effect entry. No messing about, this would have to be straightforward. There, above him. A large window made up of leaded-lights. And no lights glowing in the room beyond. He stood sharply, out of the shadows at the base of the wall. He drew back his elbow and smashed it into the bottom corner of the window three times. The leaden lattice buckled under the blow, enough for him to pull out several of the small glass rectangles. He gripped the empty lead and peeled the metal out of the wooden frame, making a hole large enough for him to crawl through.

From the far side of the building he could hear them; shouting, running, dogs barking. Perfect. There had been very little noise when he had broken through the window; a muffled thudding at most. He replaced the heavy knife in the clip strapped to his left calf, and took the Browning out of its holster. It felt good in his hand. He reached through the hole and carefully dropped the rucksack to the wooden parquet floor. Inside the AGR, his face was hot, beginning to sweat. He could hear his breathing, sucking hard to draw the air through the dense filters. He thrust the gun arm through first, then his head and shoulders, and pulled himself up over the ledge and into the room.

Stopyra had put out the lights and locked the door. The phone was dead. Out beyond the window, the fire had died quickly following the initial explosion. It had been the gazebo. Marble and stone; nothing to burn. The smoke plume that had billowed skywards was now dispersing in the clear air of the upper atmosphere. The halogen lights still blazed their illumination of the lawns running out from the chateau towards the trees. The men paid to guard him had all run from the house at the sound of the explosion, heading into the trees towards the blast. Now, as he looked down from the darkened window, they were coming back, out of the trees. Those with dogs were freeing them from their leashes, letting them run. The rest were dispersing, more organised now. They were heading back into the forest, some of them, to pursue the hit and run anarchists. Others were forming a loose cordon around the building, looking out towards the trees. But something told him that they were too late. This was not the work of anarchists. A Nemesis was in the chateau even now, hunting, searching, unstoppable.

Perhaps it was fated to be. He was not to become one with the Secret Chiefs this time around. They had sent out this

83

Nemesis to destroy the clumsy shell of his body. He was not yet ready. Next time around, maybe. All the same, he would cling to material existence if he could. He pulled open the narrow drawer in the table on which the telephone rested and pulled out an FN Barracuda revolver. He turned the Louis XV armchair around to face the room's only door and sat down in the dark, to wait.

Chapter 11

INSIDE THE CHATEAU... 11.36pm

A HEAVY-SET woman walked down a narrow corridor on the ground floor of the west wing. She had heard the commotion but it would not prevent her from performing her duties. She had much to thank her master, Emile Stopyra, for. A career destroyed at forty-five years of age, she had been alone and unwanted with nowhere to go. It had been the drugs, as she had always guessed that it would be, one day. An addiction to morphine that had gripped her since her early twenties.

There had also been a man of course and, well, he had long since gone, dead by his own hand, razor slashes in his wrists letting his life blood ebb away in that seedy Montmartre apartment all those years ago. She had been left alone, thirty years old, starting to run to fat, her looks, such as they had ever been, fading prematurely.

He had been an artist, young, full of life, fresh with ideas, studying at the *Conservetoire* on the Left Bank, when they had first met. She had been new to Paris, a newly qualified nurse working at the *Hospital St. Lazare*, just south of the *Gare du Nord*. She had met him in a small bistro on the Rochechouart Boulevard. He had sat beside her at her pavement table as she had looked up to the *Sacre Coeur*, illuminated romantically in the late dark of a warm summer evening. They had been inseparable since that evening, exploring the city, which neither of them had known, quickly becoming lovers.

He had introduced her to marijuana first and it had felt natural in the company of his friends, a relaxing remover of inhibitions. And later, when he had wanted to experiment with morphine, to expand his consciousness, to help him explore new ideas in the pursuit of his art, she had trusted him. She had stolen the drug from the hospital. She'd had access, and she'd been clever, and very careful. It had been easy. And he had told her of the sublime journeys that it had taken him on and he had begged her to join him. And again she had trusted him. And soon they were both trapped, caught in the dizzy vortex of addiction.

They had drifted this way for years. His art had suffered for it; he had become wasted and idle. Then one night she had returned home from her work at the hospital, work that she no longer loved the way she once had, work that now served only to fill the hours until she could lie with him, sharing the syringe of poison that had rotted their lives, to find him dead. His blood washed the bare floors of their apartment.

There had been an enquiry, of course, and it had all come out. She had been ruined, left penniless and empty with no job, and no friends to fall back on. Her meagre savings had been all but exhausted when a man had turned up on her doorstep. He had been well dressed, a representative of an influential benefactor. She had accepted the job that he had offered, hardly able to believe her luck. They had not been able to prove that she had taken drugs from the hospital, but the suspicion had been enough. She would never work in the mainstream again. And here was employment. In the service of a virtual recluse, in the south, where no one would know her, where she could begin again.

And she had been in the service of Emile Stopyra ever since. He had not minded her addiction, and she had never questioned the work that he had asked her to do. To be sure, there were many strange goings on; frequent visitors to the chateau, especially the bald one who was so ready to give orders and to whom her employer showed such deference. And the Englishman, so horribly crippled, his injuries having so unnatural a basis. But she had never questioned. She owed so much to Monsieur Stopyra, and she would always repay him as best she could, with unquestioning loyalty.

Now something bad was happening. Here tonight, in the chateau. She had heard the explosion outside, had heard the shouting, the footsteps of the security men running off into the night. Outside now, they sounded remote, like the soundtrack of a television drama being watched in an adjoining room. She could hear the click of her own footsteps as she marched briskly down the stone floor of the corridor. She would not panic. She would see what it was about. Help her beloved benefactor in whatever ways were possible. She was just steeling her resolve when, two yards in front of her, a door leading to a small, seldom used sitting room, flew open, and out of the darkness came... hell.

Scrambling up and over the ledge of the window that he'd crudely ripped open, Strachan had found himself in a small, darkened sitting room. Moving swiftly across to the closed, heavy wooden door, he'd stood still for a few seconds, listening for signs of activity from beyond. *Click clack, click clack,* he'd heard. Footsteps on the stone surface. Only one set. And sounding like a woman's shoes. Now he could tell that those footsteps were approaching - unhurried but with purpose. Time to move fast.

Throwing the door open, he stepped into the corridor to confront this woman, balancing on the balls of his feet, his knees slightly bent in a crouch, his left hand held out slightly, to give him balance. He looked squat and powerful in the loose fitting combat clothing, could see the terror in the face of the fat woman who stood frozen before him. Her lips were beginning to curl back, her mouth was dropping open. In a moment she would scream.

He thrust his right hand forward, ramming the barrel of the Browning hard into her solar plexus, below the rib cage, the hard steel sinking in the layers of fat until it met resistance, up under the breastbone. He pulled the trigger twice and there were two dull thuds, the fat of the woman's body acting like a silencer to deaden the sound of the explosions. The force of the bullets threw her back, fully five yards. She fell into the spray of her own blood, and was dead before she hit the grey stone floor.

The room directly below Stopyra's in the east wing also lay in darkness. But unlike the quiet, waiting calm of the room above, from this dark came muffled sounds of frenzied activity. The man in this room had also heard the explosion of course, had leapt from his bed to look out the window. And the dog, a sleek longhaired Alsatian, had jumped with him, snarling by his side, its hackles raised.

He soothed it, quietened it with whispered words and a calm stroking hand. It was *him*, of course, no question. The man from the forest. He had known that the man would be back. It would have been better if he had killed the man in back then, along with the girl. But too late he had realised that this man too, had an affinity with the gloom. Military of course, and *very* good. It had been a pity about the dog. One of his favourites. But that would serve to add extra pleasure to the final reckoning when it came.

Outside he had seen them scurrying about like ants, these ex-policemen and nightclub bouncers that his master had chosen to ensure his privacy and safety. A dozen of them. Look, eight surrounding the building to guard against an onslaught from the forest. The others out chasing shadows with the dogs among the trees. Fools. *He* had been more than a match for them already. *He* would already be inside the building. A worthy adversary at last. But there was time yet. He would take his pleasure first. And with that thought he climbed back onto the bed, called the dog to lie beside him, and began to masturbate them both, his breathing becoming fast and laboured. And as he came, he took his hand away from the whimpering animal and reached over to pick up the knife, which lay on the bedside table, plunging it repeatedly into the screaming fur and flesh by his side.

Move you fucker, move! The voice inside Strachan's head, that of Sergeant Traynor from Hereford. But he was way ahead of it, the fallen body of the dead nurse left behind him. At the end of the corridor, twenty yards in front, the passageway turned sharply left, a blind bend. He kept flat against the nearside wall, the gun now in his left hand, pointed out front as he hurried along in the dark.

Stopyra David, never forget, you can't come out of this one without seeing that fucker dead. But where will he be? A labyrinth of corridors and passageways this place, and a hundred rooms. Maybe in his private rooms, David, second floor, east wing. He pointed them out from outside that time, remember?

Yes, of course. Aim for there, but miss nothing on the way if you can help it. Not much time. And plant explosives. Ground floor for them. Let the flames rise, trap anyone you might miss.

The angle in the corridor now. Throw yourself across, back into the far angle, two hands on the gun, ready, and scan. Nothing, no one. An empty corridor again, stretching away to the east. And at the end, light. The entrance hall David, you recognise it. Head towards it, keep to the wall again. Don't give them a clear target. A door to the right. As good a place as any. Get the first of those incendiaries in place. A hand on the knob. Twist and throw the door open. Dive in low and roll, both hands on the gun, sweep the room in covering arcs. Empty, dark. Get to your feet, close the door, gently. Look around. A large room, the walls invisible behind shelves and rows of books. A library David. What could be better?

A hand, delving into the rucksack, pulling out one of the crude cylindrical bombs. Set the timer for ten minutes. It should all be over one-way or another by then. Now take out the plastic five-litre container of petrol. Pour some around the device and up over the nearest of the bookcases. Now lay a trail of it across the carpet and splash it up the wooden door. Good, excellent even.

David!

A whispered voice from somewhere. He spun, gun at the ready, but the room was empty. He was still alone.

David!

More urgent this time. He pressed himself against the wall, next to where the door hung on its hinges. He knew the voice. Oh God not here, not now. Can't afford to go crazy again here, Jesus fucking Christ. It was Jonathan's voice. From nowhere; from inside his head.

I can help you David. You're doing right, doing good. And I can take you to him, David.

He pressed himself back against the wall, not believing, unable to believe. And he was light headed, just for a moment, and slightly nauseous. But just for a moment. And then he was back. And the voice was with him, telling him where to go, what to do. And he obeyed it.

Out of the library, down the corridor towards the brightly lit hallway. He took all of his natural precautions, unable to shake off the years of training. But the voice inside his head was ever present, telling him what was safe, where to go.

He was inside the hallway now. To his right, the huge double doors were wide open. Through them he could see the backs of two of Stopyra's men as they stood watching the tree line beyond the sweep of the spotlights. Not worth bothering with. Yet.

There's no-one about, David. The servants, the staff, all of them, hiding in their rooms. You've got a free hand, David. The bombs. We've got to get them in place before we go to him.

And always Jonathan rode in his mind, showing him where was best and he planted his explosives, in strategic places, setting the timers to the same ten minutes so that there would be four separate blasts, one after the other. Four separate diversions to help disguise his escape.

He discarded the rucksack, leaving it and the remaining petrol with the last bomb, planted in a highly decorous parlour on the ground floor of the east wing. A room full of antique furniture, priceless works of art and tapestries. A room built to burn...

For the man in the room below Stopyra's it was time to move. He rose from the bed, its sheets stained red, looking black in the dark. There would be time to remove the dead animal later.

Pulling on his brown corduroy pants, he grinned, and it showed in his eyes. His face, such as remained of it, was locked in a permanent grimace, the legacy of a fireball that had engulfed him when he had tripped running forward with a molotov cocktail. That had been Dien Bien Phu, Vietnam, with *La Legion Etrangere*, all those years ago. Looking at him back then, physically at least, he had appeared human. Now, his features reflected the sadistic monster that had always been his mind.

He laced up his boots, wiped the blood from his knife and slipped it into the scabbard that hung from the belt at his waist. He pulled the handgun, a Steyr GB, from under the pillow where he kept it - always in reach - and slipped it into the waistband at the small of his back. There was no need to check the magazine. He had slipped in a fully loaded one just an hour before. Ready now, he slipped out of his room to set the ambush for his approaching adversary, pleased to be getting a second chance…

Up the stairs, David. That's it.

He could hear Jonathan's voice. It was clear in his mind, as though Jonathan was there with him, running beside him. But it was somehow superfluous too. Because this Jonathan wasn't just a voice. It was a mind and a soul that lived inside him. He and Jonathan had somehow become one. More than the synergy that as identical twins they had always shared, they were two energies sharing the one body. Everything that Jonathan had known, everything that Jonathan had experienced, was there for him to use.

No time to wonder at it though. He ran up the stairs sweeping up from the hallway, taking the steps two at a time. No need to take care, to cover his back, because Jonathan was there, an extra pair of eyes, watching out for them both. And more. Because somehow, Jonathan could see what was up ahead, could tell whether danger lurked around the next corner.

The first landing was clear, and dark again. The whole of the chateau interior seemed to be plunged into darkness, except for the lights, which blazed in the hallway below.

Not here, David. Up the next flight. The second floor, that's where we'll find him.

He ran across the landing, a rich carpet deadening his footfalls. Up another wide flight of stairs, and onto another landing. Corridors off to left and right. Right, and this time he needed no telling. Slow down, it's along here somewhere. Close, very close. It would be at the far end, where it would look out over the forest towards the gazebo.

Creeping now, picking each step carefully. The light here was very dim. The only illumination came from a large window at the end of the corridor, which let in some of the glow from the floodlighting outside. His breathing sounded harsh again from inside the AGR. Sweat dribbled down his face inside the mask. He was half way there, creeping in the quiet and the dark…

Behind, David!

The part of him that had become Jonathan screamed out the internal warning and he spun with the Browning, to have it kicked from his hand.

A brevity of time that spewed a cascade of information into

91

his consciousness. An instant in which he recognised the Spectre of Death from the forest. The grinning skull that had laid waste to Astrid. Another reason for his being here. And for that instant, they stood facing each other, Strachan automatically crouched low and menacing, with the black angular face of the AGR, the Spectre a grinning sunken mask of white scar tissue, burning into the red of a hideously disfigured naked torso and shoulders.

Jonathan, reacting fast, taking control of the motor functions, moved Strachan into action. The Spectre was holding a gun, pointed at Strachan's midriff. Standing too close. A mistake. Strachan twisted to his left, bringing his right hand around to grasp the underside of the Spectre's wrist, knocking the gun hand to one side and pulling him slightly off balance. With his left hand, he gripped the barrel of the pistol, pushing the weapon down and twisting it sideways while forcing the Spectre's wrist upwards with his right hand. The Spectre's grip on the weapon was broken, and Strachan lunged for the unprotected grinning skull with the pistol butt.

But the Spectre was too quick. Side stepping the thrust, he aimed a blow to the side of Strachan's head, using the base of his palm, where the hard bones of the wrist would make contact and cause the maximum damage. Strachan twisted his head away, just in time, and the blow glanced painfully off his collarbone, sending him crashing to the ground, the Spectre's gun sent clattering from his grasp.

The Spectre moved quickly for the kill, raising his left boot high to stamp down on Strachan's unprotected temple. But Strachan was younger, his reactions faster. He pulled his left knee tight up to his chest, then crashed it out with the vicious force of an uncoiling spring, up into the exposed groin of the Spectre. He could hear the breath being sucked involuntarily into the Spectre's lungs, even as the power of the kick lifted the monster off his feet, sending him sprawling to the floor.

Strachan was up quickly, the knife out of its scabbard on his left calf, but the Spectre was immobile. He lay, curled in a ball, his hands buried deep in his groin, his breath coming in wheezing sucks. Strachan knelt beside him, pushed the head back, and thrust the knife up under the jaw and into the brain. A quicker and more merciful death than he would have wished for the bastard, but a more important target waited.

Stopyra stiffened in his chair. He had heard it. A muffled commotion coming from the corridor outside his room. He raised the gun, where it would point, chest high, at anyone entering the room. He took some comfort from having the gun in his hand. But not much...

Strachan was focused. There was the door, at the end of the corridor. Stopyra's rooms lay beyond. And Stopyra *had* to be there; would be there. He knew it. He crept over to the door silently. He placed his ear to the wood. Silence. And from below the door, no light emerged. Fuck it, this was what he had come here for, no time to pussyfoot around now. The first of the charges would be ready to go off at any minute. He turned the doorknob and threw the door open, stepping to one side to cover the wall. Nothing. He threw himself to the floor just inside the door, rolling as he swept the room to cover himself. The room was empty. Just heavy and expensive furniture. Over on the far side, he saw a further door, and instinctively he knew. *That* was where Stopyra was lying in wait, like a hunted animal cornered in its lair. Well, he was more than a match for that soft fuck. He strode over to the door. It seemed lighter, flimsier than the doors that were a feature of the rest of the chateau. A recent and modern addition. He lay on his back directly in front of it. His legs coiled back, up to his chest, the Browning was gripped ready in his two hands.

Strachan crashed his legs forward into the door, smashing the lock and throwing it open. At the same time, the first of his improvised incendiaries blew, the noise a deafening shock in the cathedral quiet of the chateau.

Stopyra, startled by the blast, living high on tension at the approach of his Nemesis, fired wild and high into the empty space of the open door before him. And Strachan saw his chance. He rolled off his back, forwards and under the gun, catching Stopyra in the chest with his shoulder, sending the chair over backwards. Stopyra's gun was sent flying into a far corner of the room. Strachan was up quickly onto his knees. He brought the butt of the Browning down savagely onto the bridge of Stopyra's nose, feeling, and even hearing it shatter.

Stopyra screamed with pain and terror, but it didn't matter to Strachan. The need for silence no longer applied. He enjoyed hearing the banker scream. He pinned Stopyra's arms to the floor with his knees, holding him against the floor. Then he placed the Browning carefully on the carpet alongside the man's bloodied head. He knew that he didn't have much time, but Jonathan was still with him, keeping watch. He would at least have time to make Stopyra's last moments exquisitely unpleasant. He used his thumbs to gouge out Stopyra's eyes, popping them out on their fibrous stalks so that they rested limply on his cheeks. Stopyra jerked violently beneath him, struggling and screaming with pain and shock. Strachan was beginning to enjoy himself.

Hurry the fuck up, David! We don't have all night!

Jonathan, placing a mental hand on his shoulder, bringing back his urgency. He grasped the limp eyeballs in one hand and tore them out by their roots. He flung them at the far wall, which they hit with a splat, sticking for a second before sliding to the floor.

'Bye bye, cunt,' Strachan said to the twisting and screaming body beneath him.

He drew back his right hand and delivered a killing blow to Stopyra's throat.

Now he could hear the footsteps running up the staircase. Right. These bastards would learn what combat was all about. He picked up the Browning and checked that the four remaining magazines were easily to hand, stuffed into his belt. Quickly, he made his way out of the bedroom and into the corridor. Two of Stopyra's guards were facing him, fifteen yards away. He fired twice, quickly. The guards dropped, both dead from the impact of the nine-millimetre shells to their heads.

Strachan ran to the bodies, stooped briefly to strip one of them of the Heckler & Koch MP5K submachine gun that he had been carrying. He took the magazine from the other fallen weapon and tucked it into his belt. Now he ran for the staircase. He had to secure the stairs before any of the other guards could reach the top and trap him. The second explosion rocked the building as he reached the top of the staircase. Two more guards were racing up and he dropped them with two quick bursts of the machine gun.

Down, quickly. He took the stairs two by two down to the first landing. Jonathan was still with him, he could feel his presence. But he didn't need Jonathan now. This was the David Strachan of old; in a tight spot, to be sure, but more than capable of getting out of it.

The first landing was clear. He sneaked a look down into the hallway below, but could see little as the thick black smoke filled the air. He could smell the fumes even through the AGR. A large window on the first landing looked out over the floodlit lawn and to the safety of the forest beyond. The guards who had been standing looking towards the trees only a few minutes earlier were gone. Nothing between him and the forest, if he could only get out of the building.

From the hallway below, he could hear the confusion of shouting voices and running footsteps. He was pleased; panic was setting in down there. No one seemed inclined to climb the stairs for fear of being trapped by the rapidly spreading fire. Strachan looked to the window again. Two large segments were hinged and could be opened outwards. A way out. He opened one of the windows and climbed out onto the ledge. He guessed that he was about twenty feet up. A thirteen foot drop if he hung from the ledge. Nothing to a paratrooper.

Seconds later, he hit the hard ground, knees slightly bent to absorb the fall, rolling in the best airborne tradition. Then he was up, sprinting across the lawn in the full glare of the spotlights. As he hit the tree line, the last of his incendiaries exploded, and he turned to look at the chateau. Several of its windows sprouted orange flames, which glowed brightly against the black background of the night sky. Mission accomplished, he thought, now get the fuck home.

Chapter 12

JUNE 16th... 12.30am

STRACHAN PLUNGED THROUGH the forest, unmindful of the noise that he was making. The wall was just up ahead, beyond that the motorcycle, lying hidden in the undergrowth. He had made it. It had not been the out and out slaughter that he had at first planned, but the two primary targets had been hit. And a few others for good measure. The chateau and that strange gazebo with its hideous knowledge; well they would both be gone too. Just another hundred yards and he could spring at the wall and haul himself over.

A sudden crippling pain dropped him screaming to his knees. He rolled about, crunching the dried leaves that carpeted the forest floor, his hands pressing against his temples as if holding his head could assuage the violence of the pain that raged within.

He tore the AGR from his face, but could not enjoy the cool of the night air. His head seemed to be filled with a blinding, throbbing white light, which pulsed concentrated misery into his every nerve. And then, as he lay there, the light and the pain subsided and he could see inside himself. And he was living his nightmare again. The precinct lay before him, and there was the black figure going about its inevitable slaughter, eventually being cut down by an army patrol. But this was different now. He was walking through the silent precinct, approaching the fallen figure. It clung to life, the heaviness of its troubled breathing plainly discernible in the expansion and contraction of the chest. He bent down and reaching out a hand, turned the body over. The entrance wounds from the army bullets trickled blood out onto the black combat smock. He started to peel back the black balaclava, feeling a growing sense of foreboding. And when the balaclava was finally removed, his mouth dropped open to form a silent scream. It was Jonathan.

He began to rise, faster and faster, the figure of his dying brother growing small as he accelerated up and back, high into the air above. Again there was the flash of searing white light filling his mind and then in one instant, contracting into nothingness. And in that instant, he knew that Jonathan was dead.

He found himself sobbing on the forest floor. His brother was gone. He knew it for certain because the bond that had joined them as identical twins was somehow no longer there. And the Jonathan that had helped him back at the chateau had gone too. For the most part. He could still sense a little of that which was Jonathan skipping tantalisingly at the edges of certain thoughts. As though Jonathan had managed to leave a little of himself behind. And he took some small comfort from that. But now he had to get away, fast. He wiped the tears, which had trickled down his face, with the back of his hand and raced for the wall. He jumped at it on the run and pulled himself over with one smooth movement. He knew exactly where he was. On the far side of the lane, covered with fallen branches and loose brush, lay the motorcycle.

The road was empty and quiet as he scurried across and pulled the machine from its hiding place. It was a Suzuki, Japanese and new. It started first time. He gunned the throttle, slipped out the clutch and raced, the windrush biting at his face, back towards Monaco for the last time.

1.02am

The ride had been one that he would normally have enjoyed. The road surfaces had been dry, the roads themselves a series of twisting bends that the motorcycle had been able to handle at high speed. The Michelin Hi-Sport radial tyres had provided masses of grip. As it was, he had not been able to appreciate the obvious pleasures that the ride might have given him.

A few minutes ago, he had pulled the motorcycle over to the side of the road. Now he stood for a few seconds, looking down the almost perpendicular slope. It would have been around here somewhere that Princess Grace's car had left the road back in'82, sadly cutting short her life.

A breeze was coming in off the sea. The Sirocco. He could feel it on his cheeks. He was staring, losing himself to his thoughts after the exhilaration of the flight from Stopyra's Chateau. There had been no chase; no one had followed. It was all beginning to seem something of an anti climax.

But he couldn't afford to take any chances. He would have to ditch the bike, would still have to get the hell away from the Riviera coast. The police records would show that he had had cause to go after the influential and well connected Monsieur Stopyra. A little background checking with Interpol and they would know that he had the capability to go with the motive. He would have to get out.

He rolled the motorcycle off its stand and shoved it over the edge of the cliff. It crashed noisily down to the bottom of the slope as he turned his back and began to walk the remaining couple of miles into Monaco.

Strachan looked at his watch. 1.30am. He had had a few drinks but was not drunk as he walked along the *Quai des Etats* Unis towards *The Hasler*. He knew that this would be the last time that he would take this walk, back from his favourite harbourside café, and his heart sunk a little with the thought.

He reached the boat and stopped, instinctively wanting to look back, to see it all for one last time. But in the end, he thought better of it. He would look back from the sea, where he would be able to take it all in. He would put the boat on autopilot and stand at the transom guardrail, watching the lights of his adopted home until they began to twinkle and fade as he crossed the horizon.

The night was steady and dark, disturbed only by the whisper of the mild Sirocco, lit only by the inadequate light of a crescent moon. A fine night to slink away unnoticed into the waiting shadows. Strachan stepped aboard the boat with a purpose. He wanted to get under way as soon as possible, to get as much distance in the dark as he could. He was all fuelled up, he knew. He had seen to that the previous morning. Everything was ready, and all he had to do was start the engines and manoeuvre out beyond the harbour wall into the open sea. Then he would be away to find a new destiny, a final adventure, somewhere in the high barren lands of the Afghan hills with the Mujahadeen militias.

He was going to need his binoculars though. They were below decks, resting on the chart table. He crossed the saloon deck and unlocked the doors that led to the living quarters below decks. In the dark, he made his way easily down the steps leading down into the navigation area. It was pitch black down there but he knew his way around well enough. He could just make out the shape of his binoculars where he had left them on the chart table, and as he reached forward to pick them up, he was caught by a savage blow to the side of the neck, which paralysed his nervous system, sending him sinking, unconscious, to the floor.

Chapter 13

STRACHAN BEGAN TO wake from an uneasy sleep. In the twilight moments before consciousness, his mind was flitting through dreams of confinement. He was aware of a throbbing ache in his neck, and of a constant vibration that combined with the pain to make him feel slightly nauseous.

As he woke, he realised where he was, remembered what had happened. He was below decks on board *The Hasler* lashed to the chart-table chair. He opened his eyes slowly, and looked around. The lights were out and there was no sign of the assailant who had made such a mug of him. He tried to move against the ropes that bound him to the chair. There was very little give; the knots had been professionally tied. However, the rope was the blue nylon cord that he used aboard the boat, and he knew that it could be stretched. Looking out through a starboard porthole, he could see that the boat was out on the open sea. The vibration that he had been aware of as he was coming awake was a product of the twin diesel engines. The boat was obviously not under sail.

He had no idea as to the identity of his attacker (attackers?), but it had to be something to do with Stoprya, with the revenge that he had extracted on that bastard only hours before. But how? There hadn't been time, surely? And Stopyra was dead. That much he knew for certain. In the confusion, which of his men would have had the presence of mind, or even the inclination, to mount a counter strike like this? And how would they have known who he was, where to reach him? No matter, these were questions that he could ponder at a later time. He must make the most of the fact that he was momentarily alone, considered no threat by whoever was piloting the boat.

He began to work his wrists and hands against the knots that bound them behind the chair. The knots were tight and painful. The circulation to his hands had been cut off, compounding the agonising pain as he worked his hands against the rope.

For five minutes he struggled, feeling his skin chafe against the nylon cord but he must, he knew, ignore the pain. Whoever had captured him would be sure to make regular checks on him. And since he had no idea of their intentions, he must make the most of this initial period of solitude. At any time, they could come down to finish him off, weigh down his corpse and junk him over the side into the empty embrace of the sea.

The blood and plasma from his skinned wrists helped slick the rope. He was breathing in sharp bursts, between clenched teeth, his face a screwed up mask of effort and concentration. And there! The rope was beginning to give. Just a little, but enough for him to slip his blood-lubricated hands through the loop just that first few millimetres. This small success gave him renewed strength. He doubled his efforts, his grunts of exertion drowned by the throb of the engines. Almost there. He was oblivious to the roll of the boat on the waves, his nausea forgotten as he strained against the bonds. And now his left hand was free, then the right. No time to inspect the damage to his wrists; behind him in the drawer beneath the chart table was a pair of scissors. He reached back and slid the drawer open, feeling blind for the instrument. After a little scrabbling around, he found them. Quickly now; he must cut the cord which bound his feet. The scissors sliced easily through the rope and he was free. His ankles burned as the blood began to rush back into his feet. He would have to massage his legs for a few seconds, the pain was such that...

The light from the torch beam lanced harshly into his eyes, causing him to squint. It came from his right, from somewhere in the galley. As his eyes became more accustomed to the glare, he could make out, in shadowy outline, the owner of the torch. From above the beam, which stayed steady on his face, he could see white teeth grinning brightly out at him from a dark face. The man was tall; over six feet, Strachan guessed, and heavily built with it.

Mentally, Strachan was not disheartened by this set back. The

101

'sickeners' that had been thrown at him during his SAS training had prepared him for disappointment. And after all, he was no longer a trussed up sitting target. His hands and feet were free. He would have a fighting chance.

The torch was held in his unknown captor's left hand. In the right hand, Strachan could see the source of the man's smile, a confidence-inducing machine gun.

Even through the gloom, Strachan's rapidly adjusting eyesight could make out that the weapon was a Finnish Jatimatic. A new weapon, one not readily available through civilian outlets. There was no advantage to be gained from the fact that the weapon was being held single-handed; the Jatimatic was designed with the bolt carrier set at an angle up from the short barrel, which made it very easy to control.

The dark man reached quickly to his left and switched on the galley lights. Strachan recognised him. It was one of The Prince's goons.

The connections began to fall into place for Strachan. He had seen The Prince taking part in that ghastly ritual, what seemed like a lifetime ago back in Stopyra's gazebo. The Prince would have been able to identify Astrid. Would have known that Strachan was bound to have been involved. This kidnapping would have had nothing to do with his raid on the chateau. It would have already been planned. The Prince's yacht had left the harbour the day following the ritual. It would be somewhere out at sea. And Strachan was sure that they were now headed on a course to rendezvous with it. It made sense. The Prince was vain and proud. He would want to be present at the kill, to gloat at the downfall of his adversary. He would be too much of an idiot to leave the dirty work for professionals to do in their own time and at a place of their own choosing. That explained why Strachan was still alive. He had no idea how near to the rendezvous they were, but deciding that it would be best to assume that time was unlikely to be on his side, he knew that he would have to make this first move quickly.

The goon was still grinning at him; an ignorant, illiterate grin. With the machine gun, he indicated to Strachan's right hand, which still held the scissors. Obviously, he wanted Strachan to drop this potential weapon. Strachan saw this as an opportunity.

He was certain that the Prince wanted him alive, and that given the absolute power of life and death that he exercised over his servants, this ginning loon would be loathe to return a bullet riddled corpse to his unforgiving master. He would have to take a risk and play on that.

Strachan shrugged his shoulders, his face a mask of uncomprehending ignorance. He kept the scissors clenched tight in his right hand. The smile slipped from the face of the goon and he indicated again with the barrel of the machine gun. Again Strachan played dumb. The goon slipped off the safety catch and took two steps forward, towering over Strachan to the right, and jammed the barrel of the gun painfully into Strachan's right ear.

Strachan sucked in hard with the sudden pain and cowered back into the chair. He tilted his head back to look up pleadingly at the goon. The gin returned to the infantile dark moon-face. It had become a face of almost casual overconfidence.

So Strachan hit. Ducking his head forward, out of the line of the gun barrel, he brought his right hand up sharply, driving the closed scissor point deep into the goon's wrist. The goon's hand flew open on a reflex and the gun flew out of its grasp. Before it hit the floor, Strachan had twisted up out of his seat and caught the goon with the heel of his left palm to the underside of the jaw. The blow had carried with it the full force of his upward motion as he powered up out of the seat, first closing, then shattering, the jaw that had fallen open but had not quite had time to release the scream that was building up behind it.

The goon was unconscious a split second after the blow had landed and slumped backwards onto the deck. Strachan was immediately upon him, chopping savagely with the outside of his right hand onto the unconscious man's throat. It had been a quick kill and now Strachan was ready for more.

There was no way of knowing how many more of the Prince's men were above decks. Obviously there was at least one, but any others? First, he had to get away from his exposed position at the bottom of the stairs. Anyone opening the doors above would be able to take in the situation at a glance.

Strachan picked up the Jatimatic. He did not bother to search the dead man for extra ammunition clips. There would be neither time nor use for them. He did take the hunting knife from the man's belt though. He could not envisage a close quarters combat situation where a knife might not come in handy.

Ducking quickly beneath the steps leading up onto the saloon deck, Strachan slipped quietly into the small crew-cabin, which lay at the extreme aft of the boat. There were two portholes that looked back, out over the black waters of the sea. Strachan opened one. It was small, but he would be able to crawl out with out too much of a struggle.

He thrust his right hand out first, clutching tight to the Jatimatic. He would have to take a chance that there was no-one standing at the aft guardrail three feet above. It was a tighter squeeze than he had anticipated as he squirmed his head and shoulders through the circular hole, twisting his body round so that his face was looking up at the black, star spattered sky beyond the lip of the transom.

The rear of the saloon deck was empty. No-one there to glance down and scream out an alarm. Beneath his head, the roar of the engine exhausts and the prop-churned water covered the buffeting sounds of his heavy-booted feet as he pulled his legs free of the porthole. Holding on to the transom steps, he lifted his head cautiously over the lip to look out over the saloon deck. He had taken the safety catch off the Jatimatic and held it ready in case any of the Prince's goons were looking in his direction. But the situation was perfect. Just one man, skippering the boat from the raised cockpit. This man stood at the wheel, facing forward, the cockpit door open behind him, with not the slightest inclination that anything might be wrong below decks.

Strachan smiled. Just one. He would kill the man if he had to, but it would be better to take him alive. He had it in mind to make the rendezvous with the Prince, to bring terror to that corpulent, sweating face. And to do that, he would need this one.

Ducking back out of sight below the lip of the transom, he quickly pulled off his heavy combat boots. They would make too much noise on the varnished hardwood saloon deck. Cat-like, he pulled himself up onto that deck, stealthily making his way across the planking until he was pressed up against the doors, behind which descended the stairs leading below decks. The cockpit towered directly above him, a set of five steps to either side leading up to the enclosed cabin. The wheel was set to the left of the control console and the enemy stood behind it, directly in front of the open door. Strachan took a few deep, slow breaths. He would have to be as quiet as he knew how. He slid out to the bottom of the left hand set of steps. The pilot stood before him, his exposed back a tempting target.

Up onto the first step, silent, the gun ready in his right hand. Onto the second. Strachan was holding his breath now; one more step and the target would be in reach. He lifted his foot, placed it on the third step. *The Hasler* lurched sideways, caught by an unexpectedly large wave. Strachan was thrown to the right, instinctively reached out to steady himself on the stair rail, and the gun clanked alarmingly against the tubular steel bar.

Above, the pilot spun around, alerted by the noise, his face a wide-eyed mask of alarm. He aimed a wild kick at Strachan, who had regained his balance. Strachan twisted to his left and the foot lashed out into empty space. Strachan grabbed the ankle with his left hand and pulled hard. The astonished pilot was pulled off balance and fell backwards hitting his head hard on the control console behind him. Strachan kept a hold of the man's ankle, dragging him out of the cockpit and down the steps onto the saloon deck. The man was only semi-conscious as he lay sprawled on the hardwood planking, but Strachan was taking no chances. He aimed a chop to the side of the man's neck paralysing the nervous system momentarily and knocking him out completely.

Strachan moved fast, leaping up the steps and into the cockpit cabin. He pulled a coil of the blue nylon rope from a small cupboard beneath the control console. With one bound, he was back on the saloon deck. He took the knife from his belt and cut the rope into manageable lengths, then dragged his unconscious captive over to the cockpit steps. He sat the inert figure up against the vertical step-rail support and bound the feet together at the ankles and the wrists together behind the back with quick tight knots. Then he lashed the body to the upright post with tight loops around the midriff, chest and throat, making the throat knot tight enough so as to just allow normal breathing and making any lateral movement a futile, choking exercise. Now he was ready.

The man was beginning to groan slightly, beginning to regain consciousness. Strachan helped him along with a few light slaps to his cheeks.

'Come on, asshole, wake up. Wake up,' Strachan whispered between clenched teeth.

'Oooohh...' the man groaned, 'Oooohh...'

Strachan held the heavy survival knife in his right hand. His mind for a second thought of Astrid. Not smiling and full of joy, but caught in freeze-frame as the crossbow bolt had hit her in the throat. He clutched the knife tighter, hoping against hope that the man before him would be reluctant at first to talk. First though, he needed to check the cockpit above. There may be a chart, some papers, anything which might give some indication as to the rendezvous point.

He climbed the steps, knowing that his waking captive would be going nowhere, and stepped into the cockpit cabin. No charts or papers were immediately visible, but lying atop the control console was a large grey canvas zipper bag. Strachan pulled open the zip, and by the dim glow of the cabin watch-light, saw half a dozen white oblong blocks, vacuum-sealed in clear heavy polythene. He reached into the bag and pulled out one of the blocks, weighed it in his hand. About three pounds in weight. He tossed the block casually into the air and caught it again. He knew exactly what it was of course. Composite C4, 91% RDX and 9% plastic binder. It was more powerful than TNT, remarkably resilient to temperature change and the most water resistant of all the commonly available military demolition charges. Perfect for blowing holes in boats.

Strachan put the block down and scrabbled around in the canvas bag some more, eventually pulling out a black cardboard box. He took off the lid and found what he was looking for. In the box were six pencil detonators, attached to tiny adjustable radio signal receivers and a hand held radio transmitter, the size of a Sony Walkman. It was altogether obvious that Strachan and the boat were intended for Davy Jones' locker, and more obvious than ever that the only reason for his being kept alive from the start was so that the Prince could gloat at his demise. Well,

Strachan thought, we can spoil that little party for you, can't we?

He had already formulated his plan, knew exactly what he was going to do. Now he just had to discover exactly where he would be able to find the noble Prince. And that would be a pleasure...

Chapter 14

AN HOUR LATER. Strachan began to feel a tug at his heart as he placed the second of the C4 charges deep in the bilges, below the water line for'ard. Two would be enough, and placed forward, well away from the fuel tanks, there would be no billowing tower of smoke and flame to attract any boats and planes that might be within a thirty-mile radius. *The Hasler* would slide gracefully to the bottom.

Reaching into a deep pocket, Strachan took out two of the pencil detonators and set each of the radio receiving heads to the same frequency, which he committed to memory before plunging them firmly into the two blocks of explosive. He stood, sliding the bilge hatch cover into place with his foot, wiping his hands on the camouflage pants that he still wore. His hands were becoming sticky as the blood which had covered them, a mixture of his own, coming from his chaffed wrists, and that of his captive, who remained lashed in place and unconscious above decks, began to congeal.

Half an hour to the rendezvous point. He had time to take a shower. He was feeling dirty, inside and out. The cold water would cleanse the flesh; maybe only time would purge the soul. The man lying unconscious above decks had been reluctant to talk. One of the Prince's more intelligent slaves, nevertheless he had to be shown that life held greater terrors than his master's displeasure. The knife had been a malevolent teacher.

At first, the man had shown arrogance in his refusal to talk, the throaty Arabic of his speech espousing death before such disloyalty. But Strachan had long since known that death was nothing to fear, a boon to be granted easily to the shimmering altar of honour. It was much more difficult to surrender the pain of hideous torture to that impotent tin god. Some could do it, but Strachan knew that this one wouldn't.

At first he had laid the man's left cheek open with the heavy blade. A slow, drawing, diagonal stroke, letting the sharp metal bite under its own weight into the chubby flesh. Not a painful cut, but psychologically devastating. It made the man realise the helplessness of his position. He screamed and squirmed away from the blade, but the rope that cut tightly into his throat would allow no movement. His eyes bulged and he began to choke as his throat forced itself into the rope and Strachan laid the knife blade cold and flat against his face, and laughed and laughed. And eventually the choking became retching, and foul smelling puke gushed in steaming mottled torrents to cascade down the man's front. A half a dozen times the man's stomach twisted, squeezing out its half-digested contents for all the world to see, until finally he was dry retching.

Strachan took away the blade, stepped back for a moment and the man slowly gathered his breath. Tears slid from his eyes to mingle on one side with the blood that reddened his face, and green snot hung from his nose. Strachan prodded him with his boot, towering above him, and gently asked for the rendezvous co-ordinates again. The man began to sob and wail, crying 'Allahu Akbar' to a God who didn't listen. Strachan crouched on his haunches, placed the tip of the knife blade just under the man's left eye. The sobbing and shrieking continued, loud in the empty uncaring night air and Strachan ran the blade up, slowly and with great precision, parting the skin of the lower eyelid and slicing into the eyeball which opened, smearing clear jelly-like aqueous humour over the silver metal blade.

Half an hour later, Strachan had acquired the information that he needed. He had bounded up the steps into the cockpit cabin and had checked that *The Hasler* was on a course to meet the rendezvous point. It was then, after setting the autopilot to follow that course, that he had grabbed the bag of explosives and made his way quickly below decks.

The Prince's man remained alive but had slipped into a merciful unconsciousness. His clothes had been cut away from him and he was minus his eyes and his nipples. The flesh of his face had been mostly cut away and the skin had been flayed from his penis. Inside, Strachan had been a little sickened by what he'd done. He'd tried to tell himself that he'd had no choice. It had come as small comfort.

Strachan stepped from the shower, feeling fresh and revitalised on the outside. Inside he still felt a slight revulsion at his sadism, at what he had done to the man who sat wretched and dying above him.

It was a feeling alien to him. He had thought himself long ago hardened to a world of cruel expediency. This slight twanging of conscience was more like Jonathan. Christ no! He pushed that thought back into the dark cupboard from which it had emerged. There were things to do that did not allow the luxury of aimless philosophy.

He took a cut off wet-suit out of the wardrobe. The inside was powdered and he slipped into it with ease. On top of the wet-suit he pulled a pair of loose fitting cotton pants and a baggy cotton shirt, both navy blue in colour, and slipped a pair of canvas espadrilles onto his feet.

The bag containing the remaining four explosive charges lay on the bed and Strachan picked it up and carried it into the main saloon, placing it on the table. He looked at his watch; fifteen minutes to the RV.

The C4 blocks were already cased in waterproof polythene and the detonators, he knew, would be water resistant to a depth of a hundred metres. But he had to prepare the rest of his kit. He walked into the galley, stepping over the body of the dead goon that still lay where it had been dropped, and from a drawer he took a handful of self-sealing plastic bags. Returning to the saloon, he took the radio transmitter from the canvas bag and put it in one of the plastic bags. He ran the tongue and groove plastic seal through his thumb and forefinger, making sure that it was properly closed along its entire length, then dropped it back into the bag.

From a locker beneath his seat, he pulled a tin of common builder's putty. He prised the lid off and then dropped the tin into another plastic bag, sealing it as before. He checked his back pockets, and the button down ones on the front of his shirt, making sure that the remaining four detonators were safely stowed, then put the transmitter and the putty into the canvas bag, along with the C4 blocks. He was ready. Time to go back above decks.

The radar showed the Prince's yacht as a bright green dot. Strachan would soon make visual contact. For the last five minutes he had heard *them* trying to make radio contact. He had left the radio on receive. They would know that something was wrong, but they would only suspect a faulty radio. He hoped.

Their attempts at contact were constant now. Strachan decided that he would not put his trust in hope. He set his back-up radio to a frequency slightly off the one being used by the Prince. He spoke in Arabic, explaining that the radio was indistinct, hoping that through the interference, his voice would be unrecognisable. He knew that he was taking a chance, but it was better than total silence. *That* they would surely suspect.

Over the horizon it came into view, a white luminescence against the black of the sea and the night sky. Strachan shut off the radio. There would be no more games. He locked the steering wheel and made his way down the steps to where the tortured and now screaming man was still tied. Strachan looked at his handiwork. It made a gruesome picture. Still, the man had earned his chance at Allah's paradise. It was time to help him on his way.

Strachan pulled the heavy knife from his belt. He knelt down beside the screaming man and plunged the blade deep into the cavity of the man's left collarbone where it penetrated as far as the heart, causing instant death. His screams of pain ceased with a finality that was only accentuated by the wide openness of the sea and the infinity of the night sky.

He pulled the knife free again, cut the bonds that still held the inert body in place. The shiny, blood-greased corpse slumped to the varnished wooden deck. Strachan took hold of it beneath the arms and dragged it up the steps and into the cockpit. He had work for it to do before it would be allowed to find its final place of rest. He stood the limp body at the control console, lashing the hands to the wheel, then crouched down out of sight to wait.

The engines had been cut. This was the time for action. Strachan was out of the wheelhouse, crouching with his bag of destruction on the port side of *The Hasler* out of sight of the

111

inevitable watchers who would be searching for signs of activity, from the Prince's huge white yacht.

The Hasler was drifting to a halt. Strachan risked a glance over to where he knew his enemy would be waiting. About sixty metres. His judgement had been perfect. He lowered himself over the side of *The Hasler* and into the cool Mediterranean water. The canvas bag full of explosives was slung over his shoulder. The explosive charges were heavier than water and would help act as ballast.

Keeping close to the side of the boat, he made his way forward, until he could see around to where the Prince's yacht lay at anchor like a sleeping white monster which bobbed up and down, not with the motion of the sea, it seemed, but in time with its own dreamtime breathing. There was the Prince, standing at the guardrail, an armed goon at each elbow, staring intently over at The Hasler. Strachan could feel the rage emanating from that corpulent and no doubt sweating bulk. By now, the Prince would know that something had gone terribly wrong, but he would have no reason to suspect just how close his own life was to meeting its end. At worst, the lack of communication from The Hasler would present him with an infuriating 'Marie Celeste' style mystery, and one which he would want to get to the bottom of pretty damn quick. To this end, Strachan could see a Gemini inflatable being lowered into the sea from the rear of the Prince's yacht.

It was time to move. Strachan sucked in a huge lungful of the fresh ocean air, then dove below the surface of the water. It was going to be a long haul and to surface before the target was reached would mean certain death. Six feet down, he pulled with his arms, cupping his hands to use them as scoops, grabbing hold of the water and pulling him laboriously through it as his legs kicked furiously behind in an effort to push him forward. What he wouldn't give now to have been able to use fins. The darkness was absolute down there, the quiet deeply oppressive. He would see nothing until the white bulk of the Prince's's yacht loomed before him, a few yards away. If his navigation was accurate, if a slow current didn't drift him off course, if - oh hell, if a thousand and one things didn't go right. If ever there was a once and once only chance at anything, this was it.

How much further? He dared not ask himself, but the rogue thought skipped and danced in his mind anyway. His lungs were holding out okay, but he was beginning to feel a slight tightening of his chest, and the muscles of his forearms and shoulders twinged frighteningly every now and then with the effort of pulling him along and down, so that he did not drift to the surface. A minute he had been under; must be over half way, surely. Got to keep at it, got to *win*.

From above and to the left, there was a noise. Strachan twisted his head instinctively to look, but there was nothing to see in the inky black of the undersea. Still, the noise was coming closer, a water-muffled whine getting louder, very fast. He realised that it must be the outboard motor of the Gemini that he had seen being lowered from the yacht. It was going to pass right over him. The outboard prop was not deep enough in the water to harm him, but he was buffeted by the turbulence as the inflatable passed over him. He tried to visualise the angle that the Gemini would take to get to *The Hasler*, to try to work out his own position in relation to the Prince's yacht. He must be close now. *Just where the fuck was it?* His lungs were screaming, and fingers like grappling hooks sunk themselves into his brain, thoughts which tortured him to kick for the surface. Every nerve in his mouth and throat fought for him to open wide and exhale the foul gas that threatened to burst his lungs, in a powerful jet of relaxing bubbles and, on a reflex, to suck in whatever was out there, water, air, whatever, just so long as there could be at least a moment of ecstasy.

Oh Christ, the yacht must be here, it simply must be. He could take no more. The surface was just above him, the cool night air, sweet and inviting. If he could just surface for a brief moment, surely he wouldn't be seen any way, all eyes would be on *The Hasler*, not the water in between. Let him surface for a moment, to take a few more deep breaths. Fucking hell, why hadn't he jacked in that stupid cigarette habit years ago? He must surface now, he must. He would. Yes he…

And there it was before him. Whiter than he had expected it to be and no more than five yards away. Two more strong pulls with his arms and he was touching it, his hands slipping along the reinforced moulded GRP hull. He slid up its curves, letting his head break the surface of the water. The air burst from his lungs in an involuntary reflex, and with no control, he sucked in a great mouthful of the sweetest air that he had ever tasted.

The Prince stood and watched as the Gemini made its way across the still water between the two boats. A thousand curses on those ignorant incompetent animals. Two of them. And the element of surprise. How could they have possibly failed? But failed they had and he knew it. He could feel Strachan's mocking energy reaching out to him from the stilled yacht that drifted with the waves before him. Well if the British Captain was still with his vessel, he would live to regret this last slight. In the middle of the ocean, with no-one to see, no law to worry about, he would show the miserable whore's spawn what it meant to be a Prince, and show him just how that lofty estate related to the drab ordinariness of the Captain's own highly insignificant existence.

A slight breeze chilled his sweating brow as before him the Gemini pulled alongside *The Hasler*. The four-man crew used the paddles to manoeuvre the craft around to the stern where the transom steps led up from the waterline onto the deck. They were out of sight there, but the Prince was not worried. They were four in number, highly trained and well armed. After a few seconds, the Prince watched as three of the Gemini crew climbed onto the aft saloon deck, their machine guns ready. The radio held in his podgy hand crackled into life.

'No sign of life here. One man standing in the wheelhouse. He looks dead though. Am about to investigate, over.'

The Prince made no reply. Dead. If his men were really dead, that evil bastard of a Captain would pay with the living skin of his hide. By Allah he would. But surely he would not be there, aboard his boat? Surely he would know that he would be facing certain death? Ah but he was cunning that one. He would have a plan.

For a brief moment, the Prince felt the quick chill of fear run down his spine. A plan! What plan? What could he hope to...

'The man in the wheel house is gone alright.' It was the radio again. 'And you should see this here. It looks like it was Ahmed, but it's difficult to say for sure. The face has been cut clean off.

114

Lumps of it around the bottom of the wheel house steps, over.'

Ahmed gone. And there had been torture. Of course, how else would the British pig have discovered the rendezvous co-ordinates? By all that was holy, there would be violence in payment for this. But that proved it. Strachan was out here. And he would be here with a purpose. Where was he? They must find him, and quickly.

Strachan surfaced back at *The Hasler*. He had swum under the keel and had broken the water on the port side, out of sight of the Prince and his men. He had planted the explosives, set the detonating frequency. His hands felt sticky where he had used the putty to help secure the blocks of C4 explosive to the Prince's yacht. Its surfaces had been smooth and he had prayed that the putty would hold. He had wedged one of the blocks between the prop shaft and the hull where he knew that it would stay firm, but he really wanted all four blocks to go at once. He had placed them so that they would take the bottom clean out of the boat and would send it beneath the waves within seconds. Still, that one safe block would do a good job on its own if the others came unstuck. It had been good insurance.

Now he needed that Gemini. He had seen it disappear around the stern of *The Hasler* and knew that it would be moored below the transom steps. There would be one man still keeping watch in the inflatable. He had seen three climbing onto the aft saloon deck as he had come to the surface after planting the last of his explosives. One should present no problem.

Once more, he dove beneath the waves, making his way to the stern of the boat. He swam beneath the Gemini, rolling onto his back to look up at it. From the way that it sat in the water, he could tell the position of the man left on board to keep watch.

The knife filled his left hand without him consciously having to reach for it. It was as though it had slipped out of his belt to find a more comfortable resting place all of its own accord.

Only the top of his head, to eye level, was out of the water as he pulled himself along *The Hasler's* hull to creep up behind the unsuspecting watchman in the Gemini. His progress through the water was deliberate and silent. His eyes never left the target that waited before him, alert to any change in position, ready to

115

tell him to slip for cover beneath the waves if necessary. If anyone came to the guardrail above and looked down, he would be finished, but he dared not think about that. He needed the target ahead, or else all was lost anyway. The strap of the grey canvas bag was beginning to chafe at his shoulder, but it did not matter. He would soon be able to relieve himself of that particular burden.

His nose was touching the Gemini now. He twisted himself so that his right shoulder would not snag on the outboard motor with what he was about to do. The watchman sat with his back to him, unsuspecting. But the next move would have to be smooth.

Strachan held the knife tight in his right hand. His left hand curled tight around the thick nylon rope, which was attached to the Gemini's inflatable hull about half way up. He took a deep breath and launched himself up out of the water, pulling with his left hand, and in the same movement, swinging his right arm in a calculated arc so that the knife blade hit the watchman square onto the sphenoid bone, the small patch about an inch back from the eye where the skull is thinnest. The heavy blade penetrated to the hilt, causing instant death. The unfortunate watchman barely had time to tense up at the first sound of Strachan rising from the water behind him. Now he fell forward onto the floor of the Gemini, and Strachan was quickly out of the water and in beside him. There had been a little noise as he had pulled himself up out of the water, but in the still of the night on the open sea, even a little noise would carry. He had to work fast.

He dumped the canvas bag onto the corpse, which lay awkwardly inert on the deck before him. Reaching inside, he pulled out the plastic bag, which contained the radio transmitter. Quickly, he set the frequency to that of the fuses that would ignite the explosives placed deep in *The Hasler's* bilges. There was a small plastic safety cap covering the button that would cause the transmitter to send its deadly signal. Strachan flipped it open. Now he was ready.

How much time had he got? The Prince's three men would soon complete their search of *The Hasler*. They would be back on deck at any moment. He had to get some distance. No way

116

could he risk starting up the Gemini's outboard. That would be suicidal. He picked up one of the paddles and began to guide the inflatable away from *The Hasler*, moving around to the port side where he would remain out of sight of the Prince who he knew would be unable to leave his watching post at the guardrail of his own yacht.

Using *The Hasler* as cover he started to paddle for the open sea, kneeling astride the corpse that littered the bottom of the boat, and facing back towards his beloved yacht. As he got further and further away, he increased the strength of his strokes, caring less and less about the noise as he stretched the distance between himself and potential danger.

He was about sixty yards away now, a distance where he could be sure that he would be safe from the explosion that would soon send *The Hasler* to a premature grave at the bottom of the sea.

It was time. He threw the paddle to the floor of the boat and picked up the transmitter. The Prince's men would never know what hit them. He looked up at *The Hasler*, standing grey in the dark of the night. Christ, there they were! The first of the Prince's men had appeared on the saloon deck. And he'd been spotted. The man was shouting to his comrades - Strachan could hear him - and was lifting his machine pistol to point in his direction. Now! Strachan pressed the button. There was a dull, loud thud, and *The Hasler's* pointed bow was lifted twenty feet out of the water. The sea had absorbed most of the blast, but the shock sent a five-foot wave out from the epicentre, which threatened to swamp the little Gemini. Strachan held on to the sides, keeping the transmitter firmly in the grip of his left hand.

The Hasler had hit the water again with a thump, sending a white spray of water out in all directions, momentarily obscuring it from view. Strachan quickly changed the frequency of the radio transmitter. The Prince would go next. But he wanted to savour this one.

As the spray cleared, Strachan was able to see *The Hasler's* last moments as bow first, she slid gracefully beneath the waves, her flat stern rising awesomely into the night sky as the cool waters of an unemotional sea poured through the gaping hole at the front. In the few seconds that she took to disappear from sight, Strachan felt salt tears mist his eyes as he remembered how his uncle had given him his love of sailing as a boy, how he had named *The Hasler* after 'Blondie' Hasler, the leader of the 'Cockleshell Heroes' whose wartime exploits he had listened to wide eyed at his uncle's knee.

But that was all past. *The Hasler* was gone forever now, and beyond where she had lain, Strachan could see the gleaming white bulk of the Prince's vessel. And there was the fat pig, leaning forward over the guardrail his crew along side him. He could see no detail of their faces, but he knew in his mind that they would to a man be wide-eyed and incredulous with shock. His thumb hovered over the button, ready to send them to a watery hell, but he wanted them to see him first. He wanted the Prince to know!

A rifle bullet cracked past his left ear. His senses sharpened. They knew all right. They had seen him and he had better be quick. He pushed down hard on the button, as though the strength that he put into this action would in some way determine the force of the blast.

All four blocks of C4 explosive had held. There was an almighty bang as the yacht rose straight out of the water, fully thirty feet. As it hung in the air, Strachan was able to see that the entire bottom of the boat had been blown clean away. Two of the crewmembers had been thrown over the guardrail and fell through the air beneath the boat as it dropped back to the hungry sea. Strachan could not see the Prince, but he knew that he would have been thrown back onto the deck. The boat hit the water and sat, briefly, as though nothing had happened.

Strachan began to worry. What if the boat had floatation tanks built into the sides of the hull? What if it had been built, able to withstand such devastation? He began to pull furiously on the cord that would start up the Gemini's outboard motor. Bastard! It wouldn't start. He pulled again. Still nothing. And then he sat back and relaxed. The massive yacht was going down. It started slowly at first, but as the powerful sea enclosed it in its greedy tentacles, it was pulled beneath the waves in a matter of seconds, leaving no trace that it had ever been there at all, save for a scattering of floating debris. There was no sign of the Prince, or any of his crewmembers. They must have been sucked under as the massive bulk of the boat had disappeared beneath the surface. Well fuck 'em all. That had been the intention all along. Strachan pulled the outboard starter cord again and the engine burst into life, its noise seeming alarming to Strachan's ears after the effort of striving to keep as quiet as possible during the preceding minutes. He looked to the stars to give him direction, then steered the little inflatable for the coast.

Chapter 15

THE MEDITERRANEAN SEA... JUNE 16th... 4.38am

OUT ON THE ocean, Strachan cut the Gemini's outboard motor. He had been running north for about twenty minutes, but was a long way from landfall. The breeze was beginning to dry his wet clothing, but it was also starting to chill him. The breeze died though, as the boat drifted to a halt and he began to feel the warmth of the summer night caress his arms and legs.

He had to get rid of the dead body that lay in the bottom of the boat before he reached land. The sea would take care of it, of course, but first, he must search the dead man. There might be stuff that he could use. The machine gun, another Finnish Jattimatic would be of no value. He could hardly be seen walking the streets carrying one of those. On the dead man's belt he found a black leather holster. He opened the flap and took out a modern automatic pistol. It was a new Beretta 92F. Strachan weighed the gun in his hand, unconsciously nodding his approval. It was the weapon that had won hands-down the competition to find a new military handgun for the US armed forces. Nothing else had even come close and only politics had delayed the wholesale deployment of the weapon throughout the US military. Some politicians had choked at the idea of going abroad to purchase a handgun for their armed forces and this had not been unexpected in a land where guns were held in such reverence. A second series of trials were going to be arranged to give Uncle Sam's finest a chance to equal the brilliance of the Italian design. Strachan doubted that they were up to the task, but equally, he was in no doubt that the Americans would eventually plump for one of their own. Still, that was their loss. For his part, he was pleased to have the use of the world's finest automatic. He checked that the magazine was full and tucked the weapon away in the waistband at the back of his pants.

He found two more loaded magazines and pocketed them both, along with a wad of bank notes, totalling twenty thousand francs. That would come in particularly handy. He had not thought to take any cash with him from *The Hasler*.

What else would the man be carrying that he might have a use for? Strachan ripped open the camouflaged battle tunic to search through the inside pockets, but found nothing. However, there was a curious patch of white cotton cloth stitched inside the tunic behind the left breast, where it would rest over the heart. The patch was about six inches square, and Strachan was sure that it must have something important sewn behind it. Using the tip of his knife, he carefully un-picked the stitching which held the patch in place, but when he pulled it away, he was disappointed to find nothing. He had expected some documentation, or drugs, or perhaps even poison, but there was nothing to find. There was though, a large red cross, with arms of equidistant length, which splayed at the ends, printed in bright red on the reverse of the white cotton. The symbol had to have significance, or why wear it, and even more intriguing, why hide it? He would ponder this little mystery at some other time. Meanwhile, he had a job to do. He tucked the patch of white cloth deep into a pocket, then started up the outboard motor and steered once more for the Riviera coast to the north.

PARIS... JUNE 16th... 5.34am

How beautiful Paris always is, thought Michael Brachman. He was glad that he could use the excuse of business to remain in the heart of the Isle de France for a few extra days. St. Clair had made it plain that he had wanted him to remain, following the disturbance at the temple four evenings past, and he had been more than happy to accede.

The limousine, provided with uniformed chauffeur by St. Clair whenever Michael came to visit, sped smoothly down the Champs Elysees towards the Place de la Concord. It was late for such an urgent summons from St. Clair. Michael could sense trouble. Tonight was when Stopyra and the Prince of the Lands of Purity were to have dotted the 'i's and crossed the 't's. The minor troubles, which had threatened to unbalance the forces that had been brought into play during the ceremony, should be wiped into nothingness by now. Perhaps something had gone wrong. It would be a setback, to be sure, but nothing that could not be handled. They were, after all, the new Shadowmasters. The Brotherhood bands that lay at their command could cast the nets of their influence far and wide. This was a trifling affair. A little oil might have to be poured over troubled waters to calm things down. But they were too close to the completion of the new Great Work to be disturbed by trivia now. The final pieces of the jigsaw had fallen into place two nights before, politically as well as temporally. St. Clair must surely be made aware of this. Now was not the time for panic, not the season for intemperate rages.

He sat back in the deep leather seat of the limousine, his twisted spine finding its comfort as best it could. He had felt the power within himself two nights ago. A distant, tantalising taste of the power and the glory of the Secret Chiefs. St. Clair must be made to know this wisdom, to maintain a physical equilibrium with reality. Whatever had happened tonight, the right answer would be found. If St. Clair could not see that, he must have it forced upon him.

As his charge sank back into his leather seat, the chauffeur assigned to Michael Brachman by Henri St Clair, moved the car right, into the Rue de Marignan. Uncharacteristically, he had checked his rear view mirror as he had performed the manoeuvre, but had quickly averted his eyes. It must have been a trick of the lights, he thought, a reflection of glass and neon and the dark shadows of the night. Because just for a second, he could have sworn that he had seen his passenger's face change. Had he really seen tongues of fire dance from the eyes, seen the mouth drawn tight into a thin-lipped smile from which had slithered a forked reptilian tongue? He shuddered involuntarily, then continued to concentrate on his driving. But somehow, he could not seem to shake a strange and meaningless word from his mind: Choronzon.

Brachman squirmed uncomfortably in his chair, not even aware of having moved. The chair was deep and soft, but his twisted frame sat uneasily in it. He had long since grown used to having to constantly change position and he was lost in his own thoughts.

The drawing room of St. Clair's Paris apartment was large and opulent, but made to seem cosily elegant with the use of discretely subdued lighting. In the far corner, St. Clair himself paced uneasily, a cordless telephone pressed to his ear. His conversation was angry, his words hissed between clenched teeth and long pauses as he listened to the words of the person on the other end of the line. And those words evidently did nothing to ease his passion.

Brachman was not listening. There was a power inside him that spoke not in words but with pure and innate insight. It was strange and somehow dangerous, though not unpleasant. He became aware of St. Clair throwing the phone down onto a golden velvet covered chaise longue.

'The fool!' St. Clair raged. His arms flapped with Gallic exasperation. 'That Arabian idiot -'

'-Has blown it,' Brachman interjected coolly. 'No matter, the situation can easily be remedied.'

St. Clair looked cautiously at his old comrade. There was an assurance in that voice that he had not noticed before. A calm dominance. For a moment, he wondered whether perhaps he had lost the control that he had always held over his closest companion.

'We have lost two of our number, it is a nuisance, but they can be replaced. We have any number of candidates ready to take the place of those who have gone.' Brachaman's voice had lost none of its authority as he continued. Clearly, he had mastered the moment, and St. Clair found himself listening warily to the words.

'As to our original problem, we have the answer at our finger tips. We should never have hesitated from the first.'

'No, you cannot mean it. We cannot risk it!'

St. Clair was clearly agitated. He knew what was coming next. 'We know the identity of our quarry. The Prince - may Allah

123

comfort him – was able to supply us with all we ever needed to know. There will be no risk, Henri.

Was the voice a touch patronising there? St. Clair couldn't be sure. But no matter, he had to put a stop to this dangerous talk. At once.

'No Michael, I cannot countenance such an action. Not at this time. We are so close. What if...'

'If! If! Pah, *if* my aunt had balls, she'd be my uncle. Don't be such an old woman, Henri. We will awaken the Templar and that will be an end to it.'

'Michael... you do not understand... you've never encountered... Listen, the Templar will do our bidding. It is his conditioning. His duty. His training. But don't you understand? Michael, his loyalty lies with the Great Work... and what we are doing to achieve it... can you see him granting his approval? How will that stand with us?'

'Does the master now seek the approval of his servant? Fine inheritors that makes us, don't you think? You are forgetting, Henri, that it is we who control the Templar. Yes, I know his ancient charge concerning the Great Work. But what are we doing other than to accelerate that which ought to have been achieved many centuries ago. I for one imagine that the Templar might be pleased.'

St. Clair did not argue, though his inclination told him that he should. He sensed a lack of conviction, a lack of honesty, even, in his old friends words. He was not used to being contradicted. Not by anyone. But Michael's eyes had held his, and for a second, St Clair was sure that they must have caught a reflection from the living flames of the fire, for they seemed to blaze a deep reddish-orange. Whatever, he no longer felt inclined to argue with his friend. He would set the wheels in motion. He would summon the Templar.

Chapter 16

MORNING, AND LATE morning at that. The high sun shone brightly through the tree canopy. The birds twittered loudly and Strachan could barely believe that he had slept through their initial dawn chorus. His exertions of the previous night must have knackered him more than he had thought.

His head was fuzzy and he still felt a little weak as he raised himself up on his hands. Something hard was digging into his back. He reached around with his left hand, expecting to pull out a rock or a lump of wood, but what he felt was more familiar. The butt of an automatic pistol. Shit, he really was slipping. He had forgotten all about that. Still, it was all flooding back to him now.

He had sent the Prince and his crew to an early grave, had really sorted them out. The thought made his whole body glow with an inner warmth. But there were other things. The torture of the man aboard *The Hasler* for one. How could he have been so utterly vile? The man would have talked without his having to resort to that kind of barbaric mutilation. The man just hadn't had the heart for heroic resistance. Strachan had known it; had felt it the moment that he had begun the interrogation. But he had enjoyed the fear that he could see before him; it had made him feel powerful, commanding. Even god-like. Oh, that was really cute, god-like. Thinking about it now made him feel slime-like. There was no excuse. Fuck, it seemed that the medicos had been right all along; he really was a twisted bastard. A psycho.

In the empty warmth of the forest, he began to sob. The tears ran like warm salt rain down his cheeks and his shoulders shook as he gave himself up to the flood of his emotions and allowed

125

the purity of his contrition cleanse what was left of his soul. He opened his mouth wide to cry out to the surrounding forest, but –

Crunch crunch crunch. Crunch CrUNCH CRUNCH! Footsteps! Getting closer with every stride. Strachan flattened himself against the forest floor. The Beretta was in his left hand in front of him. Only his head was raised, facing the direction of the approaching steps.

'But you said you were going to try the water skiing this morning. Losing your bottle?' A girl's voice. A tourist. Of course, he'd come ashore just east of Antibes. He was lying up in the forest just a few hundred yards away from the beach. And he would be surrounded by the famous 'Tent Cities' used by budget holidaymakers. He let out the breath that he had been holding, in an audible gasp.

'Sod that. I've still got the effects of last night to sleep off.' A young man's voice now.

They were right in front of him, but he could not see more than a shadow of their passing through the densely packed trees.

'Maybe this afternoon,' the boy added unconvincingly, and was teased mercilessly by the girl.

Then they had passed by, heading towards the beach. How Strachan envied them. Why couldn't he be allowed to live like them? Why should he be denied the simplicity of their existence? O Astrid, why? *Why?*

The dark thoughts were back with him once more, but this time he wouldn't cry. Because he knew the answer to the *why*. It was in his past. It was in every minute that he had spent in the Middle East, in every East German border crossing that he had ever made and in every bandit stakeout that he had ever arranged in South Armagh. And mostly, it was back on a dark and cold wet island in the South Atlantic on a night that he still could not remember, but which would haunt him forever. It was because of Wireless Ridge.

What the hell had happened back there? The question haunted him now more than ever. A fuck up of some description, certainly, and a good man had died in the effort of saving him, getting him off the ridge and back to the sea. But why? He hadn't been physically wounded - that much was clear from the moment he

126

regained consciousness. The operation had obviously been a success. So what had happened? Why had his own trooper taken him out, and why would no-one tell him anything? Just what had he done? It had to have been something appalling. Every treatment, every debriefing, every visit to every shrink that they'd sent him to. All of it concerned violence, aggression. The word psychopath had been used, but nobody would ever give him the detail? Why?

But, enough of such pointless speculation. There were things needed doing. He would have to get out of France, and that might not be easy. He had counted on being out on the open sea in *The Hasler*, but that idea had flown out of the window. And he had hardly covered his tracks. The authorities would probably be on his trail even now in connection with the massacre at Stopyra's chateau. Still, *The Hassler* was missing from its mooring. They would be looking for him out at sea, that much was certain. At least for the time being. And if they eventually found the floating debris from the two sunken yachts, well maybe they would think that he had perished. Perhaps committed suicide even. That would be better. Would buy even more time.

A thought hit him fast, from out of the blue. Marseilles. It was the obvious choice. A large city, a military centre, an expansive working waterfront and a decidedly dodgy seedy quarter. It would be easy to lose himself in the narrow streets of the waterfront area for a few days. And Marseilles was the place where contacts could be made. The kind of contacts that he would be needing. The city was rife with every form of criminal activity imaginable from organised prostitution based on slavery to drug running. The kind of people that he would be seeking out would know how to keep their mouths shut. For a price. And he knew just where to find them.

Quickly, he stripped off the shirt and slacks that he had been wearing throughout the night's activity. They were crumpled and stiff, but the sea had dried out of them during the warm night as he had slept. With some difficulty, he squirmed out of the wet-suit, his skin beneath the neoprene covering still moist and wrinkly. He pulled the shirt and slacks back on and using his knife, dug a hole in which he buried the neoprene garment, covering it up and disguising the spot so that the casual observer would not notice that the ground had been disturbed.

He picked up the Beretta and stuffed it deep into a trouser pocket, cursing that it looked so conspicuous. But there was nowhere else to put it. He would have to walk with his hand thrust into the pocket to cover it. In the other pocket, the money was still safe in the plastic bag where it had been wrapped to protect it during the swim to the shore. The Gemini had been sunk about two miles out, the body of the Prince's henchman lashed tightly to the outboard motor. There was no chance of the corpse ever rising to the surface, and within a few days, the flesh would be gone, having provided nourishing succour to the abundant marine life, which made the coast waters home.

Strachan knew that there was a small railway station just in from the beach which was served by the coast railway. He would be in Marseilles within a couple of hours.

Chapter 17

'THEY HAVE ASSURED me that the matter is being taken care of, Sergei'

The voice was American. It came from a man who stood gazing out of a panoramic window overlooking the lake. The water caught the rays of the afternoon sun, and the view was, clichés apart, breathtaking.

'Their assurances, yes, excellent. But can they deliver what they promise?'

The first man turned sharply from the window, his mouth open, ready to reply. But the question had obviously been rhetorical. The other occupant of the room was speaking again.

'You know, Frank, they should have left it to either of us to settle. Professionals should always be tasked to carry out a professional job, don't you agree? Frank?'

Frank Redbridge pressed his lips together, rubbing them against each other. It was something he always did when he was thinking. And the man seated in front of him had a way of asking questions that demanded thoughtful reply. He looked at the man while he pondered an answer.

Christ, that was Sergei Bondachuck sitting there. Nothing special to look at, not at first glance, anyway. Just your average middle-aged man who had obviously gone to some trouble to keep himself in good shape. The way he had himself, come to that. They were of a similar age, he and Sergei. Sitting here, they could be any two high ranking business men thrashing out the fine points of detail on a mega-buck deal in the safe, neutral seclusion of a chalet half way up a mountain in Switzerland.

But Sergei Sergeivich Bondachuck held rank in an organisation that could tear the heart out of any corporate structure. Sitting in that chair, looking up at him, awaiting his reply was the head of the *Glavnoye Razvedyvatelnoye Upravleniye* - the GRU. The GRU *was* Soviet military intelligence. And General Sergei Bondachuck sat at its pinnacle.

Thank God the chalet was secure. Sergei had arranged it, so it was bound to be safe; after all, *he* had the most to lose. Not that he didn't trust Sergei, they were brothers in something that transcended the pettiness of international politics; it was just that... hell, if knowledge of this meeting should ever become public, then the shit really *would* hit the fan. It would never make the papers, would create no scandal; however, it would mean the stripping out of the entire overseas structure of US intelligence. Because within that shadowy sphere, he himself headed a department that did not even officially exist. Which in itself indicated the degree of sensitivity of the work that Frank's department did. It wouldn't make the papers simply because the papers would never recognise it as a story if it hit them in the face. And the State Department, under whose banner Frank worked, would see that they didn't even get so much as a gentle caress.

'Well, at first I thought that there would be no problem.' Redbridge answered. 'I mean, just one man. Still, now, I must say that I take your point.'

Redbridge sat, facing the Russian General. He continued: 'A fucking disaster, that. Stopyra and the Prince dead. Two more Shadowmasters to find. At a crucial time like this. Maybe it *should* have been left to one of us. Still, they have activated the Templar now. The loose ends should soon be tied up.'

'I hope that the Templar can live up to your expectations, I myself have never seen him. Who among us has?'

Redbridge sat up in his chair. 'His reputation precedes him. And remember his pedigree. A Hashishim and a Templar both. I for one have no doubts about his ability to safeguard the work.'

This defence concluded, Redbridge sat back in his chair again.

'I do not doubt, Frank, but bear in mind; this man we seek was actually *at* the Temple. He saw us. What if there were photographs? Where would that leave us? For the others, it would not be so bad; they would merely be subject to ridicule, a decadent group of wealthy men relieving their boredom with a little black magic. The newspapers will have their fun for a while then it will die away. But you and I? For us, I think, things will be different.'

And while he was letting this thought sink in, the General opened an attache case by his side and pulled out a buff coloured file, which he handed to his American colleague.

'Now take a look at this.'

Redbridge opened the file and took out the two sheets of paper that it contained.

'Little wonder that our amateur brothers have been having their problems, don't you think?'

Redbridge didn't answer. He was studying the two pages. It was a dossier, thinly sketched, of a British soldier. That it contained only the scantiest of information and no photograph was immaterial. The heading told him all he needed to know: STRACHAN... DAVID... CAPTAIN... SPECIAL AIR SERVICE. Little wonder indeed.

'Caution might prove to be a wise watchword, don't you think? At least for the time being. You may keep the dossier. In fact I would rather that you did.'

The meeting was over. The General rose to leave. The implication was clear. *His* men at least would be alerted. Strachan would be found and killed, one way or another.

'*Dasvidanya,*' he said, as he closed the door behind him.

Redbridge sat and stared at the doorway for a few moments. He would be going nowhere for a couple of hours anyway. After all, there was no point in asking for trouble. And were he, by however remote a chance, seen to be leaving the secluded chalet with a top ranking Soviet intelligence officer – Christ! It didn't bear thinking about. Although of course it *had* been thought about. Both he and the General had arranged elaborate cover stories with which to cloak their activities from their employers. But if push came to shove, how long could either of them expect those stories to hold up? No matter, there was a more immediate danger to consider. Captain David Strachan.

The file told him that Strachan had been out of the service for more than four years. So what was his interest in the Shadowmasters? Could it really be coincidence? No, surely not.

But if the British government had even the slightest inkling of their activities, why couldn't the job have been handled by DI6? Unless of course they were trying to remove themselves from association in case of discovery. If that were the case, then Strachan would indeed be an ideal recruit for a one-off surveillance job. Hell, with his background, he was probably better qualified than anyone 'six' could have come up with from out of their own ranks. Civilian intelligence operatives, although resourceful, were, more often than not, urbane. City creatures. Whereas Strachan was an animal of the jungle. Yes, an almost perfect recruitment.

No, this couldn't have been a mere coincidence; it was too incredible. But what part had the girl played in all this? Pity they couldn't have taken her alive. Stopyra's men had been crude. Amateurs. How he wished that he could have arranged for a team of his own to be there. Still, it was done now. He would put out a discreet low-level alert among his own men. He wanted Strachan alive. He needed to know what, if any, damage had been done. It was a risk. But it was better than not knowing. They were too close to the finish to have everything ruined now.

He looked at his watch. He would be back in Washington within twelve hours. That was too long. He would send out his signals from the Embassy safe room. Time was something that they did not have in abundance if there truly was a man like Strachan on the loose.

Chapter 18

MARSEILLES... JUNE 16th... 2.30pm

THE TRAIN JOURNEY to Marseilles had been uneventful. A few people had stared at Strachan on the platform, his rumpled clothing giving him something of the air of the vagrant, but he had been mostly left alone. The world was more and more becoming a place where people had learned to mind their own business, and for once he had been glad of it. It had made him conscious though, of just *how* conspicuous his appearance was making him. And if he needed anything at all right then, it was anonymity. With that in mind, he had made it his first priority to buy some new clothes. The department store had been perfect; he had been able to get everything that he had needed at one stop, which was good. Because he had wanted to get off the streets as soon as possible.

He had bought a couple of pairs of loose cotton pants, in neutral colours, three shirts, a couple of tee shirts and some underwear. And for his feet, he had bought two pairs of canvas tennis shoes. A nylon holdall had completed his purchase, and the next thing had been to find somewhere to stay.

There was, of course, the seedy quarter in Marseilles, just off the waterfront. Perfect for his needs. The streets were narrow and old, the buildings having a run-down feeling of decay. The area was dotted with bars and brothels and the kind of hotel where rooms could be rented by the hour. The people, though wary of strangers, would be warier still of the police. These were people who knew the value of silence. And also its price.

Strachan had changed his clothes in the toilet at the railway station. It made him feel cleaner, better. But he had decided to remain unshaven. It gave a coarser look to his features; would perhaps make people think twice about asking too many questions. With the Beretta stashed safely in the holdall, he made his way down to the Old Port.

Hotel Petit Louvre it said in crusty blue neon over the door. It was just what he had been looking for. Grimy pieces of whitewash flaked from the walls outside within which the entrance was nothing more than a gloomy, uninviting hole. Strachan stepped out of the shadows of the narrowly enclosed street and into the even darker lobby. It was a dingy area just inside the doorway, boasting three wicker chairs, which had seen better days. A faded print of Van Gogh's *Sunflowers* spattered with what could have been coffee stains, hung incongruously straight on one wall and there was worn linoleum on the floor, curling at the edges. There was a faint smell of stale urine about the place.

'What do you want?'

The voice carried with it a somewhat bellicose taint and was not the least bit welcoming. It came from Strachan's right where there was a small, chest-high reception desk. Glancing across through the gloom Strachan could see no one.

'Well if you don't want nothing, piss off out again. I'm not buying anything.'

Strachan smiled. He had indeed chosen well. He walked over to the reception desk and peered over the counter top. A fat, sweaty, unshaven face looked up at him.

'Well?' the face asked, its lips barely moving, keeping a foul smelling cigarette held firmly in place.

'A room,' was all Strachan said. He slipped away his smile and held the man's eyes with his own hardened stare.

The man rose up from behind the counter, and Strachan leaned up from the Formica top. As he rose, Strachan became aware of the fact that the man was pulling up and fastening his trousers at the same time. He smelled of rancid sweat and stale tobacco, but Strachan was not perturbed. He had smelled worse.

The man looked Strachan up and down, drawing now and then on the foul cigarette.

'It'll be six hundred a night,' he said. 'In advance...' this last added to emphasise an obvious distrust of all newcomers.

There came a sound of movement from under the counter and instantly Strachan's nerves put him on alert, set him ready for action. But this turned out to be no threat. A girl rose up by the sweaty man's side. Strachan regarded her. She was heavily made up, but he could see that she was young, although exactly what her age was, he could never have guessed: she could have been twenty, she could have been fourteen. She wore a faded blue blouse, which hung open to the waist, and her bare breasts were exposed to view. Even through the gloom Strachan was certain that he could discern evidence of cigarette burns on her skin.

The man noticed Strachan looking at the girl as out of sight, beneath the counter, he pushed away her hand that was feeling his crotch. She giggled and it was then that Strachan noticed the wild dilation of her pupils. He made the connection instantly. Heroin. This girl was an addict and was trading sexual favours with the fat man in return for a fix. The way that her lipstick was smudged left him in no doubt as to the particular favour that was being bestowed. Still, it was none of his business. He was not here on a moral crusade.

'I think that three hundred would be a more reasonable price.' Strachan eventually replied. He knew that the fat man had offered the inflated price as a test. Tourists never made their casual progress to the hotels in this part of town. The fat man had been trying to gauge just how desperate Strachan was to stay in the shadows.

The sweaty man pondered for a few moments then said, 'Six hundred, and you can have her aswell.' He jerked a thumb in the direction of the girl who didn't even seem aware that she was being sold.

'Just the room. And three hundred.'

Strachan's eyes bored into the man, conveying a casual but very real menace. He knew that he could back the sweaty man down, could read it in the fat moon face.

'You are a hard businessman, monsieur. But the rate is four hundred, take it or leave it.' Whoever this stranger was, he was no tourist, of that much the sweaty man was certain. But he *was* running from something. Exactly what was not his affair. But there was no reason why he shouldn't make a modest turn on that fact. 'And that's still in advance,' he added feeling a need to recover some degree of initiative from this exchange.

Strachan tossed four crumpled bank notes onto the soiled counter top. The man scraped them up and pocketed them. He reached under the counter and placed a key with neither number nor keyring, on the desktop.

'Room twelve,' the sweaty man said, before spitting the cigarette butt from his lips, over the counter top and on to the linoleum floor where it lay smouldering. There was no attempt to offer Strachan directions.

Strachan swept up the key and turned to a dark and rickety looking staircase.

'It is customary to sign the register, monsieur,' said the sweaty man.

Strachan didn't even acknowledge the remark. The sweaty man shrugged and turned back to the girl, slapping her face hard with a heavy hand. A bead of blood appeared on her bottom lip, looking pure and sweet and beautiful against the background of her decadence. She reached up a delicate hand to wipe it away but just transformed it into a crimson smear.

The sweaty man wiped the back of his hand across his glistening brow then grabbed one of her exposed breasts and used the grip to force her to the ground behind the counter once more.

'Right, let's try again, shall we,' he suggested.

From beneath the counter, the girl simply giggled.

LATER...

The mattress was hard and lumpy and sagged mightily beneath Strachan's back. He looked at his watch. 8.00pm. The bed was so uncomfortable that he wondered how he had managed to sleep at all, let alone for so long. Still, he had, and now he felt much better for it. He reached down for the holdall on the bare wooden floor beside him, and pulled out a pack of *Marlboro Lights*. His fingers had difficulty in pulling the first cigarette from the pack, as usual, but eventually they managed. The smoke

136

was warm and soothing. It helped him to think. And he had much to think about. Just what the fuck had been going on these last few days?

Astrid. He'd thought he might spend the rest of his days with her, but they'd had no more than a week or so. Stopyra. It had been his doing. And the Prince. Still neither of those would ever trouble the world again. He'd had, at the very least, the satisfaction of seeing to that. But those were human factors. Easy to understand. There was so much more that was genuinely puzzling and he didn't like where his thoughts were taking him. That night at Stopyra's gazebo for one. Okay, so there had been some sort of black magic ceremony going on, but Christ! As far as he'd always been concerned, those rituals had been nothing more than a smokescreen, an added titillation for the people taking part, whose real interest had been in the freewheeling sexual side of the business. At least that was the impression he'd always taken from reading the Sunday tabloids. Black magic was nothing more than play acting and mumbo-jumbo.

But fucking hell, there had been more than mumbo-jumbo that night and he knew it. There was no point trying to kid himself. It was possible that the participants in a ceremony of that sort might be able to hypnotise themselves to the point where they believed that they had experienced something beyond the realms of normal human understanding. But he hadn't been taking part. Yet he'd seen those things, felt the changes in the very air around him. And so had Astrid. Christ knew, it had affected her more than it had him.

And if ceremonies like that had the power to affect people who were only peripheral to the proceedings, mere observers, even if only to induce within them the *effect* of hallucination, wasn't that in itself supernatural? Wasn't that magic? And if the power to alter human consciousness existed, then surely it could be channelled. It opened up a whole new world of possibilities too dangerous for him to want to think about.

And then, what about Jonathan? In many ways, that was the strangest aspect of that horrible night. He had seen Jonathan that night, seen him standing there at the edge of the forest. It had been him; there could be no doubt. They were twins. Identical twins. He would have been able to find his brother in a football

137

crowd. Blindfold. And that was no idle boast. But if that was bad enough, what of the events of last night, when he had returned to the chateau on his mission of revenge? Jonathan had come to him there. Not a man of flesh and blood, but a consciousness, an essence. An essence invading his mind! Could Jonathan have been a part of the nightmare? Could Jonathan have been haunting his mind all along? And what of the absolute pain? He had seen his brother die that night. More than that, he had experienced his brother's death, had been certain of the truth of it. And lying there, on the lumpy bed the fact hit him for the first time. He would never see his brother again.

Tears welled up in his eyes, and he hadn't the will or desire to fight them. He allowed himself to sob, letting the gentleness of sorrow wash over him in cleansing waves. Astrid was deep in that sorrow too, standing alongside his brother to double his grief. He let the salt tears run unchecked down his face as he wept, until finally, although he had slept for so long, sleep came with its sanctuary to claim him once again.

Chapter 19

MOSCOW... JUNE 16th

COLONEL ALEXEI BESANOV looked at his watch: 8.30pm. He would be late. The General hated to be kept waiting, he knew, but there was nothing he could do about it. And the General would understand once he had been told of Bulganin's nit-picking session. God knew, the afternoon in the Kremlin Armed Forces Procurement Committee room had consisted of little else.

'Wasters and dilettantes, of use to neither man nor beast...' He could hear the General using those words to describe the vast Moscow bureaucracy. However, the thought did nothing to ease his restlessness; he himself was obsessively punctual and being late was making him feel uneasy.

The car sped across the first intersection and over into Leningradski Street. The traffic was getting heavier here, mostly taxis on the ferry run to Sheremeteva, the large international civilian airport to the north west of the city. The new *Glasnost* had seen increasing numbers of foreign visitors coming to Moscow. It seemed that one could barely move these days for foreign tourists - incredulous westerners doubtless seeing spies on every corner. And the tourists themselves probably found themselves tripping over businessmen, now eager to peddle their wares in the Soviet Union. It was a sign of the times, he supposed. And this mingling of cultures was not such a bad thing; it would help serve a cause that was dear to his heart in the long run.

He settled back into his seat and tried to relax. Peredelkino, the complex of *dachas*, the country residences given as rewards to high ranking or successful Soviet citizens, was still more than half an hour away.

The traffic thinned out dramatically as they passed the Leningradskoye Road turn off, where all the taxis filtered to the right on their way out to the airport. Speeding now, they were on the *Volokolamskoye* Road, which would take them out of the city and into the artificial countryside on the banks of the river Moscow where the *dachas* were situated. As the twilight began to fade into night, Colonel Besanov drifted slowly into a shallow sleep.

The big Zil limousine pulled up smoothly outside the large log cabin structure that was the *dacha* of General Sergei Bondachuk. Even so, this easy transition from motion to stasis was enough to waken Besanov from his dozing. His driver was already out of the car and making his way around to open the door for him, but Besanov did not wait. He hated that kind of fuss, always had. Opening the door himself, he pulled himself out onto the gravel. The driver stood to attention and saluted him, as did the two uniformed guards standing sentry duty at the bottom of the steps leading up to the cabin door. Besanov returned the salute with not a little pride. They were his men, these. Under secondment to the General, certainly, but at his call should they be needed, should an emergency arise. Under such circumstances the General would arrange for them to be returned to their units without having to be asked. God, if there seemed to be any chance of real action, he suspected that the General would probably lead them himself. But until such an emergency, the General would always be able to call on the Moscow Military District Spetznaz Brigade for his security needs. After all, guards of the Ninth Chief Directorate patrolled Peredelkino. KGB. And it was not that these worthies could not be counted upon to be vigilant in their work, far from it. But the General *was* head of the GRU and there was no love lost between the two intelligence agencies. So the General felt more comfortable with a few of his own – within the grounds of his own estate at any rate. No one had as yet questioned the arrangement, which in itself spoke volumes.

Besanov strode up the steps, the door opening up before him as he reached the top.

'Yuri, Yuri, welcome.' It was the General himself, come to greet him. This was unusual.

The General looked to his watch. 'You are late. No, don't tell me -' he raised his hands, halting any potential explanation '- I know what it is to be grilled by our civilian overlords. An afternoon in the Lubianka would be preferable, eh? Still, they have to fill their days somehow and you are here now. Come in, come in.'

The General ushered him in through the door and closed it behind him. He seemed to be in remarkably high spirits, but Besanov knew the General well enough to know that this was a front. And the reference to the Lubianka – an exaggeration coming from the lips of the man who headed the GRU. Lubianka was the familiar name for number two, Dzerzhinsky Square, the traditional headquarters of the KGB. Nowadays though, the real power was transferred to an establishment ten miles to the south west of Moscow, near the village of Teplyystan. Here the KGB had built a massive new complex, modelled on that of the CIA in Langley, Virginia. And more than that, the days when the Lubianka had been used as a dungeon and torture chamber had long gone, even before the building of this new complex. The fun, the blood and vomit and the terrified screams were now to be found in the Lefertovo prison in central Moscow. Still, the Lubianka had established its reputation as the home of terror, a reputation not lightly relinquished.

The General showed him into the lounge, a large and comfortable room, with rough log walls. It was a man's room, thought Besanov, remembering that the General had never married. The General indicated to him to sit, and he complied, lowering himself into an armchair. The General sat opposite. He had not been offered a drink, he noticed. This was not to be a social visit then.

'We have a problem, Yuri,' the General said, speaking in the hushed tones he used for command. 'Mostly, all is well. Our business in the south was a success. However...'

This was it thought Besanov, here it comes.

'...there was an intruder at the site. You do not need to know the details; suffice to say that as of this moment we are seeking to appoint two new Shadowmasters.'

There was a pause as the General let this new information sink in.

'Does this alter the timetable in any way?' Besanov asked.

'No, it should not. But the intruder is still at large and he may have photographs. You understand what that would mean, of course?'

Hell yes, Besanov understood alright. It had been twenty years since he himself had first been approached. It had been while he had been a student at the University of Moscow. He remembered well Professor Protopovsky. The introduction had been slow and subtle. There had been evenings of discussion and debate, he and other students and the Professor. They had discussed academic matters - he had read politics - and there had been heated debates at times. But there had been wine and they had been young and the Professor had encouraged and directed them.

It was difficult to say exactly when or how the Professor had engineered things so that there were evenings with just the two of them in discussion together, but certainly that was how it had turned out. Even then, his induction had been gradual. In the trust that had grown between them, they had discussed philosophy, the mind, the purpose of man. And gradually, the Professor had shown him things, had opened up to him the full potential of the human condition.

There had come a time when he had realised exactly where these meditations were leading; just a glimpse of a hidden glory somewhere out of reach yet accessible nonetheless. By then it had been too late to step back. He was pragmatic enough to realise that if knowledge of what he was practicing were to reach the wrong ears, there would be a rubber room waiting for him somewhere, liquid coshes to batter his mind. But he did not need the traditional alchemist's exhortation to silence. He had grown up in a country where secrecy had become second nature. Even so, he had seen - been shown - a vision of a different future for that country.

'There *are* others, Yuri. You - *we* - are not alone.'

'Who then? Where do we find them?' He had needed to know the answers to these questions back then, had been desperate for the comfort of comradeship. But the reply had been disappointing.

'It would not be for me to say, even if I knew. Which I don't.'

The old Professor had seen the hurt in his eyes. Must have done, because he continued: 'Look Yuri, the journey that you

142

are undertaking is not one readily understood by those who do not wish to know. Even in the west where they pride themselves on what they like to call freedom of expression, there are those like ourselves who feel the need to keep their science hidden.'

It was only then that the Professor's words had begun to hit home.

'Then what hope is there for us here?' he had asked. 'Are we destined to journey alone? There is so much that could be good, not just for us but for everyone. And fear must keep it hidden?'

'Oh Yuri, the idealism of youth burns in you right enough. But the world is changing. The ways of our science is unfolding. Little by little, knowledge is released, small doses so that it can be absorbed and understood. There is a time of change coming Yuri, believe it.'

And the Professor had explained the futility of his trying to seek out like-minds. 'If your time is come, Yuri, those who need you will find you. They will know how to find you and they will recognise you when they see you. But don't be disappointed if you are destined to travel alone. As I have said, seek out your own destiny and remember that you have a duty to pass on your wisdom to a pupil of your own, if it should come to pass that the Great Work does not claim you for itself. The cosmos can afford to be patient.'

He had remained calm outwardly, but inside he had been churning over. So there were others, they were not alone. But more, oh so much more. The Professor had not said it straight out but he had been able to read between the words: there was a plan! A plan for the world, for a better world. And although slim, there was a chance that he may be a part of it.

So many things had begun to make sense then and there had been so many more questions that he had wanted to ask. But in the end he hadn't asked them. He had realised that the Professor had told him all that he could. Perhaps all that he himself actually knew. He would just have to be patient. This knowledge had set his pulse racing but he would learn how to wait.

Which is what he'd then done. For years. He had left the university and had forsaken the approaches of the KGB recruiters, choosing instead, the army. It was something that he had felt that he could afford to do; his family connections

143

and the exemplary conduct of his life had ensured party membership and a degree of security. Which had led to Spetznaz: the obvious vehicle for his talent and ambition.

The General had come into his life ten years ago. He had reviewed a parade of the Moscow Military District Spetznaz Brigade, a rare event in itself. And he had *known*. As the General's eyes had met his own, it had hit him like a thunderbolt. Then when the General had summoned him two weeks later, he felt that he had known what the agenda for the interview was going to be. He had not been disappointed.

Ten years of learning and planning there had been since then. And in that time he had discovered, little by little, the vast scale of the great undertaking. That it was essentially GRU controlled in the Soviet Union, which made sense, because the GRU was in nominal control of the thirty thousand or so Spetznaz commandos contained as integrated yet independent units of the Red Army.

Spetznaz. How it would rock the Moscow politicians and their servile bureaucracy to see how their instrument of shock would be used. Oh, they thought that they had taken their precautions, those politicians. In their fear, they had had to. For they had sanctioned the creation of a monster easily able to turn on them and devour them. Whole divisions of shock troops, skilled in political warfare, insurrection and assassination. Only the officers were allowed to describe themselves as Spetznaz. The troops, all regular soldiers, were aware only of the existence of their own unit. They wore no special uniforms, usually adopting the dress of the nearest regular unit, more often than not a crack airborne division in its own right.

The Politburo had been right to fear this necessary evil. Right from its inception, a secret Brotherhood had seen the potential of such a surgical tool and had striven to make it its own. And it had been a relatively swift process. Yet the Brotherhood had realised the need to build their own safeguards into the infrastructure they were creating. The traditional Lodges around which the groups engaged in the Great Work had been based had been organised into a cell system. Members only knew other members of their own cell and nothing of the greater plan. Their leaders received instructions clandestinely, not because they could not be trusted, but in case of discovery. What a man didn't know, he couldn't relate, no matter how effective the psychological or chemical inducement. They would all of them recognise the pattern of the Great Work when the time came.

Now of course, Besanov knew that that time was rapidly approaching. He appreciated only too well that for them to be exposed now would be disastrous. Photographs, by Christ. Of course, there was no way of knowing if the photographs really did exist, but this was certainly not a time for taking chances.

'So what is it you propose Comrade General?' Besanov spoke with deliberate calm.

'Insurance, Yuri. The Shadowmasters have sent a Nemesis to seek out and destroy this intruder. Someone of time-proven ability. But you must know only too well the delicacy of our own situation. We must do what we can with our own resource.'

There was a pause. Besanov knew exactly what was being proposed. Spetznaz had its own field agents, specialists in assassination subversion and espionage. They operated already in the west and were well placed to carry out the seek and destroy function for which they would now be required.

'I will need something to give to our people Comrade General. They cannot operate blind. Do we have a name, anything?'

The General pointed to a folder on the coffee table between them. 'In there Yuri. Read it.'

Besanov picked up the folder and opened it. The contents took little time to peruse.

'Special Air Service,' Besanov stated simply. 'And that 'No Longer In Active Service' tag. Can we regard that as being accurate given current circumstances?'

'We can assume nothing. But we must hope that our information is correct. I don't have to tell you that if this Strachan is still serving, then by now he will be back in Hereford. Beyond our reach. We must hope that our intelligence *is* accurate, but be aware that it might not be. I must leave it in your hands.'

The interview had ended and Besanov knew that he had been dismissed, with a job to do. He rose from his chair and saluted the General. Nothing more was said as he was left to see himself out and back to his waiting car.

10.30pm. It was dark now, and the road was lit only by the twin beams of the huge Zil's headlamps. Even so, the driver showed no inclination to slow down, as though he knew the road well enough to drive it blindfold. Which was an exaggeration, but not too far from the truth.

In the back of the car, Besanov was wide-awake and deep in thought. It was a real bitch, this one. Oh, there would be no trouble in alerting the field agents of the Headquarters Brigade under his control to the task that had been allotted to them. And he would not have to justify his instructions, so there was no danger of a security breach. But the worrying question was, could there be any realistic chance of success? His mind insisted on flashing a dispiriting answer: no. After all, there was no photograph of this David Strachan, just a description. It was a hopeless situation really. A search for a fit, young, Englishman who could be anywhere in the world.

The General had spoken of a nemesis, appointed by the Shadowmasters. How good could this man be? Clearly he must be special; why else would the Shadowmasters put so much faith in him? But the General had not appeared to be fully convinced. He would not have risked the involvement of Spetznaz otherwise. These were going to be interesting times.

Besanov sank lower into his seat and closed his eyes. He wanted to sleep, but a previously unknown intruder was stalking his mind. For the first time in his life, Colonel Yuri Alexeivich Besanov was feeling the tingle of fear.

Chapter 20

THE STREETS WERE dark and narrow. Poorly lit. The walls of the buildings rose steeply out of the streets, which had little space for sidewalks. Further west, in any city in Europe or America, this area would be a mugger's paradise. Which was not to say that the Holy City was wholly without crime. But it was a fact that crime rates here were generally low and people could walk the streets in comparative safety. A fact that nevertheless brought scant comfort to Monseigneur Guisseppe Rossi as he made his hurried way through the night-blackened labyrinth.

Occasionally he would stop and quickly look behind him, as if he had been spooked by the sound of his own echoing footfalls. He had been this way many times before, of course. It was central to his mission that he should. But usually it was in daylight, in pursuance of his overt duty as a Vatican representative in Jerusalem. This was the job that the Vatican heirarchy had entrusted him with five years earlier, to see to the welfare and wellbeing of the many Catholics who would make the pilgrimage to this *Sanctus Sanctorum* each year.

'It is the greatest honour, Guisseppe,' the old fool of a Cardinal had said to him. 'To be able to walk where our blessed Lord Christ has walked. To breathe the very air that he once breathed.' The geriatric cretin had been positively beaming, as if he somehow *believed* this drivel.

'And the responsibility. Oh yes, you must never underestimate the weighty importance of what you are being asked to do. To help and assist all those who would come to Christ, to visit these Holiest of places.'

The rest of it had been lost on him. All that drivel about the footsteps of Christ - as if the miserable idiots could ever

147

guarantee that anyway, since none of them had ever been there. He himself had once visited Seville, in Spain, and just outside that most beautiful of cities, there were the ruins of the Roman town that had spawned the two famous Roman Emperors, Trajan and Hadrian. The edifices proclaiming the glory of their legacy were plain to see in his beloved Rome. No debate about the factual existence of those two. Yet there, out in the countryside beyond Seville, where he could be certain that he was treading fields that they would once have trod, he had felt…nothing. And all the while he had had to stand there, a sickly grin plastered awkwardly across his face, professing undying gratitude for the opportunity that was being handed to him.

Leave Rome! That's what it had meant. A lifetime spent on the political ziggurat that was the Vatican, ripped from under him. Of course, he could have refused. Technically, he could and they would not have forced him to go. Much effort would have been spent in gentle but nonetheless firm persuasion, but if he had stuck to his guns, they would finally have given in and chosen someone else. But where would that have left him then? Safe in the Vatican still, yes, but for how long? The outside world had no idea just how political the Vatican really was. Nixon's administration would have been devoured there. Eaten up and the bare bones spat out within days. And why not? The Vatican had had more than a thousand years to hone its political skills. There was a pedigree stretching back to the Borgias and beyond to fall back on. He would have been left alone for a few months, maybe, left to work in the Vatican's secret library, but then what?

God, the library. That, of course, had been the origin of this mess. For him at least. A library containing books of rarity, of beauty, of antiquity. And books of heresy, secret books known, he was sure, only to himself, his immediate superiors and to the now silent lips of his predecessors. Books that would shake the world to its foundations were they ever to be revealed. Under his care they had been safe. He knew the secret vaults deep under the ground where they were hidden. He had been proud of the responsibility entrusted to him. Had bathed in the power that his secret knowledge had given him. Surely his trust was not somehow in doubt? No. Never. Then why? Why was he being punished in this way?

The answer had come to him the night before he had been due to leave for the Holy Land. A Cardinal, well known to him, escorted by two Bishops, equally well known and highly respected in the Vatican heirarchy, had paid him a visit. The three visitors were, like himself, members of the Society of Jesus. Jesuits.

They had come at a late hour and after they had spoken, he had known why. They had not wanted to be seen. He had listened open mouthed as the Cardinal had spoken in hushed tones, telling him the real reason for his mission. Outwardly, he had been unable to believe what he was hearing, but his work in the secret library had given him insights. He had begun to wish for an exile in a quiet rural parish, anything but this. It had been as he had long been coming to suspect. That was what they had been telling him; that the secret heresies were true! They must have known his suspicions. How long had they been watching him? Oh dear God, had it all been for nothing then? And what of the world? What hope could there be for the world?

But he had known that he would do his duty. His calling demanded it. His training made it instinctive. Even so, how he wished that he could turn back the clock. All at once, he had realised that knowledge was not wisdom after all. And that wisdom was something that he could have blissfully lived without.

That had been what they'd done to him five years ago. He had done his duty by his masters, both overt and covert. And he had come to enjoy the overt side of his work. He had not realised how refreshing it would be to meet people. Thousands of different people of all nationalities and outlooks. It was rewarding just to walk with them, talk with them. Share their joys and aspirations for the world. Although deep inside he knew that he could no longer share their simple faith. That luxury had been lost to him forever and how he yearned for its impossible return.

Every now and then, he would be called upon to perform other duties. Ever so infrequently, but even then, more often than he would have liked. It frightened him, no point in beating about the bush; this was fear, real enough. The way things had been explained to him, it should have been wonderful, like bathing in the gold of the warm sun. But for him, it had never been like that. For him those duties represented nothing less than ulcer-

149

inducing, stomach churning fear.

And now, here he was again, hurrying down darkened streets in the early hours of the morning, his way lit not at all by the silver stars that could be discerned against the black sky between the buildings. Hurrying, moreover, to make a rendezvous that he would give a year of his life to be able to avoid.

Rounding a sharp corner, the Monseigneur stumbled, tripping on a rock that jutted out of the ground. Wordlessly he reached out and braced himself against the cool wall of a building and looked up. There before him he could see his destination. Before him, it rose majestic and silent in the still of the night. The Temple of Solomon.

NOWHERE AND EVERYWHERE... NO TIME AND ALL TIMES

The world. How brightly it shone, standing alone in the emptiness of infinite space. No sun here, and no distant stars. Just the planet, held fixed by the opposing magnetic fields generated by two massive pyramids, which stood in unsupported space to either side, invisible yet knowable and each large enough to swallow the planet whole. And the pyramids, one black and one white, revolved around this radiant silver orb, in a perpetual chase around the polar axis. It was a perfect symmetry.

But now there was imperfection. A tremor on the surface of the globe, a tremor so slight that it would have gone unnoticed had it not been for comparison with the perfection that had gone before. The straight lines of invisible electro-magnetic force that had held the tableau in balance before now amplified the tremor, magnifying it out on its way to the bases of the two pyramids. The pyramids began to gyrate wildly in the blackness of space and the lines of force between them began to buckle and crumble. The pyramids could no longer be held in balance as they came together, base to base.

And first they touched the planet, making contact on the equator. They had dimension, but not mass, yet even so, they forced the matter of the planet to collapse in on itself until the bases met and the planet was no more. The pyramids now seemed to meld into one another, faster and faster they moved together, diminishing into nowhere until their very tips became one, like a point as defined mathematically, having position but no magnitude. A position that existed in a black emptiness, but which now collapsed inwards achieving a perverse negative mass, which allowed it to shrink at a rate greater than the speed of light into an emptiness that was unimaginably greater still.

A perfect nothing that held for a second. And then there was thought.

WHAT THEN, IS IT?

A random thought, but one followed quickly by others. Others that came, rushing in like sheep so that within seconds the perfection of the empty stillness was rendered less than a memory.

A man opened his eyes. His meditational spirit had been disturbed. Now that his outer senses had regained control, he could feel the cool of the wall at his back. Smooth stone, placed there thousands of years ago. His eyes opened, but in the dark, he could see next to nothing. Still, he had spent an age here. His mind painted the pictures for him so that he could see.

There would be a visitor. One that was familiar to him. What now, he wondered? But he could feel that he would be asked, expected, to call upon his more base talents. It was so often the way in this modern age.

In the air, vibrations seemed to call out to him. A time was coming, a time that he had waited oh-so-long to see. He could feel it. But it was not necessarily how he had *expected* it to feel. There was not the purity in it that he had been led to expect. Power there was, nevertheless. He could feel God surround him and infuse him. Let it be soon, he thought. He was becoming so weary. And he had been ready for such a long time.

He uncrossed his legs and stretched them out, remaining seated on the stone floor. The circulation returned in a flood and the sensation was not unpleasant. His visitor would be here soon and now he was ready.

Chapter 21

MONSIGNOR ROSSI BRUSHED his cassock after steadying himself. It was just a delaying tactic and he knew it. Anything to slow his progress towards the Temple. The Temple had always frightened him after dark. It was an irrational fear and he had come to control it. But now, suddenly, he had come to realize with a burst of inspiration that it had never been the Temple that had bothered him at all. Nor the dark. Nor even a combination of the two. It was the man (man? Was it really a man still, after so much time?) whom his duty called him to attend. *There* was the true centre of his fear. Τὴν ἀληθεστάτην πρόφασιν, as ancient Thucydides would have said. *The truest cause.*

It had been that way for him since the very first time. And since that first time, ever had it been thus. This afternoon had seen the routine call to horror. There had been a knock at his door, waking him from the light sleep that he had grown accustomed to taking in the heat of the afternoon sun.

He had pulled himself with some reluctance and not a little annoyance from his deep armchair and shuffled over to open the door. As soon as he set eyes upon the little Palestinian boy, he had known. The boy had not spoken, had stood unsmiling, a white manila envelope in his outstretched hand. The hand and the unsmiling face had been caked in grime. The clothes that covered the urchin body had been little more than dirty rags. They had always used such creatures, whoever it was supplying him with his clandestine instructions. He had taken the envelope clutching it in a sweaty hand and delved deep into a pocket with the other, pulling out some coins that he handed to the boy. The boy had turned on his heel and ran, to be lost in the twisting streets, without so much as a bye-your-leave.

After that, he had been unable to continue with his afternoon's relaxation. There was the dread of the night to consider. The envelope had contained a simple instruction and yet another envelope. This second envelope he was to deliver to his charge, that and no more. Hopefully, he would be able to discharge this duty with the minimum of fuss. Still he had known that he would not be able to rest until the task had been performed. And now he was here.

Thankfully, at this unseemly hour there had been no one about to see as he had approached the south side of the Temple. The Jesuit-black of his cassock had melted into the shadows cast by the high walls. This was the dangerous moment, when discovery would be more than a disaster. There was a point on the wall, high up where it could not be reached and touched accidentally by some passing tourist. Rossi reached into his cassock and pulled out a heavy wooden baton, about a metre in length. Standing on tiptoes, he could reach up with the baton and push a small cube of stone that stood out from the wall. It gave, with only the barest of movements, but there was an audible click, and now he could push at the large stone block in front of him. It moved, gliding easily, twisting inwards about a foot and a half, where it stopped abruptly. The monsignor slipped quickly through this gap, not bothering to check whether he was being observed or not. Once inside, he hurried to slam the stone block back into place. It was heavy, and did not really slam, but this was not for want of effort on the part of Rossi. If anyone had been watching from outside, well, let him try to find this door for himself. God knew, it had kept its secret for centuries; it would not be easily discovered now.

How ghastly the dark corridor was. He knew that he was in a narrow corridor, although the dark was all enveloping and his eyes could offer him no help; but he had been this way before. Crouching down, he groped around with his left hand until it fell upon a pile of what he knew to be brushwood torches. He picked one up and stood, lighting the tar-soaked end with a cigarette lighter that he had fished from under his cassock. The flaming torch projected a dim light no more than a couple of metres into the darkness. But it brought great comfort to Rossi. He began to make his way down into the corridor, which sloped steeply, burrowing deep into the ground.

For several hundred metres, the path twisted and turned its labyrinthine way below. Above, Rossi knew, were the old stables of the Temple of Solomon. The Templars had been given the stables, back in the eleventh century, the original nine, who had stayed there for nine years. Many had said that these nine had found the Treasure of Solomon. And he *knew* that they had. But it had not been a treasure of gold and silver and precious stones, oh no. What they had found there had been of greater value than all the baubles of Christendom, then *and* now. If only the historians could have the courage to search without the cloying limitations of conventional science to restrict them. No matter, the Templars had kept the secrets of their treasure and better the world was for it.

He was nearing the place now. He could tell. His mind was no longer drifting with aimless thoughts, as it was usually wont to do. He could think only of what he was about to face. No more than a half dozen times had he been called upon to perform this duty. But that was more than enough as far as he was concerned. As he neared, he could feel it. Force, power, vibrations, whatever. It was real enough and it chilled him to the marrow every time. This was not of man. This was the power of God, and man had no business with it. He had never been able to accept what they had told him about the nature of God, even though he had read much the same in the secret library. But the library had given him only knowledge; words that he could know and understand merely on a flat, two-dimensional level. The Jesuit Cardinal had revealed wisdom to him that night five years ago. And now his understanding of the secret works was clear and terrifying. Outwardly, he would remain loyal. The church was all that he had known and his duty to the Jesuit Order was strong, overrode all his objections. But inside he had died that night. The Vatican had known these things, had known them all along. It was a sham. The Church was a sham and it had all been for politics. A thousand years and oh, Christ knew how many deaths, for nothing more than political expediency. Yes, his faith was gone, but he would never desert the organisation. After all, it was his job. He considered himself to be an employee, the same as any other civil servant anywhere in the world. They paid his wages and they could count on his services in return. But they could no longer expect him to believe.

There it was, in front of him. The door of dread. It was heavy, made of thick oak timbers and it was closed, blocking the passage, though he knew that it would not be locked. Those who managed to find it would always be able to enter. He stood before it for a moment, trembling in the red glow of his torch, breathing heavily as he summoned the courage to reach out and push it open.

'Do come in, Monsignor Rossi.'

The words startled him. His heart seemed to skip a couple of beats and he had to fumble to hold on to the torch, which the shock of hearing the voice had almost caused him to drop.

Still, there was no turning back now. He reached out and pushed against the rough oak of the door. As always, in spite of its age and great antiquity, it gave easily, the hinges silent and well oiled. Thrusting the torch out in front of him, as if to ward away evil, Rossi stepped across the threshold.

'Ah, that is so much better. Welcome, Monsignor, welcome.'

Rossi remained silent, standing on a flagstone landing, from which descended thirteen smooth steps. His torch cast a glow of inadequate light about the chamber, gave it a slight orange glow. There were shadows enough remaining, however, shadows that Rossi always felt would not be penetrated by even the harshest of electric lighting.

Down below, sitting with his back to the wall opposite the stairs, Rossi could see the source of the voice. He shuddered, although so deep under the ground, the chamber was warmed naturally by the heat of the earth's core. The face was looking up at him and even in the dim glow, Rossi could make out the smiling lines. Ordinarily he would have guessed that this face was a boyish forty or forty five years old. But he knew better than that.

He brushed that line of thought to one side; it was bad for his sanity. Moving carefully, he made his way down the flight of stairs, the flickering torchlight causing shadows to dance on the walls as he moved. As he reached the floor of the chamber, he was able to see the man more clearly. He had remained seated, his back resting against the wall, his legs outstretched before him. In his nakedness, the torchlight caused the thin film of sweat that covered him to glisten, reflecting the orange of the flames.

Rossi stepped with obvious reluctance towards the figure, his fear easily discernable to the smiling eyes of the man sitting before him. The Templar. That's how the Cardinal had described this man during the secret briefing back in Rome. Templar. The very name was steeped in history and mysticism. An Order that, in its day, was more secretive and powerful than his own. But that day had passed. There should have been no Templars after the year thirteen fourteen, when the last Grand Master of the Order, Jacques de Molay, had been roasted over an open fire for his heresy. But the Cardinal had told him of this one, at least. No. He could not think about it. He must perform his allotted task and be gone. Yes, that was the safest course of action. Clearing his throat, Rossi reached into his cassock and pulled out the white envelope.

'I have this for you,' he said, handing over the package.

'Thank you.' The Templar took the package.

Rossi flinched as their fingers met. He had never had cause to touch the Templar before, had always striven to avoid such contact. And now, although the Templar had felt no different to any other man, he felt somehow unclean where they had come into contact, slimy there, as though having touched a slug. He pursed his lips in a wince of obvious distaste.

'A little light please.'

Reluctantly, Rossi thrust the torch forward, where it would illuminate the page. It seemed to be Vatican notepaper, but he could not be sure. He didn't want to dwell too much on that anyway. And besides, the corner of his eye had been caught by what seemed to be a pile of rags, lying in a corner of the chamber to his right. Mostly they had been hidden in shadow, but every now and again, the torchlight flickered upon them. Had there been movement? No. Surely his imagination was getting the better of him. He must control himself. Rats. Perhaps there were rats down here. Ordinarily, that in itself would have made him shudder, but now, so natural an explanation acted as a balm to his troubled mind.

The Templar was intent on studying the page held before his eyes. There. Again. Movement. Rossi turned to look at the pile of rags. There *had* been movement. This time, he turned his head to stare, but there was nothing. The rats were probably nesting in there. The Templar had noticed his looking, had glanced up to see, but when Rossi turned back, he was studying the page once more. Finally, he placed the paper down beside him.

'My gratitude, as always, Monsignor.' The Templar's voice was light, lilting, the accent a flawless Roman Italian. 'You do your duty well. I know how distasteful you must find it.'

'Oh, not so...' Rossi protested, flustering. 'It is an honour to be of service to my Holy Order. I...'

The Templar held up a hand, silencing him, the smile still comforting on his face.

'No matter. Whatever your feelings, you have always performed your duty with the utmost diligence. And for that there will always be gratitude.'

Rossi was perturbed. He had done what was asked of him and now he wanted to be gone. In all of his five previous visits put together, he had not heard the Templar speak this many words. It marked this visit out as being special. But why? What was going on?

'You will be pleased to hear that this will be your last visit here. Your mission is complete. It has been a pleasure knowing you, Monsignor.'

Rossi's mind began to skip and dance. So this was it then. He was to be relieved of this hideously burdensome duty. Perhaps he would be recalled to Rome! They owed him that much at least, surely they did. In the warmth of such pleasurable thoughts, he forgot his fear, was uncaring of where he was. Rome. He could almost have wept.

'The honour has been always mine. Truly it has.' Rossi could barely choke out the words through his emotion. 'If there is nothing else?' He left the question open, an undisguised cry for release.

The Templar, smiling as always, gave him his wish. 'You are free to go, Monsignor.'

Rossi, to his surprise, found himself genuflecting to the naked, seated Templar, before turning to climb the stone staircase.

He did not see the smile drop from the boyish face, nor that

157

same face turn to the pile of rags that had so frightened and fascinated him earlier; and he was unaware of the way in which the rags now began silently to raise themselves off the ground, to unfold into shape as a brief shroud for a humanoid figure.

Four steps up. His chest was tight with emotion. His breathing was coming in short gasps. He would soon be out of this dungeon forever. The fifth step. Take it easy, calm down.

Behind him, the raggedy figure was standing and full. In the darkness, its features were uncertain, its skin a wizened and aged parchment, discoloured brown and dark green, plastered close to a heavy skeletal frame. The bowed head lifted an inch or two to regard the Templar. A nod and a glance in the direction of the Monsignor were all the instruction it needed. Silently, it seemed to glide over the ground towards the side of the staircase.

Eighth step. Oh Rome. Oh beloved Rome. Rossi's left foot caught in the hem of his cassock, and as he stumbled forward, his head glanced slightly to the left and he saw it. But too late. His eyes bulged wildly from their sockets in shock as a wordless scream blasted helplessly from his lungs. He tried to lunge forward, to throw himself up the stairs, but the apparition had caught him by the left ankle. Its grip was mighty and the talonous claws dug deep into his flesh; he felt the blood spurt out as thick horny nails pierced his skin.

'Nooo! Aaaagh! Noooo!' His screams were hot with the fire of panic and the air in the chamber became rancid with the smell of piss and excrement as he involuntarily fouled himself.

The rag-creature had clambered onto the staircase itself now, never releasing its grip on the struggling Monsignor's ankle. Rossi screamed like a demon, kicking and lashing out, but there was no one to hear his plea, no one to come to his aid. Except for the Templar. For a split second, he saw the Templar, standing now. The torch had fallen to the chamber floor, and in its flickering glow, the Templar was upright, glorious in his glistening nakedness, watching all with a smile of serenity still drawn across his emotionless face. The Devil. In his struggle for life, Rossi's mind was thrown back to the archetypes of his childhood. He had known since that night with the Jesuit Cardinal that there was no Devil. It was a bogeyman story conjured up to ensure the obedience of the masses. It had never been real. There was no Hell in the sense that the Church had taught it. No heaven either. But first impressions were not so easily dispelled and in that split second it *was* the Devil Rossi saw smile at him.

Then he was being dragged by the ankle, down the stairs. Still struggling and kicking, he banged the back of his head on the sharp corner of one of the steps and for a moment, his consciousness began to swim and his struggling stopped. And as he came to, after that moment, he found himself lying on his back on the chamber floor. The Templar was standing over him. He looked into the Templar's eyes, his own now flooding with tears and managed to mouth just one word: 'Why?'

He was to receive no answer. Rushing fast, like a pouncing animal, the rag-creature came between him and this fount of knowledge and with surprisingly powerful jaws, ripped out his throat in a frenzy of spraying blood and crunching cartilage.

An hour later, the Templar was sitting once again with his back to the cold chamber wall. He was still naked and his knees were drawn up tight to his chest, held there by his encircling arms. He had been thinking of Rossi. How strange it was to simply sit and think. It had been such a long time. Nowadays, he liked to spend as much time as possible in meditation. Conscious thought, even at its most exalted levels, was trivial to him now. He had long ago completed the Great Work; his mind was a living temple. But he had never been allowed to take the final step. He had seen countless Shadowmasters come and go in his time; some had been truly great men and such pleasure as he could derive from the centuries past came from his association with these men. And of these, a few had even completed the Great Work themselves, had done it in one human lifetime. That singled them out as truly masterful. Without doubt, Sons of the Sun. He mused on that fact that it had taken him three centuries to achieve that same level of attainment.

But he had had his distractions. A chosen guardian of the Science, it had been his job to carry its secrets for the future benefit of man, an insurance to ensure that those secrets would never be lost to the world. That calling had been visited on him in an older time...

'You must leave, Hassan, now.'

It had been rare for the Treasurer to call him by his old Islamic name. But they had indeed been strange times. And though centuries had passed, his memory brought those times streaming back with a clarity that was crystal and real.

'You came to us young, my friend, and still young you must leave us. We cannot allow our secrets to fall to the profane. You must take them, Hassan, secure their safety. In a different age, the world will have need of them yet.'

'But why must we skulk away like robbers in the night? Why do we not stand and fight?' My, he had been young then. And impetuous. The young never seemed able to see beyond the next day. The fuller strategy was always blind to them. That had not changed in all the years he had lived to witness it.

The old Treasurer of the Order of the Poor Knights of Christ and the Temple of Solomon had smiled benignly at the young hothead standing before him. They were in his chamber in the Temple Preceptory in Paris. A time was approaching when the French king, Philippe IV, would have his jealous revenge upon the Templars. He envied their wealth, he envied their power, but most of all, he would never forgive them for having refused him membership of their Order. It had been in the air for a long time. And Philippe, who had plotted the murder of two Popes, now had his own choice on the throne of St Peter. It had not been difficult to get a wholesale accusation of heresy aimed at the Order. After all, it was in the Vatican's interest to suppress an organization whose power now rivalled its own, and whose interests were more and more often conflicting.

But the Templars had had spies and friends everywhere. Today was Tuesday, the tenth day of October 1307. It was well known to the leaders of the Order that sealed instructions were already in the hands of Philippe's seneschals throughout France, and that those orders were to be opened at exactly the same time on Friday the thirteenth. The contents of those orders did not have to be guessed at: when acted upon, they would spell the end of the Order that had dominated Christendom for two centuries.

'Oh Hassan, you are so full of the lusts of youth, with so much to learn,' the Treasurer had said. 'Yes, we could stand and fight. We are powerful: we would probably win. But the fight would be long and bloody. And in it, we would undoubtedly lose the flower of our manhood, and here I am thinking of both sides. The whole of Christendom would be left open to invasion and usurpation. The sword of Islam is mighty. And ambitious. I should not have to remind you, of all people, of that fact.'

The young Hassan had bowed his head in acceptance. He had seen in an instant what that would have meant. If Islam had come to rule the world, there would be bloodletting on an unimaginable scale. He knew his people well. The Mullahs would generate fanaticism; the cry would be 'Islam or death.' And the Christians would choose to die. That he knew. And then there would be only his brothers, the Hashishim, the Assassins of Allah to protect the Secret Work. And alone, how long would it be before they too, became the subject of envious whisperings? How long before they would become the subject of the kind of petty political suppression that his adopted brothers were now facing? And then there would be nothing. The secrets carried down countless thousands of years would be lost forever. No, it was right that the Templars should supplicate themselves before the tyranny that threatened them. In the long run, it showed a greater strength, and not a weakness. One day the world would learn of the enormity of their sacrifice and they would receive the honour that their selflessness deserved.

'I will do what is required of me,' was all he had said.

'Good. We have no time to lose. Our documents, our true treasure, are packed and ready. You must leave tonight. A ship waits at our base in La Rochelle. The captain has the destination. Bertrand de Lyons will travel with you. Quickly now, go.'

And he had gone. To Scotland. It had been a wise choice. Philippe's influence was non-existent there, and the Pope's order of suppression had been executed in the most half hearted and reluctant fashion by the English king, Edward II. In Scotland itself, it was not executed at all, Scotland at that time having been at war with England.

They had been hard years in Scotland. It was there that the old knight, Bertrand de Lyons, had explained to him the enormity of his mission.

How clear his memory was of those times. Why, he could even hear old Bertrand's voice as he struggled to teach the young

Hassan the Hermetic processes that he would need to master to fulfil his destiny.

There was much that had happened since though. He had seen kings come and go; dynasties rise and fall. And now it was all coming to a head. Oh, he had never expected it to go on for so long. And he was so tired.

A noise to his right distracted him. He turned to look, his eyes seeing clearly, accustomed to the dark. It was his rag-creature, his Torquemada. It had torn the clothing from the dead Monsignor and knelt before the corpse, licking the urine and excrement from the flesh. He watched for a while as it used its talonous nails to disembowel the body, picking up the stomach and squeezing it, so that the rancid contents of half digested food and drink spurted into its mouth. It gulped noisily, the semi-liquid coming too quickly, running out of its mouth to spill in rivulets over its chin and down its throat; a greenish-yellow, foul smelling concoction, dotted here and there with red lumps of tomato. They reminded the Templar of aborted *foeti*.

Having drank its fill, the Torquemada turned to look at him with eyes that were milky, and white in places with lumpish cataracts. Eyes that were pleading, nonetheless. The Templar stared back, his gaze uncompromising, until the pathetic creature averted its own gaze. It backed away into the sanctuary of a shadowy corner, whimpering, and occasionally howling, a chorus of utter despair.

It had been human once. The Templar himself had reduced it to this. And the Templar would keep it so, until he could sense real contrition from that part of its mind that remained sentient. The part that was still human and knew, *knew*, the full horror of everything that had happened to it. The part that still experienced a hideous disgust at everything that it was forced to do, at everything that its once proud being had been reduced to. And even through centuries, the Templar had not felt that yet. A surface sorrow that was little more than self pity, yes, but not true repentance. Oh, the eternal vanity of the Grand Inquisitors.

To his left lay the letter that had been delivered by the dead Monsignor. A man to kill. Just one. Was he now a mercenary? A cheap political assassin? Were they so weak and trivial, these new Shadowmasters, that they could allow a single man to threaten the progress of the Great Work? It would never have happened in the days of Leonardo, of Newton, or any of the illustrious others. They had been artists all, men of vision and greatness.

Still, their days had come and gone. It was his duty to be at the call of his masters. He could at least trust himself to expedite matters efficiently and with discretion. There was at least that. The Shadowmasters could be safe in the knowledge that no trails would lead back to their door.

He picked up the letter. The name seemed to stand out from the page, beckoning him. *David Strachan*. Nothing out of the ordinary. Then why did it seem to taunt him, to mock him? Perhaps there was here a worthy opponent for a Hashishim, for a Knight Templar? Well he would see. He would be wary of David Strachan. But he would kill him. Yes he would. And then it would be time to meet with the new Shadowmasters. He had much to discuss.

Throwing down the paper, he stood and pushed at the stone, which he had been leaning on. It gave to expose a wardrobe of contemporary clothing. After all, he was hardly about to re-enter the world naked. Contemporary form would, he knew, frown upon that.

Chapter 22

MARSEILLES... JUNE 17th

IT WAS 1.00pm when Strachan finally woke. His eyes felt red and sore, his muscles lifeless with the torpor that excessive sleep can sometimes bring. In the corner of the room there was a washhand basin covered in a thick layer of dust. It had obviously not seen use in a long time. Strachan turned on a tap and to his amazement, a stream of cold clear water burst onto the grimy porcelain. He cupped his hands to gather the water, scooping it onto his face. It was immediately invigorating and he began to feel fresh and more alert. He rubbed his entire body with the cool water then used the sheet from his bed to towel himself dry.

Yesterday's clothes lay in a crumpled heap beside the bed. He would wear clean ones today. He pulled them from the holdall, ripped of the 'brand new' tags and put them on. Time to go out. He needed money and he needed a newspaper. Were the authorities still searching for him or had they found *The Hasler's* wreckage out at sea and presumed him dead? God, how he prayed for the latter. He needed time to make new plans. He pulled the Beretta from the holdall and tucked it into the waistband at the back of his trousers where it was covered from sight by his loose-hanging shirt. He was ready for the street.

The rickety staircase was gloomy, even in the mid afternoon, but Strachan managed to negotiate it without incident. In the lobby, the fat concierge sat behind his counter reading a pornographic magazine. A cigarette-butt dangled unlit from his lips.

'Leaving us monsieur?' the fat man asked without raising his eyes from the page of the magazine.

Strachan approached him. 'Not just yet,' he said. 'Don't worry,

164

I'll let you know when I'm ready to check out.'

The fat man pursed his lips. 'Well it'll be another four hundred if you intend to stay here again tonight. Payable now of course.'

Strachan dug into his pocket. Four hundred francs would leave him with only about a hundred and fifty. He tossed the money onto the counter in front of the fat man and turned to leave.

'A moment monsieur.'

Strachan was halted by the fat man's voice.

'I would prefer it if you would leave the key to your room when you leave the hotel.'

Strachan regarded the fat man's sweat-greased face. Beyond the row of blackened and crooked teeth, he knew that the fat man was testing him again, probing him to discover the extent of his need to hide, his need to avoid making a scene. Strachan had to make a stand, show this greasy fuck that he was not to be messed with. He leaned forward so that his face was inches from the fat man's, and he smiled.

'You want the fucking key?' he hissed. 'Well tough fucking shit.' He stood to his full height and jabbed a finger in the fat man's chest. 'You probably have a spare key or a skeleton key or whatever, but let me tell you, you set so much as one toe in my room while I'm gone and I'll know it. And I'll fucking kill you. Okay?'

Strachan didn't wait for an answer, just turned and walked and in five strides was out on the street.

The fat man wiped the sweat from his brow with the back of a podgy hand. He had been right; this stranger *did* have something to hide. But it was no longer the kind of secret that he itched to discover. Only a crazy man or a dangerous man would dare bring an attitude like that into this part of town. Dangerous. This one was certainly dangerous. Doubly so, because he may *well* have been crazy too. He would leave well alone where this one was concerned. His keen eyes had noticed the bulge at the small of the man's back as he had walked away. But something told him that this man wouldn't necessarily *need* the gun.

Out on the street, Strachan had found what he was looking for. A row of public telephone booths down by the marina. He made his way down past the rows of fishing boats and pleasure craft where they lay moored in neat lanes. He hoped that at least one of the phones would be for international calls because he needed to call his bank in England, and quickly.

He had a bank account in Monaco, but of course, that was lost to him now. England was where the bulk of his funds were held, and there was a risk in even accessing *that* money. But only, he figured, a slight one. The authorities would be looking for a David Strachan, but how many David Strachans were there in the UK? Too many, he supposed, for a watch to have been put on all accounts bearing that name, for every bank to have been circulated with the 'watch' information. A transaction made now may be picked up later - many days later, in all probability - but they would only be able to follow the trace to Marseilles. And by then he would be long gone. Only the manager of his bank knew him personally, and he would not need to speak to the manager to effect this transaction.

The first booth proved to be the one that he was hoping to find, one that accepted the ten-franc coins that would make his international call possible. Strachan dialled a number that he had committed to memory many years ago. The phone rang half a dozen times at the other end before it was answered.

'National Westminster Bank, can I help you?' a pleasant female voice enquired.

'I'd like to withdraw some money from my deposit account and collect the cash at a bank in France.'

'Just a moment, I'll put you through to someone who can help.'

MONACO... 1.34pm

The blazing sun burned hard on the Monaco streets. It was a busy afternoon and the harbour area was crowded with tourists, dawdling in the heat. The cafes, which lined the area beyond the swimming pool, were doing their usual wonderful business; the tables were full, with iced beer and Coca-Cola being the order of the day.

At one table, shaded from the sun's glare by a large straw umbrella, sat two men. One seemed to exude calm and looked out over the boats towards the open sea; his companion appeared fidgety, his head jerking and twitching, first to the right, then to the left. Occasionally, the fidgety one would pull a claw-like hand from his lap beneath the table and use the back of it to wipe a layer of sweat from his brow. His features were mainly hidden from view by the large sunglasses and the long peak of the blue baseball cap that he wore. Which was just as well, since those features were openly distorted, could frighten children with just an innocent glance. Not there was *anything* innocent about this man. There never had been.

The calm man sat deep in thought. In front of him, the daily papers lay folded on the tabletop, their news already digested. They had found the wreckage of the boat then, far out at sea. Strachan's boat, they seemed very sure of it. They seemed certain too, that Strachan had perished with his boat. Strachan's part - if he had indeed played any part - in the Stopyra devastation would remain forever a mystery. The speculation was that Strachan had died by his own hand, that or explosives that he was carrying in furtherance of his suspected terrorist activities had gone off prematurely.

The calm man shook his head almost imperceptibly. No accident, not with this Strachan, not where explosives were concerned. They were well wide of the mark with that speculation. He had reached out to the ocean, had felt her answer touching his centuries' worth of instinct. The ocean whispered to him, told him that she carried no Strachan in her tender embrace. So where, then, *was* Strachan? Where would he have gone? Did he carry a motive other than simple revenge to fuel his attacks upon the Shadowmasters? These were all questions to meditate upon and he would call out to the supernature of the cosmos for his answers. But, he knew he would have to be quick.

In the seat beside him, the Torquemada squirmed and jerked its head. The emaciated claw of a hand reached up once more to wipe the sweat from its brow and brought away a layer of slime, which it rubbed absently on its rough canvas trousers. The Templar glanced sidelong at it. How marvellous it would be to be rid of its festering presence at long last. Soon, he promised himself, soon. He returned to his drink and to abstract concentration. There was much he needed to consider before

167

nightfall.

MARSEILLES... 2.57pm

Back in the comfortable anonymity of the shadows of the Old Port area, Strachan sat at a roadside table in front of a greasy looking bistro. On the dirty buckled metal tabletop in front of him was a glass of beer, a couple of newspapers and an expensive looking calfskin wallet. He picked up the wallet and opened it. A face in a photograph, tucked behind a thin film of plastic stared up at him. He recognised the face of course; it belonged to the corpulent tourist from whom he had stolen the wallet a little less than an hour earlier. The fool had been walking around with it sticking out of his back pocket. Strachan considered himself lucky that he had been the first to notice it. Would some people never learn?

He pulled a sheaf of banknotes from the wallet and counted them. A thousand francs. Not a fortune, but it would keep him until tomorrow. And it would be tomorrow before he would be able to collect his credit transfer from the Banque D'Aquitaine on the *Rue D'Italie* in Central Marseilles. Tomorrow because he had wanted to collect half of his money in dollars and the local branch would need to order in an amount such as he had requested.

Tomorrow. Time for them to suspect him, time for them to set him up. It was, he knew, a risk. But if they were waiting for him tomorrow, he would spot them. He knew the signs, knew what to look for. He would cross that bridge when he came to it. He had no other choice. In the meantime, he sat back to read the papers, to discover the extent, if any, of his notoriety.

LONDON...JUNE 17th...5.30pm

From his office on the fifth floor, Robert Watson could see the traffic congesting in the City of London street below. He pondered the name of the street for a moment: Poultry it was called, a relic of the Middle Ages when the thoroughfare was the city's central marketplace for that particular commodity. To his left was the spidery interchange at the Bank, and opposite was the once splendid Mansion House, now sadly in need of repair.

Normally, the double glazed windows protected him from the incessant sounds of the city below, but now he could hear police sirens bursting their way through to him regardless, and despite himself, he found himself at the window in search of the source of the commotion.

There was nothing to see. The traffic had pulled in to the side of the road as best it could to allow the speeding police Rovers easy passage. He had just caught a glimpse of them as they rushed on their way past the building, heading for Cheapside. He didn't stop to wonder what drama had prompted their fearsome chase through such crowded streets. He was a natural banker and had never considered imagination a gift to be prized. Order, logic, correctness. They were the attributes that impressed him most, the ones he had spent his twenty-year career with the bank seeking to perfect. And in some large measure, he had succeeded and the rewards were there for all to see; the large house in Surrey with its five bedrooms three bathrooms and the paddock for the children's ponies. His neat, plain, but ever so proper wife. And more importantly than all of these, his seat on the board.

It had not been easy for him either. But then the struggle was what had made the results all the more savoury. There had been years of hard slog for his Institute of Bankers examinations, even longer hours of slog at work, and the slog of schmoozing up to the right people. He had realised early on that all the hard work in the world would amount to nothing if his face didn't fit. And being a natural banker with a natural banker's mentality, this important necessity had been the easiest of all for him to achieve.

It had even led to an invitation to join one of the City of London's Freemasonic Lodges. And in the end, it was there that he was cosiest, among his peers, everyone respectable, everyone honourable; the very pillars of civilisation, he liked to think. He had attended a Lodge dinner only the previous evening. It had been a lovely affair; excellent food, excellent wine - in moderation, of course - and excellent company.

After the dinner, a man he had come to know well over the years had approached him. Giles Henderson. Henderson was the chairman of a small but highly energetic and successful merchant bank. Henderson had caught him as he made his way to the bar after the meal and had taken him to one side.

'Watson old boy, good to see you,' Henderson had said, the very caricature of a Public School Old Boy. Then, in a conspiratorial tone he added, 'Need a small favour, old boy. Hope you can oblige.'

'So long as it's legal, Giles,' he had replied, the seriousness of his tone only half-mocking, and Henderson had allowed himself a brief smile at this attempt at humour.

'Oh God no, nothing underhand, nothing like that. Just want you to do a spot of checking around at your place, see if you have any accounts open in this name.' A small piece of paper was pressed into Watson's hand and Watson pocketed it without looking at it.

'And what if I come across something?' he asked.

'Well, I'd be grateful if you could let me know. And if there has been any activity within such an account, make a note of dates, places, that sort of thing. I really would be awfully grateful.'

'Of course, consider it done.'

That there might be an ethical, not to mention legal, prohibition against this request never crossed Watson's mind. Giles Henderson was an honourable man. If he wanted this information, there would be a legitimate reason, no doubt about it. Goodness, they belonged to the same Lodge, didn't they?

'Knew I could rely on you Watson. Here, let me buy you a drink...'

And that had been last night. It was afternoon now, and Watson hadn't given his promise so much as a thought. This had been a busy day. Still, he could look into the matter now.

He dipped his hand into his jacket pocket and pulled out the piece of paper that Henderson had slipped him. He placed it on the desk and smoothed it out. On it were written a name and an address and even a sample signature. David Strachan, it said. Shouldn't be too difficult to find, he thought, and he sat down behind his large antique desk and logged onto his computer terminal.

Chapter 23

EVENING, AND STRACHAN needed a drink, needed to get away from his own thoughts for a while. The afternoon's newspapers had brought mixed comforts.

The *Paris Tribune* had provided good news. The Riviera authorities had got him tagged as the murderer of Emile Stopyra, but they hadn't been able to dot the 'i's and cross the 't's on that for certain. From what he could make out from the newspaper report, the chateau had been completely gutted by the fires that had followed the explosions of his homemade incendiary devices. The newspaper spoke of as many as thirteen deaths with the remains of more than a few as yet unidentified. Among them he thought of the three that he knew had been despatched by his own hand; the nurse, the 'Death Man,' the bastard who had killed Astrid, and that ultimate bastard, Stopyra himself. Others he knew he had caught on the staircase in bursts of automatic fire. The smoke and the flames must have caught the rest. In his heart he felt no pity for them. It seemed to him that pity and mercy and yes, goddamnit, love, were emotions that would be forever alien to his soul.

Still, that no longer mattered since he did not anticipate a long life. And in the mountains that rose high and stark out from the Afghan Plains, those human qualities would be largely redundant in any case. It would require the darker side of nature to operate in that environment. But he would be all right; he had mastered the dark side.

The real plus point of the *Tribune* article was the fact that the authorities were indeed inclined to believe that he had perished at sea. Some wreckage from *The Hasler* had been located. It was obvious that the yacht had gone down and the police were ninety

171

per cent certain that Strachan had perished with the boat. That was good. It was by no means guaranteed that he was off the hook completely, but it meant that he had a breathing space.

The English *Daily Telegraph* had tempered his outlook. He had been scanning it for any mention of the attack on the chateau; there could well have been after all, since his name and nationality were known. It was conceivable that word might have got out concerning his background. And what sensational news that would have been in the UK. He could see the headline: *SAS Captain in French Massacre Horror*. Something like that at any rate. And the British press would be unlikely to let a story like that lie. SAS would always guarantee a story some good circulation in jingo-ridden Britain.

On the third page he had found his headline, and the half-column of copy that ran beneath it made grim reading.

Belfast Shopping Mall Killings: Man Named

He scanned the text, knowing what was coming. This was a nightmare that had haunted him for five years. Two nights ago, in the Stopyra estate, he knew that he had *felt* the ghastly conclusion, as though he had been there himself. The 'man named' was his brother Jonathan. His twin. He had read the story without needing to, morbidly fascinated to see it explained in print. Oh Jesus fucking god, what could have happened to Jonathan? He'd seen him, only a few months ago. They'd lived together aboard *The Hasler*. Jonathan had had moments of depression sure enough. But that had been understandable. He had been going through a period of readjustment after leaving the army. He himself had been there; he knew what that was like. He hadn't felt it necessary to worry too much about his brother. He had been sure, then, that Jonathan would be fine in the end.

So just what had prompted this horrific suicide? For suicide it had certainly been. Jonathan had served in Ireland often enough and would have known that there could be no hope of escaping from his actions alive. So why? *Why?* It was such an unnecessary fucking waste!

Strachan was walking, had been walking for the best part of a couple of hours, round the twisting narrow alleyways of the Old Port. He kept always to the shadows wherever he could as he

172

tried to marshal his thoughts. He looked at his watch. 7.15 pm. God, he *did* need that drink. There was a small bistro he had noticed during his wanderings; a dingy looking place tucked uninvitingly half way along a narrow alley near the waterfront. It would be perfect for him. He really needed to get a feel for this place, to tune in to its underground currents. He needed to get away fast, now more than ever. And maybe this oasis of dark would be just the place to make contacts. He knew that he would have to be gone in a couple of nights at the latest. He had no time to lose.

Christ, how he longed for the uncomplicated violence that would be Afghanistan. He was beginning to lean on the very name. It had become both a beacon and a crutch. The sooner he was there the better.

WASHINGTON...JUNE 27th...2.30pm

Whisps of steam rose in lazy twists from the cup of coffee that sat untouched on a huge leather-topped desk. The room was enclosed and windowless, the only entrance and exit being a heavy, undisguised, reinforced-steel door to the rear. The walls were antiseptically white and the discreet whirr of an air conditioning plant made the only sound.

Behind the desk, Frank Redbridge leaned back in his executive leather chair, looking up at the ceiling. It was a position that he was prone to adopt when deep in thought. David Strachan, a man he'd never met, had never even heard of until a few days earlier, was occupying those thoughts. Just who was Strachan, and what were his motives? That latter of course was the more important question, the one commanding his focus.

Perhaps Bondachuk had had the right idea. Perhaps it would be better for them all to hunt out this Strachan and eliminate him. Bondachuk would have operatives engaged on that very task even now. But there was something unsettling about this whole business. Could Strachan have really been working at some agency's official behest? The savagery of his reprisal actions against both Stopyra and the Arab Prince had suggested otherwise. But what if the operation had had *quasi-*

official status, had been under joint British and French control? Perhaps they would sanction the reprisals, have Strachan appear to be some rogue maverick as a cover for their involvement. That thought sent a ripple of apprehension down his spine. Official involvement, however distanced, would suggest that certain government agencies had become aware of The Shadowmasters. Was there also a suspicion as to the secular nature of the Great Work in which they were engaged? Beads of perspiration suddenly appeared on his forehead.

Christ, they *had* to know, they had to find out. Action must be taken against Strachan; he was in agreement with Bondachuk on that one. But what form should that action take? Termination? No, they couldn't afford that. Strachan had to be taken alive. Interrogation was imperative. It was vital that they have the answers. What *did* Strachan know? He would have to ensure that his operatives reached Strachan before Bondachuk's did.

He sat upright in his chair. On the desk before him were two telephones, both sterile and secure, a red one for outgoing calls, a blue one for incoming. Sterile and secure. He had been around long enough to know that sterile and secure did not necessarily mean from his point of view.

There was a cheap diner on the route out of the city towards Langley. It had a pay phone. He had never used it before; in circumstances such as this he made a point of never using the same pay phone more than once. Better safe than sorry. He kept in his head, the locations of many pay phones that he could access discreetly. This one was next on his mental list.

There was, he knew, no time to lose, so he rose from his chair and collected his jacket from the hanger behind him. He took out his plastic key and inserted it in the slot by the door. The steel structure slid sideways, exposing the one-foot thickness of its leading edge. He walked through, nodding acknowledgement at the two Marine guards standing without. At the end of a long passageway was an express lift ready to rush him the ten floors up to ground level. Behind him the coffee cup still steamed unnoticed as the steel door slid shut, hardening the room against a ground burst of at least one-megaton.

LONDON

It was 7.00 pm in London. On the streets, the summer light had not yet begun to fade, though indoors the premature gloom of a low sun was beginning to creep through the office blocks of the City.

Robert Watson was working late. This in itself was not unusual. However, this evening he was not working for the bank. There was the little favour he had promised Giles Henderson to consider. His late duty switchboard operators had been told that barring a thermonuclear exchange or a movement of US interest rates (and it was a moot point which of these he considered to be the more important) he was to be considered *in absentis*.

It was likely to be a tedious business, this searching through files. God, didn't Henderson have any idea of the size of their client base? The name Strachan wasn't too common, thank the Lord, but it was not exactly rare, either. There might be hundreds. And then it would come down to matching the specimen signature, and even then it might all come to nothing.

Still, it had to be done. Henderson was a prominent Mason and a Lodge Brother to boot. After all, what was the Brotherhood for if not for members to provide service for one another? Henderson was also a major City player, of course. It would do no harm to cultivate such a contact. Who knew what doors might be opened, what pathways smoothed with someone like Giles Henderson on one's side?

The monitor before him flashed up the message *Accessing Data Files. Please Wait.* "Come on, come on,' he whispered under his breath.

Finally, the screen burst with activity. Watson found himself surprised to discover that only eight David Strachans held accounts with the bank throughout the whole of the UK. Surprised but pleased, nevertheless. He would print out the account details of each and pass them all to Henderson. He could decide for himself whether the man he was seeking was among them or not. But no... that would not do. He could at least take a glance at each of these files, see if anything immediate stood out.

175

The first three were anything but interesting; nothing more than tedious ledgers detailing humdrum lives. Month after boring month of salaries paid in, bills paid out, with odd sundry extras representing the fun. Each one detailed nothing more than a *mister normal-average*.

He tapped the keys that would bring the fourth file to show all before him.

'Holy fucking shit,' he whispered. He was not usually given to vulgar cursing but what presented itself shone out like a diamond in a cowpat. First off, this cheque account had shown a credit balance of just one pound, static for over a year. Then today, fifty thousand pounds had been transferred in from an adjoining high-interest deposit account. This in itself was unusual enough given the previous running of the account, but this other - wow. There was something unusual going on here sure enough. He had never encountered a voice-activated alphanumeric coded transaction agreement before. It was the stuff of Zurich rather than a British High Street clearing bank. And more than this, the voice code had been used. Today. A conversion of sterling to dollars and a credit transfer to the South of France, collection dated for tomorrow.

Fuck the print out. Henderson would not thank him for having made him wait for this information. He picked up the telephone in front of him and dialled.

'Giles? Robert Watson here. About that little favour you asked for. Well I've been looking into it and I thought I'd better call you right away...'

Chapter 24

A DENSE MASS OF coloured roped beads barred the entrance to the bistro, so that it would be impossible to casually check out the interior from the street. This inhospitable aspect existed to serve a good purpose; it would inhibit the odd curious tourist who might have strayed into the area from crossing the threshold. The *Bistro Moderne*, as the discreet painted sign above the door proclaimed it to be, had no desire for the tourist franc; it had a thriving clientele of its own to keep it busy. The soldiers, the whores, the pimps the villains; all knew that they could find an environment both welcoming and comfortable within its grimy and ill-lit confines.

Which was not to say that it was patronised by the same faces each night, far from it. There was a hard core of regulars, to be sure; fishermen who supplemented their incomes with a little smuggling would meet there, and several of the district's prostitutes made it a base from which to sally forth after business while their minders sat fast drinking away the best part of what they earned. But much of the bistro's trade was transient. The soldiers from the Legionnaire base would gravitate there on overnight passes, for example. These were men not recruited from the more gentile of Europe's universities, and it was fair to say that few, if any, had been angels prior to joining *La Legion Etrangere*. It was natural that they should make for the kind of recreational haunt that best made them feel at home.

There were many bistros like the *Moderne* in the Old port area, but the *Moderne* had a particular attraction in that a carefree night could be spent there without having to worry about police intrusion. This was down to the patron, a monsieur Platini. Platini was a huge man who ran his establishment with a fist of

177

steel. Nothing - and he meant *nothing* - illegal was transacted in his bar. No wheeler dealing, no drug pedalling, nothing underhand whatsoever. Over the years the police had come to realise this and although many unsavoury characters were known to spend a few pleasant hours in the *Moderne*, the police were content to leave well alone. While they were in there, these criminal elements would not be getting up to mischief. This made the *Moderne* something of a safe haven, a sanctuary for those who lived on society's fringes and all were happy to conform to the house rules. Besides, everyone knew that Monsieur Platini -no one ever addressed him with familiarity, not even his wife, it was rumoured - was connected.

It was just the place for Strachan, who parted the bead curtain and stepped over the threshold. The interior was gloomy, as Strachan had suspected it would be. He made his way over to the bar and ordered a beer. Monsieur Platini had not yet arrived and a spotty faced youth served Strachan with his ice cold drink and took the money without speaking. Strachan walked to a table at the far end of the long narrow room and seated himself with his back against a wall for protection. Of course, this also allowed him to observe everything.

It was still early and the bar was as yet sparsely populated. Two men were hunched over a table in the middle of the room, deep in conversation; a group of four sat at a table on the far side, laughing and playing cards. Strachan was sure that as the night wore on, he would be able to find the contact that he so desperately needed to get him out of France. In the meantime he was content to sip on his beer, watching and waiting...

LATER...

'Hi there bud, mind if I join ya? It's getting a little crowded in here.'

It was now close on 10.00pm and the friendly American voice was right. The place really had filled up. Strachan looked up into the face of the newcomer. It was broad, split by a wide grin and topped with a neat blond crew cut. The body beneath was well built and muscular and, Strachan could tell, in great shape.

And despite Strachan's lack of reply, this stranger drew out a chair and planted himself in it.

'C'mon bud, loosen up,' the stranger said. 'Don't try and tell me you're not American. Or British. Maybe British. An English speaker at any rate. I pride myself with being able to tell these things. Straight off. With just a glance.'

The grin remained, but still Strachan felt no inclination to reply. Undaunted, the stranger thrust a huge hand across the table.

'Look, the name's Joe Lyndon. Let's just sink a few beers and talk some sport; practice our own language before we forget how to speak it altogether, eh? Whaddaya say?'

There was going to be no getting rid of this guy. Strachan cracked his features into a smile and reached for the outstretched hand.

'Okay Joe, you win. Brian Richards at your service. And your antenna served you well. English.'

'Shit, and I know nothing at all about soccer.'

'Football,' Strachan corrected him. 'And that's okay. Neither do I.'

For half an hour the two men made casual small talk and Lyndon insisted on buying all the drinks. 'My treat for disturbing your peace and quiet, eh?'

During the conversation, in which Strachan had improvised a story of his being a late-life drifter making his solitary way around Europe, Strachan began to sense that fate had indeed dropped a potentially useful contact into his lap.

'So what do you do around here then Joe?'

'Oh, this and that. A little buying, a little selling. Now and then some security work or courier work. Whatever it takes to get by, really.'

It was becoming increasingly clear that Joe Lyndon was not being entirely forthcoming with the truth. Maybe he had contacts with the local underworld. That was certainly the implication. Strachan would have to be careful, but perhaps this was indeed the very contact he had been seeking. There came a slight lull in the conversation. Just a few moments, but it was broken by Lyndon.

'Kinda blocking your view, aren't I?' he whispered, the smile

179

for once dropped. 'Well don't worry, you're safe here. The police don't ever cross that portal. Monsieur Platini sees to all that.' He gestured a thumb back over his shoulder to indicate the large Patron who had for some time now occupied his usual stool at the far end of the bar. 'He don't allow any funny business in here and the police know it. They keep away. It's a sort of unofficial arrangement, if you know what I mean.'

Strachan *did* know. He was also convinced now that the man who sat smiling before him was more than just an amiable American looking for homely conversation. But this was all potentially dangerous. He would just have to play things by ear.

From over by the bar a raucous peel of laughter erupted. The source was a group of seven shaven-headed young men who had been drinking steadily for the last couple of hours. The noise was harsh, cutting through the general hubbub and even drowning out the rock music that blared from the jukebox. Strachan looked towards them and Lyndon followed his gaze.

'Don't mind them,' Lyndon said, turning back to Strachan. 'They're Legionnaires. From the base just out of town. Probably on their first liberty, way they've been drinking. You get them in here. It's a good place for them to come and hang loose, let off a little steam. Not many places would give them house room.'

Strachan had already clocked them as Legionnaires from the moment they had walked into the bar; the shaven heads and the arrogant bearing earmarked them as members of *that* military elite. He knew well enough that it was an arrogance they had well and truly earned. They reminded him of paratroopers in the British Army. Christ, they might even *be* paratroopers - *La Deuxieme Regement Etrangere Parachutistes*, perhaps. Which would make them brothers, in a sense.

'Legionnaires, huh?' Strachan said. 'Guess we'd better not step out of line then.'

Lyndon smiled, nodding his agreement, then leaned towards Strachan to whisper: 'Listen, I got a little business to attend to with those guys. Stay here and keep the beers cold will ya? I won't be more than a couple of minutes.'

'Please, go ahead,' Strachan said. 'We all have to eat, don't we?'

'How right you are, bud, how right you are.' Lyndon stood up

180

from his chair. 'Don't go away now.'

Strachan watched him cross to where the Legionnaires were standing. He was a big guy, Strachan noticed. Not tall, but stocky, powerfully muscular, and moving with a confident gait that gave rise to the lie that he had inches to spare. Strachan watched him greet the Legionnaires as though they were already acquainted and it crossed his mind that maybe that was indeed the case. In spite of Lyndon's earlier comment speculating that this would likely be their first liberty.

And that word, *liberty*. It was military terminology sure enough, navy rather than army. Strachan pondered that there may be a greater depth to Lyndon. And from his perspective, was that going to be a good thing?

Strachan sipped his beer and watched as Lyndon played the group. The talk, which he had no chance of overhearing above the heavy metal din of the jukebox, had begun conspiratorially with all of them huddled around the charismatic Lyndon, but now it had become more animated. Must have got down to the nitty gritty, thought Strachan. Money. He didn't know what Lyndon was selling, but he had his suspicions; and because of them, Strachan didn't *want* to know.

Lyndon was gesturing towards the beaded door and two of the Legionnaires broke away from the main group, leading the way out. Lyndon turned to follow, looking over at Strachan, the wide smile an ever present on his face. He winked, then turned and stepped out of the door. No business transacted on the premises, Strachan thought. He had hardly believed that it was a hard rule in a place like this, but obviously he had been wrong.

The remaining five Legionnaires were in a huddle and a few seconds later, three of them broke away, striding purposefully towards a rear door through which Strachan suspected the toilets were located. Something was going on. Strachan could feel his hackles beginning to rise. Lyndon was being set up, he could feel it. Those three Legionnaires had not looked to be slipping away to the john together and the good-time look had been altogether missing from their faces.

He owed Lyndon nothing, Strachan thought. Christ, they'd only just met. But he felt he *needed* Lyndon, and that was important. He couldn't afford to be involved in anything that might bring him to the attention of the law, but could he afford to lose Lyndon? He was no xenophobe, but it was surely going to be easier, in a tight spot, to be dealing with a cultural brother. His mind was made up with that thought. It might be all for nothing, but he couldn't take the risk. If Lyndon was being set up to be rolled, he would have to put a stop to it. He finished his beer and rose from the table, following where the three Legionnaires had disappeared through the rear door.

The dirty toilet, with its stench of stale piss and vomit, was empty when Strachan got there. A square window, just large enough for a man to climb through, hung open on its uncertain hinges at the far end, beyond the urinals. Strachan needed no telling that his collective quarry had all clambered through it. He would have to be careful; he didn't want to get too close. Stalking was to be the name of the game, at least until he knew exactly what the score was.

Strachan peered out, just in time to see his targets disappear around the nearby corner leading into a barely lit alleyway. He pulled himself through the gap and crept after them. He stopped at the corner and peered round. The situation was just as he had feared. He found himself looking down a narrow passageway, which was blocked at the far end. The three Legionnaires he had been following stood ten yards in, spread out now, blocking any escape. Twenty yards beyond that, he could see Lyndon, fixed between these three and the two he had originally accompanied. Lyndon must have sensed this new presence behind him, because he turned his head.

'Hey, what the fuck's going down here?' Strachan heard him ask belligerently.

'You, monsieur. *You're* going down,' came the confident, amused reply.

'The fuck you say…'

Strachan couldn't afford to wait. He was only too aware of his own abilities, but he could only guess at Lyndon's. And Legionnaires were Legionnaires were Legionnaires. Stepping out from the cover of the wall, he launched himself into the alley towards the backs of the three he had followed, his rubber-soled sneakers making no noise on the cobbled floor.

The three Legionnaires sensed his presence as neared them, but too late. Reaching forward and grabbing tight to the collars of the two outer men, Strachan lashed out with his left foot, catching the centre man a crippling kick just below the left buttock. The man immediately tensed upright, the blow having sent an unbearable shock to his sciatic nerve. Pain seared through his entire left leg, flooding out beyond his abdomen. He began to crumble as the leg gave way beneath him, all muscle control lost, when Strachan twisted his kicking foot sideways, driving it home behind the joint of the knee and forcing the kneecap down harshly onto the ground.

No time to finish him off; the two whose collars he still held in his grip he wrenched sideways to his left where they both smashed against the wall. He had thrown them together so that they would not be able to come at him from different directions and in the confines of the alley would now get in each other's way. He twisted left to face them. One came back quickly off the wall, having braced himself with outstretched arms. He spun smartly, facing Strachan in a fighting crouch, stepping clear of his comrade who had fallen awkwardly to the floor. He stepped away to his left, forcing Strachan to twist to follow him. Very good, Strachan thought, very good indeed. He could see that the man was drawing his attention, giving his partner time to recover in a position where he would be able to attack from Strachan's blind side. It was textbook perfect. But textbooks were one thing; this was for real and this kid was going to find that out. It seemed that Lyndon had been right first time; these guys must have only just completed basic and had never seen real combat action. Certainly they could never have faced the terrors of close up hand to hand; because this kid had not realised that Strachan had not followed him all the way round, had kept his comrade well in sight and well in range.

The young Legionnaire lashed out, a straight arm thrust with the heel of his right hand, drawing the power from his hips. Strachan saw it coming, stepped neatly to his left, bringing his right arm up to hook inside the right arm of his assailant, locking his right palm in the nape of his attacker's neck, then straightening the arm and locking it at the elbow. Stepping forward and through, Strachan lifted his right foot and smashed his heel into the back of the Legionnaire's right knee, making the joint fold and sending the man down to the ground. Twisting smartly to the right, Strachan brought his left hand over the shaven head, hooking his fingers into the eye sockets and pulling the head backwards to meet a savage blow with his left knee. He threw the body to one side, knowing it to be unconscious; the knee-blow had been sweet, hitting the occipital bone with an audible crack.

A blow coming from the right. He twisted his head, but too late. The blow caught him on the right cheek bone, not full force - he had moved quickly enough to avoid that - but hard enough to bring a mist of tears to his eyes and cause him to stagger a couple of steps backwards.

He was off balance, vulnerable. This one was moving in for the kill. Strachan threw himself backwards onto the cobbled ground, breaking his fall with outstretched arms. It sent him momentarily beyond the range of his assailant. More importantly, flat on his back, although vulnerable, he was at least balanced. And there were only limited ways of attacking a fallen opponent. And this assailant chose the wrong one.

Unbelievably the Legionnaire was arrogant enough to believe that Strachan was at his mercy and came in unthinking, aiming a wild kick at Strachan's left flank. Strachan rolled, avoiding the crude kick and came up off the floor like a panther, catching the kicking leg in mid air and lifting it up with him as he rose. His own left leg lashed out, the side of his foot smashing cruelly into the exposed genitals of the young Legionnaire. He tipped the boy off balance, keeping hold of the outstretched foot and stamped his own left foot repeatedly into the boy's face. Then placing his left foot hard on the upper thigh of the leg resting twisted on the ground, he sharply twisted the foot that he was holding, hearing the knee ligaments snap. This one too, was now out of commission. Would be for many months.

Lyndon. How was Lyndon doing? Strachan turned to look back down the alley. One of the two Legionnaires Lyndon had been dealing with was lying flat out, not moving. The head was twisted outrageously and Strachan knew instantly that the boy was dead. That was a broken neck and no mistake. But the remaining Legionnaire was clearly a league beyond. Both he and Lyndon were circling each other in the confines of the dark alley, crouching low and occasionally probing with an outstretched hand, each attempting to lure the other into a killing zone. Through the gloom Strachan could see brief flashes of light as the bright moon would catch the polished metal of a knife blade.

Strachan knew that it would not be long before the police arrived. They had not made much noise during the fray, but they had made enough. Behind the safety of closed doors, some horrified citizen or other would have been bound to call the law. And right it was that they should thought Strachan. He just didn't want to be there when the law arrived.

Before him, the first of the three Legionnaires that he had taken out lay writhing on the floor, curled up and clutching a shattered kneecap. Strachan stepped past him, pausing to plant a heel into the man's face, smashing the head back against the cobbled floor and sending him into a temporarily blissful unconsciousness.

The Legionnaire sparring with Lyndon turned sensing Strachan's approach. It was all the distraction Lyndon needed. He lunged forward with his left hand, gripping the Legionnaire's knife-hand, twisting it, throwing him off balance. With a quick and smooth action, he brought his own blade slashing down and drew it across the inside of the boy's arm, completely severing the massive tendon inside the elbow joint. The arm fell loose in Lyndon's hand, the knife sliding out onto the floor as all motor control to the arm was lost. Blood gushed out from the wound in spurting fountains and both Lyndon and Strachan knew that the major blood vessel that ran up the inside of the arm had been cut. The Legionnaire screamed a death-wail deep into the night. There would be police now for sure.

'This way, quick!' Strachan hissed.

Lyndon pushed the soldier away from him and ran for the entrance to the alley, with Strachan at his shoulder. Strachan realised that Lyndon would know these dark, twisting, narrow streets better than he did and was content to follow. Within seconds they had disappeared into the night, leaving carnage behind them.

It was 1.00am when Strachan and Lyndon finally arrived at the *Petit Louvre*. Strachan had been right; Lyndon had known his way around. They had soon made their way out of the Old Port area and into the centre of the town where they had been safer. The initial police activity had been centred on the dark streets around the death-alley. Now they needed to talk. And Strachan's room was safe.

The fat concierge looked up from his magazine, the ubiquitous cigarette hanging from between his lips. He raised a quizzical eyebrow as the two men passed through the lobby and up the stairs. He had not taken the dangerous stranger for a queer, but who was to know? Still, it was no concern of his. He might even be able to profit from the knowledge. He knew many of the Africans who came across the sea in search of a living. There wasn't much that those hungry, desperate people wouldn't do for a price. And he would take a cut. But that could wait until morning. For now he was happy to content himself with his cigarette and his pornography. He had always been a patient man.

'Well, I guess I owe you some thanks, bud.'

Lyndon had plonked his heavy frame onto the small wooden chair in the hotel room. Strachan sat on the edge of the bed, facing him.

'I don't know,' Strachan said, 'you looked as though you could handle yourself.'

'Maybe, but five against one and I'd have been dead meat. Let's not kid ourselves about that.'

'A SEAL wouldn't be in the business of kidding then?'

The reference to the SEALs, the US Navy's Sea Air and Land Special Forces operatives had Lyndon's grin dipping a little at the corners. Strachan noticed it.

'SEAL, huh? Now what would make you think along those lines?'

'Oh, I don't know. Just a hunch. But I'd be prepared to lay money down.'

Lyndon leaned back on the chair and let out a small laugh.

'Okay, so let's say that I have had something of a passing acquaintance with those dark devils. But what about you, David?

It is David isn't it? David Strachan?'

Strachan tensed, his hand moved around to the small of his back.

'Oh for fuck's sake David, there's no need for that. Leave the gun where it is. We need each other right now, you and I.'

'Is that right? You're assuming quite a lot, aren't you? Just who is this David Strachan that I'm supposed to be?'

'Now you're starting to disappoint me. I mean, have you been living in a cave these past few days? You've been big news, Davy boy. You've been in all the papers. You must have seen, surely you must. Fuck knows, everybody else has. People have hardly talked about anything else.'

Strachan's hand remained hovering at the small of his back but he didn't draw the gun. Lyndon continued:

'I knew you hadn't gone down with that boat, I just knew it. British Army, the papers said, and a little voice inside my head said SAS. You see, you were right, Davy boy. About me, I mean. Navy SEAL. We recognise each other's handy work, don't we, people like you and me?'

Strachan was caught off guard and didn't know what to think. Was this a trap? Was this ex SEAL opening up in order to catch him out? Surely not. There was that business just now, in the alley. One Legionnaire dead for certain, one left as good as. This SEAL had as much reason to run and hide as he did. Maybe they *could* be of use to each other. He would play it cool, wait to hear what Lyndon was going to propose.

'Well, what's the matter Davy boy? Cat got your tongue?'

'Okay, let's suppose I am this David Strachan. How is it that I need you? And just what the fuck would you want with me?'

'Until just now, Davy, it was all one sided. I mean, you needed me, or at least somebody like me, but I didn't need anybody. But as you saw for yourself, I left one, probably two Legionnaires back in that alley. *Legionnaires.* Not just some half-assed street punks. There'll be some hue and cry about that and no mistake. Plus, there were survivors. They can recognise me. And you come to that. Makes this a dangerous town for us to be in, don't it?'

Strachan was beginning to relax. He remained on his guard – trust was a long way from being earned. But what Lyndon said did make sense.

'Accepting what you say - and the fact of what just happened can't be denied - I still don't see where our paths need to cross.'

'Come now David. You came here, to this part of this town, looking for an undocumented way out of the country, no questions asked, right? Right. And you came to the right place. Anything can be bought here. Anything. But you must have known that it wouldn't come cheap, so you got to have had a shit load of money. That's going to be where your contribution kicks in. Me, I haven't got a bean. But I know who to approach and the right prices to pay. And who to trust. No pissing about, we get away quick and easy. And with the two of us watching out for each other, we know we ain't gonna get rolled, right?'

'I thought you said you knew who to trust,' Strachan shot back. 'Why would we need to watch out for our backs?'

'Hey Davy, there's trust and there's trust. This place ain't no gentleman's club, let me tell you.'

Strachan couldn't help but grin.

'You bastard,' Lyndon spat out. 'You were just stringing me along.'

Now Strachan laughed. 'You got to learn to loosen up a little, Joe, you know what I mean.' He was really laughing now and he realised that he was experiencing post-combat euphoria.

'Loosen up, shit.' Lyndon was beginning to laugh a little himself now. 'Do we have a deal or what?'

'I guess so. I can access the money tomorrow. Dollars, US.'

'Tomorrow is just fine. I'll make the arrangements in the morning. This time tomorrow, we'll be out."

Chapter 25

FOR MICHAEL BRACHMAN, it was a strange feeling. He was walking, straight and upright. Walking easily, with no awkward pain. It hadn't been like that for a long time. Not since... well, it was best not to dwell on that, not even now. Physically though, the good times were returning, he could feel it.

There was a slight breeze blowing cool against his cheeks and he knew that he was tall and strong. And it was well that he was, because he had seen signs of St Clair beginning to crack. The man had been a power when things had been quiet and all was going well... but now that they were close, he could see the man coming apart with the pressure. It was good that *he* was at hand to take charge. There could be no more false starts, no more Napoleons, or Hitlers. Or, even, Gellis.

Licio Gelli. He had come closest to the ideal, only to fall so cruelly from grace. He had been exposed in the early eighties, a fat spider sitting squarely in the middle of the intriguing web of finance and sinister secrecy that he had woven around his impressive creation, the Masonic Lodge P2. Politicians, military men, bankers, industrialists; all had been seduced by the sweet lure of the secrets and the power that Gelli's vision had been able to offer. Not even the Vatican had remained untainted when the files containing membership lists had been discovered in Gelli's mountain hideaway. If only... but then the world did not turn on 'if only's.

They had spoken of Gelli only that evening, he and St Clair. He had had to point out certain parallels.

'Gelli was a fool!' St Clair had exploded. 'He could have set us back hundreds of years with his *Propoganda Due* and his financial shinanegans. He bowed to the beast of Mammon. It

189

was inexcusable,'

Brachman had sat twisted and uncomfortable in his chair listening to this tirade as St Clair paced the room in his rage. Mention of Gelli had always set St Clair off. Sometimes Brachman had been known to bring the subject up simply to watch it happen. Usually he was content to sit back and watch and listen, but this time he had felt compelled to speak.

'You're too harsh, Henri, too harsh by far,' he had said in the quiet whisper that he was coming to use with ever greater authority. 'Gelli had his failings, to be sure, but he came closer than anyone, don't ever lose sight of that. All the others have been grotesqueries; military men short of vision who thought that they could subborn the mission entrusted to them to their own egos.'

'You would belittle the achievements of Bonaparte? Did he not then get near? Or Hitler, who held it in the palm of his hand, only to let it slip away? Would you really place Gelli above these?'

'The military strategists, pah. Both wastrels and both damaging. There could never be a United States of Europe forged on the anvil of military force. Force breeds resentment, always has, always will. The Bonapartes and the Hitlers could roll their armies across countries and force them together a thousand times over but still fail in the task. The resentment would cause imbalance and imbalance when such mighty natural forces have been brought to bear will always bring catastrophe. The last time was devastating. It could easily have led to the ruination of the Work that our forerunners had spent hundreds of years ripening. It is well that the Shadowmasters have now learned that our aims will never be achieved militarily. There will be no more madness.'

'Madness? You seem to forget that from that last 'madness' our predecessors were able to forge the beginings of the European Economic Community...'

'Exactly!' Brachman interjected. 'The fledgling of a truly United Europe, a framework that Gelli was able to build upon. He was the first among us to have seen that economics and finance were the stuff that would weave the web of European unity. A vast interlocking network of fiscal dependance, growing ever grander and ever more complex until all Europe was intermingled, no one unit able to disengage itself from the whole. Then all would see the need for the boundaries to be removed, the day would finally dawn and the people would welcome it. That is what Gelli saw and what he came so close to achieving. Intellectually, he was gifted beyond the dreams of either of the military men.'

'But he failed! He was too impetuous. He had not the grandness of mind to see it through.'

Do you have the grandness of mind, my friend? Do you? Brachman found himself thinking. He said: 'Gelli wanted to see it happen. He was unable to bear the thought that he had worked so hard not to see the end result. With better support from those around him, he would have found the strength to temper his impetuosity.'

St Clair had looked down at him then. Had St Clair been aware that there had been a hint of rebuke in that last remark? Perhaps. But St Clair had said nothing.

Brachman had simply looked up, locking eyes with St Clair and the debate had come to an end. And Brachman's point of view had prevailed. And at that moment, he had sat up straighter in the chair, unmindful of the fact that it was something that he was usually unable to do.

And now, at this later hour, there was more. He and St Clair had retired to their beds in the early hours of the morning. St Clair was no doubt still comfortable in his own, but here *he* was, walking along the left bank of the Seine, along the Quai D'Orsay. Walking without the aid of a stick, walking with confidence and with a purpose that he could not yet seem to fully understand.

The streets were deserted, the darkness gloomy and encapsulating despite the flickering blobs of light reflected in the black waters of the river from the lamps that dotted both embankments. Brachman quickened his pace, walking fast towards the Isle de la Cite. On the opposite bank was the darkened grandeur of the Louvre, its bulk obscuring the view of the Sacre Coeur standing in floodlit splendour atop the hill of Montmartre.

Something was driving him on, an urge, an unscratchable itch.

He could not imagine what it was that he was seeking, just that he would know it when he found it. And in the dark Gothic monument that suddenly appeared towering before him, he knew that he had.

Notre Dame. He felt a pulse of warmth glow through him. The greatest of the Temples dedicated to the Great Work, all of its secrets woven into the stone and the masonry. All there to be deciphered by those with eyes open to see and the patience to piece together the clues. A work of overpowering mastery. And the secrets of the stones had called to him through the night air. The notes of the music of Satie, who had brooded in its interior darkness rather than study, and of Debussy, who had woven spells around it, seemed to skip and dance on the breeze, inviting the initiated to join them. He had answered the call and now he was here. But the building was showing him something, telling him of a greater mystery.

He walked to the river bank, high above the water and stared down for a moment. The answer would be found down there, he knew, so he looked around, making sure that there was no-one there to see, then slipped over the edge and into the water's slow lazy flow.

Chapter 26

NOWHERE AND EVERYWHERE... NO TIME

TREES GREW TALL in the fairytale perfection of the land. The grass was green and lush, dotted with beautiful wild red poppies on the open plains, and with swathes of bluebells in the clearings of the deciduous forests. It was the threshold of enchantment and only the rarest of humans had ever visited. In the distance, beyond the rolling downs, stood a castle, clean and grand, its stone walls shimmering a gleaming white beneath the golden rays of a bright sun in a cloudless sky.

Six days earlier, one of those rare humans, an old man, dressed simply in a coarse white robe had passed this way, humble in his solitary pilgrimage. The old man, quiet and wonderous in his humility, had been welcomed into the castle. He had found many fellow pilgrims within the walls, all treated as honoured guests of the sad young King and his virgin bride. The old man was happy to be there, but his humility would allow no display of elation. He knew that all who wished to make the pilgrimage he was undertaking would have to stop here. He himself had been here before, but as always, things had changed. The people were different, the situation alien.

Four days he had spent there, treated always with the greatest of courtesy and being honoured with the finest of everything. But always, he had been tested, his suitability to continue ever on trial. Many had failed the hidden tests and, heavy of heart, had not been allowed to continue on, their self pity a visible indication of their unsuitability.

In the afternoon, the old man and eight fellow journeymen had been escorted to a fine ship, with cloth of gold sails, to venture forth to an unknown destination. They had arrived in the late evening, the ship drawing close to an uncharted island, a perfect square of land in the middle of the blue ocean. A high wall enclosed it and at its centre was a huge tower. The pilgrims disembarked and an opening appeared in the wall, through which they filed. Once all nine were inside, the wall sealed itself once more. The pilgrims made their way to the foot of the tower and finding no entrance, laid themselves down on the lush grass at the base of the structure to sleep and wait.

Morning brought with it a visitor. The pilgrims were all awake with the golden dawn and saw a man appear from behind the tower. The newcomer was naked and the dry parchment wrinkles of his skin showed him to be old, older than any man had a right to be. But as he approached, he carried himself tall and erect, his movements lending themselves to fluidity and despite his lack of clothing, his bearing was never less than dignified.

'Hail to you, pilgrims!' shouted the ancient one, his right arm raised in greeting.

The pilgrims all bowed their heads so as not to look upon him, though he paid their embarassment no heed. Presently, he was among them.

'Now then,' the ancient one said. 'Each of you must bear with him for the remainder of this day, one of these three things.'

The sweep of his spindly arm and the direction of his gaze caused the pilgrims to turn. Behind them they saw laid upon the grass, various ladders, ropes, and curious sets of feathered wings, which had not been there before.

'Now, it is open to you to cast lots, or to choose for yourselves.'

'Let us choose.' Proposed one of the pilgrims. The old man though remained silent. He was ready to accept the will of the others. The ancient one cast a glance at him.

'No, by lot,' he said, as though having had an abrupt change of heart.

And so the ancient one arranged it and the old man was left staggering under the weight of a twelve-foot ladder. After a while, the ancient one led the band of pilgrims around to the far side of the tower, a long walk under the relentless heat of the sun.

At the far side was an opening in the wall, and the ancient one bade them all enter, following them inside. The opening then sealed itself. The interior was dark and when the pilgrims had accustomed their eyes to the gloom, they discovered that the ancient one was nowhere to be seen.

After a while, a cover was removed from the ceiling and a maiden, whom the pilgrims remembered having seen back at the castle, implored them to join her.

Those pilgrims who had drawn wings flew easily up to the hole and sailed through to the next level and now the old man was glad of his ladder, for he was easily able to climb up to the gap, where he was implored to pull up his ladder behind him. Those with ropes fared worst, having to haul themselves up to the opening and many not without blisters to show for it.

Once all the pilgrims had ascended to the new level, the maiden acquainted them each with his allotted task. The sad king and his bride had been beheaded and only the pilgrims would be able, through their efforts, to restore them to life. And so they had begun the first stage of the process, the reduction of the bodily tissues of the king and queen to a tincture by simmering their matter in a huge copper cauldron at a constant heat.

Once this process was completed, the pilgrims were called up as before, to the next level. Again, they were shown what to do to continue the process of restoration, before moving up to the level yet beyond.

Throughout the day, they continued at their labours, each new level bringing an even greater wonder for them to behold and although the tasks were often wearisome, the promise of the joy to come, of which the maiden sang, was enough to keep them steadfast at their work.

And after the sixth level, the maiden appeared at the hole above and spoke:

'It is all but complete. Come with me, whosoever would see the substance of all science.'

So once more the pilgrims, tired, though light of heart, made their ascent, one by one, into the chamber above. The old man waited. He would go last. He was in no hurry. He knew that by letting the others go first, he would miss nothing. And one of the others waited with him. A young man, handsome and with timeless dark eyes beyond which the old man swore that he could discern the depths of human history. They both bore ladders on their shoulders, waiting their turn, and were about to proceed when the ancient one appeared, placing a hand on the shoulder of each of them.

'No, my sons, no further,' said the voice of ancient wisdom. 'It is enough for you that you should reach this far.'

The old man's heart sank as if beneath a heavy weight. He looked to the young man, but saw no emotion in those black sparkling eyes. He raised his own face to look up into the aperture and saw the maiden smile down at him through the gap, just before it sealed itself. The smile sent a shiver through his being and he knew that indeed it was enough that he had come so far. Maybe another time.

He looked to the face of the young man. He would offer comfort if he could. But the age-old eyes shone back at him, a smile on the warm lips and the young man reached out a hand and gently caressed his cheek. It was a gesture of warmth and compassion and it took the old man completely by surprise. And now he understood more than ever that he had indeed come far enough. For it was to be they and not the others, who would see the living end.

'If you would be so kind, it would be to your advantage to attend to the bellows.'

They both turned to the voice of the ancient one. He was smiling at them, the first time they had seen emotion on the benevolent face. Behind him stood a huge circular furnace, filled with hot coals, a heat haze rising in visible shimmers from their surface. At opposite sides of the furnace were huge sets of bellows. And above, benefiting from the heat, were two caskets, suspended vertically in mid air, revolving slowly, back to back, with no visible means of support. Their lids were removed and within, they could see the bodies of the young king and his queen, their naked flesh white and smooth as the finest porcelain.

'Please, after you, my friend,' said the young man.

Tears of joy brimming in his eyes, the old man made his way to the bellows nearest him, his companion joined him on the opposite side. They had not noticed, but their burdensome ladders had vanished and they began to pump life into the fire.

'Yes, yes, go on,' enthused the ancient one. 'Raise the temperature gradually, keep the heat constant.'

And they did. The sweat poured from their faces from the effort and the heat, but they did not seem to notice. Outside, through a large open window, they saw the day turn to night, a black sky peppered with silver points of stars.

Above the flames, the caskets continued to spin, ever so slowly, but the bodies inside had begun to colour. The flesh was coming alive as they watched; it was almost as though they could see the new blood coursing through the veins of the king and queen.

Beyond the horizon came a golden glow as slowly, an orb of the purest of that colour rose high in the night sky. Upwards it climbed, growing in size and brilliance, until it stopped, plainly in view from the high window of the chamber, through which it shone like an evening sun.

'Enough, my sons, enough,' whispered the ancient one gently.

The two pilgrims stepped back from the furnace, their limbs aching but their spirits bright. As they watched, a beam of golden energy blazed down from the orb through the open window, where it struck the tops of the caskets. The room became bathed in beautiful swirling colours, sometimes bright and primary, sometimes soothing and pastel and the pilgrims bathed too in the glory of the new life, watching as the sad king twitched his lips in the beginnings of a smile.

Through it all, the ancient one beamed his beneficence from a face that now was bereft of age, his flesh now firm and ripe, as he took his benefit from the power that had been brought into being by the efforts of the pilgrims.

But outside, beyond the island's walls, the sea began to bubble and froth; the calm water raged and sprayed as something massive burst its way up to the surface.

Bellowing and roaring it grew, towering into view from the window of the chamber. The tower itself began to tremble with the vibration of mighty and enraged screams and the beam of life, the lightening bolt that was emanating from the golden orb, began to waver from its true path. It began to skip and fizzle across the tops of the caskets and then with a wild life of its own, it was thrashing around the insides of the chamber, blasting masonry from the tower where it hit the walls.

It hit the ancient one full in the chest and there was a momentary scream before his new flesh vaporised and where there had been life, there was now only dispersed energy.

The old man dove at his young companion, throwing him to

the chamber floor before the erratic energy bolt could do the same to him. It was out of control now, and there were explosions where it was blowing chunks out of the tower, punctuating the hideous screams of the monster that was growing out of the sea.

There was a thunderous crack as the top part of the tower was blown to oblivion. The old man and the young pilgrim were left exposed on the bare boards of the chamber floor, now an open platform atop the trembling tower. All that had been above, their fellow journeymen included, had been blown to kingdom come and when they dared look up through the rage and the noise they could see all too clearly.

The caskets, which still spun in mid air above the furnace, had been blackened by the blast. Inside, the king and queen were lost, their flesh decaying visibly, bloating with evil gas and discolouring, finally bursting, spraying foul spew onto the chamber floor. The ubiquitous maggots, those friends of festering evil appeared taking succour from what was left, until within seconds, only gleaming white bones remained. Then the maggots themselves, gorged and distended, burst open to let out brown slimy insects that buzzed over and around the platform, landing on the old man's face, crawling into his mouth and around his eyes and nostrils. The old man spat them out, almost puking in his disgust and brushed them away from his face with a free hand. He continued to spit and gag; the insects had left their filth in his mouth and the stench of putrefaction was overpowering. Beneath him, the young pilgrim was beginning to cough and splutter, as he was being similarly afflicted, the old man rolled off him, giving him the freedom to protect himself.

For a few minutes they fought, beating off the foul smelling insects, which left trails of evil smelling slime wherever they made contact. Then, as though at some unseen signal, the vile creatures rose in a cloud, high above them, circled three times and then headed out to sea.

Coughing and spluttering and occasionally dry retching, the two pilgrims followed their progress out to where the sea still raged about the beast that it had spawned. And the old man could see the beast now, properly, for the first time. Mighty it was, standing fully a hundred feet out of the sea, its flesh seemingly carved from rough and splintery dark wood, although it was supple and mobile. The powerful legs thrashed and foamed in the water and it writhed incessantly, as though in great pain and torment. At the end of its muscular arms were vast hands sprouting vicious talons, which clawed at the air about it. The head was drawn in stretched muscle and sinew, a human face with the skin flayed off, showing strips of muscle and tendon which dripped blood, hissing and steaming into the sea below. The mouth, wide and cavernous, was open constantly, screaming torment into the night, past rows of jagged razor teeth and a mane of straw-like white hair flowed long and frenzied about the shoulders.

The old man glanced once into its eyes and turned away, unable to face the blackness that screamed from empty sockets that had the appearance of being all-seeing. Blood wept from ragged tear ducts.

And the monster reached out to grasp the writhing life-beam that still thrashed erratically out of the golden orb, boiling the sea where it touched and there was a sickly smell of burning flesh from its hands. Yet seemingly unperturbed by the burns that it was sustaining, it pulled at the beam, directing it into one of its empty eye sockets. As the beam made contact, it screamed in its rage and pain, a noise so resonant and powerful that the foundations of the tower began to crumble and the edifice began to topple.

The old man was falling through space, tumbling and falling, and as he fell, he caught a last glimpse of the beast, glowing yellow as the beam illuminated its innards. There was a final almighty flash of gold, and then...

PARIS... JUNE 18th... 4.16am

'AAAAAAAAhhhh!'

The air rushed from Brachman's lungs in a scream, as he sat bolt upright in his bed. He hugged his arms around himself, for he was cold, despite the warmth of the Parisian summer night. He looked around and realised that he was in the guest chamber of St Clair's Paris apartment. And where else would he be? After all, he was St Clair's guest and this was where he always stayed when visiting beloved Paris.

But he had been travelling this night. He could not remember the detail, but there was a sense of striding through darkness, through swirling fields of cold energy, which had comforted him on his way. And many wisdoms had he encountered as he strode against this power, until the darkness had grown clearer and clearer, bursting finally over him in a burning wave of golden fire. Fire which had flamed and consumed him, gaining substance and granting power.

There had been witnesses, too. Witnesses who he knew had not approved of what they had seen. Well to hell with them; whatever had happened had been good. He felt strong now and wise. A wisdom that had no need for cheap knowledge.

Templar. Templar Templar Templar. The word, a human word, but not without value nonetheless, continued to pulse in the back of his mind. Why? He did not as yet know, but he would come to understand, he was sure.

Bang bang bang bang. There came a staccato rapping on his door, which distracted him.

'Michael, what is it? Are you all right? Michael!'

It was St Clair. He must have heard the scream.

'I'm all right, Henri, perfectly alright. Come in.'

He would play the invalid. There were things he now knew that St Clair was not yet ready to understand. The door opened and St Clair, wrapped in a silk dressing gown, rushed through and up to the bedside.

'I heard a scream. It woke me,' explained St Clair, now seemingly embarrassed at his haste to fear the worst.

'It is nothing Henri, really. I twisted, trying to get more comfortable, and my back…'

He left the sentence open, knowing that he would always have the ability to embarrass St Clair in this way. For his twisted frame had not always been so.

'You must take more care, mon ami,' said the blushing St Clair. 'This is no time for us to be losing you.'

'Never fear, Henri. You know that I am made of stern stuff.'

Sterner indeed than you could ever have imagined Brachman thought. Because he could feel his back now. And for the first time in years, there was no discomfort. His crooked back was straight again.

OXFORD... JUNE 18th... 4.16am

'NOOOooo!' screamed the voice in the darkness. An old man was slammed abruptly into consciousness. He was sitting cross-legged in the lotus position on the hard floor of a darkened room, the suppleness required of the position making a mockery of his apparent agedness. His eyes were immediately wide, the pupils dilated and he could make out shapes despite the near totality of the gloom. He was sweating and his breathing was heavy and laboured.

Rising from the tiled floor, he walked swiftly over to where he knew the window to be and tore open the heavy velvet drapes. Outside, the lights of Oxford with its cliched, but nonetheless real, dreaming spires, bought material comfort to his soul.

What had happened? What had he experienced? There had never been a terror to equal it, not even in the early days, those first tentative steps when his consciousness had shrieked away from the flooding contact with the black. He had been far into the process, he knew. There was a retained sense of the gold. But it had been corrupted, made to fall from grace by something. Had it been him? He could not bring himself to believe it; he had made the journey before and had found perfection at the end of it, and although it would never, and *should* never be easy, he thought that he had come to know the way rather well by now.

If only he were able to recall the images anthropomorphically, rather than just as sensed experiences, maybe he would be able to see. But he knew that that would probably never be. The essence of the journey remained, although the details changed with each new passage, of that much he was aware. But only a rare few of the rare few that had completed the journey had ever been able to translate the experience into a readily understandable sequence of images and events. And he had not been one with that elite thus far.

He rested his hand on the window frame, which was cool to his touch. Outside, the electric street lamps burned orange in the blackness while above the silver stars shone their ancient light onto the planet.

What had come had been corrupt, he was sure of it. It had tainted the gold, had forced it to bend to its own ends and the gold had tried to rebel. Had that been the cause of the fury? These were points on which to meditate. But he retained a sensation of hope. He somehow felt that he had not been alone, that there had been another who had witnessed and despaired. If he could only make contact with this soul, together perhaps, they could correct this imbalance. For imbalance there had been. The world would be a safer place for their efforts, mankind's future more secure. Imbalances had a way of expanding and gaining momentum before nature equalised them out.

Imbalance. A word devoid of emotion. A true representation of what he had experienced, but a cold word nevertheless. Humans had always had a more emotive word to describe the *imbalance* that he had just experienced and as he looked out to the college spires that dominated the skyline view from his window, he pondered on that word. The word was: evil.

MONACO... JUNE 18th... 4.16am

Black, dotted with white flecks and silver sparks flashing hither and thither. Black, then white flecks now vanished, but: flash! The silver again. Flash! Silver once more. Black. Black. Flash! A final bolt of silver, then blackness, a calm blackness with no motion. A perfect stillness.

The Templar opened his eyes. The room was in darkness, but in the far corner he could see the crumpled form of his Torquemada, where it lay immobile, in a heap. He was sitting naked on the floor and his body was dripping with sweat.

What were they doing, these fools, these children? Would they never learn the lessons of history? He had been there and seen the results of their doings. And he would be able to tell them that it would end in disaster. He would have to meet with the Shadowmasters and soon. Shadowmasters, hah! These were but pale imitations of the intellects who had gone before.

202

Were these really the worthy inheritors of the mantles of Leonardo, and Newton, and all the others? Never. But he would show them their duty. He would have to or it would all have been for nothing.

Outside he heard the lapping of the waves where they hit the small beach below. His suite in the Loews Hotel was one of the ones supported by huge concrete pillars out over the water.

The sea, that most appealing of nature's wonders. How he ached to become one with it, to cross the abyss and share its secrets, share its joy as a fundamental wisdom of the cosmos. Soon, he promised himself once again, soon. And this time he knew that he meant it. He could not bear to carry the future of the human race on his shoulders forever. He would find this Strachan and deal with him. Nothing could be allowed to stop them this time. He would direct them himself if he had to, make sure that their misrepresentations were corrected. Then, at last, he would be free.

Chapter 27

STRACHAN SAT UNEASILY in a large wicker chair looking into the sun. The view from the marbled patio was breathtaking, stretching down into a tree dotted valley, but he could not enjoy it. He had no idea of the villa's location, he and Lyndon having been driven there blindfolded. This was a natural precaution, given the identity of the man they were due to meet and one he had not objected to. But they had taken the Beretta from him too, another natural precaution, but one that Strachan had felt a little less comfortable with. Still he had gone along with it. Really, he had had no choice.

Lyndon sat opposite him, leaning back in the chair and soaking up the sun's rays, without a care in the world. He looked awfully sure of himself, thought Strachan. Strachan shifted his position slightly, the thick money belt containing the cash collected earlier in the day from the Banque D'Aquitaine irritating his skin. There had been no incident at the bank and that at least had been a comfort.

Two men stood, one at either end of the patio, dressed in suits by Armani and Cardin, their eyes hidden from the sun's glare behind Ray Ban Aviator sunglasses. They appeared casual, though their faces were expressionless and Strachan knew that they were both armed and were both good. He could tell that immediately from their bearing.

How much longer? Strachan was beginning to get restless. He had been sitting out on the patio since their arrival, at first alone, as Lyndon had immediately been ushered into an office inside the villa, while he himself had been escorted through the villa and out in the patio to wait. His hosts had been thoughtful, he couldn't fault them for that and a flunky was ever at hand to

204

fetch and carry drinks, whatever he wanted. He had gone through a litre of iced lemon Perrier water before Lyndon had eventually returned to join him on the patio.

'He'll be out to join us in a moment,' Lyndon said, throwing himself heavily into the wicker chair opposite. 'He just has a little business to attend to. He's a very busy man.'

'Whatever you say, Joe,' Strachan replied lifelessly. Really, he wanted *their* business over and done with quickly, so that they could get the fuck out. He hadn't expected Lyndon to be *this* well connected. And this *was* a major connection.

The procedures, the ostentation, the sheer professionalism of what had gone on so far said it all. Whatever this connection was going to do for them, it wouldn't be for want of the money that they could pay. Their funds would be mere fly-shit to such a person.

No, more likely that although money would change hands, which it would as a matter of principle, whatever was done would be done as a favour. As a favour to Joe. Perhaps he had chosen *too* well. Strachan would rather the greed of the small time criminal, which he could use and control to his own advantage, than to put himself helpless into the hands of someone who would control events from start to finish. After all, it was *his* life that he was putting on the line. Still, Joe seemed calm enough about the whole thing. Maybe he was over reacting. Maybe. But he would keep his eyes open just the same.

Lyndon could sense Strachan's unease.

'Just look at that view, wontcha?' Lyndon said. 'It'd cost you well over a million bucks to buy a view like that.'

The beaming smile was spread over Lyndon's face as he spoke. Strachan didn't react. Lyndon leaned forward towards him, serious for a moment and said:

'Hey, look, it'll be okay. These people are okay. The best. I know them; I've worked with them. Trust me.'

Strachan looked up into the big blond face and said: 'Do I have a choice?'

Lyndon leaned back, folding his arms behind his head.

'Put like that, I suppose you don't, no. We've come too far to back out now.'

'Then I'll just have to run with the tide, won't I?'

And Strachan was smiling again now, because everything was going to be okay. He felt strong again and arrogant almost. Not like a hunted animal at all.

'We both will, bud. Just as well we can swim, huh?'

'I might have known it would come to that with a fucking SEAL along for the ride.' Strachan said and they both laughed.

MONACO... 11.50am

The telephone rang in suite 103 of the Loews Hotel in Monaco. It had a muted tone, soft and unobtrusive, so as not to offend the potentially delicate and certainly well heeled occupants of the room. But the current occupant would not have cared if it had had all the subtlety of a cathedral bell. For he was not in the least bit delicate.

From his position, lying flat on his back on the huge soft bed of the plush room, with its panoramic sea view, he reached out a hand and lifted the receiver off its cradle. He put it to his ear, unspeaking.

'A withdrawal of some fifty thousand dollars, US, made from the Banque D'Aquitaine in Marseilles at 10.30 this morning,' said an unannounced voice before hanging up.

The Templar replaced the receiver in its cradle. Marseilles. He had known it all along, but here was confirmation. It had been that inadequate oaf St Clair on the line. What a pitiful charade of secrecy he was playing. His voice would be recognisable to a deaf goat at a thousand paces. If there had been any intercept on the line, his anonymity would have been safe for thirty seconds at most.

Still, that was unimportant for now. Marseilles. That was important. Of course Strachan would have made for Marseilles. It was a smuggling port, an underground port, where everything was bought and sold. He would be trying to get out of the country, anonymously and quickly, without documentation. And Marseilles could do that for him. For fifty thousand dollars, he could buy his own boat. But he wouldn't need to, this one. The Templar could sense resourcefulness and cunning in this Strachan. He would have made his contact before now, but surely

206

would not be off during daylight hours. No, such things were always better accomplished after dark. There was still time, if he could move quickly.

He looked over to the corner of the room where the ragged heap of the Torquemada lay awkwardly in its misery, the heavy rise and fall of its scrawny chest the only indication that it was alive at all.

'Come, my slave,' said the Templar, swinging his legs over the side of the bed. 'I expect I shall have need of you.'

The wretched creature lifted its head, and there was raw terror in its dull eyes.

12.22am

Another half hour had passed. The sun was burning fiercely onto the patio where Strachan and Lyndon waiting in silence, when the glass doors behind them were thrown open. Two men, dressed in the ubiquitous designer suits that were worn almost as a uniform by the occupants of the villa marched through, followed more sedately by a balding, middle aged man of slight build, who seemed in no hurry at all.

This entourage made its way over to the far side of the patio, where the balding man lowered himself exquisitely into a deep wicker chair. Strachan and Lyndon had followed his entrance, but made no move to greet him. Strachan was well aware of the power show that was going on; it would not be fitting for such an important figure to have to come to them. Even here on the patio, they would have to go to him. After a few seconds, the man gestured to them, just the raising of an eyebrow, but Lyndon picked up on it immediately.

'Okay, Dave, this is it. He wants to see you.'

Strachan lifted himself up out of his chair and followed Lyndon across the marble floor to where the man was seated. Small stools were placed before the man and Strachan and Lyndon were gestured to be seated.

The man studied Strachan in silence for a few moments, and Strachan felt a distinct unease under the penetrating gaze. Finally, the man spoke:

'So, Mr Strachan. I believe that you require a favour of me.'

It was a statement and not a question. Strachan was surprised at the near perfection of the English accent. A hint of public school, perhaps? Surely not.

'I am told that you can pay for this favour, which is good, because payment will be expected. Not too much, because what you require is such a small thing. But first, let us talk.'

The man raised his right hand, and immediately a cigarette, a pink Sobranie Cocktail, was placed between the first and second fingers by one of the expensively attired attendants. The man licked his lips and then placed the cigarette between them. Another attendant leaned forward to light it with a gold Dunhill lighter. The man sucked slowly on the burning stick of tobacco. He held the smoke in his lungs for a few seconds, closing his eyes to savour the sensation before exhaling in a steady stream through lips, which formed an almost perfect 'O'.

'Tell me, Mr Strachan; whatever was it that prompted you to deal so harsh a blow to such an esteemed and respected citizen as monsieur Stopyra?' The man noted Strachan's puzzled expression, and continued: 'You must understand that I ask, not out of idle curiosity, but because of the truth that all actions have consequences, and the consequences of your encounter with our late and lauded pillar of the banking community sent out shock waves which in a small way touched on my business interests and activities. In fact, one or two postponements were occasioned, but they were of small consequence. The business will be transacted at a later date.'

'I'm sorry if I caused you any inconvenience, Monsieur. I never meant-'

'No harm done, Mr Strachan, really, I assure you. Believe me, had it been otherwise, even the presence of Mr Lyndon here would be of little value to you.' Strachan felt his senses sharpen at the muted threat, but there was little he could do; he was defenceless and outnumbered.

'Please, just tell me your story, satisfy my idle curiosity.'

Strachan sat back and told everything, omitting not even a single item of detail. The story was half an hour in the telling and the man sat emotionless throughout, his eyes never leaving Strachan's for a moment. When he was finished, Strachan just leaned back on his stool and shrugged: 'And that's all there is.'

'A remarkable sequence of events. Really, quite remarkable. So much devastation, and all for the immediate heat of revenge.'

Strachan's eyes narrowed. Was this man cheapening what he'd done for Astrid? The man noticed Strachan's anger and saw no harm in softening a little.

'Please take no offence at my musings, Mr Strachan, for none was intended.'

Strachan felt the hot blood draining from his face. He had been too keyed up. He really needed to conclude his business and be gone. But the man was not finished. He said:

'Now, what really intrigues me is the patch of cloth with the strange red cross that you found stitched inside the jacket of the man on the Gemini. Do you still have it?'

Strachan reached under his shirt for the money belt and the two bodyguards stiffened.

'It's okay boys, the patch is in here, nothing more,' Strachan said, patting the canvas belt, which was now in view beneath the opened shirt. The man chuckled, the first sign of emotion that Strachan had seen him display and it had an instantly heartening effect. So, the man was not without humour after all. And the chuckle had been comforting, almost avuncular. He popped the stud on one of the canvas pockets and pulled out the folded patch of cloth. 'This is it,' he said.

The man studied the embroidery for a few moments and then said to Strachan: 'Please excuse me for a few moments. I will not be long, I promise.' As he stood he motioned to Lyndon. 'Come with me, Joe. I would like a word.'

Lyndon and the man, flanked by the two guards, strolled back inside the villa. Strachan was left to wonder about the patch. Was it, perhaps, the insignia of a rival organisation? Certainly it would not have been beyond the resources of the Prince to recruit underworld help in his attempt to liquidate Strachan. In fact, that began to sound like an increasingly viable scenario. The only one that made any sense at all, really. He began to relax. Taking out those goons might prove to have been a fortuitous move.

Five minutes later Lyndon reappeared, the cloth patch in one hand, two envelopes in the other.

'Well, what's the score?' Strachan asked.

'No problem, everything's taken care of. He just wanted to photograph the patch is all,' Lyndon replied, handing back the square of cloth. 'It is a curious insignia after all.'

So, Strachan mused, he had been right. A rival power base. Well, it was none of his business. 'And the arrangements?' he enquired.

'All in here.' Lyndon waved a grey envelope in the air. 'Instructions, timings, everything.'

'And the money?'

'Twenty thousand, US. Take it or leave it.' The other envelope was tossed towards Strachan. 'Put the cash in here and leave the envelope with one of the boys when we leave.'

'Twenty fucking thousand!' Strachan exploded. 'Where am I being sent to? Tokyo, for Chrissakes?'

'No. Just Sicily,' said Lyndon chirpily. 'For twenty thousand, *we* are going to Sicily.'

Chapter 28

IT WAS MID afternoon on a typical British summer's day; black clouds swooped menacingly low over the city, puncturing the steamy heat with heavy, staccato showers.

High above the urban sprawl, a large man walked in isolation across the emptiness of Hampstead Heath. Another fucking washout, he thought, smiling to himself. Today, he was perversely thankful for the rain. Firstly, he had centre court tickets for Wimbledon, the fulfilment of a life's ambition and it would have pissed him off mightily if there had been any chance of play going on. As the rain dribbled down the back of his collar, he knew that that was a definite no-no, right at that moment. Secondly, it meant that he had the Heath more or less to himself. Which meant that he wouldn't have to piss around too much waiting for soft ass get-in-the-way doodley-brained by-passers to get *out* of the way. Why, he had never seen the Heath so empty.

Abruptly, he stepped off the pathway and into a small thicket of trees. No one had seen him. There had been no one about *too* see him. Despite the unexpected emptiness of one of London's more popular summertime hangouts, he had not relaxed his operational procedure by as much as one jot. He had been in the game too long for that. And he *was* one of the game's best players, no question about it. Fuck ups just simply weren't allowed anywhere near this particular posting, it was just too sensitive. The man purred with satisfaction at the thought as he made his way through the dripping undergrowth. His diplomatic passport identified him as Robert Dibble and he was ostensibly on the Ambassador's staff at the embassy in Grosvenor Square. But it was a cover, no more than that. His true role was covert and ultra-demanding.

The Company maintained staff in London, as they did in the capitals of all of America's allies. These staff officers were known to their host governments and were accepted; after all, for international intelligence co-ordination, it was necessary to have liaison officers in each other's back yards. Hell, Dibble guessed that more diplomacy was required in intelligence liaison than in the political diplomatic scene proper. Too many egos and too many shadows, he guessed. Still, this was all okay and above board. What would really cause the solids to collide with the air conditioning was if the government of a close ally, Her Britannic Majesty's, say, was to discover a covert team operating on its soil, without its authority. Proctor & Gamble would be on overtime for a year making products to cover the stink.

But it would never come to that. Only the best of the Company's proven operatives were chosen for "inside jobs". That was why he was here, wasn't it? And his colleague, his partner in the UK, John Law, well, he was no bit player either. A quality operative and a good friend. They had both been here for two years now and everything had gone as smooth as silk. Only one wet job in all that time, which was how he liked it. Assassination always posed problems, not the least of which being that on an 'inside job', the operatives could not cause confusion and slip quietly away for home. The host authorities would waste no time in putting two and two together and coming up with four. Especially here. They were fucking tight, these Limey Special Branch types; and 'Five', for that matter. Despite old-hat misgivings back in Langley, the days of Philby, Burgess and Maclean were well and truly behind them. They were well on top of the game now. He had seen it himself first hand. Must be all that counter-terrorist action they get, courtesy of the Micks, Dibble thought.

Right, there it was, dead ahead. An old oak tree with a twisted and wizened trunk. Even in the empty woodland, he checked again to be sure that his actions would not be observed and convinced that he was alone, he approached the tree and stuck his hand into a knot-hole, shoulder high in the trunk. How the fuck Redbridge back in Washington ever got to know about places like this he would never know.

The coded wire had come through only an hour ago and had been passed on to him in his office in Grosvenor Square. It had had the appearance of a routine immigration check request, but key words had identified the sender as Redbridge, his controller. The message was contained in a complex cypher held in the wording. It was not desperately secure, but it would be meaningless to the analysts at GCHQ in Cheltenham, who would undoubtedly have intercepted it, as they would all embassy high frequency traffic. They would have dismissed it out of hand by now, as indeed they should. It was depressingly routine after all, one of many hundreds of such tedious pieces of business. From an ally too. They were looking for more interesting game at the listening station.

He pulled his arm out of the tree trunk, his hand clutching a small envelope, which he quickly tucked into his pocket. The rain had stopped now, he noticed, although heavy droplets still dripped from the leaves and the branches of the trees overhead. Looking up, Dibble saw that the clouds had parted, showing a clear sky of crystalline blue. If it stayed like this, there would be play at Wimbledon after all.

He hoped that the instructions that he had just taken from the 'dead drop' would not necessitate immediate action. If he hurried, he could be in his centre court seat within an hour and a half, allowing time to get back to his apartment to change. With luck, he might not even miss a ball.

PARIS...

Andrei Gavrilov sauntered casually along the Quai du Louvre. It was hot and he wiped the sweat from his brow with the back of his hand. He had spent the whole morning walking. Taking in the sights and sounds of the city. He had been here before, but it had been two years past. He wanted to re-familiarise himself with his new working environment. The west truly did present a culture shock after the grim garrison outside Moscow, which had been his home for the last two months. But even the rigours of garrison training and appraisal were paradise compared with that eighteen months which had been spent almost continuously on seek and destroy patrols in the Afghan hills.

He breathed in deeply, holding the warm air in his lungs until he was almost dizzy, before letting it out. Evil bastards, those Afghans. They should have known better. Why, hadn't the British failed to cow them during the last century at the height of their empire? That in itself should have told them something. Because the British had never been slouches when it came to brutal subjugation, had never shied away from the slaughter when they considered it to be expedient. They had taken the entire sub-continent of India and had held it, with an army of mere thousands. Not hundreds of thousands mind you, just *thousands*. Yet *they* had considered Afghanistan a particularly hot potato. That should have told the militarists in the Kremlin something. But of course, they only made decisions there, the *vlasti*; they never had to be on the ground to carry them out. What were the words of the poet?

When you're wounded and lying on Afghanistan's plains
And the women come out to cut up what remains
Then roll to your rifle and blow out your brains
And go to your gawd like a soldier

Something like that anyway. Kipling, that was the poet's name. Not a beautiful verse, but a knowing one. There was a poet who had really experienced. The four lines told a far greater and uglier story than the mere words they contained.

He shuddered inwardly. He had cause to remember what the Afghan women could do. After eighteen months there had been a genuine relief to be out of it. That in itself was not easy to come to terms with. For Andrei Gavrilov was Spetznaz, and used to neither fear nor defeat. But in Afghanistan he had come to know both.

Still, that was behind him now, just a hideous memory of the past. He had much to be thankful for today. Here he was in Paris, with the Louvre Palace towering up to his left, the lazy water of the Seine down below to his right and a warm and cheerful sun soothing the tensions of the whole city. And his mission? GRU again, as it had been on each of the previous four occasions when he had visited the west. But a strange one this; an order given in conditions of secrecy startling even within

214

the machinations of the Soviet Union. For a straightforward assination. Or at least it would be, if the target could be located. And that seemed a remote chance to say the least.

The briefing had come one to one from the lips of the Colonel Commanding, Moscow Military District Sptetznaz Brigade. If Comrade Besanov had felt the need to issue him with his orders personally, it must be highly sensitive and of the utmost importance.

But what a peculiar brief. An ex, *ex* mind you, not current, British SAS Captain had apparently gone berserk in the South of France and murdered a leading French banker, then had apparently committed suicide in the middle of the Mediterranean. The Comrade Colonel had reason to believe that the British Captain might still be alive and he was to do his utmost to discover the truth of this and, if necessary, dispose of the man. Extraordinary. Sounded more like the domain of Directorate 'S' of the First Chief Directorate, KGB. They held the assassination and the terrorism brief and the more shadowy aspects of the mission sounded right up their street.

Gavrilov curdled at the thought. Like most GRU and even regular army personnel, he held no affection for the Committee of State Security. In his mind, there was something dirty about them. There had to be, surely, for them to spy on their own people. He spat in the street at the thought. Perhaps the Committee was involved in some way. Perhaps there was something about this strange mission that GRU wanted to keep the Committee well away from. The very thought strengthened his resolve.

But where to start? He must move quickly, try to think logically. Assume that this Captain, this Strachan, had not died. Where was he, where would he go? He must put things in order. The South of France, you're wanted for murder, you're on the run. You can't use your own papers, but you want to be on the move, to get out of the country. How do you go about it?

There was a sudden screech of brakes as rubber tyres bit hard for grip on the asphalt and the furious blaring of a car horn. Gavrilov jumped back instinctively onto the pavement. He had been so deep in thought that he had stepped off the curb and into the busy road adjacent to the Pont Des Arts. He ignored the insulting words of the Gallic driver, a little embarrassed at making such an inexcusable fool of himself.

To his left stood a couple of teenagers. Lovers, he supposed, from the way they clung to each other. They were stealing furtive glances at him, then turning away. Laughing at him, he supposed. And he deserved it. He had been a fool. He would stay sharp from now on. But what was the motif on the tee-shirt that the girl was wearing? It was the head of a man wearing a white kepi. The white kepi of the Foreign Legion! Marseilles! That's where he would make for if he were Strachan. Marseilles, where anything was available to a resourceful man. And Strachan would be resourceful, to be sure. The letters SAS told him that.

The hunt was going to be like looking for a needle in a haystack, he knew, but it wasn't all bad. If Strachan were alive at all, then he would be in the south of France, surely. And there was no better place for Gavrilov to begin his hunt than Marseille.

He waited for a gap in the traffic, then sprinted across the road. He continued to run, the heat was nothing to him. The Gare de Lyon lay some distance ahead, beyond the Ile de la Cite, beyond the dominating bulk of Notre Dame. It would be his gateway to the south and he had no time to lose. Thank God that the French had a fast and efficient railway service. Thank God for SNCF.

Chapter 29

THE CAR RAN smoothly over the narrow mountain road, despite the ruts. It was a new Jaguar XJ6 and the engine did not so much growl as purr. In the back seat, Strachan and Lyndon leaned back, allowing the sumptuous leather upholstery to mould itself to their shapes. They were both taking time to relax; there was nothing else to do. They could not even admire the scenery because of the tight blindfolds that each had been obliged to wear.

It was the first time in days that Strachan had felt able to relax. It really did seem as though he was going to get away. He was going to make it. He had taken his revenge and was going to escape unscathed. A wave of relief flooded over him. Before his sightless eyes he could sense swirling colours, mostly reds on black as he made images from the blood coursing through the tiny blood vessels in his eyelids. He followed the patterns for a while, allowing them to draw him in, dampening the senses of his conscious mind. It became almost like sleep to him, though he retained control of his thoughts. Then the swirling red blood drifted away leaving only a sea of blackness. Strachan felt totally at peace in a way that he had never before experienced. And far away in the void, he began to discern a hazy, almost misty, slivergrey speck. It was growing, too. Slowly and carefully, the silver coming to dominate the grey, the intensity of its reflected light burning away the haze, until Strachan could see quite clearly what it was. Growing before him all the time, and now obviously recognisable was... the moon.

LONDON... 2.48pm

The streets still glistened wet after the morning's thundershowers. Curling wisps of steam rose from the asphalt as the hot summer sun almost apologetically tried to dispose of the evidence of its own shortcomings. Summer, was supposed, after all, to be the province of the Sun. It was mid afternoon and Oxford Street was busy. The smell of traffic fumes and old dust hung thick in the humid air making the whole city feel sticky and dirty and altogether unpleasant.

A man, obviously old, though not feeble, made his way carefully through the crowds, down towards Oxford Circus. He had come up from the underground station at Tottenham Court Road, deciding to walk the couple of miles or so to Paddington, his destination. Anything was better than to remain crushed and uncomfortable in the tourist-jammed underground train. The air up above, though far from fresh, would do him good. Tucked under his left arm, the man carried a small brown paper parcel; a few books that he had made the journey into town especially to purchase from a discreet little shop in Museum Street, near Holborn. Over his right arm lay a lightweight gabardine raincoat. It was more comfortable to carry it than wear it, here in the full blaze of the sun. Even the brushed-cotton checked shirt and jeans that he wore were beginning to stick to him. He would be glad to get home to shower and change; but that was some way off yet. He reached up to run his right hand through his silky grey hair, inadvertently brushing sweat up from his brow and slicking it back into the still generous locks. That made him feel grubbier still. It was, however, the same for everyone, and he would just have to make the most of it.

The sounds of the city surrounded him, wrapping themselves around him like a shroud. But he had always been a city dweller so he did not mind. The constant hum of motor car engines, the rougher note of diesel taxis and the occasional roar of a red double decker bus as the driver trod on the accelerator; these were sounds of comfort to him.

He made his way unhurried through the cosmopolitan throng. To his right, the shop windows beckoned garishly, almost begging and sometimes demanding that people should part with their money. Many would succumb. For most of them, it was the only reason they were there at all.

Approaching the Virgin Megastore, the man could hear the muzzy sounds of rock music, which spilled out onto the sidewalk. It was indistinct as yet, but something about it seemed to be calling to him. He began to feel a little buzzing in his head, a feeling that was altogether far from pleasant. Still, he felt compelled to make his way toward the sound, its plea irresistible.

The entrance to the Megastore was drawing nearer with every footstep and the sounds of the city had all but disappeared. All he could hear now was this music. And now he was close enough to make out the words through the insistence of the drums and the guitars.

> *Just a babe in a black Abyss*
> *No reason for a place like this*
> *The walls are cold and souls cry out in pain...*

The man turned abruptly to his right. He was sweating freely and now it had nothing to do with the heat. He pushed his way past people, through them even, deaf to their protests. He had to know more. The buzzing in his head had stopped to be replaced by a tightening of his mind, pulling and twisting him inside. He stepped through the entrance to the Megastore as the music continued:

> *An easy way for the blind to go*
> *A clever path for the fools who know*
> *The secrets of the hanged man - the smile on his lips*

He was in the store and the music blasted hard at his ears. *A clever path for the fools who know; the secrets of the hanged man's smile.* Well he'd followed that path, he *knew* those secrets. There could be no doubt that the words were references to the images of the Tarot. And the lyricist must have had some understanding of the Tarot, must have known it to be more than a shallow fortune telling device for the profane. The Fool and the Hanged Man, two of the Major Arcana, both having powerful hidden meanings for those who could see beyond the surface. The Fool representing a purity of innocence, an emptiness of mind, a stillness, which was the first essential of the path towards the Splendour of the Sun. The small dog yapping at the Fool's feet a pictorial allegory for the busy conscious thoughts that would fight against this stillness. And the Hanged man – a more complex image, the man suspended upside down from the bough of a tree, one leg bent over the other, forming a cross. This was the reversal of the normal thought processes necessary for an undertaking of the Great Journey. The Hanged Man had reason to smile.

The old man's head began to swim with the undisguised imagery of it all. A young girl, no more than eighteen, wearing faded blue jeans and a black tee-shirt with the words *Simple Minds* emblazoned across the chest, walked in front of him. A plastic badge, introducing her as *Sharon* was pinned just below her left shoulder. The old man grabbed her arm as she passed, startling her.

'This music...' he asked. 'What is it?'

The girl pulled her arm sharply from his grasp and took a step back, looking him up and down. She was no longer startled but mistress of this, her environment. The old man before her was obviously a fish out of water here and she wouldn't have to yell for security.

'It's *Revelation* by *Iron Maiden*,' she said, her surprisingly gentle voice betraying her home-counties origins. 'It's from the *Piece of Mind* album.'

Turning slightly, the girl pointed to a huge rack of shiny album covers. A brief grin was beginning at the corners of her mouth. There was after all, something amusing about this old man taking an interest in heavy metal.

'You'll find it over there,' she said. 'They're filed alphabetically.'

'Thank you,' the old man replied. 'Thank you very much.'

Looking past her, he made his way over to the rack that had been indicated, leaving her staring, bemused, at his back.

He began to flick through the 'I's, his fingers working fast, the twisting in his mind becoming a heavy throb. Then he saw the label: *Iron Maiden*. The band had a section all to itself, surely an indication of popular success, he rightly noted, wondering briefly why this should concern him. He began to search through the glossy sleeves for the *Piece of Mind* album but he never found it. His fingers seemed drawn to one particular cover and before he could think why, he had pulled it from the rack. At the bottom of the sleeve was the title, *Number of the Beast*, but the picture above just screamed at him; and oh, what horror! It was innocuous enough in itself, no more than a comic strip fantasy, but as the throbbing in his head grew more violently strident, suddenly he knew why this had drawn him.

Flashes of a nightmare passed through his mind; a tower exploding in a thunderflash of shattered masonry as out of a boiling sea rose nothing less than the straw-haired monster pictured before him. He became aware of his heartbeat, a huge booming drum as blood pulsed heavy through his temples. The pain inside his head became unbearable until, clutching the album cover in sweaty hands, he fell faint to the carpeted floor.

Chapter 30

SIGNES...SOUTH OF FRANCE... JUNE 18th... 2.56pm

THE TEMPLAR PULLED the hired Renault 21 into the side of the road. There was no traffic on this small country highway and the sun beat down viciously on the hard baked ground. But the surrounding countryside was still beautiful for all that. All four of the car's windows were wound open to provide much needed ventilation.

In the still quiet of the hot country afternoon, the Templar glanced at the rear view mirror. He could see his Torquemada lying crumpled in the back seat, where it had been all journey. It never stirred. It lay still now; there was not even a sign of breathing. The Templar knew that the Torquemada was once again feigning the death that it - *it* had long ago ceased to be a *he* - craved. The Templar curled the edge of his mouth in an involuntary grin at the thought. He would never allow his Torquemada to escape so easily. Even so, there was nothing to be gained at the moment by disturbing the creature's little game so he left well alone.

Marseilles lay up ahead, less than one hour's drive away. The A8 Autoroute that he had picked up just outside Monaco could have taken him virtually into the city centre. However, he had pulled of at Brignoles and headed south to complete the journey by a circuitous route. One that brought back memories of a time long past.

The Torquemada would remember this part of the world too, he knew. Time had not changed the fields and the trees and the hedgerows. Perhaps the Torquemada had caught a glimpse. Perhaps that was why it was now feigning death. Because for the Torquemada, the memories of this area, just outside Signes, would be soul destroying...

Over four hundred years had passed since they had last seen these fields, but time had not dimmed the Templar's memory. The summer had been harsh then, too; the brilliant sun no less fierce and the daytime sky a cornflower blue with not so much as a hint of cloud. And it had been a weary time; weeks of hard riding had taken him to Toulon where he would rest up for a few days before his boat was ready to sail. A Mediterranean passage to Venice awaited, a bought passage on a trading ship. This final mission, this last part of the great responsibility had been carried out without a hitch. The Templar documents that had been entrusted to him, oh so long before, by the Treasurer of the Order of the Poor Knights of Christ and the Temple of Solomon, were safe at last. They had proved a great blessing but a much greater burden, and he had had to shoulder that burden all alone for nearly two hundred and fifty years. Now at last, he knew that the treasure would be secure. The documents had been placed in a stone tomb near Arques. No one would ever look there. The tomb belonged to a family with Cathar antecedents, a family with knowledge of and love of the Great Work. People who would not see it wither and perish.

How greatly troubled times had been then; more than ever, faith was being forced to bend its pristine knee to politics, and the Inquisition of Rome was still powerful; the more notorious Inquisition of Spain was at the height of its terror. And just beginning to build a momentum was the hysteria that would sweep like a fire through Europe and would blaze for two centuries leaving more than a million men women and children dead in its wake. A blaze without boundaries, which would chill the hearts of some men even as it singed the flesh of others; where the most terrifying accusation of all would be: *WITCH!*

Certainly, it had not been a time to be carrying documents of such indicting value. There had been a pressing need to make them safe. And this, after considerable searching, had been achieved. Nothing had been left to chance; only the Templar and the patriarch of this brave family whose tomb was to hold this 'more than gold' had known the whereabouts of the documents. The Shadowmasters of that age had known that there was a key that would point out this hiding place. An obscure key, an encoded key, to be sure. But one which they would be able to decipher. The Shadowmasters also knew the whereabouts of the key. That had been decided in advance in Paris. It was from this very hiding place that the Templar had ridden hard into Toulon, from an obscure village in the Languedoc, an area historically steeped in sympathy for their work. The village was Rennes Le Chateau and, with some irony, by the light of a full and silver moon, the Templar had hidden the key within the walls of the village's only church - its inevitably Catholic Church.

Thence to Toulon. He had stayed at an inn there, for the first time in centuries relieved of his burden of care for the Templar treasure. And that first night he had taken to his bed after eating heartily at the table of the innkeeper and drinking a flask or two of the rich wine of the region. He had sunk straight away into a blissful sleep.

The next morning had seen him walking, down by the waterfront. He had always liked to be around boats. He loved the imagery that a busy harbour threw to him; the dreams of travel and adventure that the smell of the sea conjured up. How good it was to know that his burden was laid to rest at long last.

Still, *he* had been far from safe. Those associated with the protection of the Great Work were in constant danger from the Inquisitors. Cries of treason and heresy were never far away. They were dark times when the Shadowmasters had been in need of the skills of one who had learned his craft in the fortress of Alamut. In need of a follower of the great mystic, Hassan-i-Sabbah. In need of an Assassin...

At the water's edge, he had mused on the fact that from the earliest times there had been an exchange of cultures between the Christian Templars and the Sufi mystics of Islam. This was why he had been given over to the Templars. Both Orders had realised that the petty political squabbling that characterised the Crusades meant nothing. The protection and continuation of the Great Work was all that mattered, was something that both of them would strive for in the end.

It was a long and difficult path that had led him to be waiting at Toulon. Looking out over the sea, he had closed his eyes to let the morning sun tingle its early warmth across his face.

'Monsieur, if you please.'

The words had come from behind him. Quiet, but not

whispered, simply low and almost pathologically calm. His hand had moved instinctively to his sword and he had turned swiftly to face the speaker.

How clearly he remembered it all, even the very words, after all this time, and he found himself back there in his thoughts, reliving it all...

'Monsieur, I am a friend. You will not need your sword.'

He found himself regarding a slightly built man - not a peasant, but certainly not an aristocrat. His clothes were expensive enough, yes, but his bearing lacked the arrogance and rude confidence of the ruling classes. His demeanour marked him out, rather, as a moderately successful merchant or trader.

His hand staying close by the handle of his sword, the Templar looked him in the eye, waiting for him to state his business. He had led a life of intrigue for too long to drop his guard easily, even when no clear danger was apparent.

'Allow me to introduce myself,' the quiet stranger continued. 'My name is Jacques Molay.'

The Templar's eyes flashed momentarily. He had met a Jacques de Molay in those desperate times, so long ago. That man had exuded greatness and as the last Grand Master of the Order of the Knights Templar, had burned on the orders of Philippe IV rather than repudiate and compromise the truth of the Great Work.

'Yes,' the Templar said sharply. 'And what can I do to help you?'

The quiet man smiled. A pleasant, friendly smile. 'Your eyes betray you, monsieur,' he said. 'And you would be right in your assumption. My line does indeed, in an obscure way, trace itself back to your former Grand Master.'

What was he to make of this? He was thrown off guard. Instinctively his hand strayed once more to the handle of his sword. His eyes scanned the waterfront for signs of the militiamen who might be converging upon them if this was indeed a trap. But the waterfront remained serene, with just the same few fishermen working on their nets - just them and this enigma smiling before him. Once again he relaxed his grip on the sword.

Jacques Molay reached out his right hand and unclenched his

fist. A ragged piece of cloth, yellowed and tattered with age, lay on the open palm but there was no mistaking the red emblem embroidered in its centre. The Templar Cross.

'Let us walk,' the Templar said. 'And you may tell me what it is that is so important that you would jeopardise both our lives.'

In the end, they walked for over an hour as the sun climbed higher into the cloudless Mediterranean sky. And Molay told the Templar of the horror that had necessitated his taking so risky an action. There was an envoy, resting some way in from the coast with his entourage at a village called Signes. The envoy was Catholic, a representative of the Spanish Church making his way to Rome. But more than that, this envoy was representing the Suprema, the Grand Council of the Inquisition. And in Signes, he had felt it necessary to do his duty by the Church in an area where the Roman Inquisition had no representation.

What had happened was a commonplace wherever the Inquisition touched. One villager, jealous of another for some reason, had made an accusation to the Inquisitor, as was often the case and events had run away with themselves. The Inquisition was now concluded and today was to be held the *Auto da Fe,* where the Grand Inquisitor would pass his sentences on the guilty, some sixty of the villagers and surrounding farmers. In itself, this would have been of no interest to the Templar. But among this sixty was one of the Brotherhood, one of the leaders of a secret network that was only now, after the destruction of the Templars, organising itself clandestinely throughout all of Europe to continue the Great Work. In the west, this network fell under the aegis of a council of thirteen Shadowmasters.

'So it is a setback,' was all the Templar said. 'We have suffered them before. Many times. The work is great enough. It will survive any punishment proscribed by this particular *Auto da Fe.*'

'But monsieur, it is more terrible than that,' the trader Molay replied, his face now grave. 'These accusations are not of heresy. Their concern is witchcraft. This Inquisition has been a rooting out of witchcraft and there will be but one sentence. You will know as well as I, monsieur, that the sentence will be one of death by burning.'

Suddenly back in the present, his mind making a swift leap of centuries, the Templar squirmed deep into the car seat and opened his eyes to scan the surrounding countryside. What back then had caused him to do what he had irreversibly done? It had not just been to save a leader of the Brotherhood. He had felt a rage at the intolerance. He had by then, suffered it and hidden from it for over two centuries. Enough had been enough, he told himself. How could he then have stood idly by and watched as a whole village was decimated in the name of the Christ, who was credited with infinite mercy by his followers? Yes, and followers who would slaughter readily and swear by *His* name as they did so. Could he live with himself as he watched the world subjugated to a false and unrealisable dream because ambitious politicians had taken the name of an allegorical figure and made a gospel of the literal words that told His story? Of course not. He had not even had to ponder it then. And now that there had been centuries to mull over the resonances of his action, he knew that he would do it again, given the chance.

As it was back then, Molay had been right. The *Auto da Fe* had pronounced death by burning. The pyres had been built and the cleansing for Christ would begin with the dawn of the next day.

The condemned were being held in a wooden stockade some way out of the village, guarded loosely by a half dozen of the Inquisitor's military escort. Others patrolled the village and maintained a curfew lest the villagers get it into their heads to attempt a rescue of their kith and kin. The quiet of the night had about it an air of subdued terror.

As the sun dipped below the horizon and darkness fell, the Templar sat hidden on a hillside overlooking the Inquisitor's encampment in the valley below. He closed his eyes and stilled his conscious mind, taking the short path – no longer perilous to him – to regions of celestial power that he knew he could call on to help him that night. By three a.m. he returned to the life of the low and rose to be about his business. A brilliant moon shone in the clear black sky but it concerned him little; he was an Assassin of Alamut and he would not be seen.

The guards around the stockade were easy prey, falling to his knife one by one as rabbits fall to the hungry eagle. He opened the wooden gate to set free the prisoners knowing that most would have nowhere to hide and would be rounded up in a couple of days. Among them he sought out the one whose life held great value for him, his instinct guiding him to this like-mind unerringly as the villagers made their escape with surprising stealth. Finding the man he sought, he approached and pulled this worthy towards him giving a gestured exhortation to silence.

'With me,' he whispered. 'Come.'

The man said nothing and followed the swift, crouched run of the Templar. The tents of the Inquisitor and the remainder of his guards stayed dark, as the Templar knew they would. There were forces held in delicate balance, which he had arranged about the encampment to cloak his activities. He led the man to the foot of a nearby hill and pointed him to a rocky outcrop just below the summit. There, Molay waited with a swift horse and instructions of his own. The Templar's work was complete. Almost.

For years he had suffered the indignity of hiding and skulking away in dark corners. It had not been his training. It had never been his instinct. And now he saw a chance to hit back. He returned to the encampment slithering silently through the shadows. Two guards stood rigid at the entrance to the largest tent. They did not spot him as he used his craft to draw him in close. The tent was in darkness but the sound of heavy sobbing pierced cloth walls. That and an occasional grunting and giggling and laboured breathing. And faint words sometimes, barely discernable:

'Spiritus... huhg... Sanctus... huhg... Deus Forbiscum...'

The Templar shuddered to imagine the act of vile obscenity taking place inside. But he was going to find out. First, there were the two guards to consider.

They were standing shoulder to shoulder, each holding a heavy pike in his right hand, but their attitude told him that they were far from alert. They felt secure and unthreatened. Well, they would pay dearly for that.

He crept silently behind them, his eerie training granting him the silence of a ghost. His dagger was already in his left hand as he sprang to his feet, plunging the sharp blade into the side of the neck of one and wrenching it forward, tearing out the windpipe and all the major blood vessels so that a crimson fountain sprayed high and wide. The man slumped dead to the floor. At the same time, the Templar brought his right hand around the neck of the other guard from behind, clamping his hand over the mouth to prevent any scream that might try to escape. He could almost imagine the guard's eyes, wide and bulging with terror as he swung his left hand in a wide arc, bringing the blade around to plunge into the guard's left nostril. The blade's momentum carried it up, slicing through facial flesh until it pierced the thin bone behind the nasal septum and stabbed into the brain behind.

The Templar lowered the lifeless body to the ground. From within the tent the guttural sounds and tear-drenched sobbing continued. Crouching low so as to be out of the anticipated line of vision, he pulled the tent flap open an inch or two and peered inside. His eyes were already dark-accustomed and the sight that met them was sickening to him. The tent contained but few items of furniture and was dominated by a low, wide bed. On it, stretched out and lying face down was a young girl. The Templar guessed her age to be no more than eleven or twelve. She was naked and leather straps bound her wrists and ankles to the corner posts of the bedstead, in a posture of utter humility and humiliation. Lying obscenely atop her was an equally naked man of some forty years, writhing, pushing and grunting with hideous bestial lust. His weight pressed the unfortunate child into the mattress, which she bit into, in a brave effort to contain her cries and sobs.

O bliss of heaven, what child ever deserved so vile a fate? The Templar pulled the tent flap open and ducked inside. At first the man was oblivious to his presence, lost in his slavering passions. The child became aware of him first and twisted her head around to look at him, her cries momentarily suspended. Her sudden stillness alerted the man and he stiffened, craning his own neck around to face the intruder. His eyes met the shadowy dark face of the Templar as he stood like some hellish demon, dripping blood from his night's work, towering above the vile grotesquerie of this living tableau.

The man rolled off the girl-child, an involuntary whimper of shock and surprise escaping from his throat. And as he rolled away, the Templar noticed his stiff penis glistening with blood, as it slid out of the girl. The image and practice of abomination was complete. This pillar of the Holy Church of Christ had been taking his delight deep in the anus of his young victim. The girl's body, so suddenly freed from the savage pain of defilement relaxed with the visible equivalent of an audible sigh. The Templar hoped that she had sunk into a blissful faint.

The Inquisitor had dropped to his knees. His mouth was opening and a scream for help would not be long in coming. Quickly, the Templar stepped over to the kneeling form and smashed the heavy handle of his curved knife into the Inquisitor's nose, feeling it crumple beneath the force of the blow. The Inquisitor was sent crashing backwards rendered half-senseless by this violence. His nose was spurting blood and his upper lip was split neatly in the centre. The Templar moved swiftly, dropping onto the now languid and stupefied form. He grabbed the Inquisitor's hair with his left hand, stretching the neck, which he hit sharply with the edge of his right hand. The remaining semblance of consciousness slipped away from the Inquisitor and the Templar threw the inert form to the floor. He would not take the life of this scum. He had decided that upon a whim. There was a crueller fate that he had within his gift to bestow, but that was for later. Binding and gagging this monster he made sure that the knots were biting and vicious.

On the low bed, the little girl lay motionless save for the steady rise and fall of her breathing. The Templar cut the cords that bound her and she moved her head slowly to look into his eyes. He found himself looking away unable to face her misery, pain and suffering. He could not leave her there. He would have to get her away, away from this region where searching would begin with a vengeance in the morning. She would never again be safe here. After this night's work, who would?

He tucked the curved blade into its sheath beneath his tunic and tried to lift the girl to her feet. Her dark eyes blazed with the pain that seared from her ruptured anus and blood flowed in a damp trickle down the back of her thighs. But through the pain in those eyes the Templar could discern a message of almost pitiful gratitude. It was not going to be easy but he would see this child away from here.

He left the girl supporting herself on the edge of the bed and stepped over to the still unconscious Inquisitor. With an ease indicating enormous physical strength, he lifted the inert form over his shoulder then indicated for the girl to join him. His admiration for her began to grow. The pain must have been tremendous, yet she uttered not so much as a whimper. Throughout it all, she had spoken not a single word. She could have received her training at Alamut he mused, watching as she made her way on unsteady legs towards him.

Cautiously he lifted the tent flap and looked out into the deep dark of the night. He could sense vibrations in the atmosphere as the delicate net of balancing forces that had lain over the tents of the sleeping soldiers still hung heavy and torporous in the blackness. It would hold long enough for them to escape so long as they were reasonably quiet. By morning though, imbalances inherent in an anything but a pure world would cause decay, far - he hoped - from his stabilising influence.

The coast was clear, so with no time to lose, he pushed his way out of the tent. The Inquisitor lay heavy over one shoulder and the suffering child clung tight to his tunic. Like this, he made his way through the brush and scrub to the base of the hill where his horse was tethered and waiting...

Eyes opening softly. Back in the car, in the comfortable seat. Ah, so long ago it had all been. And even so, not for the first time in the moments since he had pulled the car over to the side of the road, the Templar marvelled at how little the landscape had changed. Then all at once, he felt the blood drain from his face; his mind became blank, collapsing in on itself, sucking him down past stretched and rushing stars through an infinite blackness of space.

Before his very eyes, a form took shape in the void, growing and growling, and he knew that he had seen it before. The straw-haired monster that had shattered the symmetry of his last journey to the realm of the Great Work. Suddenly it collapsed in on itself and there was a fleeting sensation, for just a nanosecond, of a presence wonderfully serene and benign. Then it was gone and he was once more staring at the scorched countryside, the

231

horizon blurred in a shimmering heat-haze.

So it was come to stay then. So be it, he would confront it. It was strong and malignant, a repulsively one-sided force of destruction. The Great Work was facing a danger graver than any posed by the Grand Inquisitors of bygone eras. That much he could sense immediately. These accursed modern Shadowmasters! Just what had they done?

Still, through it all, he had also sensed a spark of hope. There was an ally to be sought. He had felt that much. Great wisdom and strength and understanding. He had encountered this presence once before. It had been with him in the Tower on that last Great Journey. The old man. He had felt that same spiritual calm just then, the same vibration that he had encountered in the Tower. Together they might overcome this nightmare of imbalance. But where to find this ally? There were no clues as yet, but no matter; there were ways and means. First he had a more immediate matter to attend to. To the west lay the great city of Marseilles and a man named Strachan who was about to encounter his destiny.

Chapter 31

IN THE BACK of the Jaguar, Strachan was screaming, lashing out with his arms and legs, his eyes still blind behind the tight velvet cloth that covered them.

The driver of the car pulled sharply to a halt at the side of the road. Fortunately, they were still in the open countryside, far away from prying eyes.

'No! Nooooooo!!!' screamed Strachan. 'It can't be! Tell me it can't be!!! O Jonathaaaannn.' The scream subsided into a heavy sobbing, as Lyndon, who had torn off his own blindfold, wrapped his powerful arms around Strachan's writhing frame, holding him steady, calming him with soothing words.

'It's okay buddy, it's okay. Just a bad dream is all. You're safe now, everything's gonna be just fine. Relax. Take it easy. Relax.'

Gradually, Strachan's struggling subsided and he sat, sobbing heavily in Lyndon's arms. Lyndon reached up and gently pulled the blindfold away from Strachan's eyes. In the front seats, the driver and his colleague slid nervous hands inside their jackets where they carried their weapons, but a withering look from Lyndon stopped them short. They had both seen him in action and neither of them was confident of bettering him in the tight confines of the car. In any case, they both knew that Lyndon himself had not needed the blindfold. He had made his own way to and from the villa on many occasions. He was to be trusted. He had only used the blindfold to put his friend here at ease. And besides, they were almost there now; Marseilles lay only a few kilometres down the road. And the man lying sobbing in the killer's arms was in no condition to be taking bearings. They turned to each other and shrugged, then turned in their seats to look at the road through the dusty windscreen. The driver took out a cigarette and lit it. It was none of their business.

In the back seat, Lyndon sat with Strachan cradled in his arms. He did not feel in the least embarrassed, nor did he think anything less of Strachan. He had seen this happen many times, to many good men. Special Forces took men where only demons lived. Men had been destroyed by their experiences that only others who had been there would ever understand. He had been there. He knew.

Strachan's sobbing had subsided. He breathed deeply for a few seconds to calm himself, and then sat up. He looked at Lyndon, a silent thank you in his eyes. There would be no need for any explanation. Which was just as well, for where could he begin? It had been fucking unbelievable.

The moon. He had been staring at the moon, which sat full and bright in the sky, even though the light suggested that it was mid afternoon. A harsh wind whistled in his ears and he could feel the sting of sand grains which it whipped against his naked flesh. He had lowered his eyes, squinting against the breeze, to survey his surroundings. It had been like a scene out of science fiction. A desolate place, wind shaped sand dunes rising and falling in all directions as far as the eye could see.

Stretched out before him, he noticed footsteps in the sand, leading off into the distance and out of curiosity, he had started to follow them. As he walked, the wind dropped and a brutal red sun beat fiercely down on his uncovered skin. Yet still he had walked, following the footsteps for mile after endless mile over the rolling dunes. He remembered thinking that the tracks must have been fresh or the winds would have covered them with sand long ago, yet there they were. For hours he had wandered, in need of neither water nor salt, despite the blistering heat. Somehow he knew that the moon was taking care of him, cooling that which the sun would burn.

The tracks continued, dipping out of sight over the crest of one dune, only to reappear, leading a compulsive path up the slope of the next. He shuffled onwards, always following. His bare feet slipped in the deep sand, but strangely, it was not tiring.

In the distance, he could see the peak of a sand-mountain, a mighty dune that rose hundreds of metres into the blue of the hot sky. Still the moon was at his back, the blood-red sun in

234

front, drawing him on. It was as though the sand mountain had been calling out to him all along, as if it had needed his presence. He knew that it had something special that it wanted to show him, something that he would have to see. A secret.

He had moved faster and faster, eventually breaking into a shuffling jog through the slippery hot sand. And he was dragging himself up the slope of the mountain, on all fours at times, in his haste to reach the summit where he knew a great wisdom awaited his coming.

His goal towered a hundred metres above him, tantalisingly within reach and he redoubled his efforts, his breath coming in painful gasps with the intensity of the work. Occasionally, he would raise his eyes and look to the top. He could see something lying there now; a body perhaps, face down and flat to the sand.

He was struggling to reach the top, his hands digging fiercely into the sand of the steep slope, dragging him along, his feet thrusting back to propel him forward. He could see the figure at the top quite clearly, and it was a human figure. It was the body of a woman, her naked skin a copper-bronze, which glistened in the light of the powerful red sun. She lay still, her face turned away from him, pressed into the sand. She had never moved, nor betrayed any trace of having ever moved. He was almost there now and he could see blemishes on the skin of her back, like ragged holes, deep and nasty, half a dozen of them, each more than two inches in diameter. There was no blood, no sign of any bodily fluids, but he had recognised these wounds. They were exit wounds. High velocity rounds in all probability.

All of a sudden, he was overcome with a sense of grave foreboding. But it was too late to go back now, or even stop. He reached the prone body. The figure was voluptuous. She must have been a great beauty before the events that had torn at her flesh. A sensual, sexual woman. Even here, ravaged by death, the thought of what she once must have been was stirring him. He could feel that tightening of the crutch as his penis began to twitch. He had kneeled down, stroking his fingertips over the cool skin. And then he heard a voice:

'David?' It asked. 'David, is it you? I've waited so long for you to come and find me. So long.'

He had recoiled in horror. The voice had come from the

'corpse' before him, a rich ruby voice, a damp and inviting voice. Yet a voice that he had recognised in another capacity. Although the sound had been undoubtedly feminine, something about it had struck a chord deep inside him; it was a voice that he had lived with for a long time.

He reached out and rolled the body over onto its back. The six tiny bullet entrance holes were the only blemish on an otherwise perfect female figure. The feet, the legs, the flat belly, the pointed, full breasts with wide pink nipples, it was a body made in a dream, a vision of perfection.

'Will you join me, David? Say that you will, David. Please say that you will,' the voice implored.

He had thrown himself backwards with the shock, his revulsion overriding any attempt at rationalisation that his mind might have wanted to make. His mouth gaped open, wanting to answer, to say something, anything, but all that he could manage was a disgusted, strangled sound from deep in the back of his throat. For the voice that he had recognised came from the lips of the corpse, and the lips, painted with ruby lip-gloss, belonged to a face that was unmistakable. This once Siren of a woman had his brother's face. It was Jonathan.

'Oh you can't desert me now David, surely not now. We belong together. I'm part of you, you're part of me. Come and join me,' the voice entreated.

But he had shuffled back on his knees, his mind approaching panic. The ruby lips parted in a smile, a wet tongue slithered out from between them and suddenly it lashed out, long and sticky like that of a lizard, and it burned where it hit him, piercing his skin, and he could feel it wriggle painfully into the muscle below.

'Ooohh!' he had cried out in his horror and shock, and had tried to pull away, but the slithering appendage only burrowed deeper, almost paralysing him with pain. Then out of the bullet holes shot slimy tentacles, blue and disgusting. They stood vertically in the air for a few seconds, wriggling and dancing, and he could smell the scent of ripening putrefaction that they had brought with them from the depths of this body that was his brother.

He vomited explosively, his stomach twisting its contents out onto the sand, spattering the body that lay before him. The tentacles seemed to take this as a signal and shot out towards him, wrapping themselves around his arms and legs, wet and slimy, and stinging to the touch, as though they were coated in acid, dragging him in, closer. One found its way to his gaping mouth and wormed its way inside, quickly slithering down his throat, until he could feel it, squirming and dancing inside his stomach. His stomach rebelled, twisting itself again, but the intruder sensed the action and burrowed itself deep into the stomach wall, anchoring there, leaving him to dry-retch.

Another tentacle had found his penis, had probed around it until it had found the urethra. It had forced its way painfully inside; bludgeoning its way quickly up the narrow tube to bury itself in his bladder. He screamed aloud with the horror and the pain of it all.

'Only for a moment, my brother,' the voice of Jonathan cooed. 'Then we'll be together again, for always. You'll never want to leave me again David. There are ecstasies we will only understand when we're together.'

And the tentacles pulled on him now, drew him closer to their host, where the flesh had begun to split and melt, a grey-green slop forming at the edges. His own skin was splitting too, in response, and he could feel himself begin to liquefy as the two bodies were drawn closer, ever closer. He raised his eyes to look up at the sky, and let out a pathetic whimper, which sang out the finality of loss. Because the blood-red sun was shooting out liquid arms of its own that burrowed into the sweetness of the moon, drawing it closer to itself, devouring it with its power.

Then finally, he had found his voice and cried:

'Nooooo!!!'

OXFORD... 3.05pm

The old man sat in the lounge of his apartment. Spread on the floor before him were eight shiny album covers, the collected works of a rock band called Iron Maiden. Each was gruesome in its own way, and all were linked by a common theme; the development of a character that he had discovered was called Eddie the Head.

Eddie was the creation of an artist named Derek Riggs and on the early covers, he was portrayed as a psychopathic nightmare, a hideous parody of a man, lean and obviously vicious, with a penchant for crude blood letting. His domain was the darkened nighttime streets of cosy suburbia, where he stalked his prey, while the innocent lived out their drab lives behind drawn curtains. On the later covers, Eddie had forgone the mundane for more grandiose ambition. Eddie had been transformed from a perpetrator of earthly terror to an inhabitant of an otherworldly hell. He had become a master of powerful destinies.

But the old man kept coming back to the third impression in the series; the cover of the album called *The Number Of The Beast*. It was this cover that he had first pulled from the rack in the Virgin Megastore, this cover that had stirred so powerful an archetype in his subconscious that the sudden onrush of awareness had caused him to faint dead away in the crowded store. That had been embarrassing, to say the least, but he had had his age to call upon and had readily been able to assure the concerned staff who had taken him into a back room to recover, that he was really quite well.

He smiled to himself. The young shop assistants had hardly been able to keep the signs of relief from their faces; a corpse in the back office was the last thing that they wanted to deal with. He had said that he was okay, and who were they to argue? Quite right too, he thought to himself. His condition had been a symptom of weakness. But he would be more vigilant with his inner mind in future.

Now why had that particular image provoked so violent a reaction? Why that one? It was a representation of the malignancy that he had experienced during the final stages of the Great Journey he had so recently undertaken, of that there was no doubt. The vibrations, the auras, had all been identical. He had never been imaginative enough to conjure up worldly representations of his experience of the Great Work. His mind had always been too logical and structured for that. It took the instincts of a Leonardo, or a Poussin. And he knew that his talents lay along a different path. But now he had a pictorial archetype to work with. The question was, had the vision slipped into his subconscious and been associated with the forces that he had experienced out there on the edge, by his own developing mind? If so, it would seem to be asking too much of coincidence that his mind should construct an image identical to one conceived by an artist of whom he had never heard.

Fact was, he had never seen these pictures before; until today he had never even heard of Iron Maiden, let alone their hideous mascot, Eddie the Head. Or had he? He was beginning to think, to concentrate his thoughts. Might he have seen the picture before? Could he have seen it before and not paid it any notice? Think. Think hard. There must be something. Yes, of course! Of course he'd seen it. Many times.On the streets and in the college cloisters, the image had been with him for years. How could he have been so forgetfully senile? This picture was not just hidden away on album covers. It had screamed out at him from the tee shirts on which the design had been emblazoned. Tee shirts worn by the students, which were legion in this university town. It had been tucked away deep in his mind and had been brought into play when he had seen that album cover in the shop. His mind had simply associated *that* picture with the vicious force that it had wanted to represent to him.

But now to what was really important. Such power that force must have to command his attention so. It had not withered and decayed in the imbalance that had followed the shattering of Glory. It was being held in a symmetry of its own, a symmetry which could destroy the fragile balance of this physical world and retard the spiritual development of man for millennia. Only a handful of people in the west had the knowledge to hold such power and retain their own sanity. And it must come from the west.

The wise men of the east had always followed a different road to the Glory. Their paths could never cross with those of the Journeymen from the west. Different cultures, different ideals, different priorities. It was why those seekers after truth who had travelled to India in search of enlightenment had so often returned disillusioned and embittered. The way of the east was not for them; its disciplines too alien. Yet had they but stopped to see, they would have found they had a great tradition of their own to follow. But so few had been prepared to so much as seek

239

and the western tradition lay buried deep under centuries of persecution.

The Shadowmasters. They were behind this monstrosity. They had to be. Just what could they be thinking of? It had been bad enough when he had thought that a temporary imbalance had been created which would at least burn itself out in decay, but this was dangerous. Permanent. At last, at long last, he was beginning to understand just why he had felt compelled to remain with the mortal earth. They were dangerous, this new breed. Deadly with their ambition, willing to cut corners. It was the impatience of the new age, yes, but they were Shadowmasters. They should have known better.

The Secret Chiefs from beyond the Abyss had conditioned him to remain, not to join them in the ecstasy of spirit, which his endeavours had most certainly merited. He had known all along that they had been leading him along a different path, keeping him here, rooted to the physical and the repulsive pain of its imperfection, but now it was clear. They had felt the stirrings of the great imbalances that were now coming into play, and they had wanted him to combat them. O, the responsibility. Could he really have the wherewithal to combat such excess? He must. He simply must!

He had monitored the progress of these new Shadowmasters. He had felt the stirrings of great forces in the *yesod* of his being, the Qabalistic zone where instinct held sway and he knew that they were far progressed along the path. And he had sensed danger in that. There was not yet the political will in the world able to foster the climate in which these mighty forces might prosper for the good of all.

But always he had felt powerless. He had long wrestled with the idea of sounding out a warning to these new Key Holders. But would they listen to his words? If he were to show himself to them, would they not scoff at him and cast him aside. Had they had the grace to understand his choosing of the solitary path all those years ago, to break off and leave them to their own devices?

They could crush him, couldn't they? And they would, wouldn't they, these impatient heralds of the New Golden Age? Yes they would. They would most certainly try. They had not the wisdom of their mighty predecessors.

Still, he would not be alone. Awareness was flooding back into him now; he could remember feelings, vibrations that had been with him recently. There was somebody out there, somebody with a wisdom and power that transcended his own, somebody who would sympathise, somebody who would help.

Yet where to find this person? No matter, they would find each other, out there in the beyond, where like would call out to like to spite conventional physics, and this body would already be aware of the task that awaited, might even now be searching out *him*, his aide de combat. He must make himself ready. There was no time to lose.

Chapter 32

'THE TIME IS NOT yet ripe! Not yet! Can you not see that if we push this thing along too quickly we will destroy everything?'

Henri St Clair paced nervously before the huge ornate fireplace in the lounge of his apartment. He wrung his hands together before him and beads of sweat were clearly visible on the bald dome of his head. Sure signs that he was much troubled.

He turned sharply to face Michael Brachman, sitting awkwardly, as usual, in a deep leather armchair that backed onto the huge picture window with its views of the Seine.

'God, Michael, it has always been you who have kept our ambitions in check. You who have made us see when we would have allowed circumstances to run away with us. But now you speak of this... this... madness!'

'I have had time to think, Henri. This... madness... is the greatest opportunity that we are ever likely to have. Bondachuck can command the loyalty of his Spetznaz brigades, we both know that. The Soviet Union can be brought to change. Why wait? The United States of Europe is within our grasp. We can begin the consolidation of our base, we can then start to think, *really think*, about leading mankind into the New Golden Age. No more idle dreams of what we *can* be, what we *will* do. We must be brave enough to see it real. To hold it in our hands and marvel at it as at a precious jewel. It can be ours, Henri, but we must be prepared to act.'

St Clair looked deep into Brachman's eyes, trying to fathom the machinations that were taking place behind. This was a new Michael Brachman right enough, a tougher, more assertive, more dominant Brachman.

For years *he* had been the Grand Master of the Order; the

Shadowmasters had looked to *him* for guidance and wisdom. *He* had always set the agenda, and Michael had been his lieutenant. Now he could sense that that was changing.

This new Brachman was talking from strength, with a confidence that did not expect to be questioned. And St Clair knew that the Shadowmasters would listen to this new Brachman, would cloak him with the mantle of leadership. The German, the American, the Dutch, the Italian; they in particular would be receptive to these new words. It had only been Michael's smooth diplomacy that had deflected them from unnecessary haste in the past. Now they would welcome this call to move.

And Bondachuck? Well, no need to even ask about him. The Russian had been itching to make a move for years. The sooner the better for him, since each passing day brought the horror of discovery that little bit closer. An organisation as extensive and as powerful as the KGB would not be kept in the dark forever. Bondachuck had been the first Russian Shadowmaster since the Revolution. It could not have been easy for him. Perhaps Michael was right after all... No! No, it could not be. The infrastructure was not sound enough yet, it could not hold. This must be stopped at all cost.

He tried to hold his gaze on Brachman's eyes, to reassert his dominance, but Brachman was the master now, and he knew it. He found himself glancing away and the battle was lost.

'But economically, Michael... are we really ready yet, can we really make it work?' he asked pathetically, looking down at his perfectly manicured fingernails. He had to buy time, had to find a way to reach the others. 'Surely, after so much time, we can wait a further five years, as we had planned?'

Away from St Clair's gaze, the fires of Choronzon burned orange in Brachman's eyes and he felt power such as his frail physical frame should never contain. He bathed silent in its majesty for a second until it began to fade. Then softly, almost whispering, he said:

'We are ready enough.'

A tingling sensation began in his toes, shooting up through his newly strong legs, surging wave-like up to his chest where it exploded inside him in a power of bliss. It was then that he saw for the first time where his new destiny lay: he could become the master of the universe...

LONDON... JUNE 18th... 7.30pm

The underground room was dimly lit, without being dingy. What light there was came from four, red-shaded lamps set just over halfway up the bare plaster walls. Those walls were painted, olive green. Plush leather Chesterfields lined the walls with low tables, casually spread with newspapers and magazines, set before them. Other tables plain and functional in contrast to the suggested opulence of the Chesterfields and surrounded by mostly empty chairs occupied the rest of the space. At the far end, the room was dominated by a long bar, garishly lit with bright white light, attracting most of the few occupants of the room like moths to the flame of a candle.

Robert Dibble made his way from the bar, his hands cupped around the three pints of lager he was carrying. The artificial chill of the drinks bit at his fingers as he dodged his way between the empty tables. He had never seen the place so empty, he thought. Still, it was still early yet, and he supposed that as the night wore on, the old regulars would begin to show, in dribs and drabs, until the place became a seething mass of bodies and voices, the way that it always was when his mind's eye chanced upon a thought of it. And of course, this place served no passing trade, none whatsoever. No sign on the forbiddingly closed wooden door set deep into the grimy brickwork of the street just a minute or two's walk from Waterloo station, advertised the existence of the underground drinking den. Nor would it ever. Those entitled to visit would know about the place; those who didn't know were not entitled to visit. It was as simple as that. The way that it had always been with the Special Forces Drinking Club.

Robert Dibble had not visited the place in years. Certainly he had not needed to venture there since his current posting in the UK had begun, two years earlier. Even so, it hadn't changed and he was glad of the fact. It provided a cosy familiarity, a comfortable sanctuary for those who might need one. He approached two men, sitting at one of the tables and set the

244

three glasses down. He wiped the condensation from his fingertips, using the sides of his trousers, then drew out a chair and sat down.

'Cheers!' said one of the two men, picking up one of the glasses and taking a sip of the golden liquid. Dibble and the other man, his partner John Law, picked up their glasses and echoed the salute. There was a brief silence as they savoured the taste of the drink, feeling the cold of it bite at their throats.

'Okay Harry, so what do you think?' John Law broke the silence.

'Straight to the point eh, no idle chit-chat, no pleasant conversation remembering times past? Ah well, never mind. Everything's so rush rush rush these days. Progress I suppose.' Harry Crews leaned back in his chair, his head tilted up as though deep in thought.

'No rush Harry,' Dibble said. 'But we need your opinion. You knew him. Who better to ask?'

Dibble studied the man sitting opposite. He had known Harry Crews for more than fifteen years. The slight frame he knew to be wiry, not weak, the lack of inches deceiving in terms of the danger that the man presented to an enemy. For Harry Crews had been the officer commanding 22 SAS in Hereford when he had come over to England on his first exchange training course with seven of his fellow US Navy SEALs back in nineteen seventy three. He had come to respect Harry Crews right from the off and a rapport had developed between them that had seen them keep in intermittent touch over the intervening years. Now he looked into the craggy, lean face, a face that had aged well despite the frightful life that the man had chosen to lead, awaiting a reply.

'Strachan, yes. I knew David Strachan all right. And his brother, Jonathan. Both of them first class of course, no doubt about it. But there was always something dangerous about David. A touch of the killer. You could see it in his eyes now and again. Still, he kept it under control. Marvellous temperament really. A superb officer.' The former SAS chief pursed his lips in thought, before continuing: 'A tragedy, that south Atlantic business, absolute tragedy.'

Dibble and Law looked at each other. Law shrugged.

'Oh, you don't know about that eh? Well of course, it's not the sort of thing that's given to the papers. Just thought that you might have been given the detail in your briefing.'

Dibble smiled at the lightly veiled reference to the clandestine work that Harry Crews obviously knew that he and his partner were engaged in.

'No, Harry,' Dibble said. 'We don't know. Perhaps you could tell us.'

'Not much to tell. Nothing official of course; as you know, I haven't been 'operational' since seventy-eight. Still, down here, one picks up odd snippets of gossip. You know how it is.'

Dibble nodded. Indeed he did know. That was why he had come to the Special Forces Club to try to get some background. When he had spotted Harry Crews alone at the bar earlier on, he had known that he had made the right decision.

'Something about that control that I mentioned back then deserting the poor chap on an op. Rumours about him going a touch psycho, slaughtering to left and right. I imagine that the stories were nine parts exaggeration, as ever, but the way it was told, the one remaining part must have been hellish enough.'

'Go on Harry. Give us whatever detail you have.'

Crews sighed. 'Well, the way its told, Strachan was leading a team at the time of the assault on Wireless Ridge, just before the fall of Stanley. His team was sneaking up on the Argentines from the seaward side of the ridge. They were to hit those trenches and take out the machine guns, you know the drill, make it easy for the main force which was approaching by land.'

Crews hesitated a moment and looked over at Law who was working hard to stifle a yawn.

'Bit dull for you laddie? Are we keeping you past your bedtime?' Crews spat out.

'Christ Harry, lighten up,' Dibble countered, grinning. 'It was only a yawn.'

Crews turned slowly towards him. 'Well, tell your colleague that it might be good manners to pay attention and not behave as though he was having to suffer the senile outpourings of a near-dead relative. Remember, you pair bloody well asked me about this.'

'I'm sorry,' Law said, speaking for the first time. 'I didn't mean any disrespect, truly. Please, continue.'

Crews took a slow sip of his drink. 'Well, alright. Apology accepted. Anyway, when it came time for the off, Strachan was into the trench - using one of those absurd weapons of yours, I believe, the Ingrams. Mac 10 you call it, isn't that right? Apparently, he let off a whole magazine in one burst and cut an Argentine completely in half. Bloody ridiculous weapon. Terrific slaughter by all accounts.'

'There's got to be more than that Harry. I mean, the Ingrams is capable of doing what you say. But that seems none too appalling. It was war, after all.'

'There's more, if you'd just wait. See, what happened next - and this is all gossip mind, can't substantiate any of this - is that Strachan throws down the gun and grabs an Argentine who is scrambling over the parapet to escape. And he takes a knife and decapitates this lad. Just a boy from what they say, a teenager, a conscript. And one of his own troopers sees him there, kneeling in this mess of mud and intestines, holding this head up before his face, and talking to it and laughing at it. What do you make of that?'

Silence for a moment. Then Law said, 'Decapitation. He slit a poor kid's throat with a combat knife, then deliberately decapitated him with it. Is that what you're saying he did?'

There was no disguising the look of revulsion on Law's face. All of them knew that manual decapitation ranked only one degree better than cannibalism. An atrocity.

Crews simply shrugged. 'It's what they say,' he offered. 'His own man had to subdue him - no mean trick, believe me. Strachan was the best and most aggressive I've seen at unarmed combat. The two of them were rescued at sea. The trooper didn't make it though. Hypothermia. Hell of a thing he did, that boy. Getting Strachan out of there. Saved Strachan's life, no doubt about it. And the Regiment's reputation.'

'That's a hell of an image you set before us, Harry,' Dibble said. 'Kneeling in mud and guts like that, grinning at a decapitated head. Do you believe that it's true?'

Crews paused for a moment to think. 'I don't know,' he replied, cautiously. 'But the man who told me was the Major running the investigation that followed. And he would have spoken to the two remaining men in the team. And they would have seen it first hand. Certainly I trust my source, so what can I say?'

Dibble shook his head slowly, as if in disbelief. Law sat still and silent.

'It meant the end for him with the Regiment,' Crews continued. 'Shipped back to blighty to convalesce and then out. Now of course, there's this nasty business in France. Shocking really, though I suppose the world's none the worse for the loss of a few Frogs.'

Law laughed, spluttering out the beer that he was drinking.

'Shit, Harry,' Dibble managed to say, suppressing his own laughter, 'Napoleon's been long dead, you know. The French are your allies now, or haven't you been told?'

'*Your* allies, maybe. Or so you might want to imagine. You Yanks have never been good judges of character. You'll wake up with a knife between your shoulder blades one morning, see if you don't.'

Dibble shook his head. 'So what do you say Harry? Could he have done it?'

Harry Crews' face set hard at the question, his eyes glinting like blue ice chips through the gloom. The humour was gone.

'Could he have done it?' He repeated coldly. 'You were a SEAL, you know your training, your capabilities. Could *you* have done it?'

Dibble looked into the ice-eyes, saying nothing.

'You know you could,' Crews said, saving Dibble from the embarrassment of having to answer. 'The question is, *would* he have done it? Why? There has to have been a motive.'

'Could he have gone psycho again?' Law asked.

Crews turned to regard the questioner. 'Maybe,' he replied. 'It's possible. But I don't believe it. You are free to believe whatever you wish. I don't suppose we'll ever find out.'

Law nodded silently. What else was there to say? The three men sat quietly for a few moments.

'You'll have to excuse me for a moment, gentlemen,' Crews finally said.'Duty beckons.' He stood and winked conspiratorially at the two Americans, then made his way over towards the men's room.

'So, what do you think?' asked Law.

Dibble rubbed his chin, pensively. 'I think that Harry Crews rates our David Strachan very highly. Must have been one cool fucker. Crews don't spread his admiration round like confetti.'

'Damn!' said Law. 'What the fuck makes Redbridge think that this guy's still alive, I wonder? And what the fuck does he want with him? You know, even if he is alive and even if he makes his way back here to England - and fuck only knows why he'd be so dumb - we've got no chance of ever finding him. Shit, what a waste of fucking time.'

'Maybe,' Dibble mused, 'Maybe.'

There was certainly something strange about all of this, something that didn't quite gel. If only he could put the pieces together in his mind. Still, for all that this looked to be a no-win operation, he would put the feelers out for this Strachan, and if Strachan *did* come back to the UK, he would find him. There was a deep mystery surrounding this whole affair. And if there was one thing that Dibble hated, it was a mystery.

Chapter 33

THE NIGHT WAS cooler than it had been for some time. The early evening had been punctuated by summer showers, which had cleansed the air. Now the clouds had dispersed, leaving the streets to cool, watched over by the bright stars of the dark sky.

Strachan and Lyndon sat quietly at a roadside café in the centre of town, two anonymous tourists relaxing with a bottle of wine to celebrate the end of another wonderful day. Strachan looked at his watch.

'We'd better make a move,' he said.

Lyndon sipped the last of his red wine and set the glass down on the slightly rickety table. He looked at his own watch.

'Yeah, I guess so. It wouldn't do to keep these guys waiting. Let's go.'

He stood, dipping into his trouser pockets and pulled out a few crumpled banknotes, which he tucked under the base of the empty bottle, then set off sauntering casually down the narrow boulevard.

Strachan picked up the holdall containing his belongings, which he had recovered from the Hotel Petit Louvre. As he sauntered casually beside Lyndon, he reflected on how easily things had gone up to this point.

He had anticipated some confrontation with the concierge of the hotel. At least an attempt at a final shakedown. Yet surprisingly, the fat bald man had not been in his usual place, behind the lobby counter and the old, moustachioed woman who sat in his place had not even bothered to look up from her magazine as he had tossed the room key over to her. Perhaps she was deaf, or dead, Strachan thought, as the large key had clattered across the Formica counter top. Frankly, he couldn't have given a flying fuck either way and he had stepped jauntily out onto the street where Lyndon had stood waiting for him.

By then, the late afternoon had been turning to early evening and both he and Lyndon had been feeling hungry. They had eaten well at an expensive waterfront restaurant, leaving plenty of time for the food to digest before they had to make their rendezvous.

The envelope which they had brought with them from the mountain villa earlier in the day contained instructions as to the time and place of the meet. Strachan understood that they would be contacted at the RV by an intermediary and then told the arrangements for getting them out of the country. It was a simple arrangement that would distance them from the Great Man who ran things from the comfort of his mountain retreat should they encounter any unforeseen problems. Strachan was grateful for the professionalism of the set up. Now, the hold-all slung over his shoulder, he strode after Lyndon, hungry to get this show on the road…

MARSEILLES… 9.22pm

No-one, not even the underworld lookouts and informants who peopled the night-time streets of the Old Quarter of Marseilles, would have been able to swear that they had noticed the arrival of the stranger on the streets, which after dark were almost exclusively theirs. It was as if he had materialised among them, unannounced and unnoticed. And now that he was there, there was nothing remarkable about his presence, nothing worthy of so much as a second glance. Because although he was not one of them, his dress, his demeanour - everything about him was… just right. And *that* was no accident, no matter of luck or mere chance. It was a skill that Andrei Gavrilov had perfected and took great pride in.

He had arrived in Marseilles in the early evening and from the very first he had made for the Old Quarter. It had been a logical move. He was playing a hunch - an educated hunch admittedly but a hunch nonetheless - that his quarry would be in the city at all. Christ, there were so many uncertainties about this job, but his instinct told him that if there *were* a solution to

251

the problem, it would be found here. Increasingly, he was getting a gut feeling that told him that he was on the right track.

It had not been easy at first; he had had to be careful with his approaches, had had to win confidences in the cafes and bars without arousing suspicion. But he had filled his pockets with currency and that had helped. Slowly, discreetly, he had coaxed whispered scraps from the flotsom and jetsom of the area, their tongues working freer as the darkness closed in and the Absinthe poured down greedy throats.

Then just a few minutes ago, there had been a man in a grimy little bar, a dingy and dangerous place, who had intimated that there was something that he might be able to tell... for a price. Gavrilov would normally have been suspicious of this sort of character; unintelligent, dirty and worst of all, a drunk. But he did not have the luxury of time to spare and the man, who reeked of stale fish and the sea, had been quiet and unusually certain of himself despite the alcoholic haze in which it seemed that he must permanently exist.

There was a back door to the bar, which led out into a pitch-black alleyway. The man would sell his information there, away from prying eyes. He had learned over the years that it payed to be cautious. And discreet. So Gavrilov had followed him out into the darkness, his silenced automatic readily accessible, to purchase the words of this creature.

'Now monsieur, let us be quick about this,' the creature whispered, his face pressed close to Gavrilov's, a foul stench of bad teeth and cigarette smoke on his breath. 'I have no idea just whom it is you seek, but for certain, I know of something which will interest you. But first...' he left the sentence open. It was obvious that he wanted to see his fee up front.

'Of course,' Gavrilov said, 'Will one thousand francs cover it?'

'Fifteen hundred would be better,' hissed the odious breath. Gavrilov hesitated momentarily. It would not profit him to seem to be too eager. Finally he said 'Fifteen hundred then,' this time removing all trace of charm from his voice. Reaching into his pocket, he pulled out two old notes and pressed them into the calloused hand of the old fisherman. 'Make it worth my while.'

'Oh, it will be, it will be,' hissed the foul breath.

'Get on with it,' Gavrilov said simply.

'Right. There has been a passage arranged tonight, sailing at eleven o'clock. The destination is Sicily monsieur. The cargo, human.' The old man paused wanting to give drama to the little that he knew. It was always best to retain the upper hand for as long as possible in situations like this. Maybe there was more money to be prised from what he knew.

'There had better be more,' said Gavrilov quietly.

The voice was calm, but even in his drunken state, the old man could feel the violence that lay behind the words. His resolve crumbled.

'Yes monsieur, of course. I was just pausing for breath. My lungs you see. They are not what they once were.' He looked up into Gavrilov's eyes, hoping for sympathy, but found only cold fire. Quickly, he turned his head to look away.

'One of the passengers is a stranger here. He arrived only yesterday. It is said that he has paid a veritable ransom for his passage. An Englishman it is said.'

Gavrilov's face betrayed no sign of emotion, but inside, the adrenaline was pumping through his veins. This had to be Strachan. *Had* to be. It was too much of a coincidence to be otherwise.

'What else?' he asked, his words studied, matter of fact.

'Else? There is nothing else, monsieur. It is all that I know.'

Gavrilov's strong hand shot up, squeezing the old man by the throat.

'What else?' he asked again, in the same modulated tone.

The old man wheezed, coughed a few times. Gavrilov relaxed his grip slightly.

'Alright, alright,' gasped the old man. 'The boat. I can give you the name of the boat. But that's all. I swear to you, that's all monsieur.'

The old man's eyes glistened with tears and an acrid smell of urine wafted up to invade Gavrilov's nostrils. In his fear and drunkenness, the old man had pissed his pants.

'Well?'

'*L'Enfant*, monsieur. The boat is called *L'Enfant*. You will have no trouble in finding her. It is the truth. I swear it.'

It was the truth. Gavrilov could feel it. He had first hand

experience of interrogation. He was well able to sort the wheat from the chaff. And this was most definitely wheat. He knew that success was possible. He was going to achieve what had seemed to be the *impossible*. But he could not afford to leave any loose ends. The old man was frightened enough of him here and now, but how would he be when left to his own devices? This was an alien environment and he was surrounded by enemies. No time for taking risks. He reached into the waistband of his pants and pulled out the automatic. The old man never saw it as it spat out its bullet - sssshhhup - up under his chin and into his brain, blowing a huge patch of skull away as it exited through the top of his head.

There was a large waste bin on wheels at the far end of the alley and Gavrilov picked the old man up - careful to avoid the blood and spilling brains - and carried him over to it. He opened the lid and tipped the old man in, covering the body with assorted refuse. It wouldn't remain hidden for long, but he figured that it would give him until morning. He would be well out of the way by then, no matter what happened later that night. Straightening his clothes, he made his way casually out of the alley and into the mainstream of the nightlife of the area. He hadn't bothered to recover the fifteen hundred francs, which still remained clutched tight in the fist of the dead old fisherman.

MARSEILLES... 9.30pm

In contrast, they had been noticed, these two, but had been paid little heed. Night creatures they had seemed and rightly so. Especially the thin one, who wore the olive-drab trench coat down to his calves. A wide brimmed hat obscured most of his face and he followed at the heels of the other one like a puppy following its master. The other one was dressed more conventionally; a navy sweater with a ship's wheel motif on the left breast, faded Levi's and Adidas trainers. He was dark as the night and although not attracting attention to himself, he was noted by the people whom he occasioned to pass in the busy streets because as he approached, not one of them could look him in the eye. There was a forcefulness about him that

254

cried out: Beware!

This odd couple ducked into various bars and cafes, rarely stopping to purchase drinks, asking only discreet questions of the inhabitants of the shadows. Their luck was mixed, mostly bad, but recently they had had a stroke of good fortune. A name, an address. They were men in a hurry, this silent skeleton and his powerful master, as they increased their pace to reach where their informant had told them that their treasure was to be found.

The Hotel Petit Louvre. The Templar could feel that he was closing in now. He turned to the Torquemada, indicating with an irritated flick of his head that he wanted the creature to hurry, to keep up with the pace. He was becoming impatient to meet with this Strachan. Tonight at last he would. He knew that he would.

MARSEILLES... 9.45pm

'Monsieur, you have something for me, I believe?'

Strachan spun round to face the voice and for a moment was genuinely startled. He was sitting at a roadside table in the centre of town, as per his instructions. Lyndon had gone inside the café to use the john.

'Why look so surprised monsieur? Even small hotel owners have the right to earn a little supplementary income, no?' The fat, greasy owner of the Hotel Petit Louvre leaned closer and tapped his nose conspiratorially, whispering: 'And for cash, no questions asked, eh?' The sweating face split in a grin and a low, dirty chuckle bubbled from the jowly throat.

Strachan did not laugh in return. His face was set hard. He had never liked this child-molesting creature and was unhappy at having to deal with the greaseball now. But events were out of his hands. The Great Man in the mountain must trust this detritus, at least to be a messenger. He would just have to go along with things. He handed the envelope over.

'Here. Let's get on with it. And no small talk, eh?'

'As you wish, monsieur,' replied the fat creature, sitting at the table. The grin had left his face as he dipped into the pocket of his grubby yellow jacket.

255

Under the table, Strachan's hand tightened around the butt of his Beretta, returned to him by the driver of the Jaguar that had brought him down from the mountain villa.

'Ah, there is no need for alarm, monsieur,' whispered the fat man. 'Just a precaution of my own. I find it pays to be vigilant.'

Carefully, he pulled a small wooden box from his pocket and set it down on the table. He opened the lid, and took out a small vial of colourless liquid and a teat-pipette.

'Things're starting to move I see.' Lyndon had returned and sat himself down at the table. He didn't bother to ask for an introduction. 'What the fuck's he doing?' he asked Strachan, quizzically.

'It's a question of trust,' Strachan whispered back. 'You see, *he* doesn't trust *us*.'

The fat man ignored the comments and continued with his work. Using the pipette, he squeezed a few drops of the colourless liquid onto the top left hand corner of the envelope that Strachan had handed to him. Using a paper tissue, he smeared the liquid into the paper. His face was a study of concentration for a few seconds and then all of a sudden, the smile returned.

'Voila, gentlemen!' he beamed. 'All is as it should be.' He held the envelope out for them both to see. A small picture of a yellow dragonhead appeared where the chemicals had reacted with others impregnated into the paper.

'Now,' the fat man continued, leaning forward, 'You must listen carefully, for this next cannot be committed to paper.' He paused here, looking from Strachan to Lyndon, then back again, as if making sure that they understood. Satisfied, he continued: 'You must find your way to a boat on the marina called *'L'Enfant'*. 11.30 sharp you must be there. Ask for the captain and say, 'the oranges are white'.'

Strachan and Lyndon exchanged incredulous glances. The fat man simply shrugged and grinned apologetically.

'All very - how you say? - James Bond, I know, but simple code phrases like this, created on the spur of the moment, are almost impossible to crack. But then, you will know this messieurs. Now I must go. I have other business to attend to.' And he rose from the table, winking at Strachan.

Lyndon clapped Strachan on the shoulder. 'Well, this is it buddy. In a couple of hours, we're going to be gone, away, safe.'

Strachan had never been one for taking things for granted. 'I'll believe it when it happens,' he said simply. 'Now let's get the fuck out of here. I'm getting jumpy just sitting around.'

Chapter 34

GAVRILOV HAD HAD no trouble in finding *L'Enfant*. She sat low and sleek, raked back from the water, amid other such beauties tethered to a modern concrete jetty. Not the grimy old fishing smack that he had half expected, this boat was true class.

A forty-foot power cruiser; white GRP moulded hull with rear exhausts that indicated twin inboard diesels. Gavrilov would not have been surprised to find that she was capable of in excess of fifty-five knots flat out. It must have cost Strachan a small fortune to arrange a passage out on such a beast, Gavrilov mused. Such a pity that he would never live to enjoy the ride.

Now, how best to achieve his objective? It was not going to be easy; the marina was brightly lit and open and could be approached from many directions. Hardly surprising really. Who in their right mind would moor an expensive yacht in some aquatic back alley with a Victorian lighting system? No, the rich demanded at least the barest minimum of security and this obvious design feature was of greater value than all the more sophisticated electronic alarm systems put together.

The only certainty was that Strachan would have to walk along the narrow jetty to board *L'Enfant*. Here, in such an open environment, gunplay was out of the question. Even if a silencer was used, there would be too many people around to see, too much of a stir caused. No, this would require something a little subtler. Fortunately, he had the tool for the job. It was Bulgarian made and a device that he always carried with him on missions that might involve assassination in the west. A pair of binoculars, of which only the right eyepiece was genuine. Through this could be seen a true magnification, centred on a targeting cross-hair. The left eyepiece was lensed at the exposed end and would reflect light so as not to arouse suspicion, but through its centre ran a narrow barrel, no more than a millimetre in diameter. Through this barrel could be fired a gas-propelled steel dart, more of a needle really. Coated with a fast acting lethal poison, it could embed itself fully and initially undetectably, in the flesh of the target over a range of up to twenty metres in still conditions. It was powered by a built-in CO_2 cylinder and was discharged by pressing a button situated near the focussing ring. It would be perfect in these conditions here tonight.

There were many people milling about the marina and the jetties this evening, mostly tourists wandering around to see how the other half lived. He would not be noticed as he waited for his prey to near. It would only be a matter of time. In fact, he would not even bother to wait in the little alleyway, the one dark passage leading down to the open area of the waterfront. He would be less conspicuous out here in the open. He looked at his Seiko watch. It was 10.55pm.

MARSEILLES... HOTEL PETIT LOUVRE... 10.55pm

In the lobby of the Hotel Petit Louvre, the fat man had once again resumed his position behind the lacklustre Formica counter. His hideous hag of an alcoholic wife had been shooed away, back to the unkempt suite of first floor rooms that they called home, to watch television and pickle her insides with yet more Pernod. She was uncomplaining because she had long ago forgotten just what it was that she had to complain about.

Two thousand francs. That had been a good half hour's toil and no mistake. He had been surprised in a way, to find that his new guest had been so quick to arrange a passage out. At first, he had thought of attempting a little blackmail, just to try to prise a little extra from an obviously desperate man. But the American had been with him. There were whispers around the Old Quarter about that one; and even if the whispers were the usual mix of myth and exaggeration, there would be enough truth behind it all to make him a man worth steering clear of.

Besides, this could be the start of a new beginning. It had been many months since he had received any such work from this exhalted source. He had not known just what he had done to put him so out of favour. He had come to count on the money that he had been earning for providing little services such as he had done tonight. Then there was the lack of prestige within the community that the withdrawal of his high patronage had occasioned. Really, that had been the hardest of all to bear. Perhaps this night's work really did herald a new beginning. Perhaps he was back in favour once again.

He grinned to himself at the thought as he placed the little plastic bag that he had purchased from a street corner acquaintance on the counter before him. It contained ten grammes of heroin; enough to satisfy his depraved lusts for nearly three weeks. A month if he cut it carefully.

Footsteps clicking over the linoleum caused him to look up sharply. But he relaxed almost immediately. He was expecting this visitor. A small thin girl with red hair, cropped short in a crew cut. She was seventeen, but looked much younger. Yet her eyes were old before their time.

'Ah, Madeleine. Come to see Uncle have you? That's good, that's good,' chuckled the fat man. He beckoned her towards him. 'Come on, come on. Let Uncle get a look at you. Uncle has something you want, no?'

The smile on the fat man's face would have sickened a dog. He was almost drooling at the thought of what he would do with this tortured young body. He hoped that she had shaved off her pubic hair like he had told her to. He did so like that in a young girl. It made her feel so…why, young. He licked his lips involuntarily, dangling the bag of smack before his sweating face like a lure. And silently, the trembling girl squeezed behind the counter with him.

Immediately, he thrust his rough hand between her legs beneath her cotton dress, grunting lasciviously. She was smooth there, just as he had asked. She parted her legs slightly at the insistence of his pawing and he ran his fingers with surprising gentleness along the length of her slit. He was licking his lips again, closing his eyes, the better to enjoy.

He wouldn't cut the smack roughly tonight. He would be generous, give her a smooth ride. After all, wasn't she smooth for him? He pulled his hand from beneath her dress, his eyes still closed in fantasy, and held the fingers up to his nose, savouring the raw, womanly smell, before sliding them in his mouth. A taste of what was to come. When eventually he did droop open his heavy lids, he gave an audible gasp and jumped back, startled. Two men were standing before the counter. They had entered unheard. Unbelievable given the quiet of the hotel lobby and the uncarpeted floor. Yet here they were. Such men could only spell danger.

Within a split second, the fat man had regained his wits. His first concern was for the small plastic bag, which he had left in full view on the counter top. Usually, why not? His clientele would be hardly likely to protest. Half of them used the stuff themselves anyway; prostitutes who rented rooms by the half hour to pay for their habit. Those not yet haggard enough to have that source of revenue denied them by the forces of the market.

Quickly, he assumed the best welcoming smile of which he was capable, and said: 'Oh my, gentlemen, you quite startled me. How can I be of service to you? A room perhaps?'

All the while, his left hand was slowly reaching across the counter top, sneaking towards the bag containing the seductive narcotic. Best to get that out of sight as unobtrusively as possible, *whoever* these two were.

The shorter of the two strangers – although he could only have been a shade under six feet himself – the one with the burning black eyes, pinned him rigid with his gaze, the way a python holds a rabbit. The other, the tall, gangling one, twitched nervously in the background. A wide brimmed hat shaded this ones eyes, but the fat man could instinctively feel that they returned more and more to rest on the dope-lethargic teenager who stood idly to his right. Well that was alright; if the girl was what they were after, they could have her. There were many more like her. In fact, his scheming mind thought instantly, perhaps there would be profit to be had from such supply. Yet for the moment, still he inched his fingers over towards the small bag of heroin. He was by no means sure of his ground.

The short one, with the coal eyes, had caught the drift of his companion's agitation. And the Templar was reminded of another girl whom he had come across in not dissimilar circumstances, an age ago. In his psyche, he could feel the spirit still trapped within the rotting shell of the Torquemada's body, horrified, crying out with desire to rescue the girl. The Templar felt himself for the first time in decades, genuinely surprised to feel such a reaction. Perhaps it was a sign that his Torquemada was truly coming to penitence at last. From somewhere, from nowhere, a gleaming knife, with a short stiletto blade had found it's way into the Templar's right hand.

'No room, monsieur,' he said, bringing his knife hand up high and fast, stabbing the blade down into the creeping hand of the fat man so savagely that it embedded itself into the Formica counter below. In the same instant, the Torquemada had leapt across the counter, the light gabardine coat-tails flapping like bats wings, and wedged a hand of slightly liquifying grey flesh into the mouth that would otherwise have squealed with shock, terror and surprise.

As it was, the best that the fat man could manage was a muffled 'Mmyyaagghh!' and then he was limp, sobbing through the foul tasting flesh of the hand that was clamped over and partly in his slobbering mouth. From behind, the Torquemada held onto the quivering corpulent form with steel-strength. The Templar could feel the creature's skipping, flickering concern for the girl.

She had remained unmoved by what was happening and watched, her dope ravaged mind, years beyond salvage, uncaring and unconcerned. Her empty eyes were looking to the Templar though, as though she was awaiting instruction. For a moment, he could glimpse the spark of a tortured soul down there, deep in those empty pools. But only for a moment. Then it was gone. He flicked his head, indicating the doorway behind him.

'Why don't you go home,' he said, his voice gentle as a saint's. For a second, her mouth flickered with the semblance of a smile, as though she had recognised, for the first time in an age, that someone was concerned - however slightly - for her welfare. She slid from behind the counter, eyes dead, looking straight ahead, straightening her ruffled dress with her tiny white hands. Wordlessly, she stepped over to the Templar and kissed him on the cheek, before casually, without so much as a glance over her shoulder at the absurd scene she was leaving, walking out of the hotel door to be swallowed whole by the night.

'We would like to talk to you, monsieur.'

The Templar whispered the words, so that they floated across to the fat man like a caress, though the reaction of his eyes left no doubt that they had hit him like a slap. In that moment, he knew that he was doomed.

'Perhaps you have an office monsieur, where we can be more private...?'

The Torquemada had to support the obese frame now, as the fat man was close to fainting away from the pain and the fear. But the coal-dark eyes which held the fat man's own, reached deep inside to deny him the peace of unconsciousness...

MARSEILLES... THE WATERFRONT... 10.05pm

'The marina's down there.'

Lyndon indicated with a flourishing wave of his right arm towards the pool of bright light and activity that was the waterfront. He looked at his watch. 'We've still got twenty five minutes yet. Might as well grab a last drink. We don't want to get there too early. Could upset their preparations. We'll only get in the way.'

Strachan shot him an irritable glance. 'We've got to find the fucker yet. Remember?'

He was itching to be gone. Uncharacteristically, he was starting to feel a little nervy. The strain of the last few days as a fugitive were beginning to tell. And escape was so close to hand. He could feel the sweat on his brow, despite the cool of the evening.

If Lyndon sensed his irritability, he paid it no attention. 'Hey bubba, relax,' he said. 'I *know* this boat. I've sailed in her before. I'll take us right to her, never fear.'

For a moment, Strachan's mind threw him a picture of this ex-SEAL crouched low on the foredeck of a fast boat out on the ocean, a low silhouette, almost invisible in the dark of the night. What cargoes would he have been employed to guard? Why would any underground organisation hire the peculiar skills of a US Navy SEAL? But he knew the answer. Narcotics. What else would it be? Still, it was none of his business. Lyndon was fast becoming a friend. Why should it concern him? It didn't; he wouldn't let it.

'OK, just one drink then. But Christ, I'll feel a shit-load better when we're out on the open sea.'

Lyndon clapped him on the back, the happy, carefree smile creased wide on his face once more. 'So will I buddy, believe me. So will I…'

THE WATERFRONT… 10.10pm

Down on the waterfront, the Spetznaz assassin sat strategically at a table out in front of one of the many cafes. An untouched glass of white rum and ice sat on the table beside him. In his lap was a set of powerful looking binoculars. No one passed across the marina front without coming under his scrutiny. He was confident that the description of his target would be accurate. And that man had not yet materialised. But he would. Oh yes, ever so shortly, he would…

THE HOTEL PETIT LOUVRE… 10.10pm

The Templar sat cross-legged on a large, battered wooden desk of uncertain ancestry. Directly facing him, sitting upright and stiff, though without bonds to fix him, was the fat hotel owner. They were in the back office of the Hotel Petit Louvre. The Hotel had been closed up so that they could have their little chat in private. To one side of the fat man stood the Torquemada, still wearing the long coat and wide brimmed hat, hopping nervously from one foot to the other. They had remained like this, a silent and surreal tableau, for over a minute. The fat man had started to perspire wildly. The Templar's eyes bored into him for a moment and then he spoke.

'You have a guest,' he said quietly, though the words spat viciously in the quiet tension of the room. The fat man lurched back visibly with the shock of them and beside him, the Torquemada tensed, ready to pounce at any attempt to escape.

But the Templar's cold eyes held the fat man. Kept him fast to his seat. He sat quiet, waiting, demanding a reply.

'I have many guests,' the fat man blustered. 'They come, they go. Some are regular, some just passing through. You must be more specific monsieur, I can -"

He was silenced by the Templar's upraised hand.

'David Strachan. He is staying here. He arrived yesterday.' A statement, not a question.

'No monsieur, you are mistaken. I assure you I would remember such a name.' That much was true. No one of that name had registered with him to his certain knowledge. But there had been the man yesterday, the stranger, the one whom he had left just that evening, the one who had solid connections and even now was readying himself to leave the country. With the help of the most powerful patronage on the coast. There could be no doubt that this man was the object of his current discomfort. Then suddenly it hit him. That name. Good God, it had been in all the papers. A sensation! David Strachan was the name of the man who had devastated the Stopyra estate. The papers had said that he was dead, that he had sacrificed himself with his boat in the middle of the ocean. It was a great mystery. But not any more. Strachan was alive, he knew it, had seen him. And now Strachan had powerful friends. He would have to be careful. It would take all his wits to talk his way out of this one. His face fell suddenly quizzical.

'But monsieur, of course I have heard of this name. Everybody has. The papers have been full of it. Such terrible violence, such a tragedy, such a -'

Once more the raised hand cut him short.

'Enough of this drivel,' the quiet voice said. 'I do not have the time. You have information about this man. I can feel it within you.'

The fat man squirmed in his seat and looked round sharply at the Torquemada, who was still hopping from foot to foot, but was now beginning to whimper childishly. For the first time, the fat man caught a glimpse of the face beneath the wide brim of the hat and immediately looked away. He wanted to be sick, but didn't dare. He thought that he really could *feel* the Templar reaching deep inside of him, pulling out the truth. No, that was nonsense, the stuff of children's nightmares. But all the same, when he raised his head once more, those terrifying black eyes were still there, torturing his soul.

'Time runs short, too short for me to toy with you, so I will be blunt. The sands of your miserable life are running out, the time measured in minutes rather than the years that you had expected. You *do* have information that could help me. The degree of your co-operation will determine the manner of your end.'

The fat man was numbed by the words, for a few seconds unable to reply. He sat unmoving. Only the heaving of his flabby chest gave any indication of life. So this was it then. He had not expected it so soon, had hoped to avoid it altogether. But he had lived in a shadowy underworld for too long to believe that he had ever had more than a fifty-fifty chance of dying a natural death. That had been the life that he had chosen. For all his vices, he had never been a coward, and even now, while staring it in the face, he was not afraid of death. But could he withstand the final suffering if he were to resist this man? And what purpose would such resistance serve?

'So what then, are my alternatives, monsieur?' the fat man found himself asking. His voice did not waver as he spoke the words. He could have been asking the price of fish.

The Templar could feel the strength coming from deep within the disgusting depravity of the man who sat transfixed before him. For the second time within the space of a few minutes, he found himself surprised by something that the world had thrown at him. He twitched his lips at the corners, the beginnings of a quizzical smile.

'If you deny me, then this...' he said and his dark eyes flicked a signal to the twitching Torquemada. The fat man turned his head to look, was forced to by some horrible fascination.

The Torquemada drew its hands from the depths of the pockets of its trench coat, the flesh visibly grey and liquid, the nails brown and horny talons. The right hand reached up to remove the hat to expose the face to the glare of the room's single, fly-speckled light bulb. The fat man, unable to move, peeled his eyes wide to stare in horror. He wanted to scream, but couldn't, because vomit was belching from his throat and he couldn't stop it. The smell of puke mingled with the Torquemada's stench of decay

266

and danced about the room, touching every corner. The Templar remained unmoved by it. In his day, he had experienced worse.

The Templar had loosened the natural forces that he used to keep the Torquemada's flesh intact, just a little. Not enough to allow it to wither and crumble to the point where the life-force, the spirit which it contained would be free at last, free to seek a new destiny in its struggle to ascend to glory. No, his Torquemada must learn, must come to understand much, before that ecstasy could be allowed. But enough all the same.

The fat man had seen, for the first time in his soon to be curtailed life, the true meaning of horror. Much worse than the foul stench, worse than the talon like claws of the hands, worse than the rotting puss-bubbled skin and the threat of hideous and evil violence, were the twin wells of misery and despair that were the eyes. Oh such eyes. Such hopelessness.

The fat man coughed, spluttered, spraying milky vomit out before him. Beside him, the Torquemada was kneeling. It had recovered its hat and had fixed it onto its head. The Templar was strengthening it once more, as well as he was able. The decay was being forced back, the flesh beginning to tighten, losing some of its unnatural discolouration. It reached out its bony fingers and dipped them in the thick vomit of half digested meat and garlic and vegetables that covered the fat man like an apron. It examined the liquid for a moment, sniffing its fingers, then snaked out a broad and blackened tongue, to taste the delicacy. It sighed with delight. It was all that the fat man could do not to heave once again. But instead he looked into the eyes of the Templar.

'Oh, monsieur,' he moaned. 'I will tell you what I know, but spare me…' he wheezed uneasily, coughed again. 'Spare me that…'

'Then speak to me,' the Templar said.

So the fat man told him everything. It took less than a minute, for in reality, he did not know much. But what he did know was vital to the Templar, who uncrossed his legs and lowered himself down from the desk.

'Please, monsieur,' said the fat man, who knew that his time was come and was strangely now unafraid of death itself, 'please make it quick.'

267

The Templar reached over for the bottle of absinthe, which stood half empty on the ancient desk. He poured some of it into the dirty tumbler that sat beside it and tipped in the contents of the small plastic bag which he had picked up from the hotel counter. At first, the fat man was confused, but when the Templar stepped over to the Torquemada and reached inside the overcoat to pull out a sealed plastic packet containing a hypodermic needle and syringe, he began to understand. He was to die as he had lived. Surprisingly, the prospect comforted him.

The Templar drew up the liquid from the tumbler and injected it into an artery in the neck of the fat man. The rush hit him almost instantaneously, as his blood pumped the powerful narcotic into his brain. He was almost enraptured by the thrill of it all. He had never been tempted to so much as a sniff before. But now, somehow, he could begin to see, for the first time, why so many people were prepared to endure so much humiliation in their desire to posses such magic. Oh, it was so beautiful. Wave after wave of orgasmic ecstasy pumped throughout his whole body. The Templar repeated the exercise. Continued to repeat it until the tumbler was empty. Long before then, the fat man had slipped into a blissful unconsciousness. Within minutes, he would be dead. The Templar glanced at his wristwatch. 11.10. The marina was only five minutes or so away. There would be time.

The Torquemada had its face pressed to the chest of the fat man, licking at the thickly spread vomit that covered it. It looked up, sensing the Templar's eyes on it and whimpered. But it knew that it could not resist the call of its master, so pathetically, it rose.

The Templar pulled a handkerchief from his pocket and wiped the sick from around his Torquemada's mouth. 'Come,' he said, 'We have work to do.' And he turned and strode out of the office. The Torquemada glanced longingly at the feast that it was leaving, then with a barely audible whimper, skipped along in its master's wake.

Chapter 35

THE OLD MAN had pulled the drapes across the windows of the living room of his apartment. He had turned out the lights and the room was now heavy with darkness. He had spent a troubled evening. The events of the last two days weighed heavy on his mind. The Shadowmasters. It all came down to them, really. Oh the fools. They had gone beyond all reason this time. They had to be stopped; really, they had to. If he had only stayed within the Brotherhood, if he had not chosen to follow the solitary way of the alchemist... He could have stopped them from within, could have guided them, could have steered them away from their excesses. Oh but could he? Could he really? He had never been a power within the Brotherhood, had never commanded influence. That had been for others; stronger wills, mightier intellects. If only those intellects could have been tempered with wisdom, the way that they had in an age not so long since past. But perhaps he was being too harsh. It had been a turbulent century; change had come in accelerated leaps in ways that had not troubled the world in all of its history past.

The fact was, he had chosen to follow his own path and along it he had discovered the secret of Glory, had become one of those rare men who had found the path across the abyss. He had *chosen*, he thought, not to make the transition, but had used his discovered wisdom to remain with the terrestrial. He now knew that to have been the will of the Secret Chiefs. Had it been they also who had inspired him to write the book, which had become a legend within occult circles, inspired him to adopt that pseudonym, before passing quietly out of circulation, out of reach of all those who had known and loved him? He supposed now that it must have been.

Le Mystere Des Cathedrales by Fulcanelli. He remembered so vividly those cloistered days and nights when the words had flowed from deep within him. The most overt key to the pathways to glory that had been transmitted to man for more than a millennium. A key to all that was Great. Ah, but now he had found a new purpose. The Shadowmasters. It was time to disband the Brotherhood. It shocked him to acknowledge the concept. Disturbed him to feel that he could achieve such a mission. But it had become necessary. They had become megalomaniac; out of control. They had had their day and had served a great purpose in keeping the wisdom alive during centuries that might have seen it buried forever. But he could see, now, that in this Age of Aquarius and beyond, they had become an anachronism.

The world had become more receptive to new ideas; every day, the physicists grew closer to the alchemists in their understanding of the forces that governed the universe. There was no longer the necessity for a United States of Europe as a safe and powerful haven in which the Great Work could flourish. The days of repression were long gone. Each day brought the publication anew of documents that had for centuries been surpressed as dangerous heresy.

Now was a dangerous time, when the meddling of the Shadowmasters in international politics could bring disaster upon a fragile world. If he could only have the strength of the boy to aid him. But the boy was lost, he knew. The soldier was dead, his tortured soul set free on the streets of the Belfast that he had so despaired for. He had felt the loss before he ever got to read about it in the papers.

The Brotherhood had latched on to the boy, had sensed the strength in him, had groomed him to come eventually into the fold. But the boy had been perceptive. He had seen the danger in what they proposed. So they had reached him with intent to destroy. Reached him before *he* had had time to strengthen that raw mind. Such tragedy.

But there was another ally, the one to be sought out. There was only one place to begin that search and he stretched out now on the floor of his apartment, ready to put out the first feelers. Out where time and space had different meanings; where like could seek out like. Out on the Astral Plane.

Lying perfectly still, the old man cleared his mind in preparation. He had done this so many times that it no longer required any overt concentration.

For a few seconds, he felt himself rising, saw his own body beneath him as he drifted, slowly, higher and higher, through the ceiling, out above the roof, up into the star-filled sky. And then, in an instant so infinitesimal as to be beyond time, he was gone.

Out now, on the Astral. He allowed his essence to drift with the fast, smooth flowing currents of force which coursed in perfect symmetry, a network of living energy which supplied the entire universe with what it needed to prevent a withering decay.

He was carried fast, directionless, as his spirit began to concentrate and tried to focus in on the aura that he was seeking. How much simpler the task would be if this ally was also here, meditating along the astral. But he could not count on it. All he knew was that he had sensed great wisdom and strength in this prospective ally and such a complete wisdom would have a powerful aura to lock in to, even when suborned to the hideousness of consciousness. He was moving fast, carried on a pulse of power. His concentration was becoming absolute. It was time to let his instinct take over.

Suddenly right, he branched, joining another swiftly flowing energy field, a warm and sensuous power that tingled silver stars throughout his soul. It was wonderful and he allowed himself to drift along in a rhapsody of enchantment.

Then left, into another channel. Then right again, staying with this new one for some distance, then right again. His instinct had complete command, searching, feeling out the aura that he so desperately needed to contact.

All around, he could sense the colours. The swirling reds and yellows, the pale blues and purples. The occasional shimmering of silver stardust that sent ripples of pleasure through him as he passed by. Ah, such unbridled ecstasy. And all the time, his finely honed instinct probed and sensed, ever searching, feeling out for the first hint of what it was looking for.

Then at last there was something. He could feel it. Faint and in the distance, but definite and unmistakable. Left, into another power field, then down. Almost vertically down…

MARSEILLES… 10.25pm

'So here we are, bud; the waterfront. And down on that jetty over there -' Lyndon shot out an arm to point at the narrow concrete walkway '- is our ticket to ride.'

Strachan glanced in the direction of the outstretched arm. 'Fine. But let's stay cool, okay? We're nearly home and dry, so let's just stay inconspicuous and get the fuck out of here. Come on.'

He ambled casually, hands in pockets, towards the jetty that Lyndon had indicated, looking like any one of the hundreds of evening holiday makers who milled around the waterfront cafes. Lyndon strode after him.

'Sometimes boy,' he whispered under his breath, 'I get the feeling that you must have had your fun-gland removed.'

If Strachan heard, he said nothing.

Sitting at his table, his drink still untouched by his side, Gavrilov had seen the two men arrive on the waterfront. Even now, he had the binoculars up to his eyes, the targeting scope zeroed on the leading man of the pair.

God, this was him. This was Strachan. The description had been accurate. Too accurate for this to be a mistake. He had never before been in possession of such complete intelligence. Someone was to be commended for this. The detail fit, even down to the slightly crooked twist to the broken nose and the degree of the suntan.

Even so, he would need to be more certain, would need, in fact, to be a hundred percent, before he dared to make his move. For there could only be one shot at this. The man was standing, listening to his companion, who pointed to the jetty where he knew *L'Enfant* to be moored. His stomach tingled with the excitement of the coming action. The carriage, the gait, the bearing. A powerful confidence lay barely suppressed beneath this affectedly casual display. A soldier. A colleague. A peer, Gavrilov supposed. He had long held a healthy respect for the British soldiers who came out of the town called Hereford. How fortunate it was that the British saw fit to raise but one truncated regiment of such men. Fortunate for their foes, that was.

For the briefest of moments he felt a pang of despair at what he was about to do. How splendid it would be to take this man to one side, to get drunk in a bar somewhere and discuss the business of soldiering. What pleasure there would be in that for two such as they. But the moment was an aberration and passed as quickly as it had arrived. He had a job to do and he was a professional. He would complete his task and then melt into the night. Within forty-eight hours he would be back in Moscow. Then, perhaps, he could enjoy the R&R, which he knew he had rightly earned.

Now, he could see, Strachan was beginning to move, down towards the jetty. Once he stepped onto the concrete walkway, he would be in range and the sighting would be confirmed, one hundred percent - although in his own mind, he was certain already. He kept the targeting scope zeroed on Strachan's exposed neck as his finger slid over to cover the firing button. He had not noticed two figures that had appeared on the waterfront and stood no more than five metres from him, scanning the brightly lit area and in particular, the massed ranks of boats that bobbed inconspicuously at their moorings. Yet *had* he noticed them, he would certainly have registered a feeling of unease at the arrival of the pair; the lanky, nervous one who wore a raincoat and hat in the heat of the Riveria summer and his powerful looking companion with the compellingly fierce dark eyes. But his mind was concentrated on the job at hand. In these moments before the action, he would not have noticed if a Martian had sat at his table and sipped at his drink.

IN AND OUT OF THE ASTRAL... NO TIME

Down, down flashed the old man's essence at a speed that made nonsense of the concept that trans-light speed was unattainable. He was out of the astral and could see the earth growing large beneath him. The stars, no longer pinpoints of silver but flashing lines of ancient light, rushed by.

Then he was slowing, coming through the atmosphere, which offered no friction to the pure energy that was his astral essence. His instinct still had command, was dragging him towards the aura that it had sensed, way out there on the infinite, but he was confused. Could it be? Could it really have been true, what he had felt out there? Surely not. He would not have thought it possible. But there was such certainty in what he had felt. A presence that he would never forget, one that he had assumed lost to him. It was the boy.

THE JETTY... 10.26pm

Strachan ambled towards the jetty. For a moment, the hairs on the back of his neck began to prickle. It was a warning, a sign of danger that he had come to trust in the past. He stopped suddenly and turned to scan the busy waterfront behind him.

'Something wrong, bro?' Lyndon enquired. He had stopped with Strachan and was also scanning the waterfront, following the track of Strachan's gaze.

'I don't know. Just got a sort of feeling, that's all. Like we're being followed. Or watched.'

Gavrilov had seen them stop, had dropped the binoculars into his lap once more. Could they know of his presence? No, of course not. Strachan was SAS. He was just being careful, checking things out before taking any irrevocable step. It was a professional thing to do. He remained undetected, that was for sure. For he, too, was a professional and nothing about him seemed the least bit suspicious. Of that he was certain.

The Templar had also noticed the two men walking to one of the marine jetties, who had stopped to scan the waterfront crowds. Strachan. There, at last, was Strachan. He would have to move fast and this was going to be tricky. Could he intercept them before they reached the jetty? It would be touch and go, but this was the best chance that he was likely to get. He had set the poison beneath the horny nails of his Torquemada. A simple scratch would do it. Strachan would die, wracked with fever, within twenty-four hours. But what was that? His perception had sensed something extraordinary emanating like a shriek from the target. It was powerful, yet without force, coming from where it was buried deep within Strachan's soul, a soul it was tied to though not wholly part of. Had it been a cry for help, or a warning? He had sensed snatches of both, but the feeling had been stifled all too quickly for him to be certain. What he knew was that he had felt great good in that cry. Moreover, he had felt truth.

Now he was confused. Why *did* the Shadowmasters want this Strachan dead? What supreme threat could he pose to the Glory of the Great Work? He had never asked, it had never been his place to ask. His role was one of obedience. But he knew the answers to his rhetorical questions. His instincts told him. To the Glory, to the Great Work, there was no threat at all. It was to the Shadowmasters themselves that Strachan posed the threat. To their newly perverse ambitions, to their personal corruption. And for that, they wanted this man dead.

Was that what he had come to? After all these centuries, after so much that had been truly great? After suffering all the hideous abomination of material existence, while knowing the true beauty of what waited beyond the Abyss? A cheap assassin. Was that all that he was now to these new Shadowmasters? Well all that would change. He would see to that. He would accept the new ways no longer. It was time to see a new order. But for now, what was he to do?

Strachan and his companion had turned, were walking once more toward the jetty. The Torquemada could sense its master's unease, which compounded its own nervousness. It knew that there was business to complete and ached to be done with it, the quicker to be out of the gaze of a humanity that it now feared as much as it had once despised. The Templar reached out to keep it calm and clutched its wrist...

It was the boy right enough, and yet it was not. He was close enough to see now and physically, it was unmistakably he. But the aura was all wrong. There was the boy's alright, he would recognise it anywhere. But it was smothered, almost buried completely beneath a powerful, vigorous presence, which

275

unmistakably belonged to the body from which it emanated. He needed to know. He had to. He latched into the aura that he knew, melded with it to share its secrets and at once became aware of great beauty and great danger. It was there, close by. Looking back through the people who walked aimlessly across the waterfront, he could see it. The wisdom that he had been seeking. The dark man so powerfully benevolent. And the colours that swam around and about him, of such greatness, such glory, such beauty. He had found his ally. But that which was of the boy screamed its warning out to him, pointed his vision towards the man who sat at the table near to his newly discovered ally. The man who watched them through a set of binoculars. And instantly, he understood. And he knew what he had to do…

Chapter 36

THE TEMPLAR HESITATED. What was he to do? He was torn between his avowed obedience to his masters and the call of his conscience. But which to choose? He must decide quickly. Strachan and his companion were within a few steps of the jetty. Out along there was the boat that would carry them away, to who knew where? To safety.

Then it hit him. An internal scream, so loud, so devastating that it all but rocked him back on his heels. For the briefest part of a second, he was aware of the nearness of the old man. The old man, whom he knew he could trust, whose instincts were in complete synthesis with his own. And traces of the presence that he had sensed deep within the heart of Strachan were there with him, alongside the raw, wild energy that was Strachan himself.

Pictures, vivid and real pulsed through his mind; the obscenity of the ritual that had taken place at the Stopyra chateau, the faces of the two innocents slaughtered that night in the name of the Great Work. The face of Stopyra, a perversion of what a true Shadowmaster should be, in the instant before he had met his end at Strachan's hand. So this was why they wanted Strachan dead.

And strongest of all, was the scream for help, a vivid picture, transmitted live. A danger to Strachan, a danger to the old man, who was melded with the essence of Strachan and would be lost blind in the astral should anything happen to Strachan while he existed in such a fragile state. And the picture showed the source of the danger and the Templar recognised it immediately. It was the man sitting just a few yards away, with the binoculars raised, pointed - aimed - in Strachan's direction. A weapon? Yes. Surely yes. In that instant, his mind was decided. The joy, the truth that he had experienced in his brief proximity to the old man meant more to him, had greater value to him than a blind obedience to these new Shadowmasters. This old man's was a more worthy existence.

Almost imperceptibly, he tugged at the Torquemada, which he still clutched by the wrist and sent it spinning, wildly off balance, into the man with the raised binoculars. There was a clatter and a shriek of shock and frustration as Gavrilov and the scarecrow figure of the Torquemada crashed to the ground in a tangle of chairs and entwined limbs.

'Clumsy fucking bastard,' Gavrilov hissed as he scrambled to disentangle himself from the horrified creature, itself distraught at being such an overt centre of attention and flapping wildly to prevent its hat from parting company with its head.

'Why can't you watch where you're going?'

The Torquemada was terrified that this angry stranger would stare at it, would be drawn in horrified fascination to its face, like all the others. But Gavrilov could not be less concerned. His eyes were riveted on the disappearing back of Strachan as he stepped onto the jetty, flanked by his blond companion.

The binoculars had been sent flying with the fall. They lay on the concrete a few yards away. If he could only reach them, there might still be time. He scrambled out to them, watching as Strachan's legs seemed to buckle for an instant and the blond man had to support him, hold him upright for a second or two. His fingers stretched towards the black plastic casing of his silent weapon. Then a strong hand was fastened around his wrist, a strong arm was pulling him to his feet, even as another hand picked up the binoculars that represented his only chance of success.

'I'm terribly sorry, monsieur,' said a calm and evidently sincere voice. 'I must apologise for my friend. He is recovering from an illness. A serious illness. He is still a little uncertain on his feet. Please forgive him. The fault is all mine. I should have been taking greater care of him. Once again, my sincere apologies.'

Gavrilov had only half-heard the words. He was staring over the shoulder of this goddamn get-in-the-way Good Samaritan at the retreating back of Strachan. He was going to miss out. Strachan was going to get away. Oh fucking hell fire, what an absolute cunting bastard twist of fate. The fire of frustration raged inside him while outwardly he remained calm. It was his training. It was the way to stay alive in his line of work. Now what was this imbecile prattling on about?

'No damage done I hope, monsieur?' the Templar inquired.

Gavrilov raised a lazy hand to wipe his face, held the fingers in front of him to inspect. A brief smear of blood.

'No. No damage done,' he said wearily. 'Just a scratch.'

The Templar smiled. Gavrilov regarded him quizzically for a moment. Was that a smile of relief, of friendship? He could have sworn that there was a hint of triumph in there. No. It must have been his imagination, surely.

The Templar handed back the binoculars. 'Yours I believe, monsieur. There appears to be no damage.'

Gavrilov took them from him. He was feeling hot, a little woozy. 'Thank you,' he said. 'They're quite valuable.'

He was feeling slightly nauseous now, too. Why did this bastard keep staring at him? Such piercing black eyes burning deep into his own.

'You don't appear to be quite well, monsieur. Why don't you come with us? A little wine, a little food. You will soon be yourself again. It's the least we can do.'

The stranger's voice was compelling and to his surprise, Gavrilov found himself saying, 'Yes. Yes, that would be nice.'

Nice, fuck. He had things to do. He had no time to be pissing around with assholes like these. Shit, there was so much to do. There might still be a chance even now, if he could just find a boat for hire. And in this town, with the money he had at his disposal, that surely wouldn't be a problem.

Yet, just the same, he found himself walking along with the strange pair, the powerful man with the compelling eyes and the persuasive voice and his awkward, horrible, thin companion. Walking away from the waterfront, away from Strachan, walking into the one narrow alley, which led away from the sea. His mind was becoming fuzzy at the edges and he was hot. Sooo hot. The sweat dribbled down his forehead as he walked and a word kept throbbing into his brain, keeping pace with his slow steps: Lost. Lost. Lost...

OXFORD...10.30pm

The old man's eyes flickered open where he lay, still flat on the floor of his apartment. His body was wracked with pain; every fibre of every muscle ached in still protest at his first feeble attempt to move. It had been a close one that. Too close. But he had succeeded. That much he knew. He would not have been here, back with his material body had that not been so.

The dark man. He had found him! Had called on him for help in that desperate moment and had not been failed. So he had been right. He would be able to call on the friendship of the powerful companion whose presence had been with him in the Tower. Such power. Such beauty. He had never, never seen anything to compare. The aura had been rich and strong, throbbing with the colours that gave life to the very essence of the universe. They could belong only to the mightiest intellect, the most profound wisdom. He knew that he could be nought but a pale shadow alongside such greatness.

But what of the mystery? It *had* been the boy, there inside the young man. There had been warmth and love as their auras had mingled, an entwining of colours that he remembered from the past when they had ridden the astral together. Weaker, yes, only the tightest centre of the core of that which the boy had been, but locking so completely into the essence of the young man who now played host to this spirit that the young man would experience no shrieking insanity from such a marriage. And that too, *had* been so. He had lived inside there for a brief moment and had known it. He still carried the imprint of that marriage in his being. It was a strangeness that he had never before experienced. There was a mystery to be unravelled here and he would meditate upon it, discover its secret. There had been strength and courage within this young man. Great strength. Great courage. He had felt it immediately, even through the confusion of thoughts and sensations, which ran unchecked through the young man's consciousness like... like so many wild sheep. He had been able to draw upon that strength, had needed

280

to, to project the cry for help that had saved them all.

He tried to move again, to prop himself up on one elbow, but the stiffening pain in his exhausted muscles would not allow it. He had been drained of all but the merest life-sustaining fragments of his bodily energy, energy that he had drawn off to help him project his plea for assistance across the infinite astral to his dark ally. He fell back to the carpet with a sigh and closed his eyes. He would rest where he lay, would restore his energies. The morning would see things better, he was sure.

The boy. The young man. His thoughts lay with them. Could he call upon this young man? Such a raw power. But the boy was there too. The boy would help. With the boy, it would not be so difficult to channel those wild energies, that raw inner strength. And with what was to come, that strength, that energy, would need to be used to the limit.

He had found his allies, had found more than he had dared hope for. The testing times were now to come. How he hoped that they would be up to the task. The world was in great danger and beyond it, the very universe itself. There was a terrifying imbalance gathering its power. He could feel it.

He wanted to stay awake, to think things through, to make plans. But his drained body and wilted spirit would not permit it. Within seconds, he had slipped into the unconsciousness of sleep, the battle lines still to be drawn, waiting for the dawn to bring with it, new hope...

MARSEILLES... THE JETTY... 10.30pm

'Hey, easy now bud, what's wrong?'

Strachan's knees had buckled and Lyndon had caught him in time to prevent him from slumping to the concrete floor of the jetty. He shook his head as though trying to clear his thoughts.

'Don't know,' he replied. His mind was still swimming, gathering itself together again. 'There was just a blinding pain, then everything went blank for a moment. Don't know what it was.'

Lyndon held him by the shoulders at arm's length and looked into Strachan's eyes. 'You look okay now. How'd you feel?'

'Okay. I'm okay. It was just for a second. Fucking hell, let's just get to the boat and out of here, before anything else happens.'

'Well, so long as you're alright.'

Over Strachan's shoulder, Lyndon could see the commotion taking place on the waterfront. Some drunken bastard had fallen over his own feet, he thought. He smiled to himself. He wished that he could stay and witness the outcome. Perhaps there would be a fight. Then he saw the drunken scarecrow's companion and even at that distance, the ex-SEAL could recognise a power present in this dark man. And a warrior's carriage. There would be no fight. Only an idiot would pit himself against such a man. But then, there were plenty of idiots about, he mused. He himself would not have hesitated for a moment, he knew. But something in the back of his mind whispered that with this man, perhaps, that would not be such a good idea. It was, for him, a new thought, an alien thought and he had no idea where it had sprung from. It made him look again at the dark man who was helping another, a well-dressed tourist, to his feet. For a second the dark man glanced in his direction and he shuddered. That was one dangerous motherfucker alright. But he had a schedule to keep.

'Well bud, over there. There she is.' Lyndon indicated with his eyes to where *L'Enfant* lay tethered at her moorings like a white dart ready to skim over the surface of the water.

'Then let's go do it,' Strachan said, now fully recovered.

'After you sir,' Lyndon replied jauntily.

'No no, after you. I insist.'

A woman wearing a heavy pullover and navy blue canvas trousers, her long dark hair tied back in a ponytail, stood on the starboard transom of L'Enfant.

'If you fucks have quite finished, I've got a schedule to keep,' she called out, the harshness of the words unable to disguise the sexy lilt of her voice.

Strachan and Lyndon exchanged bemused glances. 'Well you'd better call up the skipper then, cos we've got a message for his ears only.' Lyndon replied.

The woman's face, though girlishly pretty, was set hard. She did not smile.

'You can fuck that cloak and dagger shit. I *am* the skipper. Now, hurry the fuck up and come aboard. I want to get the fuck out of here before dawn, if you two heroes don't mind?'

'Yes ma'am,' Strachan said, saluting as he stepped onto the aft deck. The woman looked down her nose at him as though he was something she had just scraped off her sea-boots. Lyndon followed him, saluting without saying a word.

The woman pushed roughly past them and clambered into the raised cockpit.

'Get below, assholes,' she hissed. 'We're moving out in five minutes.'

Strachan looked at Lyndon 'Hellfire, man,' he said. 'That's class. Pure class.'

Lyndon looked at her back as she bent over a chart spread over the cockpit control panel. 'Yeah, that's class alright,' he said admiringly. 'You could use her shit for toothpaste.'

Strachan roared with laughter but the sound was lost as the twin diesels burst into life, sending a shudder through the length of the boat. On the jetty, a silent crewman was uncoupling the water and electricity supplies prior to casting off. Strachan and Lyndon went below decks, past the navigation chart table and radio command area, into the for'ard saloon. Strachan just had time to light a cigarette before the throttles were pushed forward and the powerful boat eased its way out of the harbour and into the open waters of the dark Mediterranean.

Chapter 37

HENRI ST CLAIR paced hurriedly and uneasily about his bedchamber. His hands were clenched behind his back and he was deep in thought. What to do? What to do? It was all getting out of control, beyond his grasp, beyond his command. He could feel a badness in the air surrounding him, even here in the sanctuary of his own room. It was very strange, as though nature was beginning to turn inwards on herself. It was only a mild discomfort as yet; it would take someone of the greatest perception, someone like himself, to detect it at all. But that was not the worst of it. Oh no, not the worst, not by a long way.

Michael. Worst of all there was Michael. Michael Brachman, his long time lieutenant, his friend and confidant. And lover. He couldn't, shouldn't, forget that. There had been a time - not so very long ago - when there had been great tenderness between them. Now, he felt, Michael was beginning to threaten everything that they had worked so hard to achieve. Yet how could he ever have foreseen that this would have come to pass?

It had been the magic that had led him to Michael of course, all those years ago. Michael had been strong in those days, had been an athlete. Oxford rowing blue, rugby blue. And he had fenced. God, how he had fenced! He had appeared a man born out of time when he had fenced, had Michael. There had been about him the air of a cavalier, a resonance of a by-gone era. And in those days Michael had also been a lady's man. How difficult it had been at first to get Michael alone. Always so many pretty young things hanging around.

But his patience had eventually been rewarded; he had been able to fascinate the young scholar, open up for him a world of experience beyond all the dreams that had ever begged answers of the young man's enquiring mind. He had been able to use glimpses of the Great Work to lure Michael to him, had tantalised the boy with hints of the greatness that lay within the potential of all men.

Oh, how he had wanted Michael! Michael who so exactly matched the profile that he had drawn up when beginning his search for a lieutenant. Intellectual, inquisitive, born to achieve independent greatness. Michael, he had known, would fill the role that had been created for him, would be a powerful Shadowmaster. He had been sure of it. And the banking empire that Michael had been set to inherit had shown him to be a fit candidate to the others. Michael had been the final piece of the jigsaw; with Michael, the Shadowmasters - and he himself newly installed as Grand Master - had seemed set for greatness as they bestrode the threshold of the new Aquarian age. The time had seemed right for the centuries-old Great Work to achieve its fulfilment.

He had been seeking out his lieutenant, on the Astral, had almost despaired of finding someone to fit the exacting bill when he had finally chanced upon Michael's aura. And then there had been the months spent tracing this aura back to its human and material incarnation. Then when he had finally set eyes upon Michael, it had been lust at first sight.

St Clair trembled as he recalled that first time, in this very apartment, back in nineteen sixty-nine. Such joy! He had used the magic as an excuse then. The ritual had provided such pretty symbolism and he had known that it would prove a seductive tool, and Michael had found it all overpowering and irresistible.

He had made love to Michael, for the first time that night. For Michael, it had not been love, not then, not that time. For him, the sex had been a necessary part of the ritual and nothing more, as much a part of the ceremony as the salt ring and the burning incense. But the ceremony had sowed the seed; he had given Michael a glimpse of God that night and after that, the revulsion that Michael had felt for homosexuality had seemed as nothing set against what might be found beyond the Abyss. Even the pain had been made to seem trivial. And there *had* been great pain. For Michael. It had been days before he had been able to walk again. But from that night on, Michael had been his; there had been more and more ritual, more and more pleasure. He had had to take Michael up through the glory of the Great Work in mere months, a process that would normally take many years. He had used short cuts, dangerous methods.

The horrors that had confronted Michael's mind had left his body twisted and weakened. But it had been a time of success, during which they had grown very close. After each new stage in the process they had lain exhausted in each other's arms. And finally, Michael had reached for him. No magic, no ritual; just tenderness. St Clair remembered that he had wept then. And now, pacing his bedchamber, he wept again at the memory.

How quickly old Michael had grown. How horribly crippling his disabilities had become, as if in perverse inversion to his growing enlightenment. Such a waste, to have ruined so wonderful a body. Yet if Michael had ever minded, he had kept his resentment to himself. And had not the rewards been mighty? The temporally rewarding expansion of his banking empire through his involvement with the Shadowmasters being the least valuable of the gifts that his enlightenment had brought him.

Michael had indeed been a fine lieutenant, a true power within the Brotherhood, and a mighty Shadowmaster. Always he had been conscious of his duty, never once had he challenged the wishes of his Grand Master. Until now.

Now there was a new Michael, a cynical Michael who seemed to mock with gentle subtlety, his every action, his every utterance. This Michael was contradictory; this Michael was powerfully intellectual in his reasoning, confidently pointing out the most trivial flaws in strategy. And this Michael was ambitious.

There was something coldly violent about the new Michael, something calculating and Machiavellian. And this new Michael had taken control. He had to admit that now. He was no longer able to confront his former apprentice, look him in the eye and say: 'No!'

And he realised that Michael's ambitions were dangerous; too fast, too strong, too… unidirectional. There was horror and decay along the pathways Michael wished them all to follow. And the others would not have the vision to see, would find attraction in what Michael proposed. He knew it! He knew it! God, he knew them all. Good men, for the most, but far short of being great, any of them. He had been able to hold them in check, had been able to gently guide them. And they trusted him, respected his word. That was certain. So when he put Michael's proposals to them, explained Michael's new timetable to them, they would leap at the chance to be so bold.

Michael *was* going to ask him to put those proposals to the Shadowmasters. No, Michael was going to *force* him to do it. Michael was the master now and he was the puppet. He must find a way to resist, he *must!*

St Clair stopped pacing for a moment, pulled a pack of cigarettes from the pocket of the quilted smoking jacket, which he wore. His hands were trembling as he lit one of the Gauloise Caporals, and he knew that it was fear that made them twitch. Fear, yes, because he knew that there was really only one way to stop Michael now. He was going to have to kill him.

Chapter 38

ST CLAIR STOOD for a while, sucking smoke from his cigarette automatically, not even conscious of the action, deriving no pleasure from the act at all. Had that thought really come to his mind? Surely not. Yet before he knew it, he had spoken the words out loud.

There! The thought was out and free at last. He knew that it had been lurking there, like a thief in the dark, for some time. Now he had given it voice. He choked on the cigarette smoke and coughed slightly. It would have to be tonight. If he were to kill Michael, it would have to be tonight. Michael would be back in London tomorrow. God, Michael might even take it upon *himself* to contact the Shadowmasters with his plans. The prospect churned acid in St Clair's empty stomach. It simply had to be tonight. Now. He would just finish this cigarette…

'Ha ha ha ha ha.' Laughter, deep and rich. Though not overtly loud, it seemed to echo and reverberate within the confines of the bedchamber. Startled, St Clair scanned his darkened room in search of the intruder. Nothing. Just shades of dark and darker still. Was he getting jumpy? This was no time to be acting like a child, no time for foolishness. There was the task in hand. A serious task. Was he not Grand Master of the Shadowmasters? He was at that, for all Michael's newfound power. It was time for him to live the part.

'Ha ha ha ha ha!' The laughter again. He turned sharply, his back to the fireplace, eyes straining hard against the gloom. 'Who is it?' he asked, 'Who's there?' And his words carried with them the authority that a lifetime of privilege and duty had made second nature. But there came no reply. Just giggling.

'Heh heh heh!' That damned giggling. Where was it coming from and why did it echo so? He was beginning to feel afraid. The realisation it him with a rush. He was scared, here in his own bedchamber, in his own apartment, with his servants sleeping down the hall and the life of all Paris continuing around him outside. Here he was, trembling.

Suddenly the dark, which he had never before minded, seemed sinister and threatening. Perhaps it was the dark itself that taunted him. He chided himself for behaving like a child. But hadn't childhood been riven with its own horrors? Too late. The thought was with him now and spread through him like a fire through tinder. The bogeyman lived under the bed, didn't he?

The bulk of the large four-poster stood menacing in the gloom. *It* was surely crouched in wait beneath. St Clair stood very still, barely daring to breathe. This was nonsense and he knew it. He should simply stride over to the door where the light-switch was and end this right now. But he remained rooted to the spot. *It* would be waiting for him to make such a move. *It* would see his feet go by, *it* would lash out, all muscle and hair and teeth and claws and rip lumps out of him. *It* would be slimy. And *it* would eat him alive.

The power of reason was leaving him and while he was aware, still he was powerless to react. Panic was rushing in to take its place. The bed. The bed had become the focus for his terror. He had to look away. Somehow, he had to force his face to turn away. And eventually he did. Only to discover something much worse.

On the wall to his right his eyes were drawn to a grey oval shape. The initial shock of seeing it made him gasp out loud. Then came the realisation. The oval shape was a mirror, incandescent with the meagre light that shone through a chink in the curtains. 'Mirror mirror on the wall, who is the fairest of them all?' his mind asked and he knew that he was lost. He had never really forgotten it; it had lingered in the deepest recesses of his subconscious all these years. And even if he had been able to forget, it wouldn't have mattered, not any more. Because he could *see* her. Plain as day he could see her. The Disney creation. Entertainment for children they had styled it, but it had left him scarred. And there before him was *that* face, shining in the mirror.

Through the darkness, the mirror was no more than a vague patch on the wall but in its centre *she* was there, standing slim and tall, severe in black robes and a high golden crown. A white, chilling face of unsmiling beauty and eyes that shone with evil.

'Mirror mirror on the wall, who is the fairest of them all?' she asked. And she stood still in the mirror, awaiting his reply.

'Snow White. Snow White is fairer, fairer than you could ever be.'

Not words from the film, oh no. St Clair was horrified to realise that they had come from his own lips. Whatever could have possessed him?

In the mirror the Queen's cold eyes narrowed to slits as she turned to regard him. She leaned forward and out of the glass, shockingly three-dimensional; and a slender hand, an elegant white alabaster hand, reached up to caress the side of her face.

'Is that so, little man?' she asked. 'Well Snow White's dead now. See for yourself.'

The Queen leaned back into the glass, a sheet of orange flame blazing up before her and her dark laughter echoed in St Clair's mind. He was too far along the road to return now. He was lost to his imagination, Empress ruling Emperor, and would have to follow down any paths that it might choose for him. The orange flames in the mirror died but there was another image now in the glass.

It was a forest scene, all different shades of green and black. Something was moving in some bushes but it was all too far away to make out any detail. Then the picture zoomed in on the movement and he could see but he could not believe. On a bed of moss, a silver-clad knight was swarming all over a girl in a red skirt. St Clair did not have to scrutinise the scene. He knew that he was seeing the prince fucking - *fucking*, yes, because this was no gentle lovemaking - Snow White.

All the time, animal grunting came from the prince's lips; snarling, savage noises, until at last he stiffened, thrusting his hips hard against the unmoving girl. He howled a wolf's call into the trees as he came, rested limply for no more than a second before pulling himself away and rising nimbly to his feet. As he did so, the full horror of what had occurred became apparent. Snow White's clothing was savagely torn; her white breasts were exposed to view, adolescent and firm; her legs remained brutally forced wide apart and white panties, torn and ripped, clung wretchedly to the thigh of one leg. Blood and semen mingled with her pubic hair and trickled down her thigh.

St Clair's mouth hung open. He was rooted to the spot with terror. Was this his mind, his imagination, or was he really seeing all this? He felt that he knew the answer. And it was not a comforting one. In the glass, he could see that Snow White had been raped and murdered. A ligature of rope was tied tight around her neck and her face had tuned blue as the life had been squeezed out of her. This was not how it was supposed to be. Surely no! If Snow White was dead then where was the hope? Where was the goodness that finally made the suffering worthwhile?

It had *always* terrified him as a child, this cartoon creation, but the terror had somehow been negated by the thought that the Wicked Queen would be thwarted in the end and that love and goodness would surely always triumph. Now he realised that his fears had been well founded.

In the glass the Prince turned to face him and his skin came out in goosebumps. Even his shaved scalp began to wrinkle with fright. Because as the orange flames returned, he could see that the prince was not a prince after all. Despite the gnarled half-rotted penis that protruded from the body, dripping puss from its many open sores to mingle with the semen, which it leaked onto the verdant moss below, this was no mere man. No, it was the face of the Wicked Queen that laughed back at him, mocking and cold. 'Ha ha ha ha ha ha!' it brayed triumphantly. It was a laugh that threatened worse to come. And come it did...

A rustling to his left. Panic wrenched his head sharply round, away from the horrors of the looking glass. In the appalling darkness of the room, he could make out the indistinct bulk of the deep armchair, which sat, squat and solid beyond the unlocked door that joined Michael's chamber to his own. The rustling was coming from behind the armchair.

Run screaming, that's what he should do. Fleetness of foot would surely get him beyond the bogeyman under the bed. Then he could wrench open the heavy door and be out into the corridor beyond. The servants had their quarters above. Directly above. One short flight of stairs and he could be there, banging on doors, yelling for help and damn what they might think of him. But of course, he did no such thing. His fear had him paralysed and he found himself unable to move. Indeed, his chest was so tight that he could barely breathe. His eyes, adrenaline-sharp, remained fixed upon the indistinct black shadow that was the armchair. In the terrifying silence of the room, he could hear the pounding of his heart, his breath sucked through teeth clenched in fear. From behind him came the crackling of the orange flames, which danced once again in the mirror, but he did not dare turn round to look. He was waiting. And from behind the armchair, finally, it came. A black shape moving awkwardly out from the shadow of the chair. It came slowly towards him, with seeming difficulty and it remained ever squat.

When recognition finally came, St Clair dropped his mouth open to scream, but no noise was forthcoming. He tingled, shivering with electric fright and he could feel his mind begin to lose its grip. Because in the ever so slight glow radiating from the mirror behind him, he could see exactly what this new terror was. It was the greatest of his childhood nightmares made flesh.

Shuffling towards him was the Wicked Queen transformed. It was the dark hag, a creature created by the Disney studios via every child's hell. And the years had not lessened its power. The black robes rustled as it moved and now, as it neared, it lifted up its head. Beneath the huge black hood he could finally see the face, all warts and nastiness, its foul smile not managing in the least to disguise the vileness in its horrid eyes.

'Would you buy an apple from an old lady little boy?' the hag croaked.

St Clair whimpered, managed a step backwards. It was the voice that had haunted his nightmares. It was the worst sound that he could imagine in the whole world.

'Such a rosy apple,' the hag continued. 'See how red it shines.'

It reached a parchment hand, all bony talons, into the folds of its black robes and it emerged clutching the most perfect red apple that St Clair had ever set eyes upon. He managed another step back. Then another. The hag kept coming, shuffling slowly like the old woman it was. Its face continued to be split by the toothless grin and St Clair *knew* that that was a look of malevolence.

Step by step, he backed away. And still it came for him.

'Don't play games with such an old lady, little boy…' the hag said. 'So old. So tired. Don't tease an old lady so. Stay and take a bite from my apple.'

Still backwards he retreated, left foot then right foot. Slowly, painfully slowly. But as fast as he could manage. Until, from behind, cold hands slid over his face.

'Ooooaahh!' he gasped.

Momentarily, his eyes skittered about in their sockets as they sought to give vision to this new and immediate terror. He reached up, in a panic, to pull at the arms that held him fast from the rear, but his hands scrabbled at air. Yet still the cold fingers held his face, sharp nails digging painfully into his cheeks.

He could feel a chill breath on the back of his head and neck. A light breath that tingled with ice. And he could feel *her* there behind him. He backed up against the mirror.

'Stay and see what the old lady has here for you,' she said with the whispering voice of a loving mother. 'Such a pretty apple don't you think?'

The hag. Oh God hell, the hag was still there. Closer now. Much closer. He trembled, almost sobbing as his greatest fear drew closer still. She was almost indistinguishable from the gloom in her black robes. But he could see the smiling face clear enough. And it was that which chilled him the most. She came to a halt before him, all wheezy breath. Still the smile remained.

'Come now little boy,' she said in that voice which was sweet but not nearly sincere. 'Come take a bite.'

And slowly she reached up with the apple in her yellowing warty hands, up towards his mouth. But the apple was no longer red. It had withered and rotted and its blackened wrinkled skin was broken here and there. Maggots crawled within and about it and there was the buzz of bluebottles in the air, just a few that alighted and took off again, depositing their filth. The cold hands still held him immobile as the apple neared his squeezed-open lips. Behind him, the wicked Queen whispered:

'There, such a pretty apple, such a sweet apple. Go on, do take a bite.'

'No,' he whimpered feebly, but it was too late. The warty hand of the hag was at his lips, pressing the rotting fruit into them. He could keep his teeth clenched, but the pressing fingers of the wicked Queen on his cheeks forced his lips apart.

Maggots and bluebottles fell into this open mouth, were smeared against his teeth. A sour taste of decay should have made him retch with revulsion but he found even that reflex mechanism lost to him. The apple was pressed harder between his lips and finally the skin burst and liquid excrement oozed out into his mouth, finding its way between his teeth and onto his tongue. His head began to swim. From seemingly far away, he could hear the hoarse cackle of the hag as she revelled in his suffering. In his ear, the Wicked Queen was whispering.

'There, such a tasty morsel. Wasn't that good?'

But his eyes were closed and he was sobbing as he tried, half heartedly, to spit the filth from his mouth.

He sank to his knees, his eyes still tight-shut in misery and he groaned. It took him a few seconds to realise that the cold hands were gone. The taste of filth was gone. Then, even behind his tightly-shut eyes, he could see the brilliance of the light.

He blinked, rapidly, clearing the raw salt tears which had begun to flow, and knelt back aghast at what he saw. The adjoining door to Michael's room had been thrown open and a brilliant light - exotically brilliant in as much as it was *bright black* - shimmered from beyond the open portal. In the doorway stood a figure, tall and straight and strong. A white featureless silhouette in contrast to the incandescent black of the back lighting.

Two ghostly figures were converging before him, heading towards the open door. They were the hag and the wicked Queen. They came together before the door, stopped and turned to look at him. They smiled and the smiles seemed beautiful now, loving and warm through the halo of black. The Wicked Queen waved and then they turned, floated together, melded into one, before finally continuing on towards the white figure, standing majestically in the doorway. They continued on and into the figure, fusing with it, sending a shimmer of black starlight through the whiteness of its being. Then it was just the figure again, standing still and tall and strong.

From Michael's room, the shimmering black light began to dim. The blackness lost its irradiance, became once more the mere gloom of the shadowless night. The figure in the doorway was no longer white in silhouette. It was dark and featureless. But St Clair could feel the strength in it nonetheless. He remained on his knees, watching, not daring to move. The room was dead with silence until finally, the figure spoke.

'You would wish to kill me Henri? Surely not. Not so near, not after so much.'

Oh God fuck, it was Michael! But that couldn't be. Michael was twisted, Michael was crippled. Had he not seen with his own eyes how Michael had suffered for the Great Work? Then, more shamefully: had he not participated, encouraged that suffering?

Yet this was Michael sure enough. It was not just the voice, though that *was* Michael's. It was the bearing. This was the Michael that *had* been. The Michael that *would* have been; tall and athletic. And beautiful.

For a moment Michael's eyes glowed brilliant orange with flame, but the fire died in an instant. Michael took a step forward, across the threshold and into St Clair's room. And in that moment, St Clair realised that his end was come.

'No words Henri? You have never been slow to speak in the past. Come my friend; tell me why you would want me dead. Tell me, my *lover*.'

Michael took another step forward. Stopped. From his kneeling position before the fireplace, St Clair found his somewhat shaky voice.

'N-no, Michael. You are wrong, oh certainly you are. Why should I ever contemplate such a thing? As you say, we are near. So near.'

But his words lacked conviction. Even in his own mind, he could feel their insincerity.

'Really, Henri?' said the new god-Michael, taking another pace forward. 'Then tell me, was this but a dream?'

St Clair caught just a flash of the orange fire in Michael's eyes once more and then his vision was gone. His mind was full of imagery; Michael lying twisted in his bed, he taking steps towards the sleeping figure, creeping through the darkness. He taking the pillow, ramming it over the face of his defenceless comrade, suffocating the life away. And he cried out in disbelief, for he recognised the images. They were his own. The way he had imagined putting an end to Michael just minutes before. They were *his* thoughts. Exactly.

Then the images were gone and Michael was standing before him, just a few paces away. Through his own, misting eyes, St Clair caught a glimpse of the fire in Michael's eyes again and noticed the twisted snarl on his lips. It was a visage of violence. The face of a psychopath. Then the flames died and it was friend Michael, beautiful Michael once again.

'Oh Henri. So trusting, so weak, so vacillating. You could have joined me, you know. I had wanted you with me. I had... such plans. I would have given you strength, power. You would have shared domination of the universe with me. Oh pitiful fool.'

St Clair looked up into the angelically serene face of the new Lord.

'But what you propose, it is so... it will lead to...' But he knew that it was not for such as he to reason with such obvious might. Not now. It was too late. So he simply asked: "When?"

'You do not know? Even now, you cannot work it out?' There was genuine surprise in Michael's voice. 'Oh Henri, you disappoint me. Not for the first time. It was the ceremony of course. The invocation to Choronzon. I thought that it would have been obvious.'

'Michael no! You couldn't. The danger...' Realisation drew a mask of horror over St Clair's face.

'Oh such weakness!' exclaimed Brachman, exasperated. '*You* couldn't Henri, but I could. I *did*. It was easy; not fixing my mind with the balance that would have negated the influence of the Master of Shape and Form. I *felt* his glory, Henri. I bathed in his warmth and power. I... let him in.'

'But why?'

'Why? Why?' The flames burst in Brachman's eyes once more and St Clair shrank back. 'You ask me why? Was I always to be the cripple then? Was I to wallow in my infirmity, one who had given everything for the Work? Was I to see you let it go unfinished, spend my life in ruin? And you *were* going to let it pass us by, Henri, I had seen that. You lack both the charisma and intellect to see it through. You have always fallen short of greatness, Henri. Had I seen it sooner, things might have been different. But I have been a fool, too. The realisation came too late. I was already a twisted wreck by then, but I was not prepared to let that sacrifice go to waste. I allowed myself to *feel* the glory of Choronzon, heard him whisper to my mind the wonders that he could perform for me. And has he deserted me, Henri? Am I not now beautiful?'

Michael spread his arms, stood proud in his nakedness and St Clair could see that indeed he was more than beautiful. But he could say nothing. He simply knelt, mouth drooping open, over-awed by the figure before him.

'Choronzon will give me what is mine, Henri. Greatness beyond your meagre imagining. Should I really forgo all of *this*?'

St Clair's vision blazed with flames and he knew that Michael was transmitting a vision not merely into his mind, but etching it onto his soul. And he was powerless to resist.

There was the earth, from a distance, from far out in space. She sat like a jewel in the firmament, still and serene. And he saw the earth tremble, saw her split asunder. Seas drowned continents, huge volcanoes burst fire and hell from all quarters and he could *feel* the pain and suffering of millions as they died. Yet still the earth burst her crust until a being, a powerful fledgling creature emerged from the molten core, scattering pieces of the planet in a violent explosion far out into the emptiness of galactic space.

Then where there was once earth, he watched the creature in its fullness, a howling red monster born of hell, dripping fire and blood as it cried its newborn wail at the sun. Then it moved and he was moving with it, fast through space. It destroyed planets, stars, galaxies, as it roamed and grew, violent and conquering, destructive, leaving murder in its wake. And where it passed, it left cold barren waste; desserts bereft of the life that it had taken for itself. It grew in size and power, boiling where it flew and St Clair could feel the panic as it filled his mind, could feel the heat as it seized at his core. Pain, burning, the smell of roasting flesh and the agony of blistering skin. These were all his as he shared in the nightmare vision of the future of the universe to come.

There were no thoughts of salvation now. His mind had gone, the vision was too powerful, too awe-inspiring to contain. That and the pain. Then suddenly the vision was no more. Michael stood before him, no longer a being of flesh and blood but a creature of fire and molten rock and metal. The searing heat of mere proximity blistered the skin of St Clair's face, split it, peeled it back and roasted the raw flesh beneath. There was no blood, the heat cauterised the blood vessels instantly, boiled the water out of the liquid and baked what remained into a hard scabby crust.

The pain was more than excruciating but St Clair could not scream. A finger of flame had been thrust into his mouth and had burned his tongue into a charred and blackened nothingness, had devastated his throat with its violence. Then his eyeballs burst. He felt them pop. It was to be his last conscious sensation. His smoking jacket and slippers erupted in flame, as he lay curled up on the carpet, his hands and arms and feet now nothing more than withered and blackened claws. They were beyond repair and would never again be of use to him. Not that it mattered. He was already blissfully dead.

Flames rose from the shrunken foetal blob that had been St Clair, spreading in a circle as the carpet around them caught and cast an eerie flickering glow about the room. And Michael floated in the air above bobbing gently with the flames in ecstasy with what he had done.

Then, through the dense smoke, Michael Brachman ceased to be the flame-creature Choronzon and smiled. He turned to walk slowly back to his own room to dress and gather his belongings. He remained oblivious to the smoke and fumes; he was beyond all that now.

Above, in their quarters, not one of the servants stirred. They lay, to a man, dead in their beds. Each had suffered a massive coronary. Each had been visited in his sleep by a demon of such power that its mere proximity had drawn the life from them. Such power was Michael Brachman's to command.

He was ready to leave the scene of the tragedy now. In the morning he would hear the news and be grief-stricken. A close friend dead. How terrible, how unbelievable. What could possibly have happened? Inside, he knew that he had done only that which had been required. He could not afford to be held back. After all, he had a date... with his destiny.

Chapter 39

THESE WERE TROUBLED times for General Sergei Bondachuk. He sat alone, even at this late hour, in his surprisingly Spartan Office in the inconspicuous building which housed the headquarters of the *Glavnoye Razvedyvatelnoye Upravleniye* - the GRU.

On the large walnut desk before him sat a heavy glass ashtray, full to overflowing with cigarette butts. Even now, a cigarette was held, burning but unsmoked between the second and third fingers of his left hand. Through the tinted and toughened glass of the picture window opposite he could see the glow of lights from the offices of the building backing on to his own; it was the building at number two, Dzerzhinsky Square. He allowed himself a wry smile. It was true then, after all; the KGB never slept.

Is there someone behind one of those windows thinking of me, he wondered? He closed his eyes. It was such a strain, all of this. Had been for years. He was not close to breaking yet though - there was still a little left in the emotional fuel cell. But it could not go on forever. He wouldn't be able to handle the stress for many more years. Opening his eyes once more, he gazed again at the lights in the windows of the building opposite. Maybe not right now, perhaps not someone there, right at that moment; but the KGB *would* have a file on him somewhere. They would be keeping an eye on him one way or another. So suspicious they were, the bastards. But then, wouldn't their suspicions be well founded? Was he not indeed plotting to overthrow the state?

Bondachuk chuckled out loud. How easy he had become with that thought. He had the idea in his mind and the power at his fingertips to attempt to overthrow one of the mightiest instruments of autocracy the world had ever seen. It should, he knew, have sent a shudder of apprehension down his spine; but he had lived with this ambition for so long that it no longer drew a reaction from him. Was that of itself not dangerous? A sharp knock at the door broke his concentration. He stubbed the unsmoked cigarette in the ashtray, unmindful of the grey powder that spilled onto the desktop.

'Come,' he said, sitting upright in his chair, assuming the pose of a General of the Red Army.

The door was opened and Colonel Yuri Besanov stepped across the threshold. He closed the door behind him and marched across to the General's desk where he saluted and stood to attention. It was a ritual that owed nothing to rank and authority. It was all part of the game. The General's office was, after all, overlooked by the KGB building. The window was, of course, tinted and the exterior was coated with a film of reflective material, so cameras *shouldn't* be able to look in, but who could say for certain?

'Sit down, Yuri,' the General said, leaning his elbows on the desktop and resting his chin on the tips of his fingers.

Besanov sat, facing his master. 'The news is not good, Sergei.' Besanov spoke in the familiar; cameras might have posed a security problem, but he knew that words spoken in this room were going to be secure. A twice-daily sweep for listening devices was routinely carried out and parabolic mikes aimed at the office from the KGB building would be rendered useless; the glass window was vibrated electronically at random high-frequencies. These electronic vibrations of the glass would break up any sound vibrations coming from within. 'Gavrilov has missed a routine report.'

The General sat silent for a moment. 'Could there be a mundane explanation for this?' he asked.

Besanov shook his head. 'No,' he said. 'The first call, maybe, but the backup call has not been received either. He should have been able to make one or the other. There is always the *possibility* of course that there might be some acceptable explanation, but...' The Colonel raised his hands and shrugged.

'Then he is dead. Or worse, captured,' the General said.

'Captured... perhaps,' Besanov answered, though his tone indicated that he considered such a possibility remote. 'Even so, he knows nothing of us, of our plans.'

'True. But Gavrilov is a Spetznaz agent. And he was working at your own personal command. That alone might send western intelligence agencies sniffing where we would damn well prefer them not to, don't you think?'

The General noticed Besanov stiffen at this suggestion. He hadn't meant it as a rebuke. In his heart he felt that Gavrilov had not been captured. His inner instinct told him that Gavrilov, a soldier who he himself had decorated in the field in Afghanistan, was dead. This Strachan business was throwing up many curiosities though.

After a moment's thought, General Bondachuk sighed. 'He will not have been taken, Yuri. He would have taken his own life rather than fall into the hands of the enemy. You knew him well. You know that this is the truth. For us though, there can be no time for sentiment; we must consider what this means. Strachan must still be at large, don't you think?'

'Yes, he must still be at large,' Besanov answered. 'Yet it occurs to me that were Strachan acting in any official capacity, he would be back safe with his controllers by now.'

Bondachuk nodded slowly. 'And it has been a week since the ceremony that Strachan witnessed,' he said. 'You would imagine that Strachan's revelations might have provoked great stirrings by now. The Shadowmasters are prominent people.'

'Exactly,' Besanov agreed. 'And what such stirrings have there been? None. Could it be that Strachan was no more than a rogue who accidentally stumbled across that which he shouldn't? Personally, I fear the actions of Gorbachev more than Strachan.'

The General stiffened, not visibly, but inwardly, his mind momentarily distracted from thoughts of Strachan. This was new. 'And what is it about Gorbachev that makes you feel this way, Yuri?' he asked.

'His *Glasnost*, his *Perestroika*,' Besanov replied. 'Gorbachev might just have the will to force his freedom on our peoples. Already his Glasnost has tantalized the intelligentsia with its visions of an openness that will serve the masses. Already there is opposition to the Party, which goes unchecked. Once the intelligentsia have translated these ideas for the masses, and the masses have understood, there will be no going back. They will come to expect that the freedoms they are now being allowed to see in the west, will come to them eventually.' He finished his explanation there, as though this was clarification enough.

The General probed further; 'And why should this concern us or our plans?'

'Because our plans call for a military coup d'etat! We will not be seen as revolutionary or reformatory if Gorbachev's ideas have already become reality. The people's love of the Red Army will not stretch that far. And then we must consider the reaction of the West.'

'Yuri, you surprise me. I thought you would have seen. Gorbachev's plans will play into our hands. They will work *for* us, not against us. Glasnost opens up visions of freedom to the masses, yes?'

Besanov nodded slowly.

'Yet there is still much opposition to Gorbachev from within the Party. There are many - many more than you might imagine - who oppose Gorbachev. There are many who have vested interests in preserving the status quo. There is open opposition within the Politburo, despite Gorbachev's attempted purges of what he calls 'the old guard.' And that is just on the surface. There are thousands more who work behind the scenes on a practical level to thwart Gorbachev's plans.'

'Even so, would those Party apparatchiks welcome military intervention?'

'Undoubtedly. As the country turns to - dare we say it - democracy, these people will have much to lose. Any that would oppose Gorbachev, they would consider natural allies. Even the military. After all, they would be correct in assuming that the army does not contain within its infrastructure a bureaucracy capable of governing the country. They will assume that whoever deposes Gorbachev will wish for things to be run in pretty much the way they always have been. In short, they will know that they will once again be needed. Their positions, their privileges, will be secure.'

'And what of the people in general?' Besanov asked.

'The people can also be persuaded to welcome us,' the General continued. 'Already there are those who complain that Gorbachev's Perestroika progresses too slowly. In the confusion that will accompany our actions, we will be able to play on the hopes of both the conservatives and the reformers. Do you see?'

Besanov tugged at his earlobe, a sign the General correctly interpreted as indicating that there were further questions to be answered.

'And what of the West?' Besanov finally asked. 'Gorbachev has openly signalled that he wants to scale down the military readiness of the Red Army commitment to the Warsaw Pact. How would the West interpret the overthrow of Gorbachev?'

'Well Yuri, you know that the West, while welcoming Gorbachev's initiatives and, I believe, genuinely *wanting* to believe him sincere, still has those who harbour suspicions. *Their* readiness has not yet been scaled down. They strongly suspect that Gorbachev might yet be toppled from within. Our actions will serve only to paint smug smiles on the faces of those in the West who remain hawks.'

Besanov nodded his understanding. 'Yes,' he continued, 'Smiles that we will be in a position to wipe away when we announce initiatives of our own that will surpass in generosity any of Gorbachev's offerings. And when we act unilaterally on those initiatives, the West will truly, finally, embrace us as brothers. It will discredit and disarm the hawks in the West forever.'

Besanov did not have to say more. They both knew what the next stage of the plan entailed. Those in the Brotherhood who held it within their power and were privy to elements of the Golden Project, would wreak financial havoc on the markets and economies of Europe within weeks of the Red Army's success. And from the ensuing chaos, a truly Federal State of Europe would rise. People would welcome it as a saviour. The stage would be set for the Shadowmasters to bring the final glory of the Great Work to bear upon a weakened, and therefore receptive world...

It was almost as if Bondachuk was reading his subordinate's mind. 'You see Yuri; Gorbachev has served to help our cause, not hinder it.' The General allowed himself the glimmer of a smile.

Besanov pondered the General's words. Bondachuk was

right, of course. But it meant that they would have to act quickly. Gorbachev was about to free the Warsaw pact allies. Poland was all-but democratised already; Hungary not far behind. As Gorbachev pulled the Red Army back from the Cold War front line, he encouraged the peoples of these satellite states to win freedoms that he would have the Russian people take for themselves.

'You know,' Besanov reasoned, 'If the Soviet Union does not quickly follow with a process of free market reform and democratisation, we will fast become a pauper state.' He leaned back in his chair weighing up his thoughts for a moment before continuing. 'Our people would never stand for that, and Gorbachev knows it. I have a feeling that Gorbachev intends to accelerate the progress of his reforms. If he succeeds, what would we be able to offer the West, beyond what would already have been achieved? Our actions following such reforms would be seen as reactionary, not reformatory; the West would never be able to trust us, much less support us, and not even the Brotherhood would be able to alter that fact.'

The General's eyes narrowed and he leaned slowly forward in his chair. Besanov's reasoning had been astute. But Besanov was not possessed of all the facts. He would set that right, and now. 'We will pre-empt Gorbachev, Yuri,' he said, slowly and softly. 'Our plans move apace. Before the year is out we will have made our move.' He paused a moment to let the enormity of his statement sink in, then continued. 'It will be we, not Gorbachev, who will take the credit for tearing down the Berlin Wall, we who will rend the Iron Curtain. I can imagine the grovelling gratitude of a weary world, can't you?' He didn't wait for a reply. 'We will make a clever pretence of handing the Soviet Union over to its people. Such will be our popularity that we will but have to say *dance* and the world will dance. And from this, in the short term, will come our power. We will make ourselves the architects of a new, Federal State Europa.'

Besanov shrugged, then smiled. Even he didn't fully realise that his smile was one of relief. It would be over soon. Action would come soon. Preferable by far to the skulking and secrecy. And the fear of discovery, mustn't forget that.

'Am I to send another agent to seek out Strachan?' Besanov

asked.

The General shook his head gravely. 'No, not specifically, Yuri. Just have your agents in Europe maintain their vigilance. I would like to eliminate this nuisance, yes; but I am inclined to agree that he was not *official*. We would have felt the repercussions by now if that were the case.'

Besanov stood and saluted, then turned on his heel and marched smartly out of the office.

General Bondachuk leaned back in his chair once again. He had painted a rosy picture of how the Red Army would be seen as a saviour, handing all Europe its freedom; how it would then be the anvil on which would be forged the new, mighty, Federal State following the chaos that the Brotherhood had it within its power to precipitate. He had worked under strain for many years to achieve this end. Lately, though, as he pondered the ideal, he felt no warm pleasure in it. Why was it, he wondered, that he seemed no longer able to picture a United European State, peaceful and harmoniously prosperous? Why was it, during the last few days in particular, that his musings had come to be disturbed by visions of armoured divisions rolling west over the German plains?

Chapter 40

MARSEILLES... JUNE 19th... 02.30am

GAVRILOV WAS NOT dead. It felt to him, however, that he might be headed that way. His body was burning with fever, and a dull throbbing ache attacked every joint, daring him to attempt movement. Sweat rolled down his face, and he could feel it emerging from the open pores of his skin. He was drenched through and through.

His mind swam, in and out of lucidity. Where was he? And how did he get here? He lifted his eyelids – an agonisingly laborious process – and looked at the small squalid room. Oh yes, of course, he'd been brought here. The tall gangling buffoon, and the controlled, polite warrior (warrior? Now what on *earth* had given him that idea?) who had been his companion. But why? He had not been feeling well, that was it. They had been concerned for his welfare. Oh how good it was to have friends.

His mind cleared a little. Friends. But he was friendless in a friendless land, wasn't that it? Wasn't that how it was supposed to be. And then a realisation hit him. Strachan! The man Strachan. He had to find him again, had to kill him. No time for rest. Rest came later. After. He had to move.

'ΛΛΛΛAgghh!' It was a couple of seconds before he could associate the cry of pain with his own discomfort. His disorientation was such that even the intensity of his pain was strictly delayed action. But he knew that he was too weak to move. He had to get out somehow, though. He simply *had* to make his contact.

'Welcome back, friend.'

A voice. Dark, authoritative, quiet. And powerful. Gavrilov had heard it before. Where? When? Oh, it was so hard, just to think.

The Warrior. Oh, yes of course; the warrior, he remembered feebly. With great effort, he pried his eyes open once more. His vision was milky and blurred, but seated on a plain wooden chair, a few feet before him, he could see the warrior. Beside the chair stood a long, twitching figure, wearing a long raincoat and a wide brimmed hat. Undoubtedly the buffoon. The whole picture was tilted through ninety degrees. For the first time, Gavrilov realised that he was lying on his side. Off the ground, so he must be on a bed. Kind of them to have put him to bed, he thought. He really did need some sleep. Sleep off his fever. He had a job to finish.

'No, friend, no.' It was the voice of the warrior once again. 'Stay with us awhile. We really have so much to talk about. And there will be rest enough to follow, I assure you. Come, open your eyes.'

The voice was so seductive, so reasonable. A simple request from a friend who had helped. So he blinked his heavy lids open once more.

'That's better. Just a few simple questions to begin - oh, forgive me, but you do speak Russian, don't you?'

Speak Russian? So curious a question, couched faultlessly in the tongue of the Motherland. Well of course he spoke Russian.

'*Da*,' he answered emphatically, though it made his jaw ache abominably to move. '*Da, ya gov…*' Warning bells in his mind! Loud, violent, cutting through the fever-fuzziness of his thoughts, telling him to shut up. This wasn't right. He had no business talking to this stranger. This was foreign soil, and he was a man with a mission. He *had* no friends here. He had to move, had to get out. There was danger, he could feel it.

'Aaaaggghh!'

He rolled back onto the bed once more. The effort had been altogether too much for the pain that welded his joints tight.

The Templar regarded him for a moment, watching the rise and fall of his chest as he breathed heavily. Already he could feel the strength in this one. He wouldn't talk. He would suffer endlessly and die rather than give in. The Templar could see this in the fading aura that surrounded the man. It was an honourable courage, to be admired. And as one warrior to another, the Templar did admire it. It was a pity though. He would have liked

307

to have discovered this one's secrets. There wouldn't be much, to be sure, but there would have been at least one name. And from it he would have been able to discover the seriousness of the Russian involvement.

Was Bondachuck still the Shadowmaster representing all of the Soviet Union? He would have liked the answer to that one. A cunning manipulator was Bondachuck. A danger of a very temporal nature would come from that quarter. If it was to come at all. The Bear had been ambitious. The Templar had felt it in the air surrounding Bondachuck. And of itself, it had been an asset to the group as a whole, tempered and balanced by the virtues of the others. A harmony of talents was what the Shadowmasters had been for a millennium; the imbalance of the one helping to build the perfect balance of the whole.

But these were times of utter imbalance. He had felt it on the astral. Had seen the ruin that lay in the path of this imbalance were it to be allowed to run its course. And in its first tremors, he knew, Bondachuck and his ambition would have the ascendancy. It would be a dark age for the earth. An age of famine and pestilence and unceasing strife. It would be the beginning of the end. If Bondachuk still held sway.

Well he would have to wait to find out and time was running short. There was the man before him. He would have to give this man the opportunity to speak. It would give him the chance to make his end that much more comfortable. But in his heart he knew that the Torquemada, which twitched and whimpered by his side, would have its fill. He could feel the expectant excitement running through the creature as it danced and could feel the revulsion and horror that it felt deep within itself as it knew in advance, the abominable act of horror that it was about to perform. In its lust, it mewled like a cat and spittle sprayed from its blue lips as it raised its mottled face to the ceiling.

There was a foul acrid stench emanating from the creature all of a sudden, and the Templar looked round, surprised to see that it had pissed itself. God, how wretched. But he recognised the sign. The beast within the Torquemada was risen. He could control the creature, yes, but its agitation would grow, would attract attention. And that they didn't need. It would at least serve a purpose to let it sate itself on the brave Russian here. And at least the kill would be quick. Preferable, surely, to the slow burning death that the Torquemada's poisoned nails had introduced. In the Templar's mind, then, events were already settled.

'Look to me, *Tovaritch*,' the Templar said. Once more, Gavrilov opened his eyes and looked. 'I have but a question. A simple one that you can answer and save yourself great suffering.'

Gavrilov wheezed a painful breath and stared harshly at the Templar. The fire in his eyes was not induced by the poison that was spreading through his every fibre.

The Templar paused for a second, then continued, simply: 'Who sent you, *Tovaritch?*'

'*Job tvoimadj!*' spat Gavrilov by way of reply, though the effort caused him to wince with pain, and he lay for a few moments, gasping for air, which was now becoming harsh to his throat and lungs.

'My mother is long forgotten to me,' responded the Templar, to Gavrilov's crude instruction. 'Now spare yourself further suffering. You are a man of arms. Skilled in the craft. You are no stranger to death. You must know that your end is now certain. There is no antidote to the poison that plagues your weary muscles. But there is at least a day of increasing agony ahead.'

The Templar reached inside his jacket and pulled out a small plastic case. He opened it up and displayed its contents to Gavrilov. A hypodermic syringe and a small phial of clear liquid.

'This will quicken things,' the Templar said.

Gavrilov summoned his strength through the growing pain. So this was it then. The end was come. The realisation that death was holding not fear for him now that he was facing it squarely and surely, pleased him. Christ the pain was hideous though, wasn't it? Wouldn't it be easier to say the name? Colonel Besanov. That wouldn't hurt the Motherland, would it?

But inside, he knew that this had nothing to do with the fucking Motherland. This was his final test. His will against the pain. It was a personal thing, this last fight. Like all the shit that they'd had to take in selection and training, all the actions against the odds in the Afghan hills. Like the whole of his fucking military career. And he would fight the pain, here at the last. Would fight and conquer. Would leave this life at last, safe in the knowledge of the mastery of his will over pain. How could it be any other way?

'*Niet!*' he managed to force between clenched teeth, and slumped back, sobbing at the agony of the effort.

The Templar was unmoved. At his side, the Torquemada, rubbing its hands over the wet patch of urine that soaked the crotch of its pants then licking its fingers, whimpered with anxiety. The Templar did not have to turn to look at it to know what a disgusting spectacle it presented. Instead he rested his vision on the soldier lying on the bed, who even in death had the strength to defy him. Could he really allow such nobility fall prey to the disgrace that was the Torquemada?

Hurriedly, he took the syringe from its case, filled it with the liquid from the phial. He knelt at the bedside and Gavrilov opened his eyes to see him expertly slide the needle into the artery at the side of his neck. There was a slight burning sensation the plunger was depressed and the morphine solution was squeezed into his system. In the brief moment before the rush hit him, his eyes met those of the Templar. He saw pride there, and comradeship; that of a warrior, which transcended the boundaries of geo-politics. For in that moment they were brothers. And then he was gone, the pain banished as he bathed in a sea of uncompromising bliss.

Leaning over the Templar's shoulder, the Torquemada squealed with frustration. It had expected this life, had wanted to take it, had wanted to gorge itself on the juices of the life-blood. It sucked in air, about to shriek, but a sharp look from the Templar caused it to cower away. The Templar knew that he would have to let it take what remained of this life. Out here, in the world of man, he could not exercise the control over the creature that he was able to in the desolate places where they were free of prying eyes and ears. He could not risk an incident now. He would have to let the creature have what it craved. At least the memory of the warrior would be intact. He would know nothing of the abomination that was about to defile his flesh.

The Templar turned to the Torquemada, studied it for a moment with disgust and loathing. From beneath the brim of its hat, it watched him, trembling. Finally, he nodded, a sign that it could be about its business, and then turned his back on the scene.

The Torquemada whimpered with relief, and then threw itself on the prostrate form of Gavrilov. There was a sickly sound of tearing skin and muscle fibres as the Torquemada's talonous fingers dug deep into the throat of the unconscious man. It buried its face in the gore, slurping noisily at the blood, chewing roughly at the cartilage that surrounded the windpipe. It ripped open Gavrilov's clothing, exposing the tanned skin of his tough body, and gripped the end of the windpipe, pulling at it, as if trying to bring the lungs up through the rough gash that was opened up where the throat had once been. It bit into the flesh of Gavrilov's belly, coming up for air and digging with its fingers, to pull open the flesh where its teeth had opened the way. It reached deep inside the body, up to its elbows in gore, and ripped out the intestines and stomach. Sharp claws wrenched at the stomach-bag, tearing it. It squeezed the contents out into its mouth, where it drank greedily of the half digested food and bile, the grey liquid spotted with bits of hamburger and tomato slopping out to dribble down its chin and over its cheeks as it guzzled at the vomit. A foul stench had filled the room.

Squeezing the last few drops out of the stomach, it flung the empty sack to one side and delved deep once more into the corpse. Growling deep in its throat, it ripped and tore at the lower intestine, pulling out hands that were thick with brown excrement, and wiped these hands across its mouth, chewing hungrily on the foul smelling brown filth, licking off every morsel. Once more it delved into the lucky dip of flesh, and a hand emerged, clutching the bladder, the contents of which it drained into its own greedy throat. And yet once more it returned to the corpse.

'Enough.'

A word gently spoken, ineffectual in the face of such hideous violence. But it was a word spoken by the Templar. And the Torquemada obeyed its call.

It stood, its head hung down, shamefully, covered in blood and shit and vomit. Strands of raw gristle and bloodied flecks of meat were plastered in the thick vomit, which coated its cheeks.

311

Not one square centimetre of it had remained free of blood, or vomit, or piss, or shit. It had gorged itself in a frenzy of horror. Such was the nature of the beast that the Templar had all those years ago released in it.

And now that the beast had been called to heel, the soul of the man, the conscience which remained and could still feel, and think, and experience, stood in dread horror. Ashamed and helplessly wretched.

The walls, floor, and even the ceiling of the small room were washed with the blood of the dead Russian. Small pieces of him had been flung far and wide in the Torquemada's orgy of cannibalistic violence.

The Templar regarded the creature momentarily. Just why did he subject himself to the disgust that the creature's presence brought upon him? Why did he not simply destroy the creature, allow its spirit the freedom to seek out a new path, one that might raise it that little bit closer to its final destiny? It was tempting, standing looking at it, but he knew that he would not let it rest. He had carried it through the centuries, vowing to keep it in disgrace until he perceived the first spark of remorse for the deeds that it had done, remorse not in the form of self-pity, but a genuine sorrow for the victims of its obscenity. And of that there had not yet been a trace.

The Torquemada could sense his disgust. It lifted its eyes to look at him and whimpered. He knew that it was calling for help.

In the corner of the room was a dirty shower unit, dusty and dry with lack of use. The Templar walked over to it and switched on the taps. There was a hollow banging from the pipes, which must have echoed through out the hotel, but after a few moments, the water began to flow. The Templar let it run for a while, waiting for it to get warm, but it remained cool. As he turned, the Torquemada was already divesting itself of the soggy and fouled garments, which draped heavily over its puny frame. Finally, it stood there, the filth and the gore plastered over what parts of it had been exposed, red stains of blood smeared over parts of the rest, where it had soaked through the layers of clothing.

'In here,' the Templar said, indicating the cubicle where the cleansing water sprayed powerfully from the showerhead.

The Torquemada shuffled across the room, dragging its bare feet through the gore, and stepped carefully beneath the flow. It did not wince as the cold water splashed over it. It merely stood, as if awaiting further instruction.

To the Templar, it looked an utterly broken creature. Its eyes were upon him, unblinking, neither questioning nor accusing. They were eyes devoid of any hope. It was so utterly pathetic that for a moment the Templar felt a pang of pity sting his heart. But he quickly put that behind him. Reaching into the shower, he took a dry flannel from a hook on the wall, and damped it under the water. Carefully, he began to sponge the Torquemada down, divesting it of the filth that had resulted from its latest abomination, humble in the knowledge that he had been responsible for leading it there.

Refreshingly clean, and dressed in the change of clothes that the Templar had brought for it in a large canvas overnight bag, the Torquemada looked vaguely human once again. It liked the brown corduroy pants and the oxford brogue shoes. It also liked the brown cotton shirt and the tan cashmere pullover. It was sorry, though, that it had had to leave behind the long raincoat and the wide-brimmed hat. They were protective, kept it beyond the reach of inquisitive eyes. But the Templar would get it new ones, as soon as it was convenient. He had said so. And he had *always* been as good as his word, the Torquemada remembered, with not a little trepidation. In the meantime, the long peak of the canvas yachting cap would cover most of its face. And outside, the dawn was yet to break. There would be shadows.

Now they made their way carefully down the darkened stairway and into the quiet lobby. The lights were out here too, and the hotel had been locked up for the night, a hasty sign left outside the door. The Templar had seen to all that. They had been alone in the hotel, save for the drunken old fat woman, who snored in front of her television, and had been there since they had first arrived. She would awaken in the morning and discover her dead husband in his office. She would smile through her hangover at his passing, until she discovered the horror of room twelve; then her heart would fail her and she would die amid the gory remains of what had only recently been the finest of the Red Army's

Spetznaz assassins. But by then, the Templar and his Torquemada would be long gone. Unknown and untraceable.

The Templar waited, just inside the door. Outside all was quiet, but he took a moment to allow his instinct to tell him whether or not the coast was clear. After a second, he turned the key and pulled the door inwards. He stepped out, into the night and the tall figure of the Torquemada followed. There was not a soul about. Quickly, the Templar closed the door and locked it behind him once more, then stooped to drop the key down a nearby drain. Seconds later, his Torquemada gangling behind him, he had disappeared into the shadowy back alleys of the Old Quarter of Marseilles, leaving behind the *Grand Guignol* mystery that the Hotel Petit Louvre would become.

Chapter 41

FRANK REDBRIDGE OPENED his eyes, blinking rapidly to accustom them to the dark. His naked body was bathed in sweat, but he was shivering, shaking uncontrollably. As his vision began to swim into focus, the familiarity of his surroundings served to calm him. He closed his eyes once more and began to breathe, deeply and steadily. The relaxation exercise worked quickly; his pulse rate dropped and the uncontrollable shivering steadied.

He opened hid eyes once more, satisfied that he was calm, in control. Looking about him, he was comforted by the walls, all five of them in this pentagonal room, curiously decorated to resemble dense woodland; the view from the clearing of a forest. Above his head, a black painted ceiling, dotted with silver, five-pointed stars grouped in the twelve constellations of the zodiac, gave the continuance to this illusion. The bare-board floor beneath him was painted a rich verdant green, like the moss carpet of a natural forest.

This was Redbridge's private room, one that remained locked, whether he was in it or not, barring access to all who might wish to pry. Not even the middle-aged cleaning lady who came to the house once a week to dust and polish and vacuum the floors, was ever allowed to so much as glimpse beyond the permanently closed portal.

She was, Redbridge knew, a dull witted woman. He had encouraged her belief that he was some kind of big shot in D.C., some twenty miles further up the Potomac. If he wanted to keep his government secrets to himself, what did she care? One less room to worry about was the way she saw it. As she had told him more than once.

Now, Redbridge, who had been sitting cross-legged in

the centre of the room, rose to his feet. He stretched to loosen the muscles, which had tightened from the four hours that he had been at his meditations, and walked over to the door. His fingers slid across a touch-sensitive pad and the room became infused with a warm green light that came from hidden electrical mountings buried within each of the five walls. Leaning back against the wall, he allowed himself to slide, until he was once again seated on the painted floor. What the fuck had gone on out there? It was bad, he could feel it. Even now, traces of the imbalance were coursing through his system. It made him feel unclean.

A simple meditation, up through the strata of the frame work which encompassed the Great Glory. He had been there many times before; he had always revelled in the simple beauty of this, a simple meditational path. He had always used it for the purposes of relaxation. But this time?

Well, it had started simply enough, he mused. He had risen slowly, through the lower strata, letting the colours flow around and about him, moulding his being to harmonise with them as they swirled in regular concentric circles. Then taking their beauty, using the purity of their rhythm he had flowed along the lines of force, which held the Great Structure, the very life of the universe, up through the Middle Pillar, up towards the Gold. Not that he would ever reach the Gold. There was much work to be done before he would ever come to realise *that* glory. If indeed he *ever* would. But he had come close enough to feel the radiated ecstasy of its touch. And the mere fact that he had reached a stage where he could accomplish even that and retain his sanity was no mean achievement.

Sanity. That was the key. This time he had felt *insanity* up there. The swirling beauty of the colours had twisted and darkened, their uniform rhythms had been jerked and staggered by a monumental imbalance, one who's power and dimension had been huge and had infused him with an awe that had been shockingly terrifying. It had sent him crashing down through the strata, violent and uncontrolled, showing glimpses of unseen terror to wrench at his sanity as he dropped, mirroring the anguish of the Fallen Angel as he accelerated down to materialism. But his control in the lower strata had saved his

316

mind. He had absolute mastery of the lower levels. He had known how to slow his descent, using the colours and the sounds of those levels to cushion him.

But what he remembered now, what had stayed, even with his conscious mind, was a glimpse that he had had, right at the last. A disturbing glimpse of an aura of colour being crushed, screaming silently in its anguish, by the might of this imbalanced obscenity, as it was hurled, hard and fast, down into the very bowels of infinity. He had felt the torture of its pain as it passed him by. But worse, he had recognised that crumbling aura. There could have been no mistake. It had been the living aura of the Grand Master of the Shadowmasters. It had been Henri St Clair.

Redbridge sat for a moment, trying to gather his thoughts. He was still a little shaken from the rapidity of his uncontrolled descent. He realised only to well how close he had been to mental extinction. Had that really been St Clair? Well of course it had. There could be no mistake. But what had happened? Just what in the name of fuck was going on? Brachman would know. Surely Brachman would know. He had to get to a telephone. He *had* to find out.

He pulled himself to his feet once more, touched the pressure pad which clicked the door open and pushed his way into the darkened hallway beyond. He slammed the door closed behind him, and paced over to an ornate hallstand where sat a grey telephone. As he reached out to lift the receiver, it rang. The sound was harsh and loud in the quiet of the house and Redbridge let it ring a couple of times before he picked it up.

'Hello?' he said.

'Ah, Redbridge,' the caller said. 'This is Michael Brachman. I have some rather shocking news.'

'I know,' Redbridge replied. 'It's St Clair, isn't it?'

There was a pause.

'I was there, Michael. I saw it. Out on the Astral.'

'Ah,' Brachman commented flatly. 'I think that it would be for the best if you were to find an excuse to be in Europe. As soon as possible, if we are to avert a potential crisis. We have much to discuss.'

'Where are you, London?'

'Yes.'

'I just have to shower and pack a few things. I can be on the next flight out. I'll be there in a few hours.'

'Good,' Brachman responded with no emotion. "I'll be expecting you. Goodbye."

The call was over and Redbridge replaced the receiver. A crisis, so close to the event. Just what the fuck *was* going on? He felt sure from the tone of Brachman's voice that Brachman had the answers to the questions that were starting to flood into this mind. With St Clair gone, would Brachman take charge? Would they need to postpone the Great Work? There was something about the tone of Brachman's voice that suggested that all would continue, that indeed he, Brachman, was more than fit and more than willing, to smooth things through. But questions remained, nevertheless. And he would fucking well demand the answers to those questions, damned fucking right he would. In the meantime, he had some packing to do, preparations to make. In two hours time, there was an aeroplane he needed to be on...

Chapter 42

IT WAS A beautiful night, such as only the summertime Mediterranean can produce. The sea was flat calm, undulating gently like a large sheet of blackened glass. Above, the sky was clear, clear enough for the gaseous sprawl of the Milky Way to be clearly visible between the clusters of bright stars. Cutting through this serene beauty, the power-cruiser *L'Enfant* blasted through the water at a steady fifty knots, the shriek of her twin diesel engines crying violence to the empty darkness of the night.

Below decks, Strachan and Lyndon sat silent in the dark, smoking cigarettes. The burning tips glowed briefly as they flipped their ash in the direction of the ashtray which they could barely see on the table before them. They had long since given up any attempts at conversation. The howl of the diesels at just under maximum revs was competition too great. Strachan stubbed out his cigarette in the metal ashtray, causing it to skitter across the tabletop. He wanted some air. Sleep, he knew, would have been better, but his mind was moving too rapidly for that. The noise he could have coped with - he had slept in the fuselage of a C 130 Hercules transport aircraft before now - but it was the restlessness of his mind that kept him awake here.

Lyndon said nothing as Strachan, stooping slightly to accommodate the shallowness of the saloon, made his way aft, to the steps that led up to the open deck. Out in the cool of the night, Strachan breathed deep of the ozone-laden air. The windrush generated by the boat's speed rippled the loose material of his shirt, chilling the cotton and refreshing him with much the same effect as would a cold shower. He turned his face into the wind, squinting his eyes against it. In front of him, he could see the slightly raised cockpit, its interior infused with the muted green glow of the instrumentation. Standing with their backs towards him, picked out in surreal silhouette, were the skipper and her first mate. The other crewman, he knew, was below decks, his ears muffled against the noise, tending to the engines.

Strachan stuffed his hands into his pockets and stepped casually over to the open cockpit. The skipper sensed his presence behind her and turned sharply.

'What he fuck do you want?' she shouted over the noise.

Strachan smiled. She didn't mince her words, this one, did she? Perversely, he found that her crudity of language attracted him to her all the more. That he was attracted to the rest of the package needed no explaining. The woman was wonderful. Not beautiful in a pretty-pretty soft and girly sort of way. Not like Astrid had been, he thought, then quickly buried the memory. No; tougher, more self reliant and gutsy. A pocket Amazon. Her black eyes still held him, jaw set firm, waiting for his reply.

'Just getting some air,' he said. 'It's getting kinda stuffy down there.'

'Shouldn't fucking well smoke then,' she spat out, turning back to the instrument panel. Then before he could reply, she had turned on him once again:

'And if you're planning on staying out here for any length of time, just mind that you keep out of the fucking way. We're working up here you know. Coming up to the refuelling RV and we don't want to miss it for having to piss about baby sitting you, get it?'

Again the dark eyes held his, jaw set hard and slightly forward, demanding an answer. He wondered whether *any* of her questions were ever rhetorical.

'Got it,' he said simply over the noise and the wind. Then as she was turning once more to her charts and her instruments, he couldn't resist a little dig.

'Refuelling RV?' he asked, as though shocked that he should be troubled with even the mention of the mechanics of his journey. 'Shit I hadn't counted on that.'

The woman stared at him for a moment, her jaw dropping open with incredulity. Quickly she caught her self. 'Unless you want to paddle the rest of the fucking way. Of course we have to refuel. We've just come five hundred kilometres near as damnitt at a mean average of fifty knots, you dickless wonder. Just what the fuck do you think powers this baby, huh? Well, huh?'

She was glaring at him. Christ, there was a mean streak coursing through her and no mistake. But Strachan laughed at her, his even teeth gleaming through the dark and he could see in her eyes the realisation that he had been winding her up.

'Oh, go fuck a lepers cunt, asshole,' she spat at him and turned once more to her chart and her instruments, leaving him in no doubt whatsoever of her utter contempt.

What *did* she do for fun, Strachan wondered. He visualised her in the most appalling situations; leading a team of bailiffs sent in to close an orphanage at Christmas, headbutting pensioners and setting fire to the photograph albums which remained their only link to happier times gone by. But he felt that such imagery was unjust. That beneath the surface, below the over-tough professionalism there was a warm and approachable core. At least, he hoped that such warmth was to be found there, for without it, her personality would be chilling and psychopathic. And that would be a waste indeed.

He inched past the cockpit heading for'ard, steadying himself with one hand on the saloon deckhead. Seating himself in the sharp 'vee' of the bow, he thrust his face into the full force of the windrush, allowing it to wash over him. Five hundred kilometres. And now they were heading east. He could see the chart of the Mediterranean before his eyes. Out from Marseilles, destination Sicily, travelled five hundred kilometres and now heading east. They would be passing through the narrow strait which separated the islands of Corsica and Sardinia. If they were to be intercepted, this would be the place for it to happen. A gap as narrow as the English Channel. Even a cheap radar would pick them up early as they were funnelled into the channel. Interception *then* would not be a problem. This might be a tense time. But it would not do to dwell on it.

He turned his mind to other things. What would he do on Sicily? It had not been *his* choice to go there after all. He needed to get further east, to Cyprus first, then Israel. Both places where he had served with the SAS. Both places where he had contacts, where he could count on help. But on Sicily he knew no one. He would be reliant on Lyndon still.

Strange the way fate had thrown them together. They were simpatico already, he and Lyndon. Like-minds, similar values. Easy in each other's company. And after just a day. He didn't know about Lyndon, but this was rare for him. They could have become great buddies, he knew. But then, with a hint of regret, he had to tell himself that it could never be. He was dangerous company now and forever would be. Lyndon's problems had been local to Marseilles; he had connections, would be able to re-integrate himself into a familiar lifestyle soon enough. But Strachan's crimes had been international. The world's press had screamed his name and condemned his atrocity. The west would never again hold a place for him. His destiny would lie in the east. And deep down, he expected that his time would be short. The thought saddened him.

'Corsica,' a voice said over his left shoulder. He looked around. It was Lyndon. No cheery smile now. He was seeing the business side of Lyndon's expressive face.

'I expect that this is where we'll pick up the refuelling boat.' Lyndon continued. 'Just as well it's calm. Means we'll get it out of the way all the quicker. This is bandit country out here. Some of these guys are out of control. You know what I mean?'

Strachan nodded. Unconsciously, he ran his left hand round to where the Beretta sat in the waistband of his trousers. His fingers found the butt, sending reassuring messages up to his brain. He looked back out to the sea. Just slightly northeast he could see now, the black featureless bulk of the Corsican landmass where it broke the symmetry of the flat horizon. He wanted a cigarette. Despite the wind and despite the noise, it was relaxing out there in the emptiness of the sea, with the greater emptiness of infinite space opening out above. The cigarette would help concentrate his mind, allow him to contemplate such beauty. But he knew that he would have to go below decks if he wanted to smoke now. They were approaching an RV, and the flame from his lighter might be seen, might be misconstrued as a signal. He did not know the details of this pick up and he was not going to risk compromising it.

He turned to speak to Lyndon, but the American had gone. He could see him, standing in the cockpit, leaning over the captain's shoulder, as though looking at a chart. The tough woman turned on him suddenly and although he could not hear the words, Strachan could imagine the invective that would be flowing freely from her lips. Lyndon was backing away, his hands raised in a gesture of surrender, and Strachan watched as he disappeared once more below decks.

Alone again, Strachan found himself watching the nearing bulk of the Corsican coastline. Was he imagining it, or had he spotted something on the water between himself and the landmass? He strained his eyes to look, but he couldn't be sure. He blinked, rapidly, moisturising his wind-dried eyes, and looked again. Yes, there! There was something. It was closer now, still barely visible as its colouring blended so well with the island to its rear and with the dark surface of the ocean in front, but there it was. Another boat. And they were heading on a bearing that would bring them into contact with it. It could mean only one thing; they had found the refuelling supply vessel…

FIFTEEN MINUTES LATER…

They spoke in whispers, the two men who had boarded *L'Enfant* and *L'Enfant's* skipper. Even here, on the open sea, where the quiet emptiness of the night would not carry their voices anywhere near the distance to the nearest human ears, they maintained a respectable quiet. For they were on underground business and force of habit dictated their behaviour.

Tied alongside *L'Enfant* was a large fishing vessel, half her length again. Heavy rubber pipes snaked over her sides, their ends locked over the fuel-tank cocks, pumping gallon after gallon of high-grade diesel into the outsize inboard containers.

Strachan could see shimmering streams of evaporating fuel where it escaped into the atmosphere around the fuel cocks. He was still standing in the bow of the boat, looking at the refuelling process.

The two crewmen from the fishing vessel were talking in an animated fashion with the Amazon-Captain. Strachan did not envy them their dispute, but was keeping a weather eye on the proceedings anyway.

The two were scruffy, unshaven in their particularly slovenly Mediterranean sort of way. Their work was dirty, heavy, and dangerous and it showed itself in every facet of their appearance. One of the two was obviously the captain of the fishing vessel. He was well into his middle years, a big burly man of obvious strength. He had boarded *L'Enfant* first and had supervised the refuelling process so far. The other man, younger and with an outlandish walrus moustache, as though in the hope that it would lend authority to his chinless face, was obviously his son. Not that there was much of a family resemblance, the fact just seemed to present itself in the way that the two men related to one another. It was not a master and servant relationship, despite the fact that the older man *was* the master and the younger man was quick to do his bidding.

One crewman waited in the high wheelhouse of the fishing vessel. Strachan looked up to him and waved, but there was no response. Strachan thrust his hand back into his pocket. He turned once more to regard the father and son. They were still in animated conversation with the woman and Strachan felt his hackles begin to rise. There was something wrong here. Something he could not quite put his finger on, but which was making him uneasy nevertheless.

Where the fuck was Lyndon? Why was he lounging below decks? Fucking hell, he knew that there might be trouble. Hadn't he said so himself?

The younger fisherman had edged his way around, ever so slowly, ever so sneakily, putting himself between Strachan and the woman, who was still arguing in vicious whispers with his father. More and more he stole nervous glances in Strachan's direction and occasionally up to the crewman who remained static in the wheelhouse of the fishing vessel. Strachan pretended not to notice, casually linked his hands behind his back. Hoped that he looked relaxed and unthreatening. Because the reality had him sliding the fingers of his left hand around the butt of the Beretta, his thumb flicking the safety to 'off', his index finger tight on the trigger guard.

From the corner of his eye, Strachan caught the nod from the man in the wheelhouse. It was a signal. The younger man had picked up on it and had nodded back. Strachan could really feel his skin crawl. His heart rate had increased and adrenaline was pumping into his blood stream. Something was going down, no doubt about it. This feeling was an old friend. It had never let him down before. Trouble was close at hand.

Strachan took a step back, giving himself a more open view of the wheelhouse of the fishing vessel. Unconsciously, his knees bent ever so slightly as he rose to balance on the balls of his feet. The shift in stance was so subtle that it only a fellow professional would have recognised it. But it readied Strachan for anything.

'So what do you say about all this boy?' The old fisherman boomed out the question to his son, the first time he had raised his voice to a level audible to Strachan. The young man turned his head only slightly to answer the question. One eye stayed with Strachan.

This was it. Strachan knew it. It was coming now. The young man threw himself to the deck, reaching inside his shirt. Where he had been, Strachan saw the father with a gleaming blade in his right hand, his left around the throat of the woman, who was choking with shock and surprise. This was the world in which Strachan revelled, this was where he was really alive and as he saw the events unfolding around him in a slow-motion poetic ballet, he knew exactly what he had to do. He would kill again.

The Beretta 92F was out of his waistband and steadied in a two handed grip, even before the Walrus-moustache had hit the deck. He had gone down to clear the line of fire, so he was not the prime danger; the old man was dealing with the woman and wielded only a blade. Again, only a secondary threat.

Strachan spun on the balls of his feet and fired six nine-millimetre rounds into the window of the wheelhouse of the fishing vessel. Through an open, sliding section of the glass, the crewman slumped dead, his face and throat an unrecognisable mash of blood and shredded tissue, the back of his head and brain spread over the back wall of the wheelhouse. A Franchi SPAS-12, military assault shotgun clattered from his grasp onto the deck a few feet below.

Strachan turned, took two steps forward and stamped on the face of the fallen fisherman, who still struggled to remove some unknown weapon from inside his shirt. The blows from Strachan's feet smashed the fallen man's head against the deck, concussing him.

'Aaaiieehh!'

A shriek, and a gasping intake of breath. Strachan looked up to see the old man plunge his silver blade into the body of the young skipper, just below the rib cage. He saw her slump in the old man's grasp, heard her first wheezing breath. The red mist was upon him as he squeezed the trigger of the handgun, blasting two rounds into the old man's grinning face. He was close enough for the splash back of blood from the entrance wounds to shower his face and shoulders, but that didn't worry him. The bloodstained knife slid out of the woman as the old man fell to the floor.

'Lyndooonnn!!!' Strachan screamed, his eyes scanning the gunwhales of the fishing vessel high above, expecting more crew to appear. 'Lyndon, where the fuck are you!!!?'

Several heavy thudding blows sounded from the stern, causing Strachan to spin around.

'Over here; now take this. I'll cover the boat!' Lyndon screamed, and threw a heavy axe with which he had severed the refuelling pipes and the lines that had tied the boat to the fishing vessel at the stern. Strachan caught the axe awkwardly with one hand, and saw that Lyndon already had a gun in his hand and was scanning the fishing vessel for any activity.

'Go on then. For fuck's sake cut us loose for'ard!' Lyndon shouted, never once taking his eyes from the sides of the larger boat alongside.

Strachan swung the axe one-handed, parting the lines that held *L'Enfant* to the fishing vessel at the bow. The stench of diesel, which was being pumped under pressure onto the open decks of the powerboat from the severed pipes, was nauseating, but Strachan could not afford to be affected by it. He dropped the axe to the deck, gripping the Beretta once more with both hands. He was by no means certain that this was all over. Not by a long chalk.

He looked to his left. Lyndon had moved over to the cockpit. He could not see but he knew that Lyndon was kicking the crewman who had dived for cover beneath the instrument panel at the first sign of trouble. And Lyndon's words held back nothing:

'Up, you yellow cunt. We're gonna fucking need you. Now!'

Lyndon hit the large green buttons that fired up the powerful engines. The whole boat began to throb. The bedraggled navigator emerged from his hiding place to stand at Lyndon's side. His mouth was bloodied and twin trickles of dark liquid ran from his nostrils, dripping onto his white tee shirt. He barely dared even glance at Lyndon, who was busy at the controls of the boat.

'Hold steady,' Lyndon screamed over the roar of the engines. 'Here we go!'

He engaged the gear, pushed the throttle forward and *L'Enfant* pulled away from the ugly vessel that dwarfed her, the trailing fuel lines still pumping diesel hanging from her stern, spewing the fuel onto the surface of the sea.

Steady on his feet, Strachan kept a watchful eye on the fishing vessel as they pulled away. They were fifty yards out and Lyndon pulled back on the throttles, allowing the boat to drift to a standstill. Strachan strode over to the cockpit to join him. Together they looked at the dark bulk of the fisher.

'Can't leave that to be found, no fucking way,' Lyndon said. 'And the police finding it is the least of our problems.'

'An internecine Mafia affair, huh?' Strachan asked pointedly. He knew full well that they could not allow the fishing boat to be found; he didn't need an explanation or apology. He was not, after all, a stranger to destruction. The slight dig was to remind Lyndon not to get too patronising with the mysticism of this secret Mafia stuff. *He* wasn't going to be impressed by it.

Lyndon chose to ignore the tone of the question; he was buried in a locker below the instrument panel. A second later he emerged, holding a flare pistol.

'You'd be surprised how seriously they take little events like this in these parts,' he said. 'I mean, everybody will *know* just what happened here and who's done it. What is important is that the job gets finished, gets done right.' Lyndon turned to Strachan, stopped in the middle of slotting a flare cartridge into the fat pistol. 'Can you understand that?'

'Sure.' Strachan said simply. And he could. Any failure to finish the job would signify panic, weakness. And that weakness would indeed bring the authorities sniffing around where they were not wanted. They too, would know what had happened, would even have a good idea as to who was involved - in a tribal, non-specific sort of way. It would mean that heads would have to be kept well down for a while. It would mean a curtailing of business at the very least. It would not be appreciated. By anyone.

Lyndon snapped the flare pistol shut. He used to be able to make this sort of shot easily. It would be interesting to see if he still had the knack.

'Ten bucks says you'll need another shot.' It was as if Strachan had read his thoughts. Lyndon treated him to his most contemptuous glance.

'Wanna make that a hundred?' he enquired.

A groan from behind them caused them to turn around in unison, Strachan with his automatic at the ready. It was the skipper, the woman. She was alive. Christ, they'd forgotten about her. What a pair of selfish bastards we are, Strachan thought, playing games while she could be dying here.

Strachan knelt at the woman's side. Next to her, he could see the grip of a revolver protruding from the still concussed fisherman's shirt. He reached over and plucked it from the open shirt and tossed it into the sea. Then he looked at the woman's wound. Blood stained darkly through the yellow sweatshirt that she was wearing. Her eyes flickered open. She coughed a little, and Strachan looked to her lips, praying that there would be no blood. His prayers were answered; only clear spittle dribbled down her chin. The lungs had not been punctured by the blade then. That was encouraging.

She was looking up at him, her eyes still glazed with shock. 'I need a doctor and all I've got is you,' she said. 'Fucking great. You'll find a shroud in the locker beneath my bunk. Say something nice over me, wont you?'

Her eyes closed but her lips smiled. For the first time, as far as Strachan could remember. But in that smile he could see the warmth of the woman. Could read her thanks. It cheered him.

'Don't worry,' he whispered, brushing the heavy fringe of her hair away from her forehead. 'You'll be OK. You're gonna make it.'

'How is she?' Lyndon asked, still standing, gauging the distance over to the fishing vessel.

'I think she'll make it,' Strachan said, standing up next to the former SEAL. 'Lungs seem undamaged and looking at where the blade went in, I'd say that no vital organs have been hit. Just have to hope that no blood vessels have been sliced, but I reckon there'd be a lot more blood if they had. That's one lucky girl. Anyway, c'mon and get this over with. I'm gonna need you to hold her while I clean up the wound. I can't imagine there's any anaesthetic around here and it's gonna hurt like a bastard. I've got a feeling that she's got a kick like a mule. And I *don't* want to find out the hard way.'

Lyndon laughed, then raised the flare pistol.

'OK then, dude. Here we go.'

There was a dull thud, and the broad pistol kicked slightly in Lyndon's hand. Glowing brightly through the night air, the red fireball of the flare roared across the surface of the water, bounced off the hull of the fishing boat, and onto the sea, close by where the severed refuelling pipes were still pumping raw diesel onto the water.

The diesel vapour caught immediately and an orange fireball engulfed the fishing boat, the intensity of its light causing Strachan and Lyndon to shield their eyes with their forearms. Then came the noise and the heat. The initial fireball was climbing, high into the sky. Lyndon and Strachan watched it rise, billowing in on itself, burning itself out from the inside.

'Noooooooooo!!!' a voice roared from behind them. 'My babiiiiees!!!' it shrieked.

Strachan and Lyndon turned at once. It was the fisherman. He was on his knees. There was a power in the horror that sprung from his bruised eyes as he looked, bloodied mouth agape, at what had been his boat.

'What the fu…' began Strachan, but Lyndon tugged at his arm.

'Shit, man, look at this.'

Strachan looked. Rising from the sea was a dancing curtain of orange flame, a beacon that would be seen for hundreds of miles on a clear night like this. But through the flames, the shape of the fishing boat could be plainly discerned, fire consuming her every timber, though she remained as yet, afloat. But the horror came at the for'ard gunwhale. Strachan's mind recoiled at what he saw. Two children, small children, visible from only the chest up, were standing, looking over at them. They might have been crying, but their voices would never be heard beyond the roar of the flames. Strachan could clearly see their blackened faces. The skin was burning. Soon it would stretch and peel. They were burning to death. And there was nothing that anyone could so. My God, what kind of people would take their children on an errand like this? Were they really to have learned the family business so young?

Strachan's mind raced with the awfulness of the possibilities. 'What the...?' It was Lyndon. 'Fucking hell, DOWN!'

Lyndon shoved Strachan hard, sending him crashing into the kneeling fisherman. They both sprawled awkwardly on the deck, and Strachan felt a searing pain in the inside of his left knee, shooting up his left thigh and he screamed.

He rolled over, looked back towards the stricken fishing boat, in time to see what was clearly the Franchi assault shotgun in the hands of the largest child. He could see the pump being operated by burned fingers as the child readied to shoot again, but his vision was filled with yellow and red flames as the fire found the fortunately near-empty fuel tanks aboard the fishing boat.

Even so, the explosion was massive and the resulting shockwave pushed the powerboat fifty yards back through the water as debris rained all around. In the calm that followed the blast, Lyndon made his way over to Strachan. Nothing remained of the fishing boat to show that it had ever been there, save for a few charred pieces of driftwood. At least the end for the children had been mercifully quickened.

'How are ya, bud?' Lyndon asked, and there was no fun in his voice.

'Left leg's fucked,' Strachan told him, and really, the pain was dreadful. 'But I'll live.' He knew that his injury was not potentially fatal and therefore had a low priority in the situation.

'Good,' Lyndon said, matter of factly. ''Cos I don't have time to nursemaid you just yet. We've got to get the fuck outta here, OK?'

Strachan nodded, his teeth gritted with agony.

Lyndon turned, strode to the cockpit. There was a roar as the throttles were opened up and Strachan could feel the pull of the acceleration as Lyndon took *L'Enfant* up to her maximum cruising speed. Two minutes later, as they entered the jaws of the narrow strait between Corsica and Sardinia, the lights went out, and he had sunk into a blissful unconsciousness.

Chapter 43

THE MEDITERRANEAN... JUNE 19th... 4.50am

'Aaaaaagggggghhh!!!'

A TERRIBLE scream, one that managed to pierce even the constant shriek of the diesel engines, greeted Strachan as he swam once more back to consciousness. He shook his head in an effort to clear his thoughts. The wind and a spray of surf were washing over him and it helped. He realised that he was still lying on the exposed bow-deck of *L'Enfant* as she flew across the still, calm, water. A searing pain in his left knee brought him sharply back to reality. Fuck, how it throbbed and burned.

He opened his eyes and looked down at the leg. His pants had been cut away at the thigh and the knee joint was heavily and expertly bandaged, so that he couldn't even properly bend the leg. A stain of blood seeped through the thick crepe. A fucking shotgun wound. There would be no way of knowing the extent of the damage until they hit dry land and somewhere with half-decent facilities. You never could tell with shotgun pellets; it could be something, it could be nothing. Right now, it sure felt like something.

'Aaaaaaaaahhhh, no, no, please - aaaggh!'

The scream again. Strachan raised himself on one elbow, resting his weight on his good leg. Just below the windshield of the cockpit he could see Lyndon. The American was crouched down next to the naked figure of the young fisherman. Lyndon had stripped him of his clothing and had tied him, spread-eagled, lying with his back to the deck where it raked up to the cockpit windshield. He watched as Lyndon pulled a lighted cigarette, which he was holding, away from the fisherman's left nostril. Strachan could see that the skin there was blistered and burnt. The fisherman shook, sobbing with the pain.

'Having fun?' Strachan enquired. Lyndon turned to him and grinned.

'So, you're back with us at last, eh? How're you feeling?'

'A fucking sight better than him right now, I shouldn't wonder,' Strachan replied, nodding towards the helpless naked figure on the deck. 'Seems like you've patched me up pretty good.'

Lyndon took a long drag on the cigarette, held the smoke in his lungs then let it out slowly, savouring the taste.

'What about the woman?' Strachan asked, 'The skipper?'

Lyndon laughed. 'Say, you were right about her though, and no mistake. Kicks like a fucking horse.' He turned his face so that Strachan could see that the cheek was bruised and the beginnings of a first class shiner were starting to form. 'Had to stitch the knife wound. My, was she lucky. Took it all real good though, all things considered. She's down below now, sleeping off the best part of a bottle of vodka. She's gonna pull through.'

Strachan felt himself relax a little at this news. He really liked this girl. He liked her toughness. He found himself wondering what she would be like in bed. Then he stopped himself. There were other things to consider. 'How's the cabaret going,' he asked.

Lyndon looked momentarily perplexed, then realised that Strachan was referring to the fisherman and his grin returned once more. 'Oh this?' he said, tilting the lighted cigarette towards the naked man. 'Just thought I'd try to get a little information here, see just what the fuck's going on.' Lyndon took a last drag from the cigarette then tossed the glowing stub over the side. 'You know, those bastards were paid a whole shitload of dough to make that RV. I know how these things work. And yet there was some heavy-duty betrayal of trust going on back there, y'know. They were taking some fucking hell of a risk, messing with the people who arranged all that. I want to know just what was so goddamned important, or worse, lucrative, that would make them even consider it.'

Strachan said nothing, so Lyndon shrugged and continued, by way of explanation, 'Out here, bereft of all refinement, good old-fashioned torture's about all we got. Know what I mean?'

Strachan knew all right. Hadn't he been in a similar situation

333

himself, just a few short nights ago, back on board his beloved *Hasler?*

'I left you up here after the patch-up job, rather than take you down below, because I figured you might want to be involved when you came to,' Lyndon added, looking up towards the stars. Out over the horizon to the east, the black of night was giving way to purple. Dawn would come soon enough. He turned back to Strachan. 'This one's a tough fucker, and no mistake.'

'Then why bother taking it further?' Strachan asked. 'You know as well as I do that if he hasn't broken already, he's not likely to now, is he? Why not wait until we make landfall and we can bring more - shall we say - sophisticated methods to bear?'

'Because I want the fucker now!' Lyndon snapped. 'I want him to fear and I want him to hurt!'

Strachan shrugged. Frankly - as someone had once said - he didn't give a damn. He had just been baiting Lyndon. Suddenly, Lyndon realised it.

'Bastard,' he said, turning back to the fisherman. He reached into the blue windcheater that he wore and his hand emerged holding a set of chrome-plated scissors.

The fisherman lay with his head tilted back, repeating over and over, the Catholic Rosary.

'You can kiss all that shit goodbye,' Lyndon told him harshly, 'We're about to change your religion.'

The fisherman opened his eyes, saw the scissors, immediately understood Lyndon's intent.

'O mother of God, no!' he shrieked. 'Please, no, no more! Please!'

Eyes wide with panic, the fisherman struggled violently to free himself from his bonds but to no avail. Lyndon, the former Navy man, had tied the knots expertly.

'Well, ya know what I want to hear,' Lyndon said. 'All you gotta do is say the words.'

'But I caaaan't!' sobbed the fisherman. 'Omerta. Omerta!'

Lyndon leaned forward and slapped him harshly across the face. 'Omerta?' he hissed. 'Fuck Omerta. You're out of it, *capice?* You tell me or you don't tell me, there'll be no going back for you. It's to live or to die, here, now, is all. And there's dying and there's dying...'

The fisherman sobbed openly, tears streaming down his face. Lyndon felt that he had waited enough. He reached down between the man's legs and took the cold, shrunken penis between the thumb and forefinger of his left hand.

'My, but your good lady wife's not going to miss this, is she?' Lyndon sneered. 'Now, let's get you ready for the Rabbi, shall we?'

'Aaaaahhh, aaaaahhh,' gasped the fisherman in panic. He struggled again but couldn't move much.

The scissors flashed in Lyndon's right hand as he none too gently forced one of the blades up inside the man's foreskin. 'Shalom,' he whispered as he closed the blades. He could feel, and even imagined he could hear, the flesh begin to part, but in truth, the sound, which was akin to that of a sea-fish being skinned, was drowned by the fisherman's animal scream of pain and shock.

Even Strachan winced as he observed this spectacle. Yet he found himself compelled to watch. Glancing about, he could see that *L'Enfant's* navigator was leaning across the instrument panel to peer at the spectacle.

'Oh my,' Lyndon interjected after the wail subsided, 'will ya just look at all this blood? What a fucking mess.'

Indeed, Strachan was well able to see that there had indeed been a lot of blood. The chrome scissors no longer gleamed, sprayed sticky by the red liquid that had spurted from the man's ravaged organ. It had even covered Lyndon's hand and forearm.

Lyndon tossed the scissors to the deck. He still held the damaged penis between his thumb and forefinger and now he leaned forward to examine his handiwork. 'Hm,' he mused, adopting an air of mock medical expertise, 'A decent enough wound, but a little neat for my liking. Let's finish the job with a little less finesse, shall we?'

He took the edge of the foreskin where it had been parted by the scissors and with a savage wrench of his wrist, he tore at the wound, ripping it further and the fisherman screamed his high-pitched wail to the empty stars as the blood sprayed once more.

A triangular patch of skin had come away in Lyndon's fingers. Lyndon threw it to the deck. Then he reached forward and grabbed the remaining, loose-flapping piece of foreskin. 'Want to tell me something now?' he asked. The fisherman continued only to sob, so Lyndon shrugged and tore again at the skin, completing the job of circumcision, then wiped his fingers clean, using the fisherman's pants. The fisherman meanwhile was in spasm, locked as he was in his bonds, and howling and shrieking his pain, which burned him like a blaze of fire.

Lyndon reached inside the windcheater once more and pulled out a small hip flask. He flipped open the top and took a small swig. 'Better clean you up,' he said to the wailing fisherman. 'Wouldn't want that wound to become infected now, would we?' And with that, he poured the neat whisky over the man's bleeding penis and there was a loud crack - this time clearly discernible above everything - as the man's muscles tensed so fiercely with the sudden shock of pain that the contraction of the left thigh muscle snapped the bone in two. Then, mercifully for him, the pain became too much and his mind slipped into the oblivion of unconsciousness.

Lyndon turned to Strachan. 'Well I'll be damned,' he said. 'Always heard that it was possible, fucked if I ever thought I'd see it happen. Guess that wraps up our entertainment for a while.' He paused, as if contemplating his next move, then said: 'You want to go below? It's warmer down there.'

'Yeah,' Strachan replied. 'Might as well.' He nodded over at the fisherman. 'What about him?' he asked.

'I'll bring him down when you get settled. I mean, the scumbag doesn't warrant any special care, but we can't just turn up with a bloodied mascot like this strapped across our bows, can we now?'

Strachan raised a quizzical eyebrow.

'No,' Lyndon said firmly. 'Not even on Sicily. My people have influence, but they still don't own the fucking place. Now stop pissing me about, will ya? I got work to do.'

Lyndon grabbed Strachan beneath his arms and lifted him to his feet with ease. 'Don't put any weight on that damaged pin, okay?' Lyndon instructed.

'As if I need a fucking numbnuts like you to tell me that,' retorted Strachan. 'I think I might have worked that one out for myself.' Even so, he was smiling through the words. It was all just banter.

'Fuck you,' was all that Lyndon, also smiling, could manage by way of reply.

He helped Strachan down below decks and got him settled into a bunk opposite the sleeping skipper. He took time to check her wound dressing and was pleased to see that the bleeding seemed to have stopped.

'A fucking nursemaid now,' Strachan heard Lyndon mutter to himself as he turned to make his way up to the cockpit once more.

He shook his head and smiled. The thought hit him, that at last he was free. That he'd taken his revenge - settled an old score into the bargain as far as the Prince was concerned - and was going to get away. Was it enough? There had been thirteen of them. He'd killed two. And so much life had been taken along with them, for right or wrong. But he wouldn't dwell on that. The others had been infrastructure. Collateral damage. Unfortunate - but he didn't really care. Certainly he would have given those who remained from the abomination that night at the chateau, pause for thought. Yes, it was enough. He was alone now. No Astrid. No Jonathan. He would be a while coming to terms with the loss of them both. But loneliness itself would not hurt him. He had grown accustomed to it over the years. And no matter what was to follow, he knew that he would cope. Now that he was free.

He looked over to study the sleeping woman. He began to admire the serenity of her features in repose, and before he knew it, he too, had drifted off into a deep and restful sleep, with a feeling that for him, the nightmare was finally over.

Chapter 44

THE CABIN OF the 747 was almost completely silent. Well it would be - this was first class, after all. Frank Redbridge would not travel any other way. Normally he would sleep on journeys to Europe, but this journey was different. He'd had thoughts aplenty to keep him awake.

St Clair was dead. He had no way of knowing the circumstances - Brachman certainly hadn't been forthcoming - but he couldn't help but bring his mind to focus on the slim dossier that Bondachuk had handed to him in Switzerland. Strachan. Good God, could Strachan have had anything to do with the death of St Clair? It was not such a preposterous idea. Strachan had already wiped two Shadowmasters. Stopyra. The Prince. But then how did Strachan come to know their identities? How did he know to go after St Clair?

Air conditioning kept the temperature of the cabin reasonably cool, but the chill that swept through Redbridge now had nothing to do with the air conditioning. Destroying Stopyra was understandable, assuming that revenge for the death of the girl had been Strachan's motive. Stopyra's identity would have been merely incidental. The Prince too. He had volunteered to be the cleansing agent that would see to Strachan. He had met his match and paid a heavy price for it. But how could Strachan know their identities? It kept coming back to that. Because if Strachan knew of St Clair then chances were he would know all of them. Brachman, even. And himself. And Bondachuk. Christ. The chill coursed through him again at the thought.

Brachman and St Clair had activated this shadowy entity that they'd all heard of, but no one had seen, known as the Templar.

338

Bondachuk, of course, would most certainly have set his agents to kill Strachan. He had hinted as much back in the Swiss chalet. But this was not good enough. They needed to take Strachan alive. It was vital that they know all that Strachan knew, before they dispatched him.

He was going to London, yes, and ostensibly his prime motivation was to meet with Brachman to help secure what needed to be done. But for now, Redbridge gave himself a more urgent priority. First thing, he would seek out his agents in London, Dibble and Law. He would push buttons with high-ranking members of the Brotherhood who knew him and in some cases, owed him favours. They would get to this Strachan first - before Bondachuk could, and before this Templar could. Strachan could not be allowed to die without divulging what he knew. This was his area of expertise, and he would now take charge. With or without the approval of Brachman. Or anyone else. If Strachan was a lone wolf and had gone to ground, he would have to stay that way for ever. And if that happened, then no problem. But if he ever surfaced - no matter where in the world - then they would have him. It would only be a matter of time.

ENGLEFIELD GREEN... SURREY... JUNE 19th... 4.45am

In the study of his grand house in the English stockbroker belt, Michael Brachman was also in no mood for sleep. His day was coming. Soon. Yes, soon. None of them would suspect. Until it was too late.

He too, like Redbridge high above the Atlantic, had been pondering the whereabouts and motivation of David Strachan. How convenient it had been, that Strachan had been there that night, had witnessed the ceremony. How convenient that events had conspired to unleash in Strachan that propensity for revenge that had seen him destroy the Stopyra estate and bring an end to the lives of two of his - he already saw them as his, he noted - Shadowmasters. Not that he had wished them dead, of course. Indeed, they might have served some useful function. Temporarily. The convenience lay in the fact that he could lay

339

the death of St Clair at Strachan's door. This would put off any snooping or questioning by his brother Shadowmasters.

Of course, he had no way of knowing that one of those brothers, Frank Redbridge, had already come to that same conclusion. But it wouldn't have surprised him. All that mattered was that Strachan was cornered and killed. And the Templar would see to that. And if the Templar wasn't up to it? Well, no point in beating about the bush. He would have to see to it himself.

OXFORD... JUNE 19th... 5.10am

In his apartment, the old man was awake. Sleep he needed more than anything, he knew. But he could not engineer it for himself. Not just yet. There was too much to consider.

What the Shadowmasters were doing should be countered. He knew that. And he was also aware that there was another out there, somewhere in the wide world that he would have to seek out, if he was to contest them. He was no match for them on his own, of that he could be certain. But this other presence... This other presence was mighty, and together, perhaps...

But it was more than this that kept him awake. It was the boy. He had found the boy again. Found the boy, and the boy was strong. But so strange to find him there, existing symbiotically with another essence. Just what had happened?

The boy, yes. He could use the help of the boy too, with what was to come. The boy was mighty. The boy was strong.

The old man smiled to himself. Why was it that he kept referring, even now, to 'the boy'? The boy had been a man for some many years. And what a man he had become. He had grown into a man to be proud of. A true Renaissance man was Jonathan Strachan. Or at least, he had been...

CAP D'ANTIBES... JUNE 19th... 7.30am

The Templar sat at a small metal table outside a roadside café, sipping café au lait with no sugar. Beside him, the Torquemada

340

twitched as it sipped banana milk shake through a straw, but the Templar paid it no heed.

His thoughts were of the man that the Shadowmasters had tasked him to destroy. David Strachan. Strachan was now gone, on a fast boat. He was somewhere out on the Mediterranean. Perhaps he had made landfall already. No matter, he was certainly safe and beyond reach. For now.

But that was just it; safe from what? From him? Would he really continue with what had been tasked him by his masters? It had been strange what had happened back there in Marseilles, just a few short hours ago.

Strachan had been there, his for the taking. Yet there was one who had come to rescue Strachan, one whose call he had felt more honour bound to answer than that of his masters. Instead of destroying Strachan, he had saved Strachan. The call had come from within Strachan himself, but it was not Strachan doing the calling. This call had come from a powerful essence, temporarily fused with that of Strachan. But stranger yet, there had been another there, one in great balance, that was not Strachan, yet which shimmered with the very aura of Strachan himself. He would need to meditate upon this, and no mistake.

As for the immediate question facing him? He would not pursue Strachan. Not for now. Everything told him that the one to seek out was the powerful force that had been the old man when they had first met. The old man who had been horrified at what had happened back in the tower.

Would he need the old man's aid if ever he did confront the Shadowmasters? He didn't know. Would the old man be willing to help, if it came to that? Again, he didn't know. But he suspected that the answer to both of those questions would be 'yes.' So he continued to sip his coffee and ponder his next move. There was no need to hurry. For now.

Chapter 45

IT WAS DAYLIGHT, and bright below decks in the saloon of *L'Enfant*. Strachan woke from what had been a deep sleep. His knee was throbbing beneath the tight bandage that Lyndon had applied, but that didn't matter, because he was here, alive and safe. And free?

He looked across at the opposite bunk where the skipper lay sleeping still. The gentle up and down swell of her breast told Strachan that she was still breathing, and Strachan smiled. But there was the nag of that question concerning his freedom to come to grips with. This woman represented something that he would have to confront on Sicily. The people who had organised his passage. These were her people. And Joe's. Would they let him continue with his plan, he wondered? Would they help him? He didn't know any of them, after all. And they owed him - well, nothing.

There was more than this, however. Would he ever be able to kick from his mind, the memories of what he had experienced, along with Astrid, at that chateau? There was magic in the world, and now he could not dispute it. What did that mean? What did it mean that wealthy and powerful people were caught up in it? People like the Prince. People like Stopyra. How did the world really turn, he wondered, who pulled the levers and who greased the wheels? Did these people use the magic to help do their bidding? Or were they in the end mere servants to forces that they thought they controlled? It was beyond his capacity to furnish the answers to such questions.

There was something that he could consider though. He had killed two of the number that were there that night. As far as he knew, there were eleven of them left, and that was burning inside him. No matter what he did, there was always going to be a feeling deep within him that he had left a job unfinished. How free would he ever be with that cloud lowering over him?

But what could he do? He did not have the identities of the others, much less the means to seek them out. However much he could take comfort in the fact that he had escaped for now, he was still a fugitive. All Europe, hell, all the civilised world would be enemy territory to him forever more. He would have to live with that. Somehow, he would have to leave the task unfinished and be comfortable with the fact.

He wondered if that was possible. He closed his eyes, and after a while, the noise of the diesels became hypnotic, and as sleep came to shroud him once again, a vision of Astrid, smiling as she wandered through the forests of the Riviera coast, turned to him and waved. And he knew that perhaps, it could be...

END OF PART ONE

Now steel yourself for...

The Shadowmasters Part Two
Redemption

coming soon

from BloodBinds Press

www.bloodbinds.com

The Shadowmasters
Part Two - Redemption

The nightmare continues... The nightmare continues... The nightmare continues... Th

Following his violent flight from the South of France, former soldier David Strachan finds sanctuary in the Sicilian stronghold of Don Gino Altobelli, a powerful Mafioso. Altobelli, too, has reason to want the group that has murdered Strachan's girlfriend destroyed...

In *The Shadowmasters*
Part Two - Redemption

Brachman's power consolidates...

...Brachman threw back his head and laughed. How simple it all was. Already, complex financial arrangements had been made throughout Europe, arrangements which formed a rigid skeleton that held the trading solvency of the EEC within its giant framework. It was the sort of interlocking fiscal network that Licio Gelli of Lodge Propaganda Due notoriety had striven unsuccessfully to create.

But then, Gelli had had neither his guile nor his genius. Nor his patience. He alone had the greatness needed to see Gelli's grandiose ambition become reality. Indeed everything had been in place for some time now. Amazing the avenues open to a ranking Freemason, he mused. He laughed again as he thought of the oh-so proper middle class businessmen, each of them with egos the size of blimps, that he had thoroughly duped with the aid of nothing more sophisticated than a Lodge membership. Politicians, bureaucrats, financiers; their trust had been overwhelming. Almost as impressive as their greed.

Now he, and he alone held the keys to unlock the structure, bring it crashing down in a bewildering, internationally destabilising heap. How it would crush them all when they found out. But by then it would be too late. Within the year, there would be war. And soon after, the world would be his...

The Templar's awareness sharpens...

...Then, when he had visited the burned out shell of the apartment in Paris, he had been aware of a residue in the very atmosphere that hung around the place. Even with his skills, he had not been able to properly place it. An air of mischief, yes, but more than just that; an undercurrent of something unspeakably foul. Something poisonous to the Great Work itself. Something that might fester and grow until the delicate fabric of the very universe became unravelled. Something that would revel in the chaos that would follow...

...St Clair dead. There would be a new Grand Master of the Shadowmasters now. The name had come to him quickly, almost immediately; Brachman. Michael Brachman. The continuance of the Great Work would be entrusted to his hands now. St Clair had long been grooming him for such an eventuality, never once expecting it to come to pass. He would, in many ways, be a stronger Grand master than had been his predecessor. The others would rally to him and that was good. There would be need of such calming strength for the times ahead. Yet he couldn't shake from his instinct, the notion that something was horribly amiss with Michael Brachman.

There came a sound of a door handle being turned from the far side of the room. The Templar remained seated, tensed, his eyes directed towards the source of the sound. The Torquemada scuttled silently, crab-like, to hide itself behind its master's chair. The door opened slowly, yet no light flooded in from the darkened hallway beyond. A darkened figure, orange fire blazing from its eyes and mouth, took a step into the room and stopped dead. A sinister figure it presented, tall and lean. Its wiry arms were held out from its body in readiness for…what? …

Strachan joins the fight…

…He had not for a moment been taken in by the urbane suavity and gentleness of manner of his host. The guards who walked the grounds with pump action shotguns were testament to the man's importance. And that degree of importance in this part of the world would likely mean one thing - Mafia. But it had not been his place to pry. He had only spoken to the man on four or five occasions, each time over coffee in the late afternoon. Then they had only discussed trivialities; the weather, the merits of this Aegean island or that. The underground business that had provided all the wealth and power so overtly displayed was never touched upon. But there had been no ambiguity; no denial. It simply was. And now to find that Joe was a part of this family business. Just what could they want with him?

Joe could almost feel the thoughts racing through Strachan's mind. He didn't know just what, but he felt obliged to say something. 'Hey,' he said in his low voice. 'Let me tell you, when we first met in Marseilles, that was nothing more than a coincidence, man. A lucky fluke. You saving my life and all, well I'll always owe you for that. Fucking hell bud, we sure kicked some ass back there, eh?'Lyndon grinned.

Strachan maintained a wary silence.

'Well anyway,' Lyndon continued, 'Like I was saying, that was all just a happenstance. You taking one in the leg on the way over here, that was bad luck, could have happened to any one of us, y'know. But it was uncle Gino insisted you were looked after, him that insisted you stay here until you're fit again. It's a matter of honour, like. We owe you. The *family* owes you, know what I mean?'

'yeah, I know. But there's more, isn't there Joey boy? There's something you're not telling me. I can sense it behind your words. Why not just fucking tell me what's going down? If you're selling me out, just tell me. I mean, where am I going to go, what could I do?'

Lyndon looked to Angelina for support but she simply shrugged and lowered her eyes. Lyndon sighed. What was the use? He would tell Strachan the little he knew...

...They walked unhurriedly over to the seats in front of the desk and as they approached, the vile stench grew ever stronger. Even though Strachan had accustomed himself to it, the smell of filth and rot was so pervasive as to bring him out in a sweat. And there, as he sat in a chair before the desk of Gino Altobelli, Strachan at last could see the source of the foul stench. The fisherman, whose naked skin loked grey and wasted and whose lank hair lay sweat-plastered against his face, had his feet and lower legs dipped in a trough of what was obviously rotting urine and excrement, a yellow-brown liquid in which floated shapeless solids of indeterminate origin. He couldn't quite work out the purpose of this exercise, but as if reading his thoughts, Altobelli began to explain...

...Altobelli gestured behind him and one of the guards immediately moved over to the helpless fisherman. The guard slid the barrel of his shotgun beneath the fisherman's knees and lifted the legs clear of the liquid. As the rancid piss dripped clear of the limbs to disturb the floating filth in the trough below, Strachan's eyes widened at the sight that greeted them. For the man's legs and feet were almost unrecognisable as such. Where there should have been skin, there was now only gangrenous puss, a thick mucous coating. In patches, red and black raw flesh was discernable. The nails had fallen from the toes and the man wailed at the agony of having the poisoned flesh disturbed and exposed to the warm, unforgiving air...

...Strachan, provided with the means to bring down the Shadowmasters, finds himself once more in a world of violence, supernatural horror and human betrayal, where the stakes

are desperate and monstrous forces are arrayed against him. Yet unsuspected allies - the Templar and his hideous Torquemada, an elderly alchemist and a young, isolated KGB operative - race against time to find him.

Twisted by blazing demonic forces, the new Grand Master of the Shadowmasters has plans that will see the entire globe engulfed in a lake of fire, and only Strachan can prevent the imminent catastrophe...

The Shadowmasters
Part Two - Redemption

The horror is relentless - dare you continue..?

www.bloodbinds.com

contact the author:
peter@bloodbinds.com